P9-DDA-611

HAYNER PLD/ALTON SQUARE
OVERDUES .10 PER DAY. MAXIMUM
FINE COST OF ITEM. LOST OR
DAMAGED ITEM ADDITIONAL $5.00
SERVICE CHARGE

DRAGONSLAYER

DRAGONSLAYER

DUNCAN M. HAMILTON

TOR

A TOM DOHERTY ASSOCIATES BOOK

NEW YORK

DRAGONSLAYER

Copyright © 2019 by Duncan M. Hamilton

All rights reserved.

Map by Robert Altbauer

A Tor Book
Published by Tom Doherty Associates
175 Fifth Avenue
New York, NY 10010

www.tor-forge.com

Tor® is a registered trademark of Macmillan Publishing Group, LLC.

Library of Congress Cataloging-in-Publication Data

Names: Hamilton, Duncan M., author.
Title: Dragonslayer / Duncan M. Hamilton.
Description: First edition. | New York, NY : Tor, 2019. | "A Tom Doherty
    Associates Book."
Identifiers: LCCN 2018054058 | ISBN 9781250306739 (trade pbk.) |
    ISBN 9781250306722 (hardcover) | ISBN 9781250306715 (ebook)
Subjects: | GSAFD: Fantasy fiction.
Classification: LCC PR6108.A5234 D73 2019 | DDC 823/.92—dc23
LC record available at https://lccn.loc.gov/2018054058

Our books may be purchased in bulk for promotional, educational, or business use.
Please contact your local bookseller or the Macmillan Corporate and Premium
Sales Department at 1-800-221-7945, extension 5442, or by email at
MacmillanSpecialMarkets@macmillan.com.

First Edition: July 2019

Printed in the United States of America

0 9 8 7 6 5 4 3 2 1

DRAGONSLAYER

PART ONE

CHAPTER
1

Brother Poncet crouched on the scree-covered mountain slope clutching his cream robe about himself, and watched his comrade, Brother Ambrose, inch into the pitch-dark cavern before them. He remained a few paces behind, still out in the sunlight, although at that altitude it did little to warm him. Up that high, it was always cold, even in summer.

Brother Ambrose lifted his small magelamp up to the darkness. The glowing sphere was caged in a mirrored housing, so all of its power shone into the blackness before him. The light reached in, but not far enough to fall on any surface.

"See anything?" Poncet said, his breath misting on the air. Poncet hated the cold, and counted the moments until he could get back to the campfire and his bedroll. Going home would be even better, but that wasn't likely anytime soon. He had thought himself lucky when the Order had recruited him several years before. Now, he wasn't so sure. Crouching in the cold on the side of a mountain was very far removed from the adventures he had imagined back then.

"Nothing," Ambrose said, scratching his thick black hair. "Just darkness. Hellloooooooo!"

The sound of his voice bounced around in the abyss, repeated time after time.

"You shouldn't do that," Poncet said. This was his first mission, and he was determined not to see it go wrong through foolishness. Ambrose didn't seem to have the same concern.

"Why not?"

"You never know what's in there."

Ambrose laughed. "Afraid we'll get savaged by a mountain goat?"

"No." He thought for a moment and realised his comment was born from a fear of the dark, the unknown. Something only children were supposed to be afraid of—not a brother of the Order of the Golden Spur. Finally, he came up with something worthy. "A belek, perhaps."

"It's summer. Even up this high, it isn't cold enough for them. They stay where the snow is. Commander Leverre told us so."

Poncet noticed that all the mirth had left Ambrose's voice, even if he still sounded confident. Only a fool took belek for granted. Even if Brother-Commander Felix Leverre told them to the contrary and swore it on his mother's grave. "Ever seen one?"

"Once, when I was young," Ambrose said. "The Duke of Trelain used to hunt them every winter. Sometimes the king would travel west to join him. They rarely found any, but I remember one year when they did, and killed it. Not before it had killed half a dozen huntsmen and the Count of Dreville, though. They paraded its body through the streets of Trelain. Like a cat, it was, but the size of a bear. A big bear. Fur the colour of steel and fangs as long as your forearm."

Even with all of his training, Poncet didn't like the idea of meeting such a creature. He wondered if that made him a coward, or if experience would ease his fear of such things—if each mission he did would bring him closer to the calm confidence of Commander Leverre.

"We'll have to go in for a closer look," Poncet said.

"It's probably just another dead end."

"Probably, but Brother-Commander Leverre said it's close. We need to search every corner."

Ambrose sighed. "We could search these mountains for a lifetime, and not find anything. We don't even know what we're looking for."

"The commander does. It's not for us to question our superiors. We simply do what we're told. I want to be back by the fire as much as you do."

"What we're told," Ambrose said. "We'll need more light for starters. The cavern looks big; we'll be quicker if we send back to camp for the others."

"Should we bother them?"

"You said yourself that Commander Leverre thinks we're close. Every hole we look into now might be the spot. Need to be thorough."

Poncet nodded. "I suppose I have to go?"

"It's your turn."

Poncet bundled his robe up around his knees and started down the rocky slope, careful not to get his sword tangled between his legs. The mountains were littered with caves, but few were big enough to provide good shelter from the elements or to require much manpower for a proper search. Ambrose's description of the belek planted enough of a seed in Poncet's mind for his imagination to do the rest. As hard as the scramble up and down the mountainside was, he was glad they would have strength in numbers for the search. Gladder still that Commander Leverre would take charge, freeing Poncet from any difficult decisions.

Brother-Commander Leverre stared into the cavern's pitch-black maw, giving his eyes time to adjust in the hope of being able to make out something. However, the darkness was complete, and no amount of time would allow him a glimpse of what lay within. Darkness in such a remote, wild place was always unsettling, but he could do something about it.

He closed his useless eyes and held out his hand. Ignoring the shuffling and muttering of his subordinates, he focussed his mind entirely on his task. A tingle started on the skin of his hand and spread over his entire body. Leverre smiled at the familiar and welcome sensation, then smiled even wider when he felt something else—a dense concentration of magical energy. The Fount, and far more intense than he had ever encountered before. It was just as the Prince Bishop had described. This had to be what he was looking for. When he opened his eyes, he could see the bare skin of his hand glow with an ethereal blue light for a moment. He wondered if the feeling of exhilaration he experienced every time he used magic would ever leave him. Considering how long he had been at it, he doubted it.

"I don't know if we've found it," he said, "but there's definitely something here." He could see the look of relief in the faces of his people. They had been searching the mountains for weeks, and it had taken its toll on them all. Their Order was still ostensibly a secret—while their existence was not concealed, their purpose and true nature were, on pain of death. That meant they couldn't take advantage of the few comforts that could be found in these remote areas, instead having to stay away from any hint of civilisation and make their beds wherever they could find a dry, sheltered spot. The thought that their search might be over excited even him—not just the prospect of going home, but what success in his task would mean for his career.

He pointed his finger into the cavern, and focussed. A stone's throw away, a glowing orb formed, casting light on rock that had likely never felt its touch before. He repeated the process a half-dozen times until all parts of the cavern in view were illuminated. He admired his handiwork and enjoyed the impressed sounds his people made. Creating a magical light was a simple enough thing, but to cast it at a distance, many times in a row, spoke to the skill of the caster, and none of the others were nearly powerful enough to achieve such a feat. Nonetheless, he could feel the strain it had placed on his body, and knew he needed a few moments to recuperate.

"Begin the search," he said, concealing the fatigue that gripped him, so as to maintain his aura of power. He remained still as the dozen sergeants, corporals, brothers, and sisters made their way past him and into the cavern.

Only the two sergeants were able to wield magic with any strength. The rest could detect the object they were looking for if they got close enough, but most would need another five or six years of training and experience before they could do anything useful. Despite that, they were among the best the Order had. They would improve, but it was the next generation from whom the true rewards would be reaped. Such a slow process was frustrating, but even if the progress was slow, the gains were always worthwhile. Leverre's own had been few and far between recently, and he suspected he had reached the plateau of ability his late start had imposed upon him. In a few years, the younger acolytes would surpass him. Until then, though, he would enjoy the awe with which his people viewed him.

▲▲▲▲▲▲

Alpheratz opened one of his eyes and shut it immediately. The light cut through him like a lance and startled his already befuddled mind. It took him a moment to gain control of his thoughts, to place them in order and make sense of them. He tried to open both eyes, slowly this time, controlling the amount of light until he had grown accustomed to it.

He was careful to remain perfectly still. That part of his mind that sought survival over all else was in control, and it screamed danger. When Alpheratz could finally open his eyes completely, he could see there was something odd about the light. It was not how he remembered light to be—an intricate tapestry woven of infinite colours. This illumination was flatter, less interesting. There was no depth or beauty to it. It was then he realised he was not alone. He took a deep breath and listened. The sound of water dripping into a pool somewhere echoed through the chambers of the cave. It was joined by scratching, shuffling, and another sound—the voices of men.

That caused his heart to quicken, though his mind was still befuddled. How long had he slept? What had woken him? Might it only have been moments? He fought through the confusion, trying to remember what had gone before his sleep. There had been men then, too. Might these be the same ones? Warmth began to return to his limbs. Alpheratz knew he had to have slept a long time—an unsettling thought.

There was energy in the cavern, energy spilling from clumsy, unskilled magic. It was not as satiating as a proper meal, but enough to invigorate his stiff muscles. He took another deep breath and stretched his limbs. His sinews popped with each movement and he feared that he would be heard. He paused and listened once more. There did not seem to be any reaction. He could pick out pieces of conversation—they were looking for something, but it did not seem to be him. That was odd. Were they not there to kill him? *How long have I slept? Weeks? Months? Longer?*

He stood, wavering. The magic in the cavern could only do so much to restore him, and his muscles refused to obey commands. Alpheratz felt weak, weaker than he had ever known. If the men were here for him, he feared they might be able to best him. The thought of hiding in the hope that they might not notice him was tempting, but an orb of light appeared in the alcove where he had slept. His decision had been forced. He shook his head in distaste at the clumsiness of the magic used to make it and concluded that the person who had cast it was not powerful. They were unlikely to trouble him too much. The orb liberally spilled energy into its surrounds. Enough that Alpheratz was able to heat his flame glands.

Brother Ambrose carefully navigated the rocky outcrop. Its edges were sharp, the cavern floor uneven, and everything was damp and cold. A slip and fall could easily result in a cracked skull, and not even Commander Leverre had the power to mend that. Ambrose reached out with his mind to survey the area before him for the object. He felt frustrated by how little he had been told about it—*an object, magical, you'll know it when you find it*. He felt certain that even using magic, having a more detailed description would make the process easier. How do you find something when you don't know what it is? However, as he constantly heard from his instructors, it was not his to question why. Accept, have faith, open your mind—these were the only answers they ever gave him.

His heart jumped when he felt something. It was unlike anything he had sensed before; it was even different from the first time he had opened his mind to the Fount and felt its boundless energy all around him. He brushed his misgivings aside, filled with the excitement at the prospect that he might have found what the Prince Bishop so desperately wanted.

He stumbled forward, toward the edge of the light provided by Commander Leverre's magic. Two great, glassy orbs appeared before him, their brilliant emerald green reflecting the meagre light. It took Ambrose a moment to realise that this could not be what he sought, and another to realise that the orbs were far too large to be a belek's eyes. By the time he screamed, the first tendrils of flame were already rushing toward him.

▴▴▴▴▴▴

There was little left of the man by the time Alpheratz drew back his breath, but enough to momentarily quell the rumbling in his stomach. Unlike some dragons, he had never developed a taste for humankind. Too stringy, too bitter, but in a bind it would do, and Alpheratz could not remember having ever been so hungry. He could feel the effect of the warm meal in his stomach immediately. He rolled his shoulders and gently ruffled his wings as some of his strength returned. He needed a proper feed to be fully restored, and unless his ears deceived him, there were several more people between him and something he would actually like to eat. They would have to do for now.

Alpheratz stood again, his legs protesting at the movement, and started forward. Familiar features told him he was in his cavern, though it looked sadly neglected. Glancing at himself, he saw that he, too, looked worse for wear. His once lustrous scales were covered in moss, mildew, and grime. It worried him to think of how long he must have slept, and he wondered what the others thought had happened to him.

He rounded an outcrop that led out to the front chamber. A man stood before him, staring, frozen in terror. Men had always feared dragons, but Alpheratz had never seen a reaction so pronounced. He chuckled as he squirted a jet of flame at the man, turning him into a pillar of fire long enough to burn off his cream robes and any other extraneous parts; then Alpheratz swallowed him whole.

More were dotted around the cavern, shuffling about in the dark spots as though looking for something. They had always been vicious little pests, and Alpheratz didn't hesitate in slaughtering them. Their frailty came as a surprise—the last humans he had faced had been formidable indeed. He could remember, now, returning to his cavern, badly wounded. He had crawled to the back of the cave and collapsed, exhausted. The question of how long ago still bothered him.

He killed the last of the humans and forced them down, his stomach now protesting at the excess of food rather than the lack of it. He lay down in the cavern's mouth, looking out over the land before him. Farther down the slope, he could see one of the little cream-robed vermin running and tumbling downhill, trying to get away. Alpheratz considered going after him, but didn't think it worth the effort. He had cleared the vermin from his home and had eaten more than enough. He needed to rest and digest, then visit the other peaks and find his kin.

Pillowing his head on the cavern lip, he surveyed what was once his domain and wondered if it might be still, or if another young dragon had come and claimed it during Alpheratz's slumber. It looked little different, but it felt a great deal so. He could taste the magic on the air as he breathed. It was so strong—stronger than he had ever experienced. Mankind had sucked so much of it out of the world with their brutish efforts to use it, but now it had returned in full blossom. As he drifted off to sleep, he dwelled on that comforting thought to keep away all the disturbing ones that threatened to keep him awake.

CHAPTER

2

Guillot sat at his usual spot at the end of the small bar in the only tavern in Villerauvais. It was quiet, as usual at that time of day—everyone else from the village and the surrounds still toiled, either in the fields or in the village's few, small businesses.

His spot afforded him the succour of the back wall of the pokey little room when he became too drunk to sit upright any longer, which occurred at some point most evenings. Usually the tavern keeper, Jeanne—former wife of the long-deceased previous owner—let him be, only interacting with Guillot to refill his glass. Today, however, she had remained absent from the bar since his arrival.

He cleared his throat and rapped a knuckle on the bar. He was without doubt her best customer—often her only customer—and seeing as he always paid his way, he expected more attention. That was not even taking into account that he was seigneur of the village and the lands surrounding. Surely that had to count for something too.

He heard approaching footsteps, then the creak of the door behind the bar.

"What do you want?" Jeanne said.

Guillot shrugged. Was the answer not obvious? Nonetheless, her tone bothered him.

She looked at his empty glass. "We're out of wine."

Guillot chuckled, but when the stern expression on her face didn't change, he stopped.

"How can you be out of wine?" he said. "We make it in the village."

"Tax, Gill. Tax."

He wondered if he would ever be referred to as "my Lord." He supposed his father had been the last "Lord Villerauvais." He had always been "Gill," and it seemed he always would be. "Tax?" he said. "I don't collect taxes."

"*You* don't."

Jeanne continued to glare at him as though he had done something bad to her. Had he? He searched through the cloud of booze and hangovers that shrouded his memory and came up with nothing.

"Lord Montpareil," she said.

"What of him?"

"He's collecting taxes here now."

Guillot's mind was too dulled by the hangover from the previous night's drinking to rouse much anger. Insulting though it was, to have a neighbouring lord exert authority in his demesne, he felt greater concern over how to get his glass filled. He shrugged again.

"It all ends up with the king," Guillot said. "It's as well Montpareil collects it as I do. Which I don't."

The look of contempt on Jeanne's face was likewise of less concern to him than getting his glass filled. He gave her his most charming smile but she was unmoved.

"Five years, Gill. We were all happy to have you home, but you've been rotting here for five years. The village and all the lands are rotting with you. You'd break your poor mother's heart if she still lived, gods bless her soul. Don't think for a second that Lord Montpareil has authority to collect taxes here, or that a single penny of it's getting to the king. Anyhow, some of that tax money should have been spent here in the village. In case you haven't noticed, we need it. It's your job. Him collecting them is an insult to you and an injury to us."

Gill spread his hands in a beseeching gesture. He'd never expected to hear a complaint about not collecting taxes.

"Something needs to change, Gill. You're dragging us all down with you."

There were demesnes in Mirabaya where a vassal could be flogged and hanged for speaking to their nobleman like that. He was glad she felt free enough to say what she thought, but what she said wasn't to his liking at all. Who was she to say how he lived his life? He knew of plenty of others who were far more decadent than he, taxing their vassals to the bone, then pissing it up against a wall. He only pissed away his own family money.

Jeanne sighed and shrugged. "Maybe we'd be better off with Lord Montpareil. Anyhow, there's no wine today. No reason for you to stay." She turned, and with a creak of the door, left Gill alone. He swore, then stood and shambled out.

▲▲▲▲▲▲

Gill sat on his porch the following morning, after a fitful night's sleep, and watched the lone horseman ride toward the village. His once fine, but now ramshackle, townhouse on the edge of the cluster of buildings that formed Villerauvais afforded him a clear view of anyone approaching, which was a rare occurrence. He drew on his pipe, hoping this person had not come to see him. He hadn't been able to find any wine in the house and his mood had soured as a result—not that he was ever particularly welcoming to visitors. Their only saving grace was that they were rare in Villerauvais. It was a village at the end of the road. There was nowhere to pass through to.

This person was either lost, or going to make a bad day worse. Gill hadn't had a drink since Jeanne had cut him off the previous day, hadn't slept well, and was now approaching his longest period of sobriety in memory. He was in no mood to receive a guest.

The horseman was well dressed in what Gill felt confident in assuming was the latest fashion in Mirabay, and had a colourful feather in his wide-brimmed hat. He didn't look like a dandy, though. His clothes, fitted and cut to allow movement, were the type worn by men who made their living with a sword. It was hard to imagine what a man like that wanted here—there wasn't much call for professional swordsmen.

The rider drew up by Gill's porch and doffed his hat. He looked at Gill as though they knew one another, but Gill couldn't place him. That wasn't to say they hadn't met, however. There were plenty of blank spaces in his memory of life in Mirabay. Even more since then.

"It's been a long time, Lord Villerauvais," the newcomer said. "You look . . . well."

Gill remained lounging on his rocking chair, his feet resting on the low railing surrounding the porch. His dusty, scruffy boots—including the hole in the left sole—were displayed to anyone who cared to look.

"I look ill and hungover," Gill said, "which is true on both counts. But I'm afraid you have the advantage of me."

"Of course." The rider slipped down from his saddle. "Banneret of the White Nicholas dal Sason at your service."

Gill shrugged.

"There's no reason for you to remember me," dal Sason said. "I was a boy when we met at court. Before I started at the Academy."

Not knowing how to respond, Gill shrugged again.

"To business, then. The king requests that you return to Mirabay."

"Ah," Gill said, stroking his moustache. He had a response to that, but kept it to himself. If the shrug had seemed unfriendly to dal Sason, this answer would scandalise him. "I must admit that comes as something of a surprise," Gill said. "I rather thought that old Boudain had forgotten about me."

"He had. He's dead. I bring his son's command. King Boudain the Tenth."

"I hadn't heard. It can take news some time to reach us out here. When?"

"About six months now."

Gill nodded. He wondered if the news had truly not reached Villerauvais, or if he was the only one that it had passed by. The latter struck him as far more likely. First Montpareil encroaching on his rights, now this. Jeanne was right, loath though he was to admit it.

"I can't imagine you were thrilled by the prospect of coming all the way out here."

Dal Sason shrugged now. "It's the king's command, and it's my duty to obey. As it is yours."

"The *king's* word?"

"The new king is his own man," dal Sason said. "He's cut from very different cloth than his father."

"So he's forced the Prince Bishop to retire to his estates?" Gill said, his voice pregnant with irony. Prince Bishop Amaury's cold corpse would have to be prised from his throne when the happy day of his death finally arrived.

Dal Sason blushed. "He's still at court."

Gill felt his temper flare. "Let me guess. On this occasion—as with all occasions in my experience—the king's command reached you via the Prince Bishop's lips."

Dal Sason was silent a moment, then sighed. "The king's word is the king's word. Orders under his seal are orders under his seal regardless of who hands them to you. You of all people should know that."

Guillot's eyes flashed with anger. If there had been a sword within reach, he would have grabbed it.

"I apologise," dal Sason said, raising his hands and taking a step back. "I didn't mean anything by that."

"You may tell the Prince Bishop that I politely decline the king's summons. I am no longer a courtier and am needed here to manage my estate. Should the Prince Bishop choose to take issue with this, you may tell him to charge me with whatever he pleases, and I shall kill whoever the king's champion is at my trial. As I did the last time." Guillot's gaze followed dal Sason's to his gut, which strained against the button that held his trousers closed, then to the hand that gripped the arm of his chair to keep from shaking. In his heart he knew that a child with a stick could likely get the better of him now. "I apologise for your wasted journey."

He started to gently rock his chair, took another long draw on his pipe and allowed his gaze to drift out to nothing in particular. Despite his effort to effect nonchalance, his curiosity was piqued. What could possibly convince the Prince Bishop to seek him out after all that had passed between them?

Dal Sason remained where he was, his mouth opening every so often, then closing again without a word. He had barely had time to dismount and had already failed his mission. Guillot sighed, feeling a pang of guilt.

"There aren't any inns here, but Jeanne the Taverner has a back room she can let you sleep in if you want to rest before returning to the city. Go to the end of the lane and turn left. You can't miss it. The food's good too. Everything's fresh. A benefit of country life. Probably best not to mention you're an acquaintance of mine."

"The benefits of country life are clear to be seen," dal Sason said with a hard edge to his voice. "I'm sorry for having bothered you, my Lord, and wish you good day." He mounted, doffed his hat, and rode on.

Guillot watched him go. He thought of dal Sason's parting words and looked himself over. His clothes were old, his gut more prominent than it had been the last time he had paid it any attention, and it was several days since he had last shaved. Four, he thought. Perhaps five. Nonetheless, he had the irritating feeling he had not heard the last of the matter. The Prince Bishop was not a man to refuse in the old days. Gill doubted the years had mellowed him.

Still, what use might Gill be now, considering how long it was since he had held a sword or gone to sleep sober? Perhaps Jeanne was right. Perhaps he had allowed too many things to get away from him. Then again, how fastidious did a man need to be about himself to oversee lands that produced artichokes and unremarkable grapes? In a place like Villerauvais, there was little to do but drink to the sun as it passed through the sky.

Realising his pipe had gone out, he had set about refilling it when a shrill voice broke the renewed quiet.

"Gill! Gill!"

Gill groaned. He seemed destined not to have any peace that day.

"Gill! Gill!" repeated the voice.

He wondered if his first step in taking firmer control of Villerauvais should be to demand that his vassals address him with the proper formality. It seemed likely the window of opportunity for that had long since passed. No one would have dared to call his father by his given name—not even Gill had done that.

"You have to come, Gill!"

The voice belonged to one of the village boys—Jacques—who was no more than seven or eight years old. Judging by his ruddy face, he had run the whole way from the small farm he lived on with his family.

"Father says you have to come," he said, between gasps, as though adding the authority of his father—a tenant farmer working a small patch of Gill's land—would lend the request sufficient weight to assure it was acceded to.

"What is it?" Gill said, trying not to be overly harsh on the boy, who was likely only following his father's instructions.

"Father wouldn't tell me. He said to bring your sword."

This caught Guillot's attention. There wasn't much that could go wrong in Villerauvais that needed a sword to put right, and Guillot was well enough acquainted with the boy's father to know he was not an alarmist. His first thought was that Montpareil might have taken to more aggressive tactics to collect taxes that weren't his to collect. That could indeed mean a fight, and one Gill thought likely to see him bleeding out on a patch of artichokes before the day was done. It had been a long time since Guillot had strapped a sword belt around his waist. If he was being honest, he had not thought the cause would ever arise again—the region was too poor for bandits, he was no longer an officer in the king's army, and most would agree that he had no honour left to impugn. He glanced at the straining button at his belly and feared his sword belt might not fit.

"Tell him I'll be along directly," Guillot said, getting to his feet and grimacing at the creaking in his knees. Inside his house, he opened the chest in the hall by the door. The hinges protested, reminding him of how long it had been since he last opened it. A purpose-built compartment contained three rapier and dagger sets, each blade glistening with preservative oil.

Few men could claim to own three Telastrian steel swords—the rarest and finest metal from which a blade could be made. Possibly he was the only one. Two he had won, the third he had inherited. Many young men dreamed of winning the Sword of Honour at the Academy in Mirabay. Only one did each year, as he had. The medium-width blade was a jack-of-all-trades, supposed to serve the wielder equally well on the battlefield or in a duel. Whatever career a young graduate might embark upon.

The second was something few even at the Academy dared dream of, with a narrower, lighter blade, more suited to duelling than anything else. The annual Competition drew the finest swordsmen from around the Middle Sea—usually masters or graduate students from each country's Academy of Swordsmanship—and that second Telastrian sword was Gill's prize for winning it. It seemed like half a lifetime ago. He supposed it almost was. The smile the memory brought him soured quickly.

The final blade was old and named, with an indecipherable etching in old Imperial along its fuller. It was called "Mourning," although Guillot had no idea why—perhaps something to do with all the men it had killed. The hilt was unfashionable and plainer than the others, but its dark Telastrian steel, swirling with blue accents, had a quality that the others did not—a quality that said "great deeds and heroic feats have been done with me." Its origin was so shrouded by the mist of time that it was almost legend. Its first owner—a distant ancestor of Guillot's—was one of the founding Chevaliers of the Order of the Silver Circle, a famed dragonslayer, champion of the king, and all-round overachiever. *Difficult shoes to fill*, he thought. Guillot had once been a member, though the Silver Circle was but a shadow of its former self by the time of his induction, little more than a gentlemen's club with drinking, gambling, and whoring as its aims, with the occasional duel thrown in.

His hand hovered over the named blade for a moment, but to touch it felt as though it would sully it. It deserved better than he. To use it for lesser feats such as those he might accomplish was to shame it, and to display it on his waist was an appalling concession to vanity. Guillot snatched the Sword of Honour and its matching dagger from their felt-lined resting places and put them in their scabbards. A deep breath got the buckle secured at the last hole on the belt and he was ready to go. He almost felt like a swordsman again.

Jacques was still waiting outside, impatiently shifting his weight from foot to foot. As soon as he set eyes on Gill, he tore off in the direction of his home. Gill followed, albeit with far less energy.

CHAPTER
3

Alpheratz woke again, this time comfortable in the knowledge that he had slept for no more than a few days—he could still feel the bulk of his meal straining against his belly. A meal of that size would take him nearly a month to completely digest. He drank in the view that never failed to capture his imagination; great limestone peaks covered in snow soaring over verdant valleys. It was the domain of dragonkind, given to them by the gods in gratitude for their fidelity. He remembered the different peaks not by the names man had given them, but by the names of the great dragons who had called them home. His gaze lingered on Nashira as he wondered if she still lived, or if she had been killed during his slumber. The thought made his stomach twist in despair.

His memory was better now. He could recall how mankind had taken it upon themselves to hunt down and exterminate dragons. There was great wealth in those mountains—metals and minerals that they coveted. At first trade had kept them satisfied. They had farmed cattle and sheep and bartered them with the dragons for access to the mountains. Letting them in had been a mistake. They had learned too many secrets.

There were special places, sacred places. Wells of energy where the very essence of the world bubbled to the surface. Places where the gods had walked when dragonkind was young and mankind were few. Men had learned of them—sometimes with the guidance and help of dragonkind who wished to help mankind. Humanity's magicians were never satisfied. They were always hungry for more power to fuel their wasteful efforts in shaping magic. They sought out the secret places. Coveted them. They tried to murder dragons by trading diseased and poisoned meat. Their outrages continued and increased, until dragonkind would take no more. Conflict followed.

Alpheratz's thoughts drifted to Nashira. The remembered sight of her soaring around her peak still made his heart race. His battles with Pharadon to win her affection had been ferocious. Pride swelled in his heart to think that he had prevailed in the end. He still wasn't sure how. With his greater size and lustrous red scales, everyone had thought Pharadon would be the one she chose, but it had not happened that way.

He wanted desperately to see her again. It was not unheard of for males to retreat deep into the mountains for decades—even centuries—after mating, but it would have been uncharacteristic for him. The question of why she had not come to look for him, to wake him from his slumber, popped into his mind, but he dismissed it quickly.

He scanned the sky for any sign of dragonkind, but saw none. On such a magnificent day it seemed impossible that none would be soaring around their peaks, revelling in the beauty of the world. Might they be hiding? Their absence was cause for concern, but he stopped short of hasty speculation.

He stretched his wings, then hesitated. He still felt weak. The Fount had strengthened him somewhat, the meal more so, but he was still feebler than he had been as a hatchling, hiding in the folds of his mother's wings. He needed to know what was going on, and there was no way he could walk all the way to Nashira's peak.

Alpheratz breathed deeply. The Fount tingled along his teeth, down his windpipe, and deep into his lungs. He tensed his shoulders and walked forward. Extending his wings as far as they would go, he threw himself from the mountainside. At first he fell, and something that had once been second nature felt like an unknown skill. He strained, willing his wings to grip the air, feeling its cold touch as it whistled past him at ever greater speed. His heart raced as he tried to remember the movements that had once come without thought. Finally he felt his wings catch and it all came back to him.

Soaring up, he rejoiced in the sensation. The air was rich with the Fount, like fertile soil, and it tingled against his flesh where he was not covered in scales. He allowed himself a moment to revel in it—he looped and rolled and dived between peaks until his muscles and lungs reminded him that he had slumbered for a long time. He climbed high, turned toward Nashira's peak, and allowed himself to glide with the wind.

▲▲▲▲▲▲

"Nashira!" It was rude to enter another dragon's cave without permission, even if she was his aerie-mate. Alpheratz called again, but there was no answer. If she were sleeping, he would apologise for waking her, but he could wait no longer. Her cave was dark and damp. She had never been the tidiest, but it was unkempt even for her.

"Nashira!" Alpheratz said again. Still no answer.

He continued moving deeper into the cave. Entering her sleeping chamber without invitation was insult enough to fight over. Nashira would be within her rights to kill Alpheratz for such presumptuousness. He called out one last time, then walked into her sleeping chamber.

She was there. A wave of despair washed over him. What was left of her was there. Alpheratz coughed in anguish. Her once beautiful golden scales were gone. The metal contained within them was considered even more valuable than that mined from the ground by the menfolk. Their mages used it in their magics. Nashira's horns and fangs had been pulled from her skull; more ingredients for human potions. Bones were all that remained of her.

Alpheratz thought he would be sick. There were scorch marks on the ceiling, all around. Hers and theirs. She had put up a hard fight. She would have. It was her character, and part of what he loved about her so much. His heart filled with rage and grief. She was the most beautiful of spirits, the most gentle of souls, and they had killed her.

Her character was not the only reason she would have fought so hard. Half a dozen eggs were nestled in a nook at the back of the cave—all split open. One still had the handle of an axe sticking out of it. The pain felt like it would crush Alpheratz. His rage grew until he could find no clarity of thought. The eggs were destroyed. The eggs they had created together with so much love and care. All of their brood, murdered before they had the chance to crack the shells of their eggs.

Alpheratz stumbled outside, overcome with grief. He was flying back to his cave before he knew what he was doing. He headed toward his deepest chamber, far within the mountain. It was the place where he hatched, where he could always find comfort. He thought back to what he remembered of the wars, trying to work out what might have happened.

The first violence had occurred far to the south. A sacred place was violated, and the dragon tasked with its custody reacted in the only way he could. He slew the men who had done it.

The men should have understood. They had broken the agreements and deserved the consequences. Events escalated from there. Men in shining armour travelled to the mountains to earn fame by slaying dragons. There had been glory in those battles, and Alpheratz had come to respect some of those men, brave despite the impossibility of the task they had set for themselves. Some were so skilled they had even managed to kill a dragon. It was honest battle, bravely fought. Little different than when two dragons came to blows.

Then the mages came. They changed things. They always attacked in large numbers. They drew so hard on the Fount they could completely drain it, leaving the grass brown, the plants wilted, and any dragon unfortunate enough to be close severely weakened. They brought a different type of warrior with them: men touched by magic. Men who could do things, survive things, that no ordinary man should have been able to. That was when the tide had turned against dragonkind.

When a dragon was weakened by magic, the new warriors could corner it and kill it. This was not a battle; it was slaughter. Murder. The men had been unlucky with Alpheratz, however. His mountain was one of the sacred places. It housed one of the ancient stones, the wells, where the Fount was so strong it could be seen with the naked eye. The mages had drawn on it so hard they had extinguished its ethereal blue glow. Even now, it remained shrouded in darkness. Draining it was something Alpheratz had not thought possible, and in his moment of distraction, the men had dealt him a great blow.

The mages and their warriors had thought he was finished, and grew over-confident. What little Fount remained had restored enough of his strength for one more act. He had allowed them near enough to touch him. One had laid his hand flat on Alpheratz's snout and told his comrades a joke. They had not laughed however—the punch line had coincided with the brazen one being swallowed by flame, something the others experienced moments later. The memory made Alpheratz smile, but did little to quell the sorrow in his heart or the rage boiling his blood.

Perched on a rocky outcrop, Alpheratz watched the valley intently. He had never paid much attention to men until they started hunting and killing dragonkind. Then he had done his best to stay away from them. Fighting had never interested him much—except to win Nashira's affections—but now he could think of nothing else. They had murdered her. Murdered his young.

A cluster of small buildings straddled a stream some way down the hill. Stone chimneys surrounded by golden thatch puffed smoke into the air. People had been wandering about earlier, but all seemed to be inside now. Contained. It would make what he planned all the easier.

His muscles were still wasted and his flame glands were shrivelled. He didn't have the strength to chase them or to blast flame about with abandon. In their tiny houses, they would be easy prey. He waited for the light to fade a little more, giving him greater advantage with his superior eyes, then stretched his wings, allowing them to bite into the air and carry him down to the village below.

As he glided close, he squeezed his flame glands. At first, nothing happened. He worried that he had over-taxed them in the cavern. It took time for the glands to fill the bladders, but he had heard of those who had over-stressed their glands, damaging them beyond use. They had not lived long. There were only so many peaks where a dragon could dwell, and if you couldn't defend yours, your life would be short.

He breathed a sigh of relief as he felt the glands compress and tasted the welcome flavour of the fluids as they sprayed from his mouth and ignited on contact with the air. The thatched roofs were dry and caught quickly. In his first pass, he set light to every building in that small hamlet. The smell of the smoke and the sensation of the heat as he passed over a second time were a joy. The screams that followed were music to his ears. The screams had stopped by his third pass, but still he revelled in the flight, the flames, the fury. When finally he stopped spraying the hamlet with flame, little remained. The fire was so intense that the village burned to ash in only a few minutes.

He landed to take a closer look at his work. It satisfied him deeply to see how easily man could be erased from the face of the land. In a single growing season, there would be nothing left to suggest people had lived here. Though it had been easier than he had expected, it had left him tired again. In his eagerness, he had reduced the animal pens to dust, and there was no nourishment to be had.

He needed to rebuild his strength, to feed regularly. He took to the air once more, looking for food this time, rather than vengeance, though the latter was never far from his mind. Menfolk had ventured too far into dragon country. They had killed his aerie-mate and their brood. Men would ever be his enemy. They would suffer. They would burn. They would learn their place in the world and never dare to test their betters again. He would drive them back to their little island in the middle of the great sea with such prejudice that they would never dare set foot in these hallowed lands again.

Alpheratz spotted a larger village in the distance, one with outlying farm buildings that would provide plenty to eat. He needed to be careful, though. A larger settlement might mean soldiers—perhaps magicians and their special warriors—and he was not yet ready to deal with that. He looked around again and saw a farm a distance away. Better. His target picked—a large barn that he hoped was filled with cattle or something else to sate his appetite—he swooped.

Gill was out of breath by the time he reached the farm, well behind
Jacques. The boy's father, Alain, worked a small patch of land tucked
into a bend of the river that ran through the limestone valley that was
the Seigneury of Villerauvais. Upstream of the village, it was one of the most
picturesque landholdings in Gill's demesne, with a magnificent view of the
village, the manor house, and the limestone crags, pastures, and lush green
forests that surrounded them.

Jacques's agitation had grown as they had neared the farm, and Alain's expression when they arrived at his small house confirmed Gill's impression
that something serious was afoot. It seemed odd that after so long undisturbed,
two events coincided on the same day. The world could be an unpredictable
place, he thought. Perhaps he was just unlucky?

"Good afternoon, Alain," Gill said.

"Good afternoon, m'Lord."

Gill raised an eyebrow in surprise. *Serious indeed*, he thought. Other than
dal Sason, he couldn't remember the last time someone had called him
"m'Lord." "Your boy seemed rather in a state when he came to fetch me."

"Run on and help your mother, Jacques," Alain said. He watched the boy
run off before turning his attention back to Gill. "Something I need to show
you."

Gill followed him along a dirt path between two small fields toward where
Alain grazed his small herd of sheep. His curiosity grew with each step, and
he was beginning to think that Lord Montpareil was not involved. In the centre of the pasture was a large, circular scorch mark, like the black stain left by
bonfires on festival nights. Gill could see what looked like the charred remains
of four, possibly five, sheep in the burnt patch.

"A little overdone, I'd have said," Gill said. He grimaced when Alain didn't react to the attempt at humour, but considering half of his flock had been lost, that was not surprising.

"Found them like that this morning," Alain said, his eyes locked on the carcasses.

Gill's vassals rarely sought his help, and considering what Jeanne had said, he felt he at least had to appear to be making an effort. He knelt by the burnt patch and touched it with his fingertips.

"Did you see anything?" Gill said.

"Nothing."

The grass was burned to dust and there was little enough left of the sheep. It had been a hot fire, which would have needed lots of wood and taken some time to reach that temperature. It struck him as unlikely that Alain would not have noticed the effort required to create such a blaze. It was quiet there at night; you could hear the river and every insect. The fire could not have been built without making some noise, and that did not take into account rounding up and killing the sheep. Not to mention the fact that there didn't seem to be any remnants of the fuel. No wood or coal.

"Who'd do this?" Alain said.

"Who indeed?" Guillot said. Coincidence and mystery, he thought. Montpareil, perhaps? But why? The Prince Bishop? He needed to have another chat with dal Sason.

⏶⏶⏶⏶⏶⏶

Dal Sason was eating soup when Guillot walked into the tavern. Beside his bowl was a bottle of the wine Jeanne had sworn she did not have. Guillot cursed under his breath as he strode over. Dal Sason watched him approach, spoon paused mid-air, soup dripping back into the bowl.

Guillot sat down at dal Sason's table. "I'm having trouble with a coincidence."

"Really?"

"You turn up the day after something very unusual happens on my land."

"What was that?" dal Sason said.

"You tell me. Did you bring some soldiers with you? Hungry ones, perhaps? What's going on?"

"I came here alone," dal Sason said. "As fast as my horse could carry me. I don't know what you're talking about."

Guillot sat back and scrutinised him. He didn't appear to be lying.

"I was going to call on you again later," dal Sason said. "I'm not one to run home a failure. The Prince Bishop was emphatic in wanting you back in the city."

"Why does he want me?"

Dal Sason shrugged. "I'm only the messenger. I'm not privy to the reasoning behind my orders."

"You have no idea what the Prince Bishop, or the king, want of me?"

"None."

Guillot swore. Jeanne humphed from behind the bar.

"You'd be making my life a lot easier if you simply agree to come back to Mirabay with me."

"And if I don't?"

"I return alone, and who knows? Perhaps they'll send a regiment to fetch you," dal Sason said.

"The Prince Bishop wants me to come back that badly?"

"The *king* wants you to come back."

Guillot drummed his fingers on the table and studied dal Sason once more. "Look me in the eye and tell me you don't know anything about the burned sheep."

Dal Sason frowned, looking confused. It was enough to be certain he had no idea what Guillot was talking about.

"There's no need to answer," Guillot said. "There's some trouble with one of my tenants, so it's not a good time to be thinking of heading off on a jaunt. I don't want to come back and find them all at war with one another. I'm sorry if breaking the bad news goes hard on you, but I'm not going back with you. Tell the Prince Bishop to send a regiment if he wants me that badly."

⩕⩕⩕⩕⩕

Guillot woke to hammering on his door. He put on a robe and gathered up his sword. It occurred to him how quickly old habits returned as he reached the door. It was long after dawn, and the bright light hurt his eyes. He had fallen asleep on the couch, without a bottle, which was in danger of becoming the norm. Unfortunately, it felt as though he had been drinking—all the hangover, none of the fun. His head pounded and his body felt drained. All he wanted was to crawl into bed and sleep the day away. Or to lay hands on a bottle. Either would do. He opened the door, torn between feeling the need to be polite and welcoming and the desire to vent his foul humour.

"I'm sorry for disturbing you so early, m'Lord," the woman at the door said.

Her name was Celeste, a farmer's wife, although he struggled to remember exactly where their farm was. *Somewhere down the valley?* he thought. Guillot did a double take at once again being called "m'Lord." Was it the sword?

"What's the problem?"

"Philipe, my husband, sent me to fetch you. Our herd was attacked during the night." If the farm was down the valley as he thought, it was as far from Alain's as you could get while remaining on Guillot's land.

"Give me a moment," he said. "I'll come and take a look."

He went to his room and dressed quickly, then joined her. They walked side by side in uncomfortable silence, she no doubt unsure of how to make small talk with a nobleman, while he had no idea of how to make small talk with one of his vassals. They had not gone far before sweat beaded on his forehead, though it was not a hot day. His head throbbed and his stomach complained with all the characteristics of a hangover.

They passed through the village and along the lane that led to the farms farther down the valley. Philipe waited for them by a large scorch mark in his pasture that looked very similar to the one in Alain's. At its centre were the carcasses of two cows.

Guillot's stomach turned over, an odd feeling considering the air was filled with the delicious smell of freshly roasted beef. What had happened was not an isolated incident, and it stood to reason that it might happen again. Unless someone stopped it. That someone would have to be him. The thought made the throbbing in his head escalate to pounding. It was not proving to be a good day for sobriety.

"Do you have any idea what happened?" Guillot said, not hopeful of getting anything useful from the farmer or his wife, who stood behind him.

"I . . . I . . . I don't know," Philipe said.

"Tell him," Celeste said between her teeth.

Guillot raised an eyebrow.

"I was out in the yard last night taking a p—" His wife backhanded him across the arm. "I was out last night . . . doing my business," Philipe said, "when there was this whistling noise. Not too loud, mind, just like a gust of wind. Then this great big ball of fire appears and smashes down into the pasture."

The local grapes might produce more bad bottles than the average, but that didn't stop anyone from drinking it, least of all Guillot; so he was in no position to criticise, but his initial reaction was that Philipe had been in his cups the night before. There must have been something very wrong with Philipe's bottle to cause that kind of hallucination, however.

"You're certain?" Guillot said. "A ball of fire?"

Philipe nodded hesitantly.

"That's not all," Celeste said. She nudged her husband.

"After the fireball hit the ground, and my cattle, there was something else. A shadow. A great, dark shadow came down from the sky. It ate them."

Guillot frowned and turned back to the burnt remains. There was barely any meat left on the bones, as had been the case with Alain's sheep, but Guillot had assumed there that the flesh had been burned away and hadn't investigated further. He walked up to these remains and gave them a proper look. Here and there he could see white, rather than burnt black, bone. The pale patches looked as though they had been hit with a large, heavy blade. An axe, or a great sword, perhaps. The rapier strapped to his waist could not have caused marks like them. What kind of animal could leave a mark like that?

He shook his head. The answer had to be far simpler: the Prince Bishop was toying with him. He must already have men in the area, and soldiers needed to be fed. He had sent men to wreak havoc on Guillot's demesne to convince him to agree to whatever he wanted from Guillot. It was infuriating, but there was little Guillot could do. The further he had fallen, the higher the Prince Bishop had risen. Guillot could raise his levies and patrol the farms at night, but they would need weeks of training to stand a chance against soldiers, and like as not his force would only arrive after an attack had occurred.

The Prince Bishop knew all that, of course. It was galling to know the man could still reach out from Mirabay and play with Guillot's life. Perhaps Guillot was being too sensitive—after all, it had been many years since he had left Mirabay and he had not spoken with the old king since the day he'd left, nor the new one. He had no influence, no career, no fame. What did he have that might make the Prince Bishop jealous? Could the man's old hatred still burn so deeply?

Gill supposed it could be a belek. They rarely came as far down from the mountains as Villerauvais, and never at this time of year, but he supposed they could inflict wounds such as those on the carcasses. Might a rogue one be stalking the demesne? It seemed unlikely, but more plausible than the alternatives he was coming up with. A belek didn't explain the scorch marks, though. The fireball, he reckoned, could be put down to bad wine and an over-active imagination. Guillot had seen equally strange things while drunk, only to discover the next morning that they had occurred nowhere but in his head.

"What did it look like?" Guillot said. "The shadow?"

Philipe blushed. "Don't rightly know, my Lord." Another nudge from his wife. "Feels foolish saying it out loud," Philipe said, "but it reminded me of how dragons are described in the old stories."

"Dragons?" Guillot said, doing his best not to laugh.

Philipe shrugged.

"Dragons," Guillot repeated, looking back at the charred bones, wondering if perhaps the time had come for him to have all the seigneury's vines pulled up and replaced with something that could not be fermented.

▲▲▲▲▲▲

No banneret in the king's service could be expected to give up easily, all the more so when the Prince Bishop was involved in handing out the instructions. Dal Sason was inspecting fruit at a market stall when Guillot walked back into the village. The visitor greeted Guillot with a nod and a warm smile, which Guillot made no effort to return. He still felt sick and now had the added worry that either his demesne was under attack by dragons or his vassals were going mad. Perhaps he had imagined the whole thing? His mother had always said if something seems too good to be true, it probably is, and the thought of insanity being the explanation did indeed seem too good to be true at that moment.

He couldn't forget the old stories of the Chevaliers of the Silver Circle, that gilded fraternity of decadent wastrels. He'd thought the older Chevaliers were simply trying to frighten him with the hocus-pocus of their midnight initiation ceremony at a strange, ancient carved stone in the crypts beneath the old citadel in Mirabay. He had thought them nothing more than an idle ceremonial bodyguard to the king, a place where a safe career could be made while he settled down and started a family. The Chevaliers had seemed like the perfect solution for a country nobleman of modest means and his beautiful young wife in a big, expensive city. The fame he had won with his victory in the Competition had opened the path to advancement and he had seized it with both hands.

Guillot was drawn to the Chevaliers. As a boy, he had loved the old tales of their deeds, of dragon-slaying and derring-do—stories of Andalon, Ixten, and Valdamar, the most famous of the dragon-slaying Chevaliers. As a man, he had never been under any illusion as to what their modern brethren represented. He even questioned how much of the old stories was true. After all, he'd never seen any dragon remains. Even after so long a time, with so many said to have been slain, surely some trophies would remain? So far as he knew, none did.

While stories of the Chevaliers had filled his head with too much nonsense to completely discount Philipe's tale, he could not quite believe it. As he watched dal Sason squeeze and smell fruit and vegetables, he wondered how much more the man knew than he was letting on. Questions would have to wait, however. He felt terrible and knew that only sleep would ease his suffering. Dal Sason and the mystery in the fields would keep until morning.

CHAPTER
5

Amaury dal Richeau, the Prince Bishop of Mirabay and the Unified Church, First Minister of Mirabaya, blinked the sweat from his eyes and launched into a fast combination of cuts and thrusts, driving the salon master back down the fencing gallery.

"Excellent, my Lord, excellent," the fencing master said as he retreated.

Amaury smiled at the praise. The salon master—an Ostian by the name of Dandolo—was regarded as the best private trainer in Mirabay. He was always frugal with his compliments, irrespective of his trainee—professional duellist or nobleman—so to get it was worth one of Amaury's as-rare smiles.

Out of the corner of his eye, the Prince Bishop could see one of his assistants appear at the gallery's doorway. The momentary distraction allowed Dandolo the opportunity to riposte and score a hit, and the Prince Bishop stretched another smile and nodded to acknowledge the blow.

"I think that will be enough for today, Maestro," Amaury said, raising his rapier in salute. He waited until Dandolo had returned the gesture before turning to his assistant.

In his clerical robes, the assistant looked out of place in a fencing salon, but at least he had the presence of mind to offer Amaury a towel and a glass of water. He took both, then wiped the sweat from his brow and took a drink before speaking.

"What is it?"

"The king wishes to see you, your Grace."

"Of course he does. Did he say why?"

His assistant remained silent.

"Ah," Amaury said. "Silence can often say far more than you might think. There's a lesson in that. Tell him that I'll attend him directly."

With a nod, his assistant left. Amaury placed his training sword in its leather sheath and went to the changing room. As he peeled off his sweaty fencing clothes, he could not help but glance at the place on his hip where he had carried a wicked scar for the greater part of his adult life. The memory of it, and of the resultant ruination of his career, would be forever with him, even if the physical damage was all but gone. A less powerful man might have had to explain the disappearance of a severe limp, of a lingering injury that had ended any hope of a career as a swordsman or soldier, but not he.

No one had so much as raised an eyebrow when he started walking normally again. The leg was far from perfect, merely healed to the limit of the healer's magical ability, but with a little luck, his plans would come to fruition. Then he could personally finish what the Order's healers had started. He wondered why people had been content to live without magic for so many centuries. Indeed, they positively hated it. If only they knew the benefits it could bring, he felt certain their opinion would change. A few repaired joints, a few cured children, and they would welcome magic back with open arms. He needed to be careful picking the time, but it was growing near.

He would not be able to keep his order of mage-warriors secret forever. The old king had known of them, as did the new one. No secret known by three men was much of a secret, even if one was dead. The young monarch's scrutiny of his recently inherited kingdom had been inconvenient for Amaury, but thankfully King Boudain the Tenth had seen the sense in his project. He'd set it in motion soon after discovering a treasure trove of ancient and forbidden knowledge in a great vault beneath Mirabay's cathedral. The archive had re-opened the way to the practise of magic, something that had been outlawed for centuries, since the bannerets of old had overthrown the mages who had, in their turn, usurped the empire. The opportunity had been too tempting to pass up, so he had, in secret, established the Order of the Golden Spur. The Spurriers. He had known it would be a long-term project, one that would take decades to bring fully to fruition.

Training new mages properly was a lengthy task. Work had to start when the candidates were children, and they would be of little use until they were grown. Some progress could be made with adults, but the later one came to magic, the less power one would ever be able to wield. That was Amaury's own curse. Parlour tricks were the most potent magics he could create, and he knew he was too old to ever get any better.

The books spoke of those born with a natural affinity for magic. He had found one or two such people, but no one with the kind of power he had read of. The books also spoke of the Cup—and that could change everything. He had to find it first, however, and that was proving more challenging than he liked. He knew he had to be patient—never his strong suit. But the day would come when it was in his possession, and the power the Cup would bring with it would be awesome. No nation in the world would be able to stand against Mirabaya. No leader would be able to deny the absolute primacy of the church. *Amaury's* absolute primacy.

As he took his bishop's robes from the locker, Amaury wondered if he would have achieved even a fraction of his wealth and power if he had lived his life with a sword in his hand, rather than a prayer book. It seemed unlikely. Not until he'd been cured had he fully realised how much he had missed fighting with a sword in hand, though only now, after several months of practise, did he feel he was approaching any sort of competence. His skills were still a long way from what they had once been, but to have reclaimed anything at all was deeply satisfying. Nonetheless, it wasn't seemly for the Prince Bishop of the Unified Church to be frittering away his time in fencing salons, so he had done his best to keep his hobby a secret.

Covering himself in a hooded cloak, he left by the back entrance. It was only a short distance to the palace from the salon, so he wouldn't keep the king waiting for long. He briefly considered taking the elevator up to the palace, which sat on a hill overlooking the city. The elevator was a wooden contraption used to haul supplies and the less mobile members of the king's court up to the top of the hill and powered by oxen turning a great windlass at the top. After a moment, the Prince Bishop decided to walk the winding avenue up the hill's side. Since having his injury taken care of, he enjoyed the novelty of walking with ease.

The palace guards knew him on sight and waved him through every checkpoint between the main gate and the king's private office. Only then did he stop, knock, and wait to be invited in. Boudain the Tenth sat behind a desk piled so high with papers that Amaury struggled to see him without standing on his tiptoes. The young king seemed to want to directly deal with every matter his father had left to others, and Amaury wondered how long that would last.

"You wish to see me, your Highness?"

The servant who had shown Amaury in slipped out silently, leaving the two men alone in the dimly lit room.

"I do. I received this note by pigeon this morning." King Boudain scratched his neatly clipped beard as he scanned his desk. He pushed a rolled note toward Amaury before sitting back and waiting.

Amaury unrolled the note, scanning for the general gist rather than reading it. His stomach sank; returning to the beginning, he began to read properly. It irritated him that the king had received word of these events before he had—he maintained a very expensive network of spies and informants to make sure he was always the first person to know what was going on. Now it seemed the new king had managed to make his own intelligence services do some work—for the first time in generations. He had gotten halfway through the note when the king spoke.

"I presume this is our problem made real?"

The paper spoke of a rural hamlet completely reduced to ash. It was described as being "nothing more than a smudge on the ground." The sheet was stamped at the bottom with a small staff, skull, and sword—the sigil of the Intelligenciers. If nothing else, it was evidence that in his short reign, the king had shown the strength to bring one of his more independently minded hunting dogs under control. If that trend continued, he could become far more difficult to manage than his father was.

"It seems likely," Amaury said.

"You assured me this wouldn't become an issue."

"We're venturing into the unknown, your Highness. There will always be problems that we cannot foresee."

"This could become quite a big one. More so if your little secret army is discovered. The people aren't ready for magic, and you know as well as I do how the citizens of Mirabay respond to things they don't like."

It had only been about a year since the last riot, and Amaury remembered it well. A group of rioters had broken into his house on the south bank of the River Vosges and tried to set the place on fire. Amaury believed the riot was an expression of discontent with an ageing and increasingly dissolute ruler. He expected the change of monarch would put to rest that type of behaviour and give him peace for a decade or so—enough time to put his plans in motion. A major upset to the city's population could change that in a matter of minutes. Nonetheless, he didn't like the king's implication. Boudain had known about the Spurriers since taking the crown, and had been more than happy to have them developing in the background.

"It's *your* secret army, your Highness. You agreed with me that it was vital to the kingdom's security. Both the Ostians and the Estranzans are reported to have used mages recently. It will only happen more frequently, and when it does, we do not want to be left behind. *Great foresight and initiative*, I believe you said when we first discussed it. We have access to records that give us a great advantage. We would be fools not to put their contents to use."

Amaury sat down, forcing the king to move the papers on his desk to maintain eye contact. He wondered if he was taking a liberty. Although he'd known the king most of his life, for most of that time, he had been a prince. When they came into power, Amaury knew, some people got all sorts of foolish notions of having to assert themselves. He had yet to work out if Boudain the Tenth was one such person, but there was only one way to find out.

"In any event," Amaury said, "I'm sure it won't come to that. This is only a minor hiccup that will be dealt with in due course. It won't alter the timeline of our plan. The Spurriers won't be revealed to the people before they are ready to accept the idea."

"Minor hiccup?" the king said. "You woke up a damned dragon. A real, fire-breathing, people-killing dragon. It's already started its rampage. A small rural village we can keep quiet. What happens when it attacks a major town? It's been so long since one has been seen, I dare say most people don't even believe they ever existed. Think of the panic it will cause."

"If it lives, it can be killed, your Highness, and kill it we will. We have the resources at our disposal. It's only a matter of time."

The king sat back in his chair. "I'm entitled to be nervous. The first year or so of a new reign is always difficult, and what you are endeavouring to do with the Spurriers will turn a millennium of tradition and law on its head. This . . . could change everything. The first king in centuries to have to deal with a dragon? This could define my reign. It could put a stop to your plans."

What we *are endeavouring to do.* Our *plans*, Amaury thought. If things went wrong, he wasn't going to take the blame alone. King or not, Boudain would share the consequences. If this boy thought he could leave a man like Amaury dangling in the wind when the going got tough, he was sorely mistaken.

"I understand, your Highness, but this is not the time to vacillate. Quite the opposite. We must double our resolve and see it through. If we do, it will all work as I have planned. To put your mind at ease, I can tell you that I've already taken steps to deal with this. With luck, the next news you have of the dragon will be of its slaughter. In the worst case, we'll lose a few more remote hamlets, and have some old wives' tales and rumours of strange goings on in the countryside to dismiss as being ridiculous. Better still, with a little time to apply my mind to it, I'm sure I can come up with a way to turn it all to our advantage."

Boudain steepled his hands before his mouth, then let out a sigh. "What steps?"

"For the time being, I'd like to keep that to myself. Rest assured, I've consulted the ancient texts in the cathedral library and found a workable solution."

"Some giant, dragon-killing ballista?"

Amaury laughed. "No, your Highness, nothing so crude. I hope you will be pleasantly surprised when I'm in a position to reveal what I'm working on."

▲▲▲▲▲▲

Amaury sat in the study of his town palace, overlooking the River Vosges and the twinkling lights of the old citadel on the island that sat at its centre. The Cathedral was hidden behind a packed cluster of buildings, only the tops of its two steeples visible, silhouetted against the stars. The Prince Bishop held an old document, one that could get a lesser man sent to the Intelligenciers' dungeons. It might even be enough to get *him* sent there, should he be caught with it. Although the information it contained was little more than a story, it came from a time when magic had reigned supreme, and was thus considered as illegal as anything could be.

It recounted the early days of the Chevaliers of the Silver Circle. Amaury had wanted to count himself among their number ever since he first heard of them. They had been the doyens of bravery and chivalry in Mirabaya since the days of the Empire, until they were all but extinguished by a bad-tempered, young country nobleman. Admittedly, by that time, little about the Chevaliers held true to their original fame. They were a bunch of arrogant, debauched ingrates who lived off a fat royal pension and spent their days gambling, whoring, and causing trouble. Amaury's ambition to be a Chevalier had been erased the first time he met one.

The Chevaliers originally formed in the later days of the Empire, to deal with a problem largely peculiar to what was then called the Imperial Province of Mirabensis. Dragons. Although at that time a dragon could be encountered in any mountainous part of the Empire, there seemed to be a higher concentration of them in the peaks in western Mirabensis. The emperor had come to the provincial capital and established the Silver Circle, formed of the bravest bannerets in the Empire. They had already been magically enhanced in any number of ways by the Imperial Magi during their initial training as bannerets, as all bannerets were in those days, but these select few received further boons to equip them to hunt down and slay dragons. They became both mage and swordsman, and over the course of the next few centuries slew every dragon in the Empire. Perhaps every dragon in the world. Except this one, it seemed.

Of course, it might all be legend. The document was irritatingly vague, and ever described things in the most general of ways. Many of the documents the Unified Church had rescued from the burning of the mages' colleges had proven to be fantastical nonsense, and Amaury could easily imagine the arrogant Chevaliers embellishing their reputation. That he heeded the document at all was testimony to how concerned he was. He stood, leaving the parchment on his desk, and walked to the window. He tried to imagine what the citadel would look like with a dragon hovering above, blasting everything with flame, and shuddered. He had no great love for the citizenry, but if Mirabay and all its great buildings were reduced to ash, all he had worked so hard for, all his wealth, power, and influence, would count for nothing.

Returning to his desk, he looked at the document again. Each Chevalier, up to the present day, underwent a secret initiation ritual presided over by the incumbent Chevaliers. They had joked and laughed about it, always hinting at its mystical nature to others, but never elaborating. He thought it unlikely there was still anything magical about the ritual—the Intelligenciers would have dragged the Chevaliers off if there had been. However, as he was learning from the documents and the Spurriers' experiments at the Priory, its headquarters in an old monastery in the north of the city, you didn't necessarily need to know you were doing magic to do it. Words focussed the mind. Intent and desire focussed the mind. A focussed mind shaped magic.

Because of that, somehow, Guillot dal Villerauvais might now be the answer to his country's problem. He was the last surviving Chevalier of the Silver Circle.

He had sent a man to fetch Gill as soon as Commander Leverre had returned with news of the dragon. It had been a knee-jerk reaction and the thought of their shared history gave him some concern. His hip ached when he thought on it. What troubles, he wondered, would Guillot dal Villerauvais bring him this time?

Ever the enterprising one, Guillot solved his problem by siphoning off half a dozen bottles from the tanks in the fermenting hall on the edge of the village. The wine was weak and tasted terrible, but by the time he had drained the second bottle, it had chased away most of his demons. When it grew dark and Villerauvais quieted for the night, he was left with his memories and his thoughts—a poisonous combination. He slouched in an easy chair in his room by the window and looked out over his small village as he filled and drained glass after glass, pushing memories away and making thought difficult.

The night was clear; he could see the moon and the stars. The pale moonlight was blotted out for an instant, so briefly Guillot almost missed it. His heart began racing before his mind had absorbed what he'd seen. He stood and rushed to the back window, pressing himself against it to get the greatest field of vision. After a moment of searching, he spotted it, a great, unmistakable shape blotting out the stars as it moved lazily through the night sky.

Guillot watched it disappear, then sat. From the feeling in the pit of his stomach, he knew it was Philipe's "shadow." He suddenly felt very sober, and was not one bit grateful for the fact. It was the bottle. It had to be the bottle. There was something wrong with the fermenting tanks—mould, perhaps. That was the obvious answer.

No matter how hard he tried to convince himself, he knew that in the morning, there would be a knock at his door to tell him more livestock had been killed. As he drifted toward a troubled sleep, slouched in his chair, he prayed it would only be livestock.

⌄⌄⌄⌄⌄⌄

The small farms made it easier for Alpheratz to feed. He did not have the stamina to go chasing through the mountains after ibex or chamois, but with sheep, goats, and cattle parcelled out in pens or small fields, the farms allowed Alpheratz to gorge without having to exert himself. He fed each night, then spent the morning gliding over the mountains, seeking out others of his kind. So far he had not even seen a hint of their presence, and he began to despair that what he had felt in his gut from the moment he woke was the truth. He was the last of his kind.

Only when he was exhausted—though his stamina grew each day—did he return to his peak to rest, forlorn. Each afternoon when he woke, he felt stronger than the day before, but still hollow at the thought that all those he knew and cared for were gone. He knew in his bones that they had all died violent deaths and consoled himself with the fact that it would not be long before he could start to exact revenge.

As he lay down at the mouth of his cavern, waiting for the night, he studied the valleys before him. In the distance, he could see the twinkling lights of another village, and wondered if he should visit there the next day. He knew the humans would eventually learn to hide their livestock from his nightly attacks and would eventually call their soldiers for help. One or two more trips to the village he had visited three previous times would clean it out completely. He would strip it bare, then destroy the human population and move on to the next village, satiating the hunger created by years and years of slumber. He smiled at the twinkling lights out on the horizon. The people who lit them had no idea what was coming.

The only thing extending his patience was the feeling in every limb that his body was growing strong again. He hungered for the moment when he burned the first large town to ash. Only then would the humans understand the pain and suffering their greed had caused. Only then would they learn the price of their arrogance.

⌄⌄⌄⌄⌄⌄

There were the mornings, after he'd consumed a particularly bad vintage, when Guillot could think about nothing other than how ill he felt. There were mornings when he woke thinking of nothing at all—those were his favourites. Then there were the mornings when he woke with the past ten years forgotten, and looked to his left, expecting his wife to be there in the bed beside him. Those were the worst.

That morning, his first thought was of the shadow. How it moved silently, blotting out the stars as it went. His dreams had been of fire and destruction. The notion that alcohol was finally driving him to madness was actually welcome. The alternative, that something from children's myths was wreaking havoc on his demesne, was too difficult to cope with.

One way or the other, Guillot knew he could not sit idle. He had been so careless in his responsibilities that a neighbouring lord was collecting taxes in his demesne. Worse, he could do nothing about it. Now his vassals' livestock were being killed. If they ran him out of town, he couldn't blame them. The peasants and villagers of Villerauvais were his responsibility, and he had to take action. Half a dozen villagers regularly trained at arms, his levy should the king ever call upon him to satisfy his feudal obligations. They had not been mustered since his father's time, and he had no idea if any of the able-bodied men required to answer the call would respond. Nonetheless, that was his next step—he needed eyes and ears on the ground to report what was happening.

When he finally managed to rise from his bed, he headed to the village hall to see the mayor. The building had pride of place next to the church with its tall steeple, overlooking the small galleried square that formed the centre of Villerauvais. As seigneur, he had the right to enter unannounced, but knocked first regardless. The mayor, René, was also the village's winemaker, and Gill knew he wouldn't be popular considering Lord Montpareil's recent tax raid. The sense of shame he felt as he entered took him by surprise, and it occurred to him that the last time he'd been in the village hall was when he was a boy, with his father. Little had changed—a long table sat in the centre of the room, surrounded by chairs on the flagstone floor.

Windows fronting onto the square let in some light, but not enough. In the absence of a village meeting, René had foregone the expense of lighting any candles, so the interior was dim. The Villerauvais coat of arms was carved into the wall at the back of the hall. It loomed over Guillot like a great shaming statement.

"Is this about the slaughtered cattle or the wine?" René said. He looked up from the pile of papers spread before him, delicate wire spectacles perched precariously on the bridge of his nose. "Jeanne said she'd geld me if I give you a bottle from the barrels."

"The cattle," Gill said. "Something needs to be done."

"I agree. Richard's herd was attacked last night. Three head gone. Things will be tough on him and his family without them. Alain, Philipe, Richard, and I have agreed to patrol the fields around the village from dusk until midnight for the next two evenings. I'll make a report of our findings and send it on to Trelain. I'm sure the duke will send soldiers."

"I, well, it's good to know that everything's in hand." Gill stood there a moment longer, a sickening feeling of disappointment in his gut. What had he expected? That they would sit around in the forlorn hope that he would get himself together?

"So, about that bottle?" he asked. "Is there any chance at all?"

Anger replaced disappointment as Guillot walked away from the village square without the bottle he had been hoping for. It seemed the mayor was just as afraid of Jeanne as everyone else. He saw dal Sason lurking outside his townhouse, so executed a quick right turn to avoid being spotted. The lane he found himself on led out of the village and toward his family home, Villerauvais Manor. His father had run the seigneury from there, maintaining a lofty distance from his tenants and only venturing into town if he had good reason. That was the more traditional way of doing things. Guillot knew he was far from the perfect lord, but he liked to think the people felt more comfortable around him than they had with his father.

Guillot rarely called at the manor house. It was overly grand for the demesne it presided over, and from the look of the ruins scattered about its grounds, it had once been grander still. Parts of the building were very old, with more recent extensions here and there. His father had claimed that the oldest parts of the house dated back to Imperial times, but Gill had never believed that. Claiming a direct connection to the very ancient past seemed to be a mark of pride for nobles, as if estates, wealth, and fine houses were not already enough. The place had never been much of a home to him; he'd been sent to school in Mirabay at a young age, and from there directly on to the Academy. He had always thought he and his wife, Auroré, would turn it into a home and start a family. The gods had other plans, however.

The current caretaker was the family steward, an old banneret called Yves, who did his best with it, but with limited resources and an absent lord, he could be forgiven for allowing the upkeep to slide. It was a bit of a walk from the village, but without anything else pressing on his time, it seemed as good a destination as any.

Gill breathed a little harder than he would have liked by the time he arrived, but felt as though the walk had done him good. His head had cleared somewhat and his body felt more like it was his own. The double doors creaked as Guillot pushed them open. The shafts of light that followed him in illuminated a soup of dust floating through the air.

"Hello!" Guillot said. There was no response, so he waited a moment, then called out once more. Perhaps the old house had finally become too much for old Yves.

Yves appeared out of the gloom a moment later, clutching a bundle of papers. "Come to deal with the correspondence, my Lord?" he said.

Being called "my Lord" after his visit to the village hall felt particularly damning. Guillot nodded, trying to give a purpose to his meandering attempt to avoid dal Sason, and took the proffered bundle of papers. Yves had seemed old when Guillot was a boy, but he did not look to have grown any older in all the years since. Tall and wiry—the perfect build for a swordsman—he was meticulous about his appearance, as many old soldiers were.

Guillot followed him into the study, where the caretaker had already laid out a pen and fresh bottle of ink—he must have seen Guillot coming up from the village. The pair enacted this routine a couple of times a year, beginning when Guillot moved back to Villerauvais. For the first few years, Yves had regularly asked when Guillot intended to move back to the manor house, but he no longer did.

There were bills to be paid, accounts to be signed off, and numerous other pieces of less formal correspondence to deal with. Guillot had made a great deal of money during his time in the city, and despite his best efforts, he'd squandered very little of it. Even in this, it appeared he was a failure.

He looked at a smaller bundle of sealed notes. Despite the scandal of his disgrace in Mirabay—from which he'd been exonerated thanks to his skill with a sword—he was still a bachelor, with lands capable of generating a good income. For the second or third daughter of a nobleman, Guillot remained a reasonable marriage prospect. *Well*, he thought, *perhaps not reasonable. Tolerable.* As such, he regularly received a number of invitations to balls, garden parties, and all the social niceties of Mirabayan aristocracy. He ought to decline them politely but instead ignored them.

The rest of the tedious work always took the better part of the day. Without anything to drink and a worsening hangover, it was more tedious still. That was ever the problem with drinking—life tended to intrude long enough for a hangover to take hold. Yves closed the door quietly and left Gill alone with the ghosts of his father and all the other Seigneurs of Villerauvais who had occupied that office. Despite the distraction the paperwork provided, he couldn't shake the troubles in the village from his thoughts. The last thing he wanted was to return and discover there had been another attack.

When Yves brought him lunch at midday, Guillot was not even halfway through the paperwork, and the optimistic notion that he might be done before nightfall was fading.

"Is there anything in the cellar to wash it down with?" Gill asked.

"I had everything sent down to the house in the village," Yves replied.

"Yes, of course," Gill said. He had long since drained the cellar of both properties. "Yves, your family have been in the region a long time, haven't they?"

"Even longer than yours, my Lord."

"Do you know if there are any dragon stories specific to the region?"

"Nearly all of them," Yves said.

Guillot raised an eyebrow.

"The limestone mountains are full of caverns. Some say this was where they first appeared, before spreading across the world. It's no coincidence that your family were granted this land. A Villerauvais lord was one of the founding Chevaliers and this land was your family's reward for their service. Make no mistake—this was dragon country.

"Will there be anything else?"

"No, I have everything that I need."

"Will you be spending the night?"

Guillot thought for a moment. He didn't reckon dal Sason would spend the whole day waiting outside his house. "No. I'll head back to the village when I'm done."

CHAPTER
7

It was close to midnight before Guillot finished the final piece of correspondence and let himself out of the manor house; Yves had long since
retired for the night. There was a chill in the air, as there often was in those
parts on a clear night. His hand ached from all the writing, and had grown
so sore that by the end of the task he had started initialling letters.

It sounded like the wind was getting up, which was unseasonal for that
time of year. Gill pulled his cloak tightly around him. He was glad it was still
summer. In the winter, the winds funnelled into the valleys and made life a
misery for three or four days at a time, tearing slates from roofs, shutters from
windows, and making walking in the open nearly impossible. Although he
could hear the wind, he couldn't feel it. That was strange enough to make Gill
stop and listen more carefully.

Might alcohol withdrawal also make him imagine things? It seemed you
were damned if you did and damned if you didn't. Too much wine and you
see things, too little and you hear them. Which was worse? The night was completely still, yet he could definitely hear the swoosh of the wind. Almost a
whistle. He looked up in time to see a great, dark shape pass overhead. His
stomach twisted as he was gripped by a fear so primal that he thought he would
be sick. The shadow.

The whistle became piercing as the sky lit up with a bright flash. A great
stream of fire appeared in the middle of the sky and raced to the ground, striking with a thundering crash and a spray of sparks. For a moment, it illuminated its source, a shining black mass. It had eyes. And teeth. And wings. And
claws. A dragon.

Guillot was running before he knew what he was doing. Once he'd been
called the bravest man in the kingdom, a title that was certainly exaggerated,

but he had never been a coward. Nonetheless, he ran, and he couldn't make himself stop.

He glanced back at the place where the fireball had landed. The flames had subsided and he could see nothing. There was sound, though. The sound of a beast feeding. He assumed that some unfortunate goats or cows had been on the receiving end of the flames, until he remembered that Mayor René and the others were patrolling the fields.

▲▲▲▲▲

The bright jet of flame had ruined Guillot's night vision, so though the night was clear and the moon a decent size, he could see nothing. Also, he was unarmed, and even if he had been carrying a sword, there was little he could do now. Whatever the flame hit was well dead by now. Nothing could be gained by remaining where he was, so Guillot continued toward the village as fast as his legs would carry him.

He couldn't remember the last time he had run anywhere, but it must have been some time ago, as his lungs and legs were burning long before he reached the village square. What to do next? He looked around. Alain, Richard, and Philipe all lived outside the village. Only René had a house within it. What would he say to René's wife? He felt sick. Was there more he could have done? Would being a more diligent lord have made any difference? He tried to convince himself that it wouldn't have, but deep down he knew he had left the defence of the village to a winemaker and some farmers. Had he taken control of things, he with the finest military education that could be had and over a decade of soldiering experience, it could very well have been different. He was a Chevalier of the Silver Circle. Slaying dragons was supposed to be his primary function, if the old stories were to be believed. With what he had witnessed that night, he was very much a believer.

He tried to pull a clear thought from his pickled brain. Should he not go back and see what had been hit by the flame? Surely the beast would be long gone by the time he got back there. What should he do? Raise the alarm or investigate further? There was a time when he wouldn't have hesitated—when he would have known how to react to danger, and wouldn't have hesitated to do so. Then people had called him a hero and he might actually have deserved the title. He needed to get himself together.

In the village square, he turned around slowly, trying to remember which house was René's. As he did, he spotted light from behind the village hall's window. Rushing over and throwing open the door, he found René and three farmers sitting around the table. They all turned to look at the interruption.

"Gill?" René said. "What brings you here at this time of night?"

"Thank the gods," Gill said, sucking in a deep breath and letting it out with a sigh. The candles fluttered in the breeze he had let in, casting shadows in all directions. "I thought you'd all been killed."

"Killed?" Richard said.

"There's been another attack," Guillot said. Even in the candlelight, Guillot could see the colour drain from their faces. "By the road out to the manor."

"Franc's farm," Alain said.

Guillot nodded, noticing the open bottle of wine on the table and realising how thirsty he was. His nerves were shot and he reckoned he deserved a drink after what he had been through that night. Without waiting to be invited, he walked forward, poured himself a cup, downed it, then refilled the cup. The liquid washed down his throat and the tense muscles in his neck eased almost immediately. He let out another sigh as calm started to return to him.

"Nobody is to go out at night," Guillot said. "Not until we've dealt with it. I'm going to go for help in person. The king wants a favour of me, according to the fellow just arrived in town. Perhaps he'll do me one in return."

"Banneret of the White Nicholas dal Sason," René said.

Guillot nodded. "You know him?"

"We've met. He's staying at Jeanne's."

"Indeed," Guillot said. "I'll go to Mirabay with him and bring back soldiers."

"Why don't we just send to the duke in Trelain?" René said. "Mirabay is a far longer journey."

"The Duke of Trelain is a drunken degenerate," Guillot said, then blushed, realising that the men at the table could think much the same of him. "He spends most of the year at court in Mirabay anyway. I'd have to go there to speak with him. If I'm going that far, I might as well speak with the king. We'll need everything he can give us. I saw it with my own eyes. You were right, Philipe. It's a dragon. A huge black dragon. Believe me, we'll need more help than the Duke of Trelain can provide."

René started to shake his head in disbelief. In Guillot's opinion, the man's years away studying winemaking and viticulture left him thinking he was a little smarter than everyone else, Guillot included. He looked at Philipe, who refused to meet Guillot's eyes, probably embarrassed that the only man who believed him was the town drunk.

"Tell them what you saw, Philipe."

Philipe hesitated for a moment, then nodded. "It's true, Mayor. I saw it too. With my own eyes. A great black beast with wicked claws and enormous wings. You know I'm not a man to exaggerate. I saw what he says. Gill's not making it up."

René nodded, but slowly, clearly not convinced, and Guillot felt his anger build. Any lord worth his name would have a vassal flogged for such contempt. That wasn't his way, however, and in that moment he realised his anger was directed at himself. He had allowed this situation to come to pass. If they respected him, there would have been no pause for consideration. He was the only one to blame for that.

"You'll need to leave at first light," René said. "Who knows when this beast will decide it prefers the taste of human flesh to cattle and sheep. If it is as you say, we need help, and we need it soon."

"At first light," Gill said. "I'll need travelling provisions," he added, trying to take some of the initiative back from René. He considered putting down his cup of wine to punctuate his statement, but the desire to drink it first was too great. He drained the cup, then set it down with a thud. "At first light," he repeated, wiping his mouth as he left.

Dal Sason was eating breakfast when Guillot walked into the tavern the next morning. He had not been up this early in some time and he felt out of place.

"Good morning," dal Sason said. "Would you care to break your fast with me? As you said, the food here is excellent."

Guillot hadn't slept much, and the early start had done nothing to improve his mood. "I'm going to Mirabay with you," Guillot said, the words sticking in his craw.

"That's very good news," dal Sason said. "Mayor René mentioned as much to me this morning. Do you mind me asking what changed your mind? I've heard whispers of some livestock killings. Is that it?"

"I don't think you and yours are behind it anymore, but I'm not convinced you don't know exactly what's going on. Even if you don't, I reckon your master does."

"I'll need a few minutes to pack," dal Sason said.

"Be quick. I don't intend to wait for you. Meet me outside my house."

Dal Sason nodded, stood, and headed for the back room, leaving his food unfinished.

"I've travelling provisions for you," Jeanne said. "René told me to tell you that he sent Jacques to bring your horse down from the manor."

Guillot nodded his thanks and took the bag of supplies she handed over. He had determined not to take another drink until after he got back from Mirabay, so didn't check to see if she'd given him a bottle—and he could tell she was watching to see if he did. Not drinking was an easy resolution to make first thing in the morning, if his rising time could be called that. He would have to see how easy it was to stick to as the day progressed. He didn't want anyone in Mirabay—particularly the Prince Bishop—to see what he had allowed himself to become. He was nervous about returning to court after all these years. He had left a failed disgrace, and it shamed him to think he was going back even worse.

The first things to pop into his mind were foolish, superficial concerns. Would his good clothes be moth-eaten? Would they still be fashionable? He cut himself off at that thought, almost laughing at himself, realising how glad he was that he no longer made his life at the capital.

At his house, Jacques waited for him with a saddled horse. He glanced up at the sun, which had risen higher than he'd hoped. The day was getting away from him, and they needed to get going soon if they were to make it to Trelain before nightfall. Gill gave Jacques a nod of thanks and a penny, unfastened the saddlebags, which he threw over his shoulder, then went inside. He went to his bedroom and cleared the empty wine bottles from the top of his trunk before opening it; he was pleased to see the clothes within had not been reduced to dust. A quick inspection proved he would not shame himself in them, so he threw them into the saddlebags along with Jeanne's provisions and returned downstairs.

Next, weapons. A duelling rapier was most suited for the city, so he strapped on its sheath and belt—relieved that it fit—and slid the sword home. Just then, dal Sason appeared at the door.

"Can I help with anything?" the younger man said.

"No. Almost ready."

Dal Sason studied the only painting on the wall, of a young woman with gently curling chestnut hair. "I was told your wife was a great beauty, and now

I see that she was. I'm very sorry for your loss. It's always a tragedy when the gods choose to take someone so young."

Guillot almost said something, then thought better of it, then felt churlish. Dal Sason was only following his orders. Guillot's grievance was not with him. "Thank you," he said. He patted the coin purse on his belt to confirm it was still there, then looked around to check for anything he had forgotten. There was nothing. "I'm ready to go."

Solène slid the wooden peel into the stone oven and pulled it out in a fast, practised movement, leaving the loaves of raw dough inside. The heat of the oven's fire warmed her face but made her tired eyes water. Ignoring the sting, she fixed her gaze on the loaves, sitting deep in the oven's red glow. A focussed thought was all it needed to ensure each loaf baked perfectly—crusty on the outside; light, fluffy, and delicious inside. More importantly, that would guarantee a repeat customer and ensure the queue outside the bakery door every morning continued to grow.

Still, she was ambivalent about using magic. Even calling it magic seemed silly, but it was hard to argue that it could be anything else. Part of her wanted to turn her back on it entirely, while part of her thought she might as well take some advantage of the talents that had brought so much trouble to her life.

At times, when she felt tired and alone, she wondered if *they* might be able to find her because of it. Every so often she would see one of them, the black-cloaked spectres—Intelligenciers—moving about the town as though they had some great, important business to attend to. Trelain wasn't big enough to warrant their permanent presence, which was why she chose it, but as she had quickly learned, they made it their business to be everywhere and unpredictable. Caution was her only shield, a tricky thing when she had only the most basic understanding of her gift and affliction. She had fled from her home as soon as the villagers had discovered what she could do, hoping her disappearance would be enough—that they would forget her rather than report her to the Intelligenciers. Bastelle was a small village, far from everywhere. Few there thought much beyond the pastures surrounding the village and it was the sort of place where a person lived and died within a few paces of where they were born.

They were good people, people she had known and cared for all her life, and their fear of her had wounded her deeply. Friends. Family. She supposed she couldn't blame them—they were farming folk who took their traditions and superstitions seriously. They couldn't imagine magic as anything other than a force for evil—sorcery—and fear drove them to do things they might not have otherwise.

The Intelligenciers were dangerous and relentless, and had centuries of experience in hunting down users of magic. If they found out about her . . . She couldn't bear to consider the consequences. She knew it was risky to use magic to aid her loaves, but how else could a girl with no family or friends, and hardly any money, get ahead in a town where a little misfortune could lead to a life on the street? It was so small a thing—surely it would continue to go unnoticed, as long as she was careful. She sighed, comforted by the smell of the cooking bread. She might be a fool, but in that moment, she was a happy one.

She closed the oven door and turned back to the work top where a book waited for her. In an hour, the doughy shapes would be the best bread in the town—perhaps the best anywhere—and she could go home with a hot loaf tucked under her arm. The baker seemed glad to not have to get up before dawn, leaving her in peace for the early morning bake, but he was not glad enough to pay her well.

She could never have guessed that something as simple as baking bread could be so satisfying, nor that she would dream of having her own bakery some day. It would take time, hard work, and sacrifice, but she had a plan now, one that gave her hope for a happy future.

The early hour was no imposition for her—no one waited for her in her small room at the back of a carpenter's workshop, and staying busy helped her forget how alone she was. It wasn't as if she had to get out of bed to get to the bakery, either. She worked at a nearby taproom as well, and by the time she had finished cleaning up there after the last patron stumbled out the door, it was time to light the ovens at the bakery.

Lighting a fire was not a problem when you had a special gift, so she was able to get the ovens up to heat quickly. With the dough safely deposited, she could relax and lose herself in whatever she was reading. This was her favourite part of the day, the time where she could let go of her problems, let them drift far away.

Solène scooped several mugs into the crook of her arm and wiped the table with the damp cloth in her other hand. No sooner was the table ready than it was filled by new occupants. The taproom was full and noisy, as it was most evenings. The owner served good wine and cider at fair prices, making it the most popular tavern in the district. She navigated her way through the press of bodies and deposited her burden on the counter, then headed out to repeat the process.

Although Trelain was the capital of the duchy it resided in, it was what a character in one of her favourite books would have called *parochial*. It might have been as cosmopolitan as could be found in western Mirabaya, but the vast majority of the people living there were from the town, and Solène's accent—though only subtly different from theirs—gave her away as an outsider, and it was very obvious that that mattered to the locals. It meant making friends was a challenge and she was lonely at times, but she hoped this job would help her integrate.

Every evening, the patrons saw her in the taproom and her face and accent grew a little more familiar. When she had enough saved, she would open her bakery, and they would be comfortable enough to buy her bread. Once they'd tasted it, they'd never buy bread anywhere else. She recalled something from a book of philosophies she had read several years before, while still a teenager, that gave her comfort when the difficulties in her path seemed too many: *great things aren't achieved in a day, and the things that can be are not great*. In that, at least, the philosopher had been correct.

"Get me a jug of last season's red," said a man, part of a group at the next table, pulling Solène from her day dreams as she gathered another batch of empty mugs for washing.

"I don't work the bar," she responded. "You know that, Arnoul."

The other men at the table looked uncomfortable with his behaviour. Arnoul seemed to need to order other people around to make himself look big in front of his friends. He kept trying to show off, every time he came to the tavern, but never seemed to impress his drinking companions, and tonight was no different. He was either stubborn or stupid. Solène suspected the latter.

"Why don't you come over here and keep me company then," Arnoul said. He laughed, looking at his friends, clearly expecting them to join in. They didn't, and Solène wondered why he couldn't tell his behaviour wasn't impressing them.

"I don't do that either," she said. "Go to the bar to order, like everyone else. Go to the brothel if you're looking for company."

That drew some chuckles from his friends and Arnoul's face darkened. He grabbed Solène by the leg. When she pulled free, one of the mugs fell from the crook of her arm, splashing wine all over Arnoul's trousers and shirt. His face twisted with anger, but Solène could not restrain the tongue that had so often gotten her in trouble.

"That looks like last season's red to me," she said. "Enjoy."

Laughter erupted from the other men at the table. Arnoul smouldered. Solène gathered up the fallen mug and disappeared into the crowd, wishing she'd smashed the mug on his thick skull.

⌃⌃⌃⌃⌃

Solène didn't think for a moment that being given the keys to the tavern indicated the owner's growing trust; it merely meant everyone else working there wanted to get home as early as possible. By the time she finished cleaning, they were all tucked up in bed. Nonetheless, it gave her the chance to prove she was trustworthy, another small battle in the war to integrate. It might mean a promotion to the bar, more pay, and her bakery a few weeks or months sooner. After double-checking the lock, she started the short walk to the bakery.

Usually she avoided the shortcut, a narrow lane clogged with rubbish, but tonight she was running later than usual and the ovens needed to be lit. A fight in the tavern had resulted in a bloody nose and it had taken an age to scrub the blood from the floorboards. She picked her way down the lane, through the debris as best she could by moonlight, and froze when she heard a voice.

"Big city bitch."

The voice came from the darkness, but Solène knew who it was. Only Arnoul could be ignorant enough to think her accent came from a big city.

"Think you're funny?" he said.

"Your friends did," Solène said, backing out of the laneway. She put her foot in something squishy and forced herself not to react.

He loomed out of the darkness, his face twisted with anger. "I'm a big man around here. You can't speak to me like that. I'm going to give you something to help you remember your manners." When he raised his hand, she saw moonlight reflected on the blade of a knife. She could tell from the look on his face that he meant to do what he threatened.

"Why don't you go home to your wife, Arnoul?"

"Not until I've taught you some manners, serving bitch."

He lunged forward, grabbing her by the lapels of her coat. Her heart leapt and she tried to pull back, but Arnoul's grip was too firm.

"Let. Me. Go," Solène said.

"Do big city bitches bleed like us simple townsfolk?" Arnoul said, his mouth twisting into a vindictive smile. He pressed the blade to her cheek.

Fear flooded through her. Arnoul had always been a talker. She'd never thought he would actually do something. She closed her eyes for an instant.

The next sound she heard was a squeal. A pig's squeal. The knife clattered to the ground.

Solène stepped back and smoothed the front of her coat. Transformation magic always surprised her. She had only done it a couple of times, and never intentionally. It seemed as though it was her default defence when seriously threatened, which had been the case every time she had cast it. The first time, she had turned a rabid dog into a nose-twitching rabbit; the second, she'd changed a bully into a goat. That had been the incident that had forced her to flee her village. She knew from past experience that Arnoul would not remain a pig for long—a few minutes at most, unless she actively worked at prolonging the magic—and as soon as he reverted to his human form, she had no doubt he would denounce her as a witch.

It was Bastelle all over again, and it saddened her to think that her time in Trelain was over. Where would she make her bakery now? All the hard work she had put in in Trelain was for naught, all for want of being able to control her affliction. Still, what was the choice—having to move on, or having to carry a scar on her face for the rest of her life? Or worse? Angry, she was tempted to give the pig a good, hard kick, but it wasn't in her nature. In any event, time was precious now. She needed to pack up her few possessions and flee. Where to?

She took a final look at Arnoul the Pig, wallowing in muck, snuffling about for food, and looking far more at home in the rubbish than he ever did in the tavern. Such a shame she didn't have the time to enjoy it.

▲▲▲▲▲

Solène jerked awake in the chair by the door in her small one-room home. Light came in through her threadbare curtains, and her travelling bag sat by her feet, where she had put it when she'd decided to rest for a moment before setting off. There was a barrage of banging on the door—the follow-up to the blow that had woken her. How long had she slept? Her heart raced with panic when there was more pounding on the door.

She swore. The same thing had happened with the dog and the bully—she had slept for hours after both incidents. She always felt tired after she used magic, but never as bad as when she transformed something. She should have remembered. She should have forced herself to keep going, not allowing herself to rest until she was miles from Trelain.

Arnoul would have been back in his usual form for hours. More than long enough to call the Town Watch, or worse, an Intelligencier.

There was another bang at the door, and she knew she had to act. There was one small window at the back of her room. Peering out, she saw two shadowy figures lurking outside. It confirmed her worst fear—men were coming to arrest her and there was no way out.

She took her black cloak from the nail on the wall, wrapped herself in it, and with no alternative, opened the door. There were a dozen people waiting to greet her, most of them soldiers. At their head stood an officer of the Town Watch. She recognised him—he drank at the tavern regularly—but they had only exchanged a few words. He had a dark expression on his face. At least he wasn't an Intelligencier.

"You need to come with us, miss," he said.

"Why? What's wrong?" she said, but she knew the reason.

Someone shouted "witch," and two Watchmen firmly grabbed Solène and dragged her out of her home.

CHAPTER
9

Trelain was the first stop on the road to Mirabay. It hove into view not long after nightfall, but many hours since Guillot's backside and thighs had gone numb, unused to so much time in the saddle. The twinkling lights in its taller towers, which reached up above the town's surrounding curtain wall, were a welcome sight. Guillot and dal Sason had spent the day in silence. He continued to feel unwell, but the symptoms were subsiding. Nonetheless, he sweated heavily and felt uncomfortably hot. His head ached and the anxiety that had gripped him on encountering the dragon was as imposing as ever. A cup or two of wine would have been welcome, but he had made himself a promise and was determined to stick to it. Those at the king's court were welcome to think him a disgrace, but he had no desire to prove it to them by arriving drunk. The little pride he had left would not allow him to sink that low.

"Shall we stop for the night?" dal Sason asked.

Guillot nodded.

"The Prince Bishop is covering all the expenses?" Gill said.

"Of course."

"We're staying at the Black Drake, then."

He had been worried that dal Sason might insist they press on. Although he had said nothing about it, he desperately longed for a break from the saddle. Pressing on and exhausting themselves would slow their journey in the end, not hasten it. In the morning they could exchange their horses at the Royal Waypost in town; the fresh mounts would let them make better time.

They rode into Trelain, passing through the gate with not so much as a glance from the tired guards. Trelain was far from the troubled western marches, and was shielded from the Darvarosians to the south by a range of impenetrable mountains. However, Mirabayan noblemen were famed for warring on one another. Thanks to intricately woven family ties, when inheritance time came around, there were often a great many cousins with a claim to press. Even in a province insulated from outside danger, sturdy walls were a necessity.

Though Trelain was a large town, it would still neatly fit within one of Mirabay's districts. The wealth generated by the region's winemaking was evident in the buildings that lined the streets, from the private homes of wealthy burgesses to the decorated limestone public buildings that dominated the skyline. The surroundings were a taste of what Mirabay would be like, and it made Guillot even more anxious.

Dal Sason went inside to book their rooms, while Gill brought their horses around to the inn's stable yard. Given that the Prince Bishop was picking up the bills, Guillot had given dal Sason the name of the most expensive inn he knew of in Trelain—the Black Drake. The sign swinging over the ornate stone doorway, with its finely painted and fierce-looking black dragon, sent a chill through him, reminding Gill of what Yves had said—this was dragon country.

If he was being honest with himself, he was nervous about what lay ahead, about how he would feel, how he would be treated by people he had not seen in years. His fatigue hammered home how far removed he was from the man he had been. There was a time when he had been able to ride through the night and fight the next day. He knew he wasn't yet too old for such feats. His poor conditioning could not be blamed on the ravages of time, only his own choices. He wondered if he could possibly undo the damage the last half-decade had wrought.

Looking at the people still on the streets at that hour of the evening, he wondered what they would think if he told them a dragon was attacking farms to the south. They would assume he was mad, obviously, and as he drifted ever further from the influence of alcohol, he began to wonder if he had imagined the whole thing. The attack he had witnessed was too vivid to be a hallucination. He could still smell the burning and feel the heat on his skin. The sinister black shape, its scales glistening in the moonlight, was an image that would never leave him.

Nevertheless, if the Prince Bishop wanted him for something, believing Guillot's story and helping deal with it was the price he must pay. Assuming the Prince Bishop and the dragon were not in some way connected. As ridiculous as the notion seemed, Guillot could not shake it off. It seemed too much of a coincidence that dal Sason turned up just after the first attack.

There were other hamlets in the area, some closer to the mountains, and Guillot now regretted not riding out to see if they had experienced similar problems. There hadn't been time, however. Even now, he feared there was little he could do to save his tenants' livelihoods. The next village over, the ever-popular Montpareil, would benefit from Guillot's actions. He couldn't think of a time less suited for going without wine.

As he reached the stable yard entrance, he spotted a gathering of people adding wood to what looked like a hastily erected pyre in a small square at the end of the street. It was an odd thing to see at that time of day, so, curious, he rode over.

"What's going on here?" Guillot asked the first townsman whose eye he caught.

"Gonna burn a witch," the man said, looking at the pyre and the small group of men who appeared to be in charge of the proceedings.

"A witch?" Gill asked.

"Aye, a witch."

It had been some time since Guillot had heard of a witch trial. The Intelligenciers tended to deal with such things quietly.

"The duke's holding witchcraft trials?" Guillot said.

"Duke's in Mirabay," the townsman said. "We found this 'un ourselves."

"Then the duke's magistrate tried her?"

The man shook his head and smiled, his expression one of excited euphoria.

Guillot nodded slowly. Nothing said justice like mob law. "When is she to burn?"

"First thing in the morning. Want to get the business done before the men in black show up."

Guillot nodded again, and turned his horse back toward the stable yard entrance. He was caught between horror that mob justice was being done in the duke's absence, and the satisfaction that he was not the only one who had allowed matters in his demesne to slide beyond his control. It was none of his business, however, and his thoughts quickly returned to the prospect of a warm bed.

⟞⟞⟞⟞⟞

Guillot woke in a state of great comfort, compounded by the thought that the Prince Bishop was paying. It took him a moment to realise his headache was gone, but he knew that was largely down to the fact that the previous night, a

single nightcap had become a bottle, which had become two. He couldn't remember if there had been a third, but could not discount the possibility.
Either way, he was still drunk, and furious that his resolution of sobriety had
not even lasted one day. Breakfast was as good as the bed, and he renewed his
oath of temperance until he had finished what he had set out to do.

They waited at the entrance to the stable yard for the horses to be brought
from the Royal Waypost by one of the inn's stable hands. Gill's own horse
would be taken back to Villerauvais for what he considered to be a very reasonable addition to the Prince Bishop's tab. For the rest of the journey, they
would obtain fresh mounts at way stations along the road, a service provided
for royal agents and mail carriers. Dal Sason had already been riding such a
beast, so the exchange was easily made, but he'd had to send his official orders
with the stable hand to have a horse made available to Gill.

"Fine morning," dal Sason said, staring toward the light blue band of sky
on the horizon.

Guillot shrugged.

"What do you make of that," dal Sason said, pointing to the pyre as the
stable hand jogged up, leading their horses.

"They're burning a witch," Guillot said, being careful not to slur his words.
He could feel the first hints of sobriety returning. "They were building the pyre
last night when we got in."

"That's not like the Intelligenciers."

"It's not them. It's the locals. As best I could tell, the duke isn't even involved."

Dal Sason muttered something under his breath that Guillot couldn't quite
make out. Gill could feel his anger rise. He knew only too well what it was
like to be on the receiving end of mob justice. For some reason, this morning, the thought of what was about to happen resonated with him far more
deeply than it had the previous night.

Dal Sason studied him. "This is none of our business," he said. "Things like
this can get nasty fast, and we don't have time for that."

"It's already gotten nasty," Guillot said, hauling himself into the saddle.

"A good soldier follows his orders and doesn't get sidetracked. You can't
allow your personal feelings to interfere. We've more important matters to deal
with."

Guillot could tell dal Sason wasn't speaking out of fear, but rather out of a
belief that his mission was more pressing than a woman's life. He shrugged.

"I suppose I never was a particularly good soldier." He urged his horse forward.

"What's going on here?" he said when he reached the group of people gathered at the pyre, who surrounded a young woman wearing a black cloak. Guillot could see a wisp of red hair protruding from the hood, and a few links of the chain that shackled her hands. Even though a black robe covered her, Guillot could tell she was shaking.

"Burning a witch," one of them said.

The man very much fitted Gill's mental image of a mob member, with an expression of feverish excitement and righteousness on his face. He had probably never experienced any type of power before. Now he was drunk on it.

"That much I know," Guillot said. "On whose authority?"

"On ours!" the townsman said.

The crowd behind him roared in agreement. Their blood was up and they wanted to see someone die, and soon. He needed to be careful to ensure it wasn't him.

He laughed, feigning levity. "I'm afraid that really isn't good enough, unless you're a royal magistrate. Are you a royal magistrate?"

"No. Are you?"

"Are you, my Lord," Guillot said, allowing the angry edge to return to his voice and accompanying it with as damning a glare as he could muster. "As it happens, I'm not. But I am Banneret of the White Guillot dal Villerauvais, Seigneur of Villerauvais, Chevalier of the Silver Circle, and former champion to King Boudain the Ninth. Those titles and duties give me the power of life or death over every free man and woman of Mirabaya."

Dal Sason appeared at his side, his horse as agitated as its rider. "We should leave."

Guillot glared at him, then turned back to the gathered crowd. "She should receive a fair trial."

The townsman stared at him. "Witches don't get trials. They could use their magic to get off. She's a witch for sure."

"Could you tell that from the sinister black cloak she wears?" Guillot said.

Several people in the crowd laughed.

"Don't matter," the man said. "We're doing the king's work."

"It's not your place to decide what the king's work is."

The man shut his mouth, and for a moment, Gill thought he was cowed. Then he spoke again.

"Arnoul saw her doing magic."

"Arnoul?" Guillot said. He looked about the crowd. "Which one of you is Arnoul?"

The townsman pointed to one of the men holding the robed woman.

"You saw her do magic?" Guillot said.

The man—Arnoul—nodded.

"What magic?"

The crowd grew silent.

"I, I saw her . . ." Arnoul's voice was low and hesitant. He looked around for support, but received none. He took a deep breath. "I saw her turn into a goat!"

The crowd gasped.

"A goat?" Guillot said, with as much disdain as he could muster.

"A goat," Arnoul said, more confident now.

"Has anyone else seen her do magic?" Guillot said.

Silence.

"This woman's family?" Guillot said. "Where are they? Where is her husband?"

"She only moved to Trelain a few months ago. No husband or family," the townsman said.

"I see. And Arnoul is a long and upstanding member of the community?"

The townsman nodded. "Master of the Tanners' Guild."

Guillot shook his head in exaggerated disgust. "Draw back her hood."

"We can't, my Lord," the townsman said. "She'll hex the whole town. Put the evil eye on us."

"Rubbish," Guillot said. "Show me her face."

The man hesitated for a moment before walking over and drawing back the woman's hood. There was a collective gasp and some of the people in the crowd flinched. Revealed, the woman seemed to be in her late twenties, with burnished copper hair. Her pale skin was lightly freckled and her eyes were crystal blue. She was beautiful. Guillot wondered how many times the woman had rejected Arnoul's advances before he'd levelled these claims against her.

"Let me summarise," Guillot said. "On the word of one man, a man with a face like a dog's arse . . ." He paused for the crowd's laughter—a crowd rarely failed to laugh at a nobleman's joke—and took a moment to enjoy seeing Arnoul squirm. He wanted to make sure the mood was cheerful. ". . . you are willing to burn a young woman to death. That doesn't sound like the king's work to me. That sounds like murder." He looked around. None of the men seemed quite so confident now.

"There's only one way to deal with murderers," Guillot said. "And the king expects me to carry out that task in his name." He rested his hand on the pommel of his sword.

Arnoul looked around at the others, most of whom refused to meet his eye, then back at Guillot. Guillot ignored him, looking instead at the woman, whose face now displayed the hope that she might live. Finally, Guillot looked back to the townsman.

"Well? What will it be?"

"What would you have us do, my Lord?"

Guillot's heart raced. If the crowd turned ugly, no amount of titles would save him and dal Sason from the same fate the young woman faced. Many in the crowd—perhaps all of them—still believed Arnoul, but were afraid to speak out. They thought she was a witch, and they wanted justice, so he had to give them something to ensure an easy escape.

"Release her to my custody," Guillot said. "My companion and I are on our way to Mirabay. We'll hand her over to the Intelligenciers there. If she's a witch, you can be certain they'll find her out. She will see justice—on that, you have my word."

There were some murmurs in the crowd, but Guillot could not tell if they were favourable. For the time being, however, he was a lord, and his word was law. They were too conditioned to take orders from their betters to immediately question him. They might, eventually.

"Very well, my Lord," the townsman said.

Arnoul's face turned puce, and Guillot knew that as soon as he was out of earshot, the scorned man would start to agitate against him. Then things would get dangerous.

"We're leaving directly," Guillot said. "We need a horse for the prisoner and the keys to her shackles. My man will see you're well paid for the horse. Quickly now. I don't have all day." He gestured to dal Sason and let out a discreet sigh of relief.

"That was a stroke of luck," dal Sason whispered.

Guillot didn't respond. There was a time when doing things like that was a regular feature in his life. When he hadn't needed to rely on luck to get through them.

"Pay for the horse quickly," he said softly to dal Sason. "I don't care if it only has three legs. We need to get out of here fast. We need to put as much distance between us and Trelain as we can before this lot start to think about what's just happened."

CHAPTER 10

They rode through the day, only stopping when they had to rest the horses for as short a time as possible. As evening drew near, Gill decided they had gone far enough and declared it time to venture off the road and find somewhere to camp for the night. They looked around for a while, Gill's primary focus being that they were far enough from the road to light a fire without being seen. When they finally found somewhere he liked, they began settling in. The fire was lit, the horses fed, watered, and secured. All that remained was the awkwardness of trying to make small talk with the woman he had rescued.

"What are you going to do with me?" the woman said, finally breaking the silence.

Guillot looked at her over the flames of a fire that had taken him far more effort to start than it should have. "I'm going to take you another twenty or thirty miles along the road, and then I'm going to let you go."

Her eyes widened in surprise, as did dal Sason's.

"Are you sure that's wise, Lord Villerauvais?" dal Sason said.

"You might as well call me Gill. Everyone else does, and no, I'm not sure, but I'm going to do it anyway."

The woman cast dal Sason a filthy look. "Why have you left these on, then?" she said to Gill, holding up her manacled hands.

"Truthfully?"

She nodded.

"I forgot about them."

She rattled the chains.

"Yes, of course," Guillot said. He stood and made his way over to her, fumbling in his purse for the key.

"My Lord. Gill," dal Sason said. "I really don't think this is a good idea."

"I've had plenty of bad ideas," Gill said, "and none of them have killed me yet."

"You said we were going to preserve her for a proper trial, not to simply let her go. What if the people were telling the truth?"

"Come on, did you see the man who accused her? I'm under no illusions of what happened there. Am I correct?"

The woman shrugged. "He tried to get into my skirt. He wasn't going to take no for an answer. I hit him with a brick and got away."

"And thus a woman becomes a witch," Guillot said. "I've seen it before. The duke needs to keep a tighter hand on his subjects. Spending more time in Trelain would be a good start." He unlocked the manacles, which she removed; she began to rub her red, raw wrists. Gill grimaced at the sight. He'd been so preoccupied with getting away from Trelain, the bonds had genuinely slipped his mind. The woman hadn't complained once all day.

Well, it was his first rescue in many years. He couldn't be expected to get everything right the first time back.

"What's your name?" he said.

"Solène."

"You don't sound like you're from Trelain," Guillot said.

She shook her head. "No, I'm not from anywhere you'd have heard of."

Guillot nodded. "Fine, there's no need to tell us. I'm Guillot dal Villerauvais. This is my . . . This is Banneret of the White Nicholas dal Sason. Until we part tomorrow, you can consider yourself under my protection, and completely safe." It had been a very long time since he had played the gallant knight-errant, but it came to him more easily than he had expected. Certainly more easily than lighting the fire.

"I'm grateful to you, my Lord," Solène said. "Have you anything to eat? I'm starving."

Guillot raised a hand in apology for this second omission. He handed her some bread, cheese, and an apple from his saddlebags before sitting down again. Solène started on the food with intent, pausing only to give both men a brief, foul look as they stared at her. As she worked her way through his provisions, Gill's hopes for a decent breakfast faded.

"What's a banneret of the white?" she said, between mouthfuls.

"It means you're a very good swordsman," Guillot said. "That you've been to a special school and trained for years to earn the title. Bannerets are good; Bannerets of the White are even better."

Dal Sason cleared his throat. "The trouble in Villerauvais?" he said, changing the subject. "Is that what convinced you to come back with me?"

"Should it have convinced me?" Guillot said, his simmering suspicions heating.

"I have no idea, I only wondered. It was all anyone was talking about in the tavern; animals burned to a crisp in the middle of the night. The people were afraid."

"I'm going to try to bring back some soldiers to deal with it."

"Any idea what was doing it?" dal Sason said. "Some of the villagers thought it was a demon." He laughed, but with a hesitant, nervous quality to the sound, as though he had not quite discounted the possibility.

"They're a superstitious lot. The village chaplain reckons half of them still pray to the old gods behind closed doors. No, it wasn't a demon."

Dal Sason smiled and nodded.

"It was a dragon."

Dal Sason's face went white. Solène stared at Gill with wide eyes.

Guillot studied dal Sason long enough to be certain this was the first he had heard of the dragon. That didn't absolve the Prince Bishop, however. He was never one for keeping underlings informed of the bigger picture.

"I'm going to turn in for the night," Guillot said. "Sleep well."

Dal Sason made no mention of Guillot's dragon comment the next morning, although Guillot could tell that he was itching to. It amused him to have made such a profound statement so casually, but the stilted conversation at breakfast was probably his fault. They ate what little remained of their travelling rations after Solène's meal the previous night, then prepared to set off.

Guillot had not slept well and was irritable as a result. He had woken regularly during the night, either too hot and sweating profusely, or freezing and shivering uncontrollably. He found himself longing for a drink to take the edge off. One voice in his head said he had to stop, that drink would be the ruin of him, while another said that deep down, he didn't want to stop. He could control his consumption if he chose, so there was no good reason why he shouldn't allow himself just a taste. Enough to settle him.

He squeezed his eyes tight and massaged his temples. The only thing the first voice had in its favour was that he was miles from anywhere he could get a drink. The fact did little to improve his mood, however.

"I think we've put more than enough distance between Trelain and us," Gill said as he mounted. He turned in his saddle to face Solène. "You are free to go." Before she could answer, he turned to dal Sason. "The Prince Bishop is paying *all* the expenses of this mission?"

Dal Sason nodded.

"Excellent. Solène, please keep the horse. It's a gift from the Prince Bishop of Mirabaya, Arch Prelate of the Unified Church. He can be an incredibly generous man at times. This too." He tossed her the extra purse of coins he had brought with him, which he would be sure to charge to the Prince Bishop when they got to Mirabay.

Solène caught the purse, looking confused. "Where should I go?"

Guillot shrugged. "Does it matter? You're alive and free. Do as you like. Go wherever you wish."

"What's Mirabay like?" she said.

"It's an open sore on the face of the world," Guillot said.

"I heard it's called the 'Jewel of the West,'" she said.

"It all depends on your perspective. However, we really must be going. It was a pleasure," he said, feeling a touch of panic that he might be burdened with a greater responsibility than he had foreseen. He doffed his wide-brimmed hat, which had long since lost the feather that had once decorated it, and spurred his horse on at a trot.

Dal Sason had to canter to catch up to him.

"Are you just going to leave her there?"

"Yes," Guillot said. "I thought you'd be glad to be rid of her. What more am I supposed to do? I risked my life to save her from being burned at the stake. I can't be responsible for her forever."

"You're a Chevalier of the Silver Circle. There's a higher standard. I didn't think we should have gotten involved, but we did, and now? It's just not the done thing, leaving a young lady alone on the roads, is it?"

"I *was* a Chevalier," Guillot said. "The last I heard, they are no more. And if you think they held themselves to a higher standard, you're sadly mistaken. A greater bunch of poxed-up whoresons you were unlikely to find."

They rode in silence for a time.

Finally, Gill said, "Don't sulk. If I was going back to Villerauvais, I'd probably take her, but I wouldn't bring my worst enemy to Mirabay. I'm doing her a favour. Gods only know where she'd end up, in that city with no money or friends. This way, she has a horse. She has some coin."

"Mirabay's not that bad a place."

"As I said, it all depends on your perspective."

"The full story got out after you left," dal Sason said. "People really felt for you."

"That was decent of them," Guillot said, his words full of venom. "I'd been disgraced, arrested, and had to fight for my life by that point. Hindsight *is* lovely, though."

"People thought it shameful. The old king was losing his mind, though no one realised it then. We learned later that the Prince Bishop and the new king, gods favour him, were pressing him to abdicate. It was only his sudden death that stopped that from happening."

"He shouldn't have been so quick to judge," Guillot said sharply. "I served him with every ounce of myself up to that point." He paused for a moment, not confident of his statement. He had certainly been more diligent than the others, had always taken his duties seriously, but every ounce? That was what was expected of someone in a king's service; what *should be* expected of someone in a king's service, and deep down, he knew he had fallen short. Had he been too proud, too confident? Would anything have made a difference on that day?

"I wasn't supposed to be on duty that day," Guillot said, "and I got drunk the night before. It had been my wife and child's funeral, after all. It's always struck me as curious that of all the Chevaliers guarding the king's person that day, I was the only one arrested for negligence. The one who wasn't supposed to be on duty. What of the man who was absent—the man I filled in for while he was cuckolding the Count of Harvin at his country estate? Was he arrested?"

Dal Sason shrugged. "You were the old king's favourite. They said you were the one he felt most let down by, fairly or not—"

"Enough," Guillot said. "I'm not interested in talking about it. The king to whom I pledged my life turned his back on me when I needed him the most. And don't think for a second I don't know that bastard Prince Bishop was involved up to his neck. He always hated me, and he twisted the knife the first chance he got. I should have killed him before I left the city. I'd have been doing a public service."

Guillot quickened his pace.

"Where are you going in such a hurry? You'll exhaust your horse."

"The nearest coaching inn. I need a drink."

CHAPTER
11

They reached the first way station mid-morning. It was small and offered no refreshment beyond water. Gill wasn't sure whether he felt relieved or disappointed.

"She's following us," dal Sason said, as they mounted their fresh horses.

"What?" Guillot said. There had been some traffic on the road—merchants with carts and wagons, travellers, alone or in small groups—and Gill hadn't noticed.

"I said, she's following us."

Guillot groaned inwardly. "That's her business. Like I told her, she's free. She can do whatever she wants." They had passed a number of junctions on the road, giving her plenty of opportunity to head in a different direction. If she was still behind them, Guillot couldn't help but agree with dal Sason's assessment.

"When are you planning on stopping?" dal Sason said.

"When I find a coaching inn."

"The nearest one's still a fair distance away. We'd have reached it this evening if you'd kept the proper pace. As it is, we'll pass it this afternoon, too early to stop," dal Sason said. "Which means another night on the roadside."

Guillot swore. "If you don't enjoy the hardships of travel, perhaps you should have told the Prince Bishop to piss off. I know I regret never having taken the opportunity to."

Dal Sason didn't respond.

"Let's get going. We've fresh mounts. We should be able to drop her before sunset. She'll be close enough to the inn to have somewhere safe to spend the night."

They pushed on without pause for lunch, stopping only briefly at the inn to replenish their travelling provisions.

"I think we should stop," dal Sason said when the sun hung low over the horizon behind them. "I'd like to have our firewood gathered before it gets dark."

"Fine," Guillot said, casting a glance over his shoulder. He couldn't see any sign of Solène. Likely she had stopped at the inn they had passed a few hours earlier. "We'll stop."

They found a patch of grass higher than the level of the road, dry and hidden by some tall bushes. Guillot dealt with the horses while dal Sason went to find firewood. Guillot tethered both animals to a branch that would give them access to plenty of grass. At a sound, he turned to what he thought was dal Sason.

It was someone else. A man Guillot had never seen before.

"Good evening," the man said.

"Good evening, yourself," Guillot said. "This campsite is taken."

"Now then, that's not a friendly way to greet a weary traveller."

"You're not a weary traveller," Guillot said, taking in the man's slender, athletic build, his soldierly looking but well-worn clothes, and the sword at his waist. If this fellow wasn't a highwayman, then Gill wasn't a drunk. "And I'm not a friendly person."

The man shrugged.

"I'm feeling generous," Guillot said. "If you go now, I'll forget I ever saw you."

The man cocked his head and smiled.

"I'm not alone," Guillot said. "Even if we were poor swordsmen, the odds would be against you. I assure you that we are not."

"You've one friend," the man said. "I've got . . . more. The odds are with me."

Two additional men stepped out from the undergrowth. Guillot reached for his sword and the first man shook his head.

"Doesn't have to go like that," he said. "We'll take your coin and your horses, but we'll leave your food and your boots. I'll never have it said I'm uncivilised."

"It's not going to go like that, I'm afraid," Guillot said.

"Banneret?" the man said.

Guillot nodded.

"You lot never want to hand over what you think you can keep with your sword."

Guillot shrugged.

The man drew and lunged in one movement, faster than Guillot had anticipated. He jumped backwards, not covering as much ground as he had hoped, and drew his sword just in time to parry the next strike. Guillot realised this was the first time since his judicial duel that he'd parried an attack made in anger. Perhaps he wasn't as out of practise as he feared? The man nodded in approval. Such chivalry was not something Guillot expected of a common highwayman.

"Are you a banneret?" Guillot said.

The man laughed. "Of course not."

Guillot lunged. The attempt was disappointing. He was far more familiar with the feel of a bottle in his hand than a sword, and his tip went far wide of its target, so much that it was almost charity that the highwayman chose to parry it at all.

With Guillot's rapier swatted to the side, he was an open target, but the highwayman paused rather than exploiting it and raised an eyebrow.

"Banneret? Really?"

Guillot shrugged and the man thrust. Guillot parried with a clumsy effort that left him with no opportunity for a riposte. His sword had once felt like part of his arm—now it felt like part of a tree. The man followed up with a more determined effort, and Guillot felt a flash of fear. He had never before been in a sword fight without believing he would win. He managed to parry, but could feel the muscles in his forearm protesting at the unfamiliar use. A boy of seventeen or eighteen taking his Academy entrance exams could have beaten him.

Once, Guillot had been fêted as the finest swordsman in the world. He had won the Competition, and had the Telastrian steel sword in his hand to prove it. How could he have allowed himself to fall so low?

"We don't have to continue with this," the highwayman said. "Dying over a few coins and a couple of horses doesn't make much sense in the grand scheme of things. If you continue with this, you *will* die. I may be a thief, but I'm not ordinarily a murderer."

Guillot roared with rage and attacked. He prayed to whatever god would listen for an instant of the dazzling skill that had once come so easily to him. The highwayman parried once, twice. He didn't even have to move his feet. Before he knew it, Guillot's sword was flying through the air and his opponent's blade was at Guillot's throat.

"If you don't mind me asking, is that a Telastrian blade? I've never actually seen one before."

Guillot said nothing.

The man's eyes widened. "It is! Well, ain't that a thing. Usually I wouldn't even think of taking something like that from a man. There's robbing someone, and then there's *robbing* someone. Still, a blade like that really doesn't deserve to be stuck with someone like you."

Dal Sason emerged from the trees, holding a bundle of sticks, a fourth man's dagger held tight against his throat.

"Search their things and take the horses," the man said as he went to collect Gill's sword, never taking his eyes from Gill. He hefted the Telastrian blade in one hand. "I actually feel bad about this, I really do, so I'll tell you what. I'm Captain Fernand, Estranzan by birth, infamous by life." He doffed his hat. "If you ask around, you should be able to find me, should you ever want to get this magnificent blade back. How does that sound? I'm not so bad, am I?" Abruptly he let out a short grunt and crumpled to the ground.

Guillot raised his eyebrows and looked at dal Sason, but the other banneret seemed just as surprised as Guillot.

Another highwayman dropped where he stood. The man with the knife at dal Sason's throat collapsed an instant later, leaving Guillot no further impediment. There seemed little point in grabbing a sword, so he charged, slamming his shoulder into the remaining highwayman.

The element of surprise enabled Gill to wrestle his way to the top of their sprawl. He rained blow after blow onto his enemy, pouring out every ounce of his rage and shame. His anger carried him along as he drew his dagger and plunged it down. By the time he stopped, the man was dead.

Getting to his feet, Guillot looked around. Dal Sason met Gill's gaze with a puzzled expression, clearly no wiser than Gill as to what had felled the other three. Guillot moved from body to body—all were out cold, but showed no signs of injury. Being a gentleman of the road was an executable offence, and the responsibility for that was one of the many tasks Guillot's seigneurship imposed upon him. As distasteful as dispatching a defenceless foe was, there was no telling who these men might harm, given the chance to do so. He made it quick, and took what little solace he could in knowing they wouldn't feel any pain.

"You two all right?" A female voice called from the dusky gloom.

"We are," dal Sason called back.

Solène appeared from behind a bush, a stone in one hand and a loop of cloth in the other.

"Looks like you boys got yourselves in some trouble."

"Looks that way," Guillot said.

"It's getting cold. You should probably make a start with that fire," she said to dal Sason.

"Don't bother," Guillot said, retrieving his sword. "I'm not sleeping next to these vermin. There was another reasonable camping spot a short way back. If we move fast, we can be set up before we lose the light completely."

They walked in silence, leading the horses. Guillot chewed over two things. The first was his humiliation during the swordfight. He had never experienced that before, not from a lowly highwayman, nor the most esteemed of fencing masters. Even at his low ebb, he had expected to be capable of more. The second thing was Solène's makeshift slingshot, and her seemingly lethal accuracy with it.

Once the horses were secured at their new camp, dal Sason set about building a fire. Even as Guillot started to whittle tinder from a stick, he thought about how much he loathed himself—how could he have allowed the one thing he had been so good at escape him?

He took a seat by the assembled firewood, drew out his flint, and started to work it against the edge of his dagger, creating a peel of sparks with each pass.

"That was quite an impressive display with the slingshot," Guillot said.

Solène shrugged.

"I didn't see any stones flying through the air. Or hear them."

"Not my problem if you don't see or hear well," she said. "But I reckon that must have gone some way to settling my debt. Hurry up with that fire. I'm freezing."

He looked at her. She was shivering; it was a mild evening, but she looked as though she had crawled out of a freezing river. And missed a few nights' sleep.

"The thing is," Guillot said, "the men you hit . . . None of them had a head wound. They didn't have any wounds at all." He fixed his gaze on her.

"Oh, for gods' sake," she said, shivering hard. "I saved you. Does it matter? Just be grateful."

"I am grateful," Guillot said, pausing in his effort to set fire to the tinder. "Very. Thank you. Only, I'm a little confused." The colour was gone from her skin, and her eyes were heavy. She looked as though she was about to drop from the cold.

"Light the bloody fire, would you," she said. On her utterance, it sparked to life, a long tendril of flame rising from the centre of the pile of wood. She hugged her knees to her chest, her eyes wide. The expression on her face was like that of a guilty child.

"I, uh . . ." Guillot looked at his untouched tinder. "Well," he said, "that really is something."

Dal Sason had been close to falling asleep, but now was fully awake and staring. If he was as surprised as Gill, he certainly did a better job of hiding it.

"Tell me," Guillot said, his voice calm, "did you really turn into a goat?"

"Of course not," Solène said. "I turned *him* into a pig. Only for a couple of minutes, though."

Guillot laughed. Dragons. A sorceress. What would be next? The Prince Bishop announcing he was going to donate all his wealth to the mendicants? No, that would be too far-fetched. Dal Sason remained silent.

"You aren't afraid?" Solène said.

"Why should I be?" Guillot said. "I've just seen you drop three grown men without laying a hand, or a stone, on them. If you wanted to hurt me, you'd have done it long ago. Come closer to the fire. I'll stay awake with you until you've warmed up some."

CHAPTER
12

Each morning, there seemed to be something new for them all to digest. First, it had been Gill's revelation that dragons roamed the land once more. Now, their new travelling companion was a user of magic.

They packed up their camp in silence. Guillot kept his mouth shut, not out of any discomfort at being in the presence of a mage, but rather because of the memory of his fight with the highwayman. He had been a great swordsman for so long, the idea was part of his very being. To have it stripped away left him feeling hollow. He had always thought it would simply be there, waiting for him, if he ever needed to call on it again. How to get it back, though? He feared that he didn't even know where to start.

They set off for Mirabay once again. There seemed to be no question of her not going with them. Guillot didn't bring up the matter. She seemed to know how to look after herself, and if she wanted to go to Mirabay, he had no reason to stop her.

"What you said about the Intelligenciers," Solène said after they had been riding for a little while, the first word any of them had uttered. "You wouldn't actually do that, would you? Knowing what you know?"

Guillot shook his head. "It's not my business."

"You said you were the king's representative . . ."

"Not really. Not for a long time."

"It was a lie?"

Guillot smiled. "It wasn't. I swore you would get justice, and I reckon setting you free did that. I still do. I don't believe for a second what you did to Arnoul was anything other than self-defence. Admittedly, before last night, I didn't believe you'd done anything to him at all. Still, I'm not going to lose any sleep over my decision."

"Why'd you stop them, then? If you didn't intend to hand me over to the Intelligenciers?"

He sighed. "Let's just say I don't like injustice, and leave it at that."

"Why aren't you afraid of me, like everyone else?"

For the first time that day, Gill realised he didn't have a headache, and was grateful for the fact. "You've already asked me that."

"I want a better answer."

He shrugged. "I've been around enough people who wanted to do me harm to know what they look like."

"And I don't look like that?"

Guillot couldn't restrain a chuckle. "No, you don't. Then again, I'll bet those highwaymen would have said the same thing."

They rode in silence awhile longer before Guillot's curiosity got the better of him. "Did you know you were a . . . sorceress, before you came to Trelain?"

"Please don't call me that."

"Why not?"

"Because sorcerers hurt people. I've read about them, and they did terrible things. I'd never do anything like that. I'd never want to be like them. I didn't ask for what I can do, and I'd never use it to hurt someone unless they were trying to hurt me. Or my friends."

"I apologise," Guillot said, "but did you know you can do what you can do?"

She nodded. "Back home, I already knew I could do things—light fires, move objects around without touching them—but I was always careful. One day, I wasn't careful enough." Her voice grew flat. "I was worried that the parish priest might denounce me to the Intelligenciers, so I ran before he had the chance. I thought I could hide in Trelain. Compared to where I'm from, it seemed huge."

"I don't know if Mirabay is going to be any better for you. It's larger by far, but there will be more Intelligenciers there. Lots more."

"I have to try. You can't hide in a place where there aren't many people. In a city I can disappear. It nearly worked in Trelain. It would have, if it wasn't for Arnoul."

Guillot didn't know what to say to her. He hadn't spent much time listening to other people for a long time, at least not while sober, and he was out of practise. Like swordplay, chivalry had once come easy to him. Now it seemed completely alien. Was he obligated to do more for her than he already had?

"You seem like someone with good intentions," he said awkwardly. "Mirabay isn't the place for that. You'll need to be very careful."

"What's it like there?"

"It's hard to put into words. On the surface it's beautiful; the buildings, the music, the art, the food. Underneath?" He shrugged. "There's rot everywhere. They just dress it up better in the city."

"Thank you for helping me," she said. "I've never met anyone who would do something like you did for a complete stranger."

Guillot blushed.

"It must have taken a lot of courage to ride into an angry crowd like that and make them hand me over. You saved my life."

The praise made Gill feel uncomfortable. He was a drunk who had pissed his life away because things hadn't gone his way. He thought about admitting that he had still been drunk when he'd rescued her, but couldn't bring himself to say it. Instead, he shrugged, echoing the habit of country folk who didn't want to respond to something. The thought of being someone's saviour felt like a heavy burden. Would he have done it had he been sober? He liked to think so, but he honestly didn't know. He looked at his hands. The shaking had stopped, which came as a relief—as did the fact that his craving for a drink was far less intrusive than before. He still felt off, but "off" was better than he'd felt in a long time. Nonetheless, it was long past time to change the subject.

"You're very quiet back there, Nicholas."

"Simply trying to complete my mission with as little aggravation as I can," he said.

"Oh, don't be like that," Guillot said, refreshed by not being the most miserable person present. "It's not so bad."

"Dragons? If I tell anyone at home about this, they'll have me locked up. I mean, *dragons?*"

Guillot didn't miss the fact that he hadn't commented on Solène turning out to be a mage. Was dal Sason afraid of drawing her ire?

"Wouldn't have believed it myself until I saw one," Guillot said. "But it was as real as any of us, and it's only a matter of time before it starts killing people, if it hasn't already."

"I don't mean anything by this," dal Sason said, "but I couldn't help noticing all the empty wine bottles in your house. I've been the worse for the bottle on more than one occasion, and I'd have sworn I saw things—"

"It was a dragon," Guillot said, "or something that looked very like one."

"I was there for a couple of days. I didn't see anything that gave me to think—"

"A dragon," Guillot said, his firm tone indicating the conversation was over.

▗▄▄▄▄▖

"Always provokes a reaction, doesn't it," dal Sason said when they crested a hill later that morning and Mirabay finally hove into view.

The city basked in bright sunshine. It was a stunning sight—even Guillot, who had nothing but bad memories of the place, couldn't disagree. Surrounded by high walls and towers, the city spread along the banks of the River Vosges, with its heart and ancient centre on an island that split the river in two. The buildings were mostly built of a creamy white local stone, capped with grey-blue slates. He spotted familiar landmarks—the old castle and the cathedral on the island, the palace on the hill on the south bank, overlooking the river. His gaze lingered there a little longer, his memory drawn to the duel in the great gallery that had won him his life and freedom, but had guaranteed his disgrace. He felt bile rise in his throat.

"I don't think it's provoked quite the reaction that you mean," Guillot said as the sight of the place filled him with contempt, and worse: fear. "No point sitting here gawping." He urged his horse on. "I assume the Prince Bishop will have accommodations prepared for us?"

"That was left to my discretion," dal Sason said. "I'm not sure he actually expected me to succeed in bringing you back to the city."

"Excellent. We'll need two rooms at Bauchard's, then." Guillot watched carefully for dal Sason's reaction, but there was none. "Three, if you need somewhere to stay. The private dining room reserved for us every night we're there." Still no reaction. "And Solène can't go around the city dressed like she is. We'll need a seamstress to attend her. She needs at least three new sets of clothes. Day and evening wear, and at least one set of travelling clothes, I should think." Still nothing. Guillot floundered for a more extravagant demand, but couldn't think of anything. He wondered how much latitude the Prince Bishop had given dal Sason; how badly he wanted Guillot to come to the city?

Guillot waited for an answer, but none was forthcoming. "Am I to assume by your silence that the Prince Bishop will pay for this?"

"I don't foresee a problem," dal Sason said.

"Excellent," Guillot said, regretting more intensely than ever his decision to stop drinking.

⣦⣦⣦⣦

Bauchard's had been the most expensive inn in Mirabay when Guillot lived in the city, and it had not lost any of its lustre. The rooms were opulent, the beds were luxurious, the food was sublime, and the bill always enormous. That it would be satisfied from the Prince Bishop's funds made the experience even more enjoyable.

The very best Mirabayan wines were on offer at Bauchard's, as well as those from places farther afield, the famed Blackwater vintages from Ostia among them. It strained Guillot's willpower to its greatest extent to ignore them. With a seemingly limitless line of credit, one he desired to abuse as much as possible, the temptations were hard to resist, but he had made a promise to himself. To the people who relied on him.

Something about his return to Mirabay felt like a homecoming. As he sat on one of the luxurious couches in Bauchard's lounge, he could, at times, forget all that had happened. He could recall a nervous afternoon sitting in that very room, waiting for Auroré to arrive for their first date. Their marriage dinner had been held in the inn's dining room. His stomach twisted with a mixture of grief and shame, and he wondered what he had been thinking, choosing Bauchard's for their stay. Of all the places in Mirabay, this should have been the one he most wanted to avoid. Why had he been fool enough to come back here? Had he really thought the past would stay where it belonged?

He felt hot, started to sweat, and thought he would be sick. He looked about for the fastest way to fresh air, but knew there would be no respite outside either. Too many familiar sights, sounds, and smells. He wanted more than anything to jump on the nearest horse and ride for Villerauvais as fast as it would carry him. He clutched the ornately carved armrest of his chair, squeezing it hard for what little anchor it gave him amidst the maelstrom of memory, regret, and pain.

"Guillot? Are you all right?" Solène asked from her seat opposite.

Dal Sason reappeared, having booked rooms. He frowned and said, "Is he all right?"

Gill took a deep breath and swallowed hard. "Yes, came over a little dizzy is all. Probably hungry. I've been salivating over the thought of the dining room here for hours now."

"Me too," dal Sason said. "I've booked our rooms, so I suggest we all take a few minutes to freshen up. As soon as you're ready, we can go get something to eat."

"Perfect," Guillot said, wondering if he'd be able to hold anything down. He didn't want dal Sason to get any hint of what was really happening, but hiding it wasn't going to be easy. "When do you need to report to your lord and master?" Guillot said, trying to direct his mind to something else.

"I already have. I sent word ahead from the city gate. I expect he'll send for us as soon as he's ready."

CHAPTER
13

Amaury told his private secretary that he didn't want to be disturbed, then closed the door to his office. Practising magic gave him little of the guilty thrill it once had—now it resulted mainly in frustration—but he persevered. His predecessors had chosen to ignore the contents of the great, ancient archive beneath the cathedral, out of either fear or the blinkered attitude that magic was evil, but Amaury had seen the opportunity it represented. He wondered why they hadn't destroyed it all, but that might have meant admitting they had it in the first place, and he knew firsthand that the Intelligenciers weren't averse to introducing members of the priesthood to the purifying nature of fire.

Every so often a priest on the fringes of church control would get it in their head that they had some great insight the church had overlooked in its two-thousand-year existence, and set up shop as a mystic. It rarely took the Intelligenciers long to rid the church of the problem they presented, and useful as that was, Amaury realised there was something of an irony that his interests would make him a target. At least he had the brains to keep quiet about his plans.

Sadly, the Intelligenciers were not the only problem. Most people feared and loathed magic—and that represented the greatest obstacle to his plans for the Spurriers. He would overcome it, as he had every other roadblock he'd encountered, but how to do so wasn't clear to him yet. If he were a religious man, he would pray. The thought made him smile.

Seated in a comfortable chair, away from his desk, Amaury took a deep breath, forcing himself to relax as much as possible for a man of his responsibilities. He closed his eyes and did his best to push all of the matters vying for his attention to the back of his mind. When he opened his eyes, he fought to ensure there was only one thought in his head—the image of a glowing mote of light that gave off no heat. His brow furrowed as he tried to maintain the mental discipline needed to keep the question *is it working?* from popping into his head.

A glowing ember formed in the air in the centre of his office, no brighter than the wick of a dying candle. His breathing quickened but he forced himself to remain calm and focussed. The glow started to grow stronger, though it was still less bright than a candle flame. Sweat beaded on his brow and the veins in his forehead pulsed. He concentrated on the image in his mind's eye rather than what he saw forming before him.

Leaning forward, he strained to put more of himself into the light. His muscles tensed. As suddenly as it had appeared, the glow vanished. Slumping back in his chair, Amaury sighed. It was ever the same, and he was reluctantly coming to accept this as the limit of his magical ability. He wondered: if he had found his way into the archive as a child, would he be capable of more? If only he could find someone with real power. He knew they existed; he had even thought, on a couple of occasions, that he had found one, but though they were able to do more than others, they were not strong enough for his needs.

He knew he was really talking about a weapon: a natural-born mage who would be capable of defending the Order until the children they were training came of age. More than one would be better, but even one would do. Natural mages were a curious thing. Even the old texts didn't explain how they came to be or how to find them. He had thought of liaising with the Intelligenciers, who had a wealth of experience in such matters, but that would draw too much attention to things he did not want noticed.

It all came down to the Fount, and how attuned one was to it. It was a mysterious, fascinating thing; it was everywhere, but to benefit from it, to use it, one had to be aware of it, to accept it, to develop an affinity with it. Some had to be taught, while some crawled from the womb able to draw on it almost before they could draw breath. From that moment—whether they realised it or not—they used magic in everything. With his knowledge, he could train such a person to so great a degree of potency that the Intelligenciers would be a mere trifle.

As attractive as that was, it raised another problem. How could he hope to remain master of an order if he was its weakest member? At least he had a prospective solution to that worry: the Cup. From his hours poring over the Imperial papers in the archive, he had learned it could give a person of any age a strong connection to the Fount. The wasted years would be washed away when he drank from it, and he would become as powerful as any mage and secure in the leadership of the order he had created.

It was hard to fathom how such an important object could be lost, but he realised those had been difficult times. The Empire had been coming apart at its seams—the Imperial family had been overthrown and murdered, the College of Mages had stretched themselves to the breaking point, trying to maintain control. Their long-faithful servants, the bannerets, had found the extent to which their masters would go to hold onto power too horrific to allow.

Against that tumult, the Chevaliers of the Silver Circle, who chose to remain true to their duty of protecting mankind from dragons rather than take sides in the civil war, decided to take the Cup—their most sacred relic—to a place where they thought it would be safe. It never got there.

They had been transporting it and their treasury to their new headquarters, somewhere in the southeast of the country. Dragons had attacked their convoy and carried off the treasure, along with the Cup. Dragons were said to hoard gold in their dens, so it seemed to Amaury that the treasury, and the Cup, would have ended up in one.

At first it had seemed like looking for a needle in a haystack, but he had discovered that an object of such great magical potency left a footprint on the Fount. Seeking that footprint was the way to find the object. Fortunately, that could be done by even the weakest of mages—*even me*, he thought.

According to Leverre's report, the commander was certain he had found the Cup's location. It was damned bad luck that the cavern where it lay also held a dormant dragon. Worse still that they had managed to wake it up. It seemed each solution to his problems created more problems. To get the Cup, he needed to kill the dragon. To kill the dragon, his only solution so far was to use a disgraced drunk, and Guillot was sure to bring problems with him.

Amaury was distracted from his thoughts by a knock on his door. It creaked open and his secretary peered in.

"I told you I wasn't to be disturbed," Amaury said, tired and not interested in having to deal with anyone, or anything.

"I'm sorry, your Grace. You said you wanted to be informed immediately when Banneret of the White dal Sason arrived back in the city. He's sent this note."

Amaury sighed. "Fine," he said. "Leave it on the desk. Thank you."

⋀⋀⋀⋀⋀

Amaury forced himself not to run with excitement as he walked the polished marble floors of the palace toward the king's private offices. Dal Sason's note reported that not only had he succeeded in bringing Guillot back to Mirabay, but they had rescued a very interesting young woman from a mob in Trelain. Amaury couldn't recall the last time he had felt so giddy. Possibly he never had, but he certainly did at that moment. Opportunity and disaster, hand in hand. The world was a place of great irony. Given the choice, he would already be on his way to meet with dal Sason and the new arrivals, but even Amaury had to pay lip service to the king and report to him first.

So far, the king had been fastidious in attending his duties, keeping court every day and working at his desk long into the night. Should he develop too high an opinion of his own ability, it might become a problem, but thus far he had shown himself to be receptive to Amaury's suggestions. He might even prove to be the perfect puppet that Amaury desired, but it was too early to determine that.

He reached the king's office, irritated by the need to knock and wait under the scrutiny of the guards standing there. When the king's secretary finally opened the door, he remained in the doorway, blocking entry.

"I have business with the king," Amaury said.

"His Majesty is very busy and has asked not to be disturbed."

"It's urgent," Amaury said.

"Then perhaps you'd like to wait, and I'll inform the king. I'm sure he'll see you the moment he is free." The secretary smiled, and gestured to a plush velvet couch in the guarded antechamber to the king's private office.

Amaury had no option but to wait. Once the king knew he was there, Amaury couldn't leave until given permission. He forced a smile, nodded, and sat.

⋀⋀⋀⋀⋀

Amaury had counted three peals of the cathedral's bells before the king's secretary opened the door and gestured for Amaury to enter Boudain's private office. When he went in, he found the king sitting at his desk with his face buried in a document.

"The first piece of my plan is almost in place, your Majesty."

"Good," the king said, looking up from his work. "Please do enlighten me."

"You might recall an incident five years ago with one of the Chevaliers of the Silver Circle."

"The assassination attempt on my father?"

"Indeed. The Chevalier who was prosecuted for dereliction of duty and treason has, on my instruction, returned to the city."

"Dal Villerauvais. I remember him. How could I not? At times I thought father preferred him to me. Father was so proud when he won the Competition—a son of Mirabaya! Prouder still to have him here at the palace and in the Silver Circle. It went hard on him when dal Villerauvais let him down. Why would you bring him back?"

"With a dragon loose in the mountains, is it not natural to turn to the only member of an order of dragonslayers still living?"

"The last time the Silver Circle slew a dragon, there were people still alive who had been born Imperial citizens," the king said. "If I recall my history correctly, the last dragons were slain during the reign of my forebear, Boudain the Second. Guillot dal Villerauvais did a great many things, but I don't recall slaying a dragon being one of them."

"Yes, but it's not just a matter of expertise or experience," Amaury said. "It's always struck me as a tragedy that none of *my* forebears paid more attention to the ancient papers in the cathedral's library. I spend every spare moment there, seeking things that might aid your reign. Our current project, for instance, can trace its birth to one of my late-night reading sessions.

"I've learned things about the Chevaliers. They were imbued at their initiation with a number of abilities that made them more effective when fighting dragons. Indeed, the Chevaliers were something closer to what we are trying to create with the Order—both warrior and mage, not one or the other."

"That was a magical ceremony, and a practise that was stopped a thousand years ago. I don't need to read your ancient papers to know that. However the most recent Chevaliers were initiated, I expect it did little more than test their capacity for wine."

"Indeed, your Highness, but there might still be something to it, and I think it would be remiss to ignore the possibility. The Chevaliers had a secret initiation ritual. From what I've read, it may be that the ritual, possibly unbeknownst to the participants, retained a magical quality even long after the days of magic had ended. I have hope that the ceremony by itself will have given him an advantage in the fight against this dragon."

"Why is that?" the king said impatiently.

The Prince Bishop calmed himself. If it hadn't been for him, the king's father would have been pulled from his throne years before, and the best Boudain the Tenth could have hoped for would have been exile, or a quick death. As it was, he sat on a throne secured for him by other men. He would need to learn that, and learn it quickly.

"One thing we have discovered from our experiments and training in the Order is that words focus the mind, and focussing the mind shapes magic. If the user has an affinity with the Fount, whether natural or trained, in the correct circumstances, nothing more is needed. It's possible some of the Chevaliers were crafting magic during this ceremony without realising it."

"It sounds rather tenuous," the king said.

"I admit that it is, but I still think it's worth a try. If nothing else, it allows us to take action immediately, while we consider other alternatives. It might even work. There's only one way to find out."

The king steepled his fingers and leaned back in his chair. "You plan on having dal Villerauvais kill this beast for us."

"Yes. Yes, I do," Amaury said.

"You think he's up to it? I heard he's been rotting away at the end of a bottle since the trial."

"I'm not sure."

"What about the Order of the Golden Spur?"

Amaury blushed. The dragon already represented the greatest blot on the Spurriers' short record. "I think it safe to say that the brothers and sisters of the Order aren't yet ready for something like this."

"Even the more experienced members?"

"This project is still too short-lived to yield results, Highness. The day when they can is close, but not yet here."

"What about the Chevaliers' ritual? Why can't the Spurriers conduct that? The old bannerets weren't mages, simply enhanced warriors. Might we not be able to do the same for ours?"

Amaury raised his hands. "While many sources mention the ritual, I've yet to come across anything that actually describes it."

"Dal Villerauvais, then. Surely he can tell you what you need to know?"

If he was sober enough to remember any of it, Amaury thought. "That's a possibility, Highness, but I'd rather not reveal the true nature of the Order to someone with as checkered a reputation as he for as long as possible. I plan to interview him before I send him out. If I think he might be able to help us in that way, rest assured I will pursue it."

"It's a shame the Order isn't able to aid us in our time of greatest need. That's what they're for, aren't they?"

"Indeed, Highness," Amaury said.

"Are we wasting time and resources on them?"

"Far from it," Amaury said, "but to send the Spurriers out now would be to waste their potential. My next order of business is to work out a targeted training plan, so they can deal with this threat in the event that dal Villerauvais isn't up to the task. In a few weeks, I expect they'll be better able to tackle the dragon, if it hasn't already been dealt with."

The king steepled his fingers beneath his nose again, as he had a habit of doing when he wished to appear wiser than his years, or his ability. The gesture was quickly coming to irritate Amaury.

"I want our people to have whatever it is he has. Before we send him off. If words were said that might have effect, I want to know what they are. They might even carry more weight when said by one of the Order's mages, even if they made no difference for dal Villerauvais and his lot. Still, I'm not convinced the initiation to the Silver Circle was anything more than a drunken debauch."

"Be that as it may, it's prudent to investigate all avenu—"

"Yes, I agree," the king said. "Now, I've a great deal of work to do. Please see to what we've discussed as expeditiously as possible."

Amaury bit his lip, bowed his head, and left. He glanced out a window as he exited the antechamber under the gaze of the ever-vigilant guards. It was dark out, and he was tired. It was late to arrange a meeting with the new arrivals, though ordinarily that would not have bothered him. However, he wanted to be at his best when he encountered Gill again, and he needed a good night's sleep for that.

CHAPTER 14

Dal Sason was waiting for Gill when he went down to the dining room for breakfast the next morning.

"The Prince Bishop is ready to see us at our earliest convenience," dal Sason said, making no effort at a greeting.

"I thought it was the king I came all this way to see?" Guillot said, sniping at dal Sason to exorcise the bad mood he seemed to wake up in each morning since going sober.

"It is, but the Prince Bishop would like to speak with you first."

"I wouldn't want to keep him waiting." Gill waved to a waiter. "I'll start with fruit and yoghurt, followed by a full cooked breakfast with toast and preserves. Orange juice to wash it down. Then, I think pastries. Just bring me a selection. And coffee of course—strong, with hot milk." *That should take a while to get through*, he thought. Then, remembering the Prince Bishop was footing the bill, he added, "And the same for my friends."

Dal Sason settled into his chair with a resigned look on his face. Gill was disappointed—his tactic had probably been expected. Realising you were predictable always came as a letdown. He also felt a little guilty—dal Sason was, after all, only a servant of the Crown, following orders, much as Guillot had once been. The fact that the Prince Bishop had stuck his beak into the mix wasn't the young banneret's fault. Gill's conscience threatened to get the better of him, and he was on the verge of cancelling the pastry course until he saw a plate of them being brought to a nearby table; gluttony beat conscience back into the hole where it belonged.

Solène joined them as the fruit arrived, showing all the benefits of a good night's sleep—and many miles distance from the angry mob that had wanted to burn her alive.

"I expect you'll have a busy day ahead," Guillot said as she sat. "I think I'll be needing some new duds myself, so be sure to ask the seamstress if she can recommend a good tailor."

"That will have to wait," dal Sason said. "His Grace wishes to meet Solène too."

Her eyes widened. "Why?"

Her quavering voice betrayed the fear her blank expression was doing its best to conceal. Guillot's mood darkened further.

"What did you tell him?" he asked, anger in his voice. He was damned if he had saved her from the pyre only to deliver her to the Prince Bishop's warped sense of justice.

Dal Sason raised his hands defensively. "It's nothing like that. I'm given to understand he takes a keen interest in her . . . unique talents. He merely wishes to speak with her."

Guillot narrowed his eyes. "What do you mean by that?"

"I really can't say any more. He will explain when you see him."

"Does she have your word as a banneret and a gentleman that she will not be harmed, and will be free to leave of her own accord whenever she wishes?"

"I can give you my word on that." He faced Solène. "You have my word, as a Banneret of the White, and as a gentleman and seigneur of Mirabaya."

"And the Prince Bishop doesn't mean me any harm?" she said.

"I have no reason to believe that to be the case. In fact, quite the contrary."

Guillot nodded slowly. "All things considered, I don't think you can expect any better than that. The only alternative is to get up from the table and leave the city this instant."

She shook her head. "No, I'm tired of running, and I'm curious to see what such a powerful man might want of me," she said, her voice firmer than before. "If Nicholas says the Prince Bishop's intentions are good, I'm willing to see what the man has to say."

Guillot popped a piece of grapefruit into his mouth and mulled her decision as he chewed. He supposed that if things went sour, she could always turn Amaury into a pig—he'd pay money to see that. He realised curiosity had overcome gluttony, and after one last, longing look at the pastries on the next table, he turned to dal Sason.

"The suspense is likely to kill me, so I suppose we should be on our way."

The palace of Mirabay was a marvel in white stone: a collection of graceful, colonnaded walls amidst the lush green surrounds of a craggy hill at the edge of the city. The guards recognised dal Sason and waved them through the main gate. It had been like that for Guillot once, but these men didn't seem to have the first idea who he was or had been. Perhaps that was for the best. Some people had been sympathetic to his plight, as dal Sason had said, but others were only too delighted to attack at the first scent of blood, the Prince Bishop leading the way.

The interior of the palace was just as impressive as its façade. The king's grandfather had commissioned the great Pierro Lupini, the Auracian artist, to paint the walls and barrel-vaulted roof of the entrance hall with scenes from the histories of the Chevaliers of the Silver Circle. It was heroic pose after heroic pose as Guillot walked into the palace. The paintings had once impressed him, but no longer. He wondered if any of the events they depicted had actually happened. He noted with irony that a frieze representing his generation, one full of drinking, gambling, and whoring, was absent. At least that one he could have guaranteed as being accurate.

Near the end of the passageway, he stopped, his attention grabbed by a painting: a lone horseman, bow in hand, chasing a huge dragon. Guillot tried to remember the story it depicted—*Andalon and the Wyrm*, he thought. He supposedly shot the beast from the sky, but it seemed like a ridiculous notion, so great a thing felled by a tiny arrow.

"Are you coming?" Dal Sason had gone on several paces before realising Guillot had stopped.

Guillot wondered if it might be worth reviewing the story for any useful information. It would be foolish to die following the advice of a work of fiction, but treasures could be found in the most unlikely places, and it might prove very difficult to get any reliable information on how to kill a dragon anywhere else.

"Coming," he said.

The Prince Bishop worked from private apartments across the hall from the king's, convenient to the throne room and close to the ear of his master, although in the days of the old king, Guillot reckoned the line between master and servant had become blurred. He had made the journey to these rooms many times, but never with any enthusiasm.

The Prince Bishop was a born schemer. Even when they had both been students at the Academy, Amaury had always been able to dodge the things he didn't want to do. Where a busy man might be expected to live at his desk, confronting an endless pile of paperwork, when his secretary showed them into his office, the Prince Bishop stood by a large open window, looking out on the garden below. Poised, relaxed, smug. Just as irritating as Guillot remembered.

"Banneret of the White, Chevalier dal Villerauvais, your Grace, and . . . Solène?" dal Sason said.

She gave him a curt nod that made it clear there was no more to add, or that if there was, she wasn't telling.

"Thank you, Nicholas. You may leave us," the Prince Bishop said, turning to greet them.

He had aged little in the years since Guillot last saw him. His hair was a little greyer, his waist a little wider, but his beard and moustache were styled the same way, and he continued to wear the powder-blue vestments of his office.

"My Lord dal Villerauvais, welcome back to Mirabay," Prince Bishop Amaury said.

"Are we going to play at being old friends first, Amaury?" Guillot said.

"I really don't see the point, Gill. The kingdom has need of you. All things considered, playing to your patriotism strikes me as a wasted effort, so I will simply say that you will be handsomely rewarded for your service. The luxury of your accommodation in the city is but a drop in the sea. Lands, an elevated title, coin."

Try as he might, Gill could not deny it was tempting. He was the product of too many generations of aristocratic breeding not to be attracted to an offer like that. It was also flattering to think his name still carried some weight. There was a time when his name was a curse in both Estranza and Humberland. Fame in battle had come easy then and he had revelled in it. He wondered how the Prince Bishop proposed to use him—as muscle in some diplomatic negotiation? "Revealing your cards a little early, aren't you?"

"There's no time to waste."

"I'll take all of that, but I need something else as well. I need to borrow a company of soldiers—ones who know what they're about. I can't make any promises as to the condition they'll be returned in."

"Why?"

"Do you care?"

"Humour me."

Guillot would have preferred to punch him in the face, and was tempted to embark on a course of "tell me yours and I'll tell you mine," but his problem was at least as pressing as whatever Amaury's was, so he gave in. "Something is killing livestock in my demesne. I want to kill it before it turns its attention to my villagers."

The Prince Bishop let out a rare laugh. "How very noble of you, but I suspect the problem you speak of is the same as my problem."

Inside, Guillot roared "Ha! I knew it!," but he maintained his froideur and allowed his satisfaction to sink beneath the gravity of the situation. "Go on."

"I had hoped to engage you on this matter before the problem reached as far as your demesne, but it's of little import. It's been many years since we last exchanged a civil word, but that did not blind me to the fact that you are the finest swordsman this country has ever produced. You are also the last remaining Chevalier of the Silver Circle. Mirabaya has need of your skills, which is why I have called on you. As ridiculous as it sounds, it seems there is a dragon at large in the southern foothills. That is what is killing your livestock."

Gill nodded and the Prince Bishop's eyes widened with surprise.

"You've seen it?"

"I believe I have."

"Large? Black? Breathes flame?"

"That's what I saw."

The Prince Bishop smiled. "Well, at least it seems that we aren't dealing with two of them."

Guillot ignored the attempt at humour, noticing that Amaury seemed genuinely relieved. "Where did it come from?"

"The mountains," the Prince Bishop said. "I've been getting reports about it for a couple of weeks now. We took action as soon as they reached us."

"But *where* did it come from? How has a dragon suddenly appeared after none having been seen for centuries?"

"That's not of importance. All that we need to consider for the time being is that there is a threat to the king's subjects, one that needs to be dealt with quickly. By the time word of this spreads, we want to have it firmly under control."

"If one's suddenly appeared, don't you think it might be important to spare a thought as to why? And to wonder if more are going to arrive?" Guillot studied him for a moment. "Unless you already *know* why it's appeared."

"That there is one is all I intend to discuss. The rest is irrelevant."

"A great many things are irrelevant to you when they don't suit your purpose," Guillot said, his temper rising.

"What's that supposed to mean?"

"You know damn well what it means."

"Ah," the Prince Bishop said. "I suppose it was naive of me to hope we might leave all that in the past, where it belongs." He cleared his throat. "I did nothing more than my duty. Had you done the same, the whole situation would have been avoided."

Gill wondered if he could kill the Prince Bishop and get out of the palace before the guards caught up with him. Probably not. He wondered if he could convince Solène to turn Amaury into a pig. Permanently.

"I wasn't supposed to be on duty that day."

"One of the other Chevaliers was ill. His post needed to be filled."

"Ill? He wasn't ill. He was screwing the Count of Harvin's wife. *I* was ill. I'd buried my wife and child the day before."

The Prince Bishop shook his head. "This will get us nowhere. It was tragic, and I'm very sorry for your loss, but you of all people should know that service to the Crown comes above all else."

Guillot dug his fingernails into his palms. He did know that, but he had not been treated fairly. He tried to quell his anger and speak without emotion. "What would you do if I told you to find someone else to do your dirty work?"

"I'll find someone else. Someone who would be given all of your lands and titles should they succeed. Would you really choose to leave the protection of your lands to someone else? Lord Montpareil, perhaps? I can assure you, by the time our *problem* is finished with Villerauvais, there will be nothing left of the village. You were the best, Gill. The king is hoping you still are."

"And if I said I wasn't up to it?"

"The same as I've just outlined, and you get to live the rest of your life knowing you failed the greatest task set you by your king. This is far more important than fighting duels against men who have displeased the king. This is the greatest service you will ever provide. A quest that will erase all past . . . failings."

"You are the last Chevalier of the Silver Circle," a new voice said. "Slaying dragons is supposed to be what you are all about."

Guillot turned to see who had spoken. There was no mistaking the new king as he walked into the room and nodded to the Prince Bishop. Five years ago, he had been a princely dilettante with whom Guillot had little interaction, but he had gained presence since, with his neatly trimmed black beard adding character to his youthful face.

"Your Highness," Guillot said, bowing his head and standing.

"I will be the first to admit you were treated harshly," the king said. "I was very sorry to hear about your wife. Had I been involved, I like to think things would have happened differently. I would never have put you on duty after such a tragedy, and I don't believe it was warranted that you shouldered the lion's share of the blame over what happened subsequently. But I was not king then, and my platitudes cannot change what happened.

"*I* am your king now, and I have need of you. Are you my man?"

"I am, Highness," Guillot said. No fibre of his being would allow him to turn down a request from his king.

"That is what I wanted to hear. Thank you."

"If I might ask, your Highness: why didn't you appoint any new Chevaliers?"

"You know as well as I do that the Silver Circle had become a club for drinking, gambling, and whoring. I saw no reason to reinstate it. It is an irony that we now find ourselves in need of their service."

Guillot looked at the Prince Bishop, who smiled benignly. He thought of his brief encounter with the highwayman. Were they expecting things of him that he could no longer do?

"I suspect that they would have inevitably fallen short of the achievements of their forebears," Guillot said. "As I might. I'll give you my best, Highness, but I'll need help. Nobody knows how to fight these things anymore."

"Excellent," the king said. "The people of Mirabaya will be in your debt." With that, he left. The Prince Bishop's secretary closed the door behind him.

"You'll have help," the Prince Bishop said. "All you need. The finest men we have at our disposal. We've been researching the matter since it arose, and we've uncovered some information that may be of use. There won't be much time to prepare, however. I'm sure you'll agree that we need to move quickly."

Guillot nodded. He realised that they had never doubted he would accept. He supposed men of such power never did. His obedience obtained, the Prince Bishop turned his attention to Solène.

"Now, my dear, I've been very much looking forward to meeting you."

CHAPTER
15

T ell me, you are from where?" the Prince Bishop said.

Realising he didn't have the first clue about where Solène had been before Trelain, Guillot sat in silent curiosity.

"Bastelle-Loiron," Solène said.

"I haven't heard of it," said the Prince Bishop. "Where along the river is it? In the Duchy of Trelain? Or the March of Aurdonne?"

"I wouldn't expect you to know it," she said. "It's in the Duchy of Trelain."

The Prince Bishop nodded in acknowledgement. "There's no need for you to be afraid," he said. "Indeed, I expect you'll look back and see today's encounter as an extraordinary piece of luck. Now, show me what you can do."

Solène looked at Guillot, her eyes full of questions and doubt. In the office of the second-most-powerful man in Mirabaya, she had little choice but to do as he asked. Guillot nodded. The young woman looked back at the Prince Bishop, then at his desk. A piece of blank paper was set out, probably waiting to become some important missive. With a bright flash, the sheet burst into an intense flame that died out as quickly as it had come to life, leaving behind a small coating of ash and a wisp of smoke.

The Prince Bishop let out a laugh and sat back, slapping his palms on the armrests of his chair. "Well, that is quite something. Quite something indeed."

Guillot had never seen the Prince Bishop so impressed. He seemed to have been born with the look of bored disinterest it took many aristocrats years to perfect.

"Guillot, there are a great many things I am sure you need to see to before you set off on your . . . quest. There's no need for you to be here for this; you may feel free to attend to whatever it is you need to attend to. The men I'm sending with you will make themselves known to you and will make sure you have everything you need."

Guillot frowned, looking at Solène. She was difficult to read, but he had spent enough time with her to see the fear in her eyes and tension in her face—just like when he had first met her.

"I promised Solène I'd stay with her." At his words, she seemed to relax, increasing Gill's resolve to remain exactly where he was.

The Prince Bishop frowned and glanced at Solène, who remained resolutely mute.

"Very well," he said. "You'd find out much of what I'm about to say soon enough, but I need your word that you will keep everything you hear to yourself. State secrets and all."

Guillot thought about being obtuse, just to aggravate the other man, but that would only prolong his time in the Prince Bishop's presence. "You have my word."

"Good. To break it would be treason, and you're already familiar with how that plays out."

Guillot smiled. That was the Prince Bishop he knew so well. Guillot had agreed to the king's request, so Amaury no longer had to play nice.

"Solène, have you had any training?" the Prince Bishop said. "From the Szavarians perhaps, or the Darvarosians?"

She shrugged. "No. None."

"None," the Prince Bishop said, his smile looking stiff. "I don't mind telling you that I've spent quite some time and expense searching for someone with natural magical talent. I was convinced such people were out there somewhere, and now here you are, arrived on my doorstep."

The Prince Bishop's enthusiasm appeared almost childlike to Guillot, which was worrying. That Amaury had taken such a keen interest in matters considered heinous and criminal was even more so.

"I hate to cast doubt, or to make demands of you, but what you just did . . . Can you repeat it?" the Prince Bishop said. "Do other things like it?"

Solène nodded.

The man opened a drawer, took out another piece of paper, and placed it on his desk. As soon as he pulled his hand away, flames erupted, turning the paper into nothing more than a few flakes of ash.

"Good," the Prince Bishop said absently. "Excellent." His usual intensity returned. "I've established an order where people study how magic might benefit the kingdom. Here is what I can offer you, Solène. First, a safe place to live and work at that order. You will never have to worry about Intelligenciers, or as Banneret dal Sason informs me, impromptu mob justice.

"Second, you will be able to explore your talent in a safe environment, surrounded by like-minded individuals. We can show you how to focus your ability, and more importantly, how to control it."

Solène stared at Guillot. He wondered if the comments he'd made about the Prince Bishop during their trip to Mirabay were playing on her mind.

"Can I think about it?" she said.

The Prince Bishop chewed his lip for a moment. "Yes, of course."

He smiled again, but Guillot knew him well enough to see that it was forced. He wanted Solène in his little club, and he wanted her now.

"I would add one thing, out of concern for your well-being," the Prince Bishop said. "Don't take too long to consider. I can only guarantee your safety if you are part of my organisation. As long as you are not, the Intelligenciers remain a danger."

"I understand," she said. "You'll have my answer soon."

They left the Prince Bishop's office in silence, Guillot trying to make sense of the task he had been given and how the Prince Bishop knew so much about what was going on. He supposed the man had a network of informants, but when it came to the Prince Bishop, it was never a good idea to take anything at face value.

He shook his head. However mentally dominating his challenge was, the quandary Solène faced was more pressing. As they walked along the main hall, Guillot turned to her.

"If we head straight back to Bauchard's, you can be riding out of the city within the hour," he said.

She laughed. "To where?"

"That's a good question."

"I'm going to agree," she said, "but after everything you'd said about him, I wasn't going to make it easy. Where else can I find what he's offering?"

Guillot shrugged. "You can never trust him. I did once, and it cost me. He's a snake with unbound ambition. He doesn't care who he has to destroy to get what he wants."

"I'll be careful," she said. "I've lasted this long, I'm sure I can figure out how to survive here. I might even learn something."

Guillot had an overwhelming sense of unease but in the absence of a better idea, perhaps this order was the best option for her. "You might be right," he said, "but in my experience, Amaury never gives anyone anything without expecting something in return."

She was about to respond when they rounded a corner and were greeted by dal Sason, who apparently had been waiting for them.

"An interesting day," dal Sason said.

"You could say that," Guillot replied.

Dal Sason nodded. "The Prince Bishop's asked me to accompany you on the hunt. He'll be sending a few others with us, people from his personal bodyguard."

"That sounds encouraging," Guillot said, hoping everyone could detect his sarcasm.

"I've met a few of them before. They're top drawer. He only takes the best for his order, so I'm sure they'll be useful when the time comes."

"It strikes me as curious that the head of the great and wonderful church needs a personal bodyguard. I always thought *I* was the only one who didn't like him."

Dal Sason glared at him. "His Grace is also the First Minister of Mirabaya. That role requires the making and enforcing of decisions that aren't always popular. A bodyguard seemed necessary. He recruits the best from the Academy and has them trained at an old priory nearby. It's said he trains his spies there too."

"Really?" Guillot said. He cast Solène a conspiratorial look. "I wonder who else is trained there?"

"Anyhow," dal Sason said, "I'm here to bring you to the others who'll be working with us. Thought it would be best if we had a chance to get to know one another before we set off."

"I might go back to the inn and take a little more advantage of the Prince Bishop's generosity," Solène said.

"Thinking like that makes me glad to know you," Guillot said. "I'll see you there later."

With Solène on her way to hopefully make some extravagant purchases, dal Sason led Guillot to another room of the palace, where a man in a cream doublet and britches waited for them. Entering, Gill realised he'd been there before, years ago—the palace map room. Sections of the walls were lined with pigeonhole shelves, some with scrolls visible inside. Other parts of the walls were covered with former campaign maps, most still bearing marks made by the commanders who had used them in war. Gill recognised one as being from a battle he had fought in and did his best not to dwell on the slaughter he had witnessed there.

"This is Banneret-Commander Leverre, of the Prince Bishop's personal guard."

Leverre clicked his heels together and nodded in a banneret's salute, which Guillot returned. Just because Leverre was the Prince Bishop's lackey didn't mean his professional accomplishments were not worthy of respect.

"I took the liberty of bringing some maps," Leverre said.

Guillot nodded and moved toward the large map table that dominated the centre of the room. "Will it just be the three of us?"

"No," Leverre said. "Three more of my people will join us, but there was no need for them to be present at this meeting."

"Fair enough," Guillot said, "I'm interested to hear any thoughts you have on how we might kill the beast."

"Track it to its lair and slay it while it sleeps," Leverre said.

"Ah, the traditional approach," Guillot said. "Tell me, though. How do you propose to track a creature that flies? The lack of spoor might raise some problems."

Leverre cast dal Sason a nervous look. "We believe we might be able to overcome that issue with intelligence gathered by royal agents."

"Really?" Guillot said. He gave dal Sason a knowing look. "I'm going to be frank. I don't appreciate being treated like an idiot, and if you think you can pull the wool over my eyes, you're sadly mistaken." He pulled a chair out from the table and sat. "Now, why don't you tell me the truth? You either already know where the dragon's lair is, or you're part of Amaury's little commune of magicians. Or both. Well?"

Dal Sason nodded and directed his attention to Leverre. "The Prince Bishop said it was all right to make Banneret dal Villerauvais aware of the true nature of your abilities when it became expedient. I had hoped we could wait until we were out of the city, but I suppose now is as good a time as any."

"Fine," Leverre said. "It appears that the beast is magical in nature. We should be able to track the magical trace it leaves. Then I'm sure we'd all like to see a demonstration of the Chevaliers' dragon-slaying abilities."

Guillot forced a smile. Leverre wasn't going to be a pushover. He didn't know whether to be pleased or disappointed. "I think we're all taking a leap into the unknown and it's a waste of time to suggest otherwise," Guillot said. "Maybe being a Chevalier of the Silver Circle will help me, maybe it won't. I think the latter is most likely, but I'm willing to step up and try, and I expect you and your lot to do the same. I'm not going anywhere if I can't count on everyone to pull their weight."

"We're as committed to the mission as you are," dal Sason said.

"I want to hear *him* say it," Guillot said, looking pointedly at Leverre.

"We are responsible for ridding the land of this beast," Leverre said. "We intend to see that it's done."

"Good," Guillot said. "There are a number of things I'll need, and time is obviously limited, you'll have to use the Prince Bishop's influence to expedite things."

"That won't be a problem," dal Sason said. "Give me a list and I'll make sure everything is ready in time."

"No time like the present," Guillot said, tearing a scrap of paper from a map—much to dal Sason's horror. He took one of the cloth-wrapped map pencils from the table and started jotting down a list, suggesting the most expensive suppliers he could think of. The main item was a new suit of armour, and there was only one place to go for one, particularly if someone else was paying. When he finished he handed it to dal Sason, who looked it over and nodded.

"If that's all," Guillot said, "I look forward to seeing you all when we depart."

CHAPTER
16

Amaury stood at his window, staring down into the garden at the white marble fountain below, and if he listened carefully enough, he could hear the water. The gentle sound helped him relax. Though he always appeared to others to be in control, the dragon had placed him under a huge amount of stress. The creature had the potential to ruin his carefully laid plans.

With time and application, Amaury was certain they could recover the knowledge and skill of the Imperial mages, and build on them, but that day would come long after he passed. It wouldn't benefit him, and he was not a patient man. He wanted what they had, and he wanted it soon. The Cup was the key, and now that he knew for certain it existed, he would not rest until it was in his possession. Ancient writings indicated that people had been using weak magic from before the earliest times recorded, but it was not until Amatus, the First Mage, that the power became something worthwhile. Amatus, a scholar, had spent several years travelling the world in search of knowledge. At some point he encountered the Cup, an object from a time before men. It was the spark that lit the fire. When he returned home, he could do magic unlike any ever seen before. He used it to help his friend, the first emperor, build the empire that came to span the Middle Sea. The acquisition of knowledge had been enough for Amatus; the man was never interested in the power his ability could have brought him.

Amaury thought him a fool for that. With all his power, the Empire could have been his. He would never understand why Amatus had foregone that in favour of scholarship. Amaury firmly believed that the latter brought the former. What use was study otherwise?

The moment he first read of the Cup, he knew he had to have it. Like Amatus, he could lead the world into a new era of magical exploration and achievement.

His Order would learn from the mistakes of the mages and bannerets of the past, combining skill with magic and skill with a sword in each person, rather than dividing it between a master mage and a bodyguard banneret. No servants to turn on their masters.

It was taking too long, however. It was only a matter of time before word of the dragon leaked out. At first, it would be a disbelieved rumour. As more stories reached the cities, they would gain credence and Amaury would have another mess to clear up. However, if he gave people his version of the facts first, he could own the story. Particularly since he would offer it to them complete with a solution.

A solution they would love—the last of the Chevaliers of the Silver Circle riding off to defeat a beast not seen in centuries. The people would lap it up. The tale would be told in taverns, inns, and coffee houses across the land. Or, perhaps not the last of the Chevaliers. Perhaps the first of the Order of the Golden Spur.

It was very unlikely Gill would succeed in killing the monster. What hope could one hungover has-been have against a creature like that? No amount of special anointing would save him from something that was already racking up quite a numbers of kills. If word of *that* reached the public, it would not go down well. He would look a fool for sending a brave man to his death. Worse, he would look a villain. The solution was to make sure Gill succeeded, or he found a way to turn the man's death into an advantage. It had not taken him long to see the cloud's silver lining. He had realised he had the opportunity to kill three birds with one stone—slay the dragon, settle his score with Gill, and introduce the Order to the people in a way that wouldn't result in backlash.

Unlikely as it was, he had seen Guillot pull himself from more than one jam that would likely have killed any other man—even one of Amaury's contrivance. That meant he needed to make sure the dragon died and Guillot did the same. Then the Order could take the credit and would be welcomed by the people with open arms. He wasn't willing to leave that to chance.

Thinking about how to achieve it made him think of *her*—Ysabeau dal Fleurat. Her skills and reliability would be a gift at that moment. She had become the best problem solver he had ever encountered—the killer of a king. Hers was an invented title, but he couldn't have his daughter, illegitimate though she was, walking around as a commoner. He wondered where she was, whether she hated him for what he had asked her to do. For the consequences of what she had done without question. He couldn't understand the feelings the thought brought up in him. It surprised him that he cared.

Even now, he struggled to accept that he had a daughter. Her mother had come to him when Ysabeau was already an adult, seeking him out as a last resort. Their daughter, of whom he had known nothing until then, was a mage, and had been discovered by the Intelligenciers. Barely remembering his youthful encounter with her, years earlier, Amaury intended to ignore her plea for help, but curiosity drew him to the Intelligenciers' commandery to look at the girl. The family resemblance had been so strong there was no way he could deny her. Even the man guarding her had done a double take when Amaury arrived. Having her freed had nearly cost him his career, yet he had done it—though he was not, to this day, certain why.

He had been surprised and delighted when Ysabeau demonstrated that she had far more magical skill than anyone he had previously encountered. He had allowed himself to hope she might be the person he needed, the person Solène now appeared to be. Sadly, Ysabeau's power had proved to be insufficient. How she used what she had, though, was something to behold. She could merge with the shadows, blend into a crowd, and wield a blade with such skill that she could have rivalled Amaury himself at his best. These skills, the result of growing up in a tough environment, had made her a superb spy and assassin. Was he wrong to have guided his child down that path?

That she was exactly the person to deal with Gill when he had served his purpose—exactly the person Amaury needed at that moment—gave rise to an odd sensation. It took him a moment to realise that it was pride. Still, she was gone, and he had no way to contact her. He had to make do with other means. In Ysabeau's absence, Leverre would deal with Gill if the dragon failed, but it was difficult to muster the same level of confidence he would have had if the job were hers. He needed it done, and wanted a backup to make sure that it was.

A knock on his door pulled him from his thoughts and the tranquil garden view. His secretary peered around the door's edge. "Your Grace, your next appointment is here."

Amaury nodded. The backup. "Show him in."

"Nicholas," Amaury said, when dal Sason stepped into the room. "I have a little something extra I might need you to do for me."

⬥⬥⬥⬥⬥⬥

With only one appointment left in the day, Amaury relaxed, knowing he would soon be free to delve back into the secret archives. The thrill of the unknown, of what discovery he might make, caused his heart to quicken. He also needed to think of a way to entice Solène, in case she did not see the wisdom of accepting his offer. If he could show her the Priory, the organisation she could be part of—be at the forefront of—he was sure she would agree to join. With Guillot whispering in her ear, that probably wasn't going to happen, but he would be out of the city soon enough, and then Amaury would have her all to himself. Dal Sason was barely gone when there was another knock on the door.

"Banneret-Commander Leverre, your Grace," Amaury's secretary said, peering around the door.

"Show him in."

Leverre walked in a moment later, his back straight and his head held high—as was almost always the case with bannerets. The Prince Bishop had been the same, once upon a time.

"Thank you for seeing me at this hour," Amaury said. "Please sit. I'll try not to keep you too long. I'm sure you have a great many things to do."

"It's hard to tell, your Grace," Leverre said, in his usual humourless way. He adjusted his cream robes as he sat. "We're venturing into the unknown. We may already have more than we need. Or we might not even be close."

"Indeed," Amaury said. Although Leverre's rigid personality was tiresome at times, he had proved an insightful choice for marshall of the Order. A superb swordsman with none of the pretensions usually borne by those with noble titles, he had shown an aptitude for magic rare in those Amaury had recruited from the Academy. He was a prized find. "That brings me to the matters I need to discuss with you," the Prince Bishop said. He was not looking forward to the conversation. He knew what must be said would not sit well with Leverre's sense of honour—bannerets could be so stubborn about such things. "The appearance of this dragon, while appearing to be a disaster on its face, may have a silver lining."

Leverre shifted in his seat but said nothing.

"The king feels that it's beyond time for the Order to be brought into the open. Our comparatively limited ability to perform magic will be easy to introduce to the people. Then, over time, as members of the Order grow more powerful, they will be accepted more easily."

Leverre nodded. "How do you propose to do that?"

"The Order's cream robes are not an unknown sight within the city, but people see the Order as merely my bodyguards or as the successors to the Chevaliers of the Silver Circle. I feel that our current predicament can be capitalised on to broaden knowledge of the Spurriers."

"I think I understand," Leverre said.

"The part, but not the whole," Amaury said. "Mirabayans have long viewed the Chevaliers of the Silver Circle as their sword and shield. So much so that the king has even spoken of re-establishing them. I've argued strenuously that the Order will be able to far better fill that role, and thus far he has agreed with me. If the people were to see the last of the Chevaliers fail in the face of a great danger, they would naturally embrace those who succeeded."

"You need Guillot to fail, and you need us to succeed in his place," Leverre said.

There was no humour in his voice; Amaury couldn't determine if that meant he disapproved, or was simply stating facts. Put so succinctly, it sounded underhanded, but statecraft always carried a cost.

"Precisely," he said. "Guillot doesn't have any hope of slaying this creature, but neither do we if we don't learn more about it. That's why I'm sending you and our best people with him. I want you to find out all you can about the dragon, then withdraw with minimal losses. Let him to try to kill it. Let him take the risks alone. He's spent the last five years trying to drink himself to death, and judging by the shaking of his hands, the skill he was once famed for has long since departed."

"And if he hasn't lost his skill? What if he kills it?"

Amaury smiled. Now they were at the crux of the matter. "Then it's a hard problem solved, and an easy one created. The Order is vital to the future prosperity of Mirabaya. It needs to be brought out into the open, and welcomed.

"I'm happy for you to choose your moment. If it looks like the dragon's going to kill Guillot, let it. You can even let him kill the beast, if he still has it in him—I really don't care. Just make sure he doesn't survive to return to Mirabay."

"That sounds like murder to me," Leverre said, his voice full of indignation.

"You love your country, Felix?"

"Of course I do."

"The country needs the Order, even if they don't know it yet. The Order needs to get the credit for slaying the dragon."

"Why? No one knows anything about the dragon. If they learn everything after the fact, why will they care who killed it?"

"I haven't come to this decision lightly. Gill and I were once closer than brothers. Statecraft is an ugly business, and sometimes hard decisions and sacrifices need to be made. You can be sure the Estranzans and Humberlanders are investigating magic. We know the Usurper of Ostia employed an eastern mage. We will be carved up between our neighbours if we do not have our own mages—you of all people should agree with me on that."

Leverre nodded, but Amaury could see he was very uncomfortable. "I realise it goes against the principles of honour all bannerets hold true. Don't forget, I'm a banneret too." Amaury forced himself not to squirm at how fake he sounded. Honour among bannerets was about as common as honour among thieves, but Leverre seemed to view it as a tenet by which a banneret should live his life. "Being the marshall of the Order means you need to set aside those romantic notions for the harsh practicalities of the world. Can I rely on you to do it?"

Leverre remained motionless, and Amaury started to worry.

Eventually, Leverre slowly nodded his head. "If the dragon doesn't manage it—" He paused and grimaced. "I'll see that it's done."

Amaury leaned forward on his desk and fixed his gaze on Leverre. "Be sure that you do."

Guillot woke the next morning with a long list of things that still needed to be done buzzing around in his head. He had spent the previous afternoon acquiring many of the things he thought he might need, beginning with new boots, gloves, a suit of clothes, and a good oilskin coat—he didn't want bad weather to get him before the dragon did. He still needed a suit of armour. He had no idea how he would obtain that in the time available, as they had agreed to depart the city the following morning.

He felt he was neglecting Solène, but he had too much to do and she had her own preparations to make, since she intended to accept the Prince Bishop's offer. They breakfasted together briefly, then went their separate ways for the day.

It was possible to get pre-made armour, but there was nothing worse than spending long hours in a suit that didn't quite fit properly. Nonetheless, that would be the best he could do right now. There was no way he was hunting a dragon without a comforting layer of steel between him and its claws. He had left sundry matters like horses, provisions, and suchlike to the Prince Bishop's people. It was easy stuff and Leverre had seemed solid, so Gill wasn't worried. But armour, he had to take care of himself.

In keeping with tradition, the Chevaliers of the Silver Circle were all given a fine suit of heavy armour. There was one with Guillot's name on it rusting somewhere, but he had no idea where—he had left it in the city after fighting his judicial duel and departing for Villerauvais. He'd regretted leaving it behind—it was worth a fortune. If he'd sold it, it would have paid for renovations to the old manor house in Villerauvais, or for the replanting of the vineyards.

Armour might ultimately be useless against the dragon, but the old

Chevaliers had worn something similar, so it might just stop him from getting killed. Not to mention, a fine suit of armour would add a substantial amount to the Prince Bishop's bill.

Whatever a person wanted could be found in Mirabay. A concentration of so much wealth drew merchants from every corner of the world. The finest bakers, drapers, jewellers, and smiths resided there. Craftspeople of a skill to rival those of any city, even those of Ostenheim, said by many to be the centre of the world.

There was a smith whom everyone of importance used for their armour in the old days—Jauré. Only he made armour for the Silver Circle, overseeing every step from smelting the ore to the final piece of filigree. He likely had something in stock that Guillot could use, and it was almost certain to cost a small fortune. Guillot walked through the city toward Jauré's workshop, trying not to remember the times he had been happy in Mirabay, when Auroré had been alive and life seemed like a great adventure that would never end. The memory was difficult to shake and brought him no joy. Too much had changed. Too many dreams had been shattered.

The workshop looked much as Guillot remembered, more like an expensive tailor's shop than a smith's. It sat on a street of refined-looking shops catering to the wealthy—goldsmiths, silversmiths, gem cutters, tailors, and spirits merchants. Elaborately painted signs announced each business, and he knew a person could drain a family fortune before reaching the end of the street. Jauré's front wall was lined with lead-camed windows of expensive, crystal-clear glass, allowing everything on the inside to be seen with almost no distortion. The front room was wood-panelled, carpeted, and filled with leather couches, while the walls were decorated with armour sketches by the master himself, mounted in gilt frames. He walked in, feeling sick to his stomach, remembering his first appointment to be fitted after being inducted to the Silver Circle. The loss was more pronounced when he revisited familiar places. He craved something to dull the pain. Wine, Ruripathian whisky, anything that would cloud his head enough to shroud the memories.

"Good afternoon, my Lord," the young clerk said, coming to greet him. "How may I help?"

In an establishment such as that, it was always assumed the customer was a lord. Few others could afford the prices, and the wealthy burgesses had no need for armour—they were too busy making money to entertain notions of getting themselves killed for king and country. Even the Prince Bishop would notice the stomach punch to his purse a purchase at Jauré's would bring. As cheering a thought as that was, it did little to ease Guillot's melancholy.

"I believe you might be expecting me. My name is Guillot dal Villerauvais. I'm here for a harness."

"Of course, my Lord. We got word that you'd be calling. The maestro has worked through the night to modify something based on the old measurements we have for you in our records. I'll make some updates and pass them over to Maestro Jauré. He'll further refine the plates, and then you'll need to return this evening for a final fitting. All being well, the harness will be ready for your departure in the morning."

The assistant pulled a measuring tape from a pocket in his apron and set about taking Guillot's measurements. He amended the page several times, making an affirming grunt each time he did. "Not so far removed from what they were," the clerk said. "A little less on the shoulders, a little more on the waist, but it's not at all bad. It's not often a gentleman can say that after more than a decade."

"I appreciate the flattery," Guillot said, finally breaking into a smile, "but I can see what you're writing down."

The clerk gave a sheepish smile. "No man is immune to the passing years, and it really is far better than we usually see. I'll bring these measurements to Maestro Jauré, but I suspect he'll wish to speak to you before you go. If you'd care to wait, it shouldn't take long. Can I offer you a glass of wine?"

"Yes, please," Guillot said, the words tumbling from his mouth before he had the chance to consider them. Although it was early, many noblemen took a glass or two of watered wine with their breakfasts. Moreover, a tipsy customer would likely spend more than originally intended. He felt his mouth water and his heart quicken. Then he thought of Jeanne's disapproving glare and swallowed hard. "Actually, it's a little early for me. I don't need anything."

The clerk gave him a nod and disappeared through a door. Guillot wondered if it was too much to hope that Jauré had something that would fit him outright. Armour was such a personal thing—particularly armour of this quality and expense—so the smiths didn't tend to keep very much in stock, ready to have minor alterations made.

The clerk reappeared with another man, whom Guillot recognised as Maestro Jauré himself. He had aged some; his formerly grey, cropped hair was now resolutely white, but he still had the broad, defined shoulders of a man who beat metal for a living.

"Banneret of the White dal Villerauvais, I'm honoured that you've returned to my smithy," the master armourer said.

"There wasn't anywhere else I'd consider," Guillot said. "Although I can't help but feel bad for the trouble so hurried a piece of work must be causing you."

Jauré smiled genially, then gave Guillot an appraising look. "Far from it— it's rare that I find myself challenged these days and I have to admit I'm enjoying the test immensely. I think you'll be pleasantly surprised. I had something remarkably close to your needs in stock, so it's simply been a case of reshaping in a few places. The suit was made for the Duke of Fontonoy. Indeed, he was due to collect it the day after the duel in which he was killed."

Guillot nodded. If it had been made for a duke, the armour would be of excellent quality. It would also be ridiculously expensive.

"The suit is among the finest I've made. The duke's heir doesn't want it. He didn't even go to the Academy." Jauré gave a disapproving shake of his head.

"Might I see it?" If it fit, there was no way Guillot would refuse it. If he had to face a dragon, he wanted to do it wearing a suit of Jauré's armour, even one designed for the garish tastes of a court dandy.

"This way, my Lord," Jauré said, leading him into the back room.

The armour was the first thing Guillot saw, arranged on a wooden mannequin. It was shining steel with a dark filigree that rimmed the edges of each plate.

"Finest steel with blackened silver filigree," Jauré said.

"The duke had particularly fine taste," Guillot said, genuinely meaning it. He didn't have the imagination for such things, but if he were to have a suit made for him, it would have been this one. It was far more to his taste than his previous suit, filigreed as it had been with the Silver Circle's imagery.

"If it's convenient, we can do a test fitting now? Between that and the measurements we've taken, I think it will save you a return visit this evening."

Guillot nodded and stepped forward, lifting his arms to allow Jauré and his clerk to start putting the pieces on him. They worked with practised efficiency, but Guillot grimaced every so often when he was pinched by a plate that did not quite fit. With everything on, Guillot had to work hard to breathe. Although the armour was well balanced, it placed weight on his chest and shoulders, which were more accustomed to inactivity than burden. This had nothing to do with an ill fit or poor craftsmanship and everything to do with his prolonged idleness. Certainly only a few days of wearing the armour would change that, but that meant he needed to wear it for the whole journey if he hoped to be used to it by the time he faced the dragon. That he would be riding out to his almost certain death in discomfort was not at all a warming thought.

Jauré went around the suit, making marks on the steel with a wax pencil. He took a step back and looked the suit over for a moment before attacking once more with his pencil.

Eventually he stopped. "I think that should do it. There's not much to be done, and considering the time constraints, I think it will work out better than could have been hoped. I will have it delivered to your inn first thing in the morning."

Guillot had no idea what kind of tools were required for dragon-slaying, but he didn't reckon his Competition sword was up to the job. It was perfectly suited for its intended purpose—duelling—but he wouldn't take it onto the battlefield against armoured opponents and he certainly wouldn't use it to attack a dragon. No, he'd bring his old family sword—Mourning—with its broader, general-purpose blade. The blade was old—very old—and might have seen use in the days when his ancestor was alleged to have been a dragon-slayer. Still, he didn't think that by itself, that sword would be enough.

He would need weapons that could be used at greater distance. He feared that if he was close enough to use his sword, he might already be halfway down the beast's gullet. He had no great skill with a bow, so that seemed pointless—hopefully one of Leverre's people would be able to fill that need, either with a real bow or some sort of magical one. If Solène could knock men out without laying a hand on them, perhaps someone from the Prince Bishop's order would be able to knock the dragon out of the sky, leaving Guillot with the job of finishing it off.

That seemed too much to hope for, however, and he didn't want to turn up at the dragon's lair wishing he had something he hadn't thought to bring. In the past, he had encountered few problems that lance or sword couldn't put right, but the most important element was not the weapon, but rather the arm wielding it. Unless he practised and regained some of his ability, he would be a lamb to the slaughter. How to do that without revealing that he was a burnt-out old hacker was going to be tricky.

As he walked away from Jauré's, he considered what he would need in a lance. It would have to be modified from the type used against a horseman. Something more akin to a belek spear might fit the bill. The work would be easy enough, and wouldn't take long, and he knew of a pole turner who made tournament lances. The weapon would need to be long enough to keep him out of reach of claws and teeth, stiff enough that he could drive it home true, and barbed to make sure it caused the maximum amount of damage. That he was walking along contemplating how best to kill a dragon continued to amaze him.

CHAPTER
18

The air felt crisp the next morning when Guillot got up, the heat of the day having yet to fill it with all the smells of the city. The sky was pale blue and the sun was only moments from breaking the horizon when he looked out of his bedroom window. There was time for a good breakfast, and then they would leave. To slay a dragon. He shook his head, allowing himself a smile. Still such a ridiculous notion, one that brought amusement rather than fear. He knew that would change, however, and sooner than he might like.

When he got downstairs, Jauré and an assistant were waiting to greet him. It didn't look like either of them had slept, suggesting that the armourer's declaration that only a few changes needed to be made had been something of an understatement. Guillot would have felt guilty were it not for the amount Jauré was likely to charge.

"My Lord dal Villerauvais," Jauré said. "Your harness is ready. I'd like to check the fit. We've arranged for the use of a room here."

"Please do," Guillot said, following Jauré and his assistant into a private coffee room.

Jauré and his assistant unwrapped their greased-paper parcels, carefully placing the pieces of the armour on the large coffee table—not out of fear of scratching the table, but rather of marring the mirror finish on the highly polished metal. Such care seemed a daft thing to Guillot, considering the plate would have three hells bashed out of it if used for its intended purpose. He supposed few who purchased armour from Jauré's wore it for anything other than ceremonial purposes. That did not change the fact that it was the best, and that in Jauré's steel he was more likely to survive his mission.

"Before I start," Jauré said, "I want to say how much I admire your bravery, and what an honour it is that you have chosen me to make your harness. These are terrifying, unimaginable days, and every Mirabayan is lucky to have a man like you to protect us."

Guillot looked at him, puzzled, then spotted the morning's news sheet, left on the coffee table for guests to read. The headline said everything he needed to know. Word of the dragon had reached the city, and it had been announced that he was going to kill it. Gill felt sick. That news could only have come from one place. What could Amaury hope to gain from letting it out?

Jauré's assistant, clearly an expert in dressing an armoured man, manhandled Guillot into a more receptive pose, then got to work. The cuisses went on first, overlapping horizontal plates that covered his thighs from waist to knee. The assistant secured the pieces with soft leather straps. The cuirass was next, its tassets—the metal plate skirts at its bottom—draped over the thigh armour, ensuring no attacking blade, tooth, or claw could find a way to flesh. The cuirass was made of the same overlapping plates as the cuisses, allowing a remarkable range of movement while still providing superb protection. The assistant tugged on the fixing straps, then looked at his master.

Jauré stroked his moustache and studied the problem. Guillot took a deep breath, but it did nothing to impress the old armourer. "Perhaps it might be best to skip breakfast this morning," Jauré said. "There was only so much we could do in the time we had. Perhaps skip it tomorrow also."

Guillot almost said something smart in retort, but Jauré spoke again.

"And the day after."

Though he remained silent, Guillot was as determined as ever to enjoy the bounty of Bauchard's kitchen once more before leaving the city. Pauldrons, gorget, and helmet finished the suit, all of which thankfully fit. He didn't think a few skipped meals would make his head any smaller.

"Move around a little," Jauré said. "Try to get through the full range of movement to see if there is any restriction or pinching."

Guillot did, delighted at how easily the overlapping steel plates moved over each other, and how light the whole suit felt. The subtle alterations made it feel like far less of a burden than it had the previous day. Although it felt a little tight around his gut, he had a hard time noticing any reason to skip a few meals. "It's superb. As though it was made for me."

"A tailored suit is unlikely to fit much better," Jauré said. "Unless there's anything else, my Lord, I think the armour is as perfect a fit as we can hope for."

"It is," Guillot said. "You have my gratitude, Maestro Jauré. Please add twenty crowns to your bill for the inconvenience I put you through."

"I feel I should make a gift of the suit, my Lord, considering the task you are undertaking."

"Not at all," Guillot said. "The Prince Bishop was insistent that he would cover all expenses."

"His generosity matches your bravery." Jauré gave a curt bow, then he and his assistant departed, leaving Guillot still in his armour.

Guillot looked about in puzzlement, wondering how he was supposed to get out of the suit on his own, when dal Sason appeared at the door.

"The Prince Bishop wants you to be armoured as we ride out of the city. I've to crawl into mine now, then it's time to leave. If you've still to eat, do it fast."

Time, rather than Jauré's advice, dictated Guillot's more modest than planned breakfast. When seated, he noticed the armour was a little tight around his waist. While it was merely a trifle uncomfortable at the breakfast table, the small impingement on movement it would cause in battle might mean the difference between living and dying.

It was not far off the right fit, though, and with a little luck and moderation, it would be perfect by the time he encountered the dragon. As he sat there, doing his best to ignore the curious stares from other patrons, he noticed that Jauré had etched Gill's family arms into the blackened filigree pattern that ran along the edges of each plate. Considering the timeframe, it was an impressive touch.

When Guillot went outside, feeling self-conscious with every clatter of metal plate, dal Sason and Gill's riding and baggage horses were waiting for him, but the others hadn't arrived yet. Guillot could immediately see why Amaury wanted them to depart the city in full armour. People lined the streets as far as the eye could see, and the City Watch maintained a corridor through which the dragon hunters could pass. He was making a big show of this. Gill wondered what he hoped to gain.

"Quite a crowd," Guillot said, finding the numbers of eyes on him far more intimidating than he had in the past, even at the Competition.

"The news has spread around the city like wildfire," dal Sason said.

"People are afraid, but they've been told not to worry, that a Chevalier of the Silver Circle will save them. Probably best to try looking heroic as we ride out."

A clattering of hooves announced the arrival of Banneret-Commander Felix Leverre. He was followed by a group of similarly clad riders—three men and a woman. Guillot had to admit they looked a magnificent sight in their shining breastplates and cream robes—every bit as impressive as the Chevaliers had been in their prime.

Leverre gave Guillot a respectful nod, far more respectful than Guillot had expected.

"I suppose it's time to go," Guillot said.

"No point in delaying," dal Sason agreed.

"I'm surprised the Prince Bishop isn't here to see us off," Guillot said. "He's never been one to miss out on attention."

"His Grace has many pressing matters to deal with," Leverre said, "of which this is only one."

Guillot shrugged, still more suspicious than curious. If the expedition failed, it would be easier for Amaury to distance himself from it if he hadn't been seen personally endorsing it.

"Guillot," Solène said from Bauchard's doorway.

He walked over to her.

"Good luck," she said. "I hope you make it back safely."

"I hope so too," he said.

"I'll never forget what you've done for me."

Guillot shrugged. "You still plan on joining the Prince Bishop's order?"

She cast a glance at Leverre and his men. "Yes. Cream has always been a good colour on me."

Guillot laughed.

"I think it's the best option for me," she said. "If it doesn't work out, I can always run again. If it does, I might have finally found somewhere I can call home."

He nodded. "I hope it works out, but be careful around the Prince Bishop. He's not someone you should ever place your trust in."

"I won't, but you're the one who needs to be careful. Don't try too hard to be a hero."

Guillot laughed. "No fear of that."

They stood in silence for a moment, Guillot's awkwardness compounded by how ridiculous he felt in his armour. He heard Leverre clear his throat. "I best be off. Good luck, Solène."

"You too."

Guillot walked to his horse, which was being held by one of Bauchard's grooms. When he mounted, the crowd erupted in cheers. He forced a smile, and in as heroic a fashion as he could muster, held up one hand and waved. The cheers grew louder, though he wanted nothing more than to find a dark corner and hide in it.

Leverre rode up beside him. "Not going to say anything, my Lord?"

"Nope," Guillot said, casting a final look back at Solène, who gave him a sad smile. She knew as well as he did that he was most likely riding to his death. "Let's get going."

▲▲▲▲▲▲

There was a saying among dragonkind that Alpheratz recalled first hearing when he was not much more than a hatchling. It said that if you waited until you were ready, the moment would never come. It was particularly poignant when one considered how long dragons lived. He was strong. Perhaps not as strong as he had ever been, but given that he was much older, he couldn't expect to return to his prime. How much older remained a mystery, but in the grand scheme of the world, it no longer seemed important.

He had exhausted his patience, or perhaps he was merely being practical. It was time to start his vengeance proper, to test himself against something more substantial than peasants and farm animals. On his long flights, seeking his kin, he had spotted the ideal place: a stone fort with a dozen soldiers.

Launching himself from his perch, he swooped down toward the fort. As he drew near and the men went from being moving shapes to living things, he felt his first pang of uncertainty. The men he had killed at his mountain peak, he had taken by surprise. He had killed them in self-defence, due to fear and surprise. Killing to feed was one thing. Killing to survive another. But killing out of rage? From a desire for revenge? Was that not what he wished to punish *them* for?

What if these men were stronger than those he had killed at the peak? They were soldiers, after all. Soldiers had killed all of his kind, had nearly killed him. They had killed Pharadon, the greatest fighter among dragonkind. Fear twisted his stomach. He had never killed out of hate before.

He heard a shout from the battlements. They had seen him. He wondered how they would respond. Was it too late to turn back?

The first arrow bounced off his hide harmlessly. He thought of Nashira, how they had taken her scales. Slaughtered their young. His quest was just. They had to die. They had to be punished for what they had done. They had to be driven back from the sacred places in the mountains. Alpheratz took a deep breath and sprayed fire across the battlements. As he swept over, he heard screams, and felt relief. He was strong enough to do what he had set out to do.

Pharadon had often talked about the joy of battle. Alpheratz had never felt that, but there was satisfaction in carrying out righteous retribution. He could understand what Pharadon had felt, for he knew it now for himself.

He turned back toward the fort and glided down onto the battlements, gripping them with his claws. A man scurried up the steps and froze at the top, his face a picture of fear. He made a halfhearted attempt to jab his spear at Alpheratz. The dragon laughed and swiped at the man with his claw. The man let out a grunt at the impact and went tumbling over the battlements, his scream piercing enough to be heard over the sound of flames, like the lead note of a great musical composition. It was the symphony of righteous retribution.

Alpheratz looked around but saw no others. His initial sweep of flame had caught them by surprise and must have killed most of them. He felt disappointed. He had expected this to be a challenge, but it was no different than slaughtering sheep in a pen. He walked around the battlements until he was above the fort's front gates. Two people were fleeing down the muddy track. Alpheratz spread his wings and dove from the tower.

Flying barely above the ground, he went straight past the first man, who shrieked in terror. A swipe of his tail was all it took to deal with him, although the corpse got stuck on one of Alpheratz's barbs. The second man, he grabbed in his claws, then flapped his wings hard, soaring directly up. He shook his tail, ridding himself of the first man's body.

The man in his claws screamed for all he was worth. How had such cowardly wretches slain Nashira? Defending their eggs, she would have been ferocious. This human was no more than a worm wriggling in a bird's talons.

Satisfied he was high enough, Alpheratz released his grip and hovered, watching the man flail toward the ground. He saw the impact, but the sound was stolen by the breeze. He looked back at the tower, now an inferno. It was satisfying. It was joyous, but there was still a hole inside him, and he had barely even begun to fill it.

PART TWO

Winning the Competition must really have been something," dal Sason said, riding up alongside Gill.

It took Guillot a moment to realise that dal Sason was addressing him. "Yes, I suppose it was. I'm sorry, but are we to be friends now?"

"We've a long and difficult road ahead. It would certainly make life easier if we were."

For a moment Guillot felt churlish, but dal Sason was still Amaury's errand boy, and he reckoned that justified his antipathy. He shrugged. If nothing else, a chat would help pass the time. "In answer to your question, yes, it really was something. It was life changing. Still haven't worked out if that change was for better or worse, though."

"I was knocked out in the first round," dal Sason said. "I spent years dreaming about it, but I suppose I never really believed I could do it. So many great swordsmen to beat. How did you do it?"

"One at a time," Guillot said. "It was a long time ago."

"Still, the doors it must have opened. And to get that Telastrian sword. That's it, isn't it?"

"It is," Guillot said. "Not that it'll be much use for the job ahead. I've something else in mind for that." Guillot thought about unsheathing the blade and handing it to dal Sason, but decided not to. "As for doors? It opened plenty, but I can't say I liked everything that was behind them. It wasn't all pots of gold and beautiful women."

"I'd love the chance to spar with a Competition winner."

Guillot's gut twisted and a chill ran over his skin. "I doubt there'll be time." The thought of having to spar with a properly trained swordsman filled him with terror. He changed the subject. "What's your reason for coming along on this little quest?" Guillot said. "Devotion to king and country?"

Dal Sason laughed. "If only. The answer to your question is far baser, sadly. Money. I've a manor house in ruins, an estate on the verge of bankruptcy, and two sisters who need dowries."

"Being an only child has its advantages," Guillot said.

"As will being one of the men who killed the dragon."

"Fame as well, then?" Guillot said.

Dal Sason shrugged. "What swordsman doesn't want more fame? It lets you pick the jobs you want, instead of having to take whatever you can get."

"There's that," Guillot said, "although too much puts you back where you started. Everything that no one else wants to do lands on your doorstep, and a famous hero never turns down a challenge. Be careful what you wish for."

"I'm a working swordsman, just like you," dal Sason said.

"I hope, for your own sake, you're nothing like me," Guillot said. Silence followed, awkward enough to inspire Guillot to start a new conversation. "What do we call you and your people, Leverre?" he said, turning to look at the riders behind him. "Collectively, I mean. The Order of the Golden Spur is a bit of a mouthful."

"*Spurriers* seems to be the one most people are going with," Leverre said, joining Gill and dal Sason ahead of the rest of the group.

"You're something like the Prince Bishop's private version of the Chevaliers of the Silver Circle?" Guillot said.

"There's nothing about the Silver Circle that I'd want to be compared to," Leverre said.

"That's a fair comment. And your fellow Spurriers?" Guillot said. "Are they allowed to speak?"

"Of course," Leverre said. "They're not slaves."

"So do we get an introduction?" Guillot said. "*Skinny, Short, Ginger,* and *Girl* don't seem to be a mannerly way to address people."

Leverre shrugged. "*Ginger* is Brother Hallot, *Skinny* is Brother Quimper, and *Short* is Banneret Eston. *Girl* is Sergeant Doyenne, my second-in-command."

"Brothers, sisters, sergeants, and commanders," Gill said. "Quite a collection of different ranks you've got there."

"There's been some . . . friction about the ranks within the Order. A great many inductees are Academy graduates, and I'm sure you can understand they are reluctant to give up their hard-earned title of banneret. They don't feel they should be placed on an equal footing with those who haven't been through their training."

"No surprises there," Guillot said.

"Banneret, Brother, and Sister are all considered the same rank, though a banneret will usually be given command over the others. Their years of training justify it, I think. After that, promotion and seniority is all merit based. The day will come when the Order will train its own from youth; then, outside influence will count for little."

"That will be a great day indeed," Guillot said.

Leverre cast him a suspicious look, but Guillot maintained a broad smile to confuse his intent as much as possible.

"Yes, it will," Leverre said.

▲▲▲▲▲▲

The dragon hunters spoke rarely during the journey, but they were riding hard and needed to concentrate on the road. Even when they stopped to change horses at the royal way posts, there was little chatter. What lay ahead was daunting. Guillot had been in situations like this before. Everyone wanted everyone else to think they were brave and fearless. He himself had claimed to be unafraid when riding out on his first campaign. During that journey, he had used his helmet more than he did later, during the actual battle—it had been perfectly sized to hold the contents of his stomach every time he threw up. The loudest talkers were usually the most afraid and the most inexperienced, so Guillot took it as a good sign that everyone in his party was quiet. It meant they had been in harm's way before, and hopefully wouldn't panic and run when things got rough. Of course, it could equally have been that they were too afraid even to pretend they weren't.

Guillot did not have the first clue as to how they were going to kill a dragon, and other than Leverre's bog-standard bear-hunting approach, no one offered any worthwhile suggestions. He didn't want to get himself or any of the others killed while they were learning from their mistakes. The old stories were just that—embellished beyond the point of use. The heroes were all superhuman and relied on abilities that were either completely made up or magically enhanced beyond belief. Still, that was what made the old stories great. As stories. They weren't of any help now that Guillot needed to kill a dragon.

He filled the hours with trying to work out how to go about that and determine what might go wrong with each approach. It was difficult to work through the possible results since he had no real idea what the dragon was capable of and what its weaknesses might be. Guillot had been on many hunts, of course: deer, boar, bear, and even a belek on one occasion. None of them quite matched the size, agility, or power of a dragon, however.

Men's bravery was measured by how they behaved on a belek hunt. Might a man's madness be measured by the fact he would even consider going after a dragon?

He constantly came back to tracking it to its lair. There were a number of attractive things about this, most notably the fact that they would be a long way from innocent bystanders. He was eager to minimise the number of people put in danger. The method that seemed to offer the most reasonable chance for success—luring it out and ambushing it—would likely place something or someone in harm's way, and that was enough to make Gill discount it so long as there was an alternative.

"Is there somewhere near we can stop for the night," Leverre asked, "or should we start looking for somewhere to make camp?"

"There's a coaching inn not far ahead," Guillot said. "Last one before Trelain. After that we'll be roughing it."

"How far ahead?" Leverre said.

"Don't trust me?"

"Just wondering is all," Leverre said. "Like to have an idea of things in my head."

"You'll see it over the next rise. I'm sure you'll love it."

"I'm sure I will."

Guillot wondered if he was friendlier when he was drunk. Leverre had not done anything bad to Guillot, yet Guillot had taken an instant dislike to him. That Leverre was the Prince Bishop's man counted for some of Gill's antipathy—perhaps all—but if they were going to work and fight together, Guillot knew he had to get past that. He wondered, though, if that was all that bothered him, or if there was more to it. Though the connection to the Prince Bishop clouded his judgement, that didn't mean there wasn't something else to be wary of. Was he being paranoid, or was there something in the cold, impassive way Leverre looked at him? They would be relying on one another for their lives before too much longer; if it was all in Guillot's head, he needed to get over it.

True to his word, the inn came into view as soon as they crested the next rise on the muddy road. The weather had clearly been bad there not long before, but they had been lucky so far and had missed the worst of it. Rain had kept the road quiet, with few travellers choosing to venture out. Once word of the dragon attacks spread, Gill was sure the roads would be clogged with people fleeing the area.

With Trelain being a major town, and the seat of a duke, there were a number of coaching inns along the road between it and Mirabay. The distance between them was, for the most part, a day's travel by carriage. They became less useful when you were on horseback and trying to make good time—in Guillot's experience, it always seemed to get dark when you were exactly halfway between two stopping points. On this occasion, however, he had timed it well. They would have warm, dry beds for the night and Guillot would have one last opportunity to abuse the Prince Bishop's bank balance.

With the sun setting, the innkeeper had clearly not been expecting any more customers. The sleepy establishment burst into life when they arrived, although their less than luxurious mode of transport meant he showed then straight to a communal bunk room.

Guillot looked the room over and grimaced in distaste. "I don't think this will do," he said. "We'll need individual rooms. The best available."

Dal Sason cast him a sideways glance, but Guillot had been abusing the Prince Bishop's funds enough for him not to show too much surprise. The innkeeper nodded eagerly, not about to turn away the extra money. He showed Guillot to a room farther down the corridor: small but well turned out, the type of thing a travelling merchant might choose.

"I like to have space about me," Guillot said.

"I have just the thing," the innkeeper said, his smile broadening.

They continued down the corridor to a room at the back of the inn. Farthest from the road, it would be the quietest and thus the most expensive. The innkeeper opened the door with visible pride, so Guillot made a show of looking around and nodding with approval.

"This will do perfectly," he said.

The room ran the full length of the back of the inn; its lead-latticed windows looked out over the small kitchen garden behind. The bed sat at one end and the remainder of the space was filled with a small two-seater sofa and a coffee table sitting on a drab rug. Guillot waited until the innkeeper had left, closing the door after him, then dropped his travelling bag on the end of the bed and let out a sigh. He couldn't have cared less about the room—he had slept on the floor, in the gutter, and in various spots on the street between Jeanne's tavern and his house. What he wanted now was space and privacy.

The bed was inviting after the long ride, but he had to resist the temptation. He removed his armour—a difficult but not impossible task to accomplish alone—and stretched his aching muscles. He needed his body to get used to the plate again, and wearing it was the only way to do that. Once he had loosened some of the knots in his shoulders, he pushed the couch and coffee table up against the wall. After a moment of deliberation, he got down on his hunkers and rolled up the rug before placing it to the side. That done, he took his sword from its scabbard and started doing what was known in the Academy as "the positions."

From the age of five or six until his early twenties, every day had started with the positions. It was a slow and methodical progression through guards, attacks, and defences, the focus being on controlled, precise movement at a reduced pace. Over time, the movements became second nature, and when needed at speed, they would be clean, accurate, and hopefully lethal. At his peak, Guillot had even added positions of his own devising to his routine. He couldn't remember the last time he'd done them.

Studying his feet, he made small adjustments to their position until they were where he wanted them. There was a time when they would have naturally fallen into the correct spots, but that was no longer the case. He flexed his knees and winced at the creaking sounds they made. The position felt strained and unnatural and he knew he could not blame his hours in the saddle for that.

He raised his sword hand and took his guard. The tip of his rapier bobbed about like it had a mind of its own, where once it would have been perfectly still. He tried to console himself with the thought that it was impossible for all his skill to come back to him in an instant, but he was on his way to try to slay a dragon and he didn't have much time to get back in shape.

He started to work through the positions, which were so firmly ingrained on his memory that he would never forget them, no matter how much he drank or how much time had passed. His form was ugly. His blade waved about like a piece of cloth flapping on the wind. If he tried to thrust, he was confident only that he would be able to hit the wall in front of him.

After only a few minutes, he sweated from the effort. His forearm screamed under the strain of a sword that felt made from lead. His form, already poor, worsened with fatigue, so he stopped to take a break. He slumped down on the sofa and allowed the tip of his sword to bite into the floorboards. *At least the dragon won't be using a sword*, he thought. The thought made him smile, but only for a moment. How could he have allowed himself to sink so low?

He had never set out to drink himself to death. It had helped ease the pain in the days after Auroré's death, but those days had seemed to run on and on, into months and years. The moment had never come when he thought it was time to stop. Might it now be too late?

CHAPTER

20

Solène felt nervous every step of the way to the palace. The power of the Prince Bishop frightened her, but she was more afraid of the Intelligenciers and a repeat of her experience in Trelain. She knew she couldn't expect to be so lucky a second time, and the Order was the only place she could find safety. There was no way to know what she was getting herself into, but the unknown seemed like a promising alternative to the world she already knew.

At the palace gate, she was stopped and had to wait for word to be sent to the Prince Bishop. To her surprise, he arrived in person a few moments later, followed by a retinue including two men in the cream robes.

"I'm very glad to see you," the Prince Bishop said. "You've made your decision?"

"I have," Solène said. "I'd like to take you up on your offer."

"That's very good news," the Prince Bishop said. "Very good news indeed. These men are members of the Order of the Golden Spur, and will bring you there. You're about to embark on a very exciting journey, Solène."

▴▴▴▴▴▴

Solène had never ridden in a carriage before, let alone one as fine as the Prince Bishop's. The comfort did little to quell the butterflies in her stomach. His haste in sending for his personal carriage as soon as they had spoken suggested that he wanted to get her to the Order's headquarters before she had a chance to change her mind. She was flanked by the two men in the cream robes, both young and intense-looking. She tried to engage them in conversation to satisfy her curiosity and temper her anxiety, but they said little. They were courteous enough, however, and if anything, she would have said they were wary of her.

The Priory—the Order's home—was situated on the city's north bank. At first glance, it was an austere, walled complex that did little to build her enthusiasm. The buildings looked like they had been built many years earlier; certainly long before the Order came into existence, and judging by the density of buildings around it, before this part of the city was as populated as it now was. Her sense of foreboding grew and she questioned if she had made the right choice. However, she knew she couldn't spend the rest of her life running. The Order might represent her only opportunity to stop. It didn't need to be the land of milk and honey that the Prince Bishop had painted it. It only needed to be safe.

The carriage rattled to a stop outside heavy old gates recessed into the wall. The two men got out of the carriage and engaged in a brief conversation. After a moment, one of the men popped his head back in.

"His Grace's carriage is too large to fit through, miss. This is as far as it can take you. We'll take your baggage and bring you in."

Solène smiled at the thought of having baggage. The seamstress had arrived at the inn with her new clothes only moments before she had left for the palace. She would not have believed how good a fresh set of well-made clothes could feel, but after fleeing Trelain with only those on her back, it was a sensation she hoped she would not forget, nor ever take for granted.

Her companion offered Solène his hand, to help her out of the carriage, and she could not help but notice the effort they were making. The Prince Bishop wanted her, and wanted her badly. Was she really so special?

"Thank you," she said, peering through the open gate to get her first glimpse of the place she might be calling home. Her eyes widened in surprise. From the outside, she would have described it as bleak. The inside was a very different matter. A courtyard garden caught her eye first; it rivalled anything she had seen at the palace for beauty. It was lush, shady, tranquil, and as far from what she expected as she could imagine.

"This way, miss," the man carrying her bags said. "Word of your arrival was sent ahead, so you'll be expected."

She smiled and followed him, trying to take everything in. As she passed through the gate, the path changed from mud to smoothly raked gravel that crunched pleasingly underfoot. A large fountain adorned the garden's centre, and the sound of flowing water lent the courtyard an air of serenity. She wanted to lie down on the grass and listen to it all day. Men and women in cream robes were scattered about the garden, sitting and reading, or walking together, deep in conversation. Her immediate reaction was that this was somewhere she wanted to be.

The buildings that had seemed so dour from outside were exemplars of architectural beauty from this side. Many looked far newer than the walls themselves, and she felt her misgivings being replaced by the exciting thought that this might be somewhere she could be happy.

A tall, slender woman with blonde hair tied back in a ponytail approached the new arrivals.

"Solène?" she asked.

"I am."

"Excellent. My name is Kayte dal Drezony," she said. "I'm the Seneschal of the Order—that's a fancy name for one of the senior officers. Welcome to the Priory."

"Thank you," Solène said.

"Where are you from?"

"A tiny village called Bastelle-Loiron."

"I hear the Loiron valley is very beautiful," dal Drezony said. "I'll take you to your room and tell you how things work while we walk."

"I'd appreciate that," Solène said, feeling overwhelmed. "It's beautiful here."

"Not what you expected?"

Solène shook her head. "No, it looks very different from the outside."

Dal Drezony laughed. "That's not entirely unintentional. The Prince Bishop felt that maintaining as low a profile as possible was for the best. I agree with that, but we discovered early on that if people are happy in their environment, they make better progress, so we hide our little paradise behind ugly walls.

"This way," dal Drezony said, indicating an archway leading into another courtyard garden. "I'm to be your mentor while you're training. If you have any problems settling in, I'm the first person you come to." She pointed to a long building. "That's the library over there. It's not the largest around, but it's being added to nearly every day and it holds a lot of books you won't find anywhere else. Not just on magic, but a broad range of things that might be useful to us, or just of interest."

Solène glanced at the building and wondered how many books it might contain—certainly more than the shelf in the chapel's annex in Bastelle.

"There are two types of people here," dal Drezony said. "Fencers and conjurers—although one day the Prince Bishop hopes for us all to have the same skills, and there are a few who are passable at both. I don't see it happening myself—at least not to the level the Prince Bishop wants, but he can always dream. The first type—the fencers—are Academy graduates. Commander Leverre, the Order's marshall, is the only banneret who can create worthwhile magic. The bannerets are pretty lethal with a sword, though. Most of them have been swinging one since they were infants, and it shows.

"All the swordplay goes on in there," she added, pointing to a low building. "The refectory is over there." She indicated a long building that took up one side of the courtyard. "We try to take meals together as a community. Helps to create a sense of collegiality. The food's pretty good—one of the benefits of having so many people here of noble backgrounds. You can train them into the ground, but if the food isn't up to standard, it's mutiny." She laughed.

"Your room is through here." She escorted Solène through another arch, into a galleried lane. "The conjurers—you and I—are usually academics or people who've shown a bit of talent. You can swing a sword from dawn until dusk—and you'll have to until you get the hang of the basics—but you won't match a banneret's skill. I like to think we have an edge when it comes to the mental agility needed for magic, though, so it balances out. Now." She stopped at a door and opened it. "Your palace."

While the room did not quite match Bauchard's standards, it was certainly far closer to a palace than Solène's room in Trelain. She looked around—a large bed with what was clearly a feather mattress, comfortable chairs, spotlessly clean. It was far more than she could have hoped for.

"Will it be all right?" dal Drezony said.

"It's excellent. It's better than excellent."

"Good, good. The Prince Bishop is very eager to see that you're happy. We'll take lunch in an hour—the bell will let you know when. Come across when you hear it. Until then, settle in, relax, and feel free to take a look around. If you've any questions, don't hesitate to ask."

The woman left, as did the men after delivering Solène's bags, and Solène sat down on the bed, surveying her new home. She couldn't stop herself from grinning like an idiot. All she had ever done was survive. Now the possibilities seemed limitless. Her mind boiled with questions. When would her training start? What would it involve? She wondered what she might learn. Would it seem too eager if she went to the library to take a look around?

As much as exploring her magical talent appealed to her, the idea of learning how to use a sword excited her. She had seen bannerets about the place, the swords that only they were entitled to wear strapped to their waists. She had always wondered what it would be like to use a blade, and now it seemed she would get the chance to try.

CHAPTER
21

Alpheratz had visited the village a number of times, filling his belly with the humans' cattle and sheep. The inhabitants had done their best to make feeding difficult for him, but he had stripped away their herds nonetheless. Now that it had little value as a source of food, it was time to finish the place and move on.

He circled the village from above, trying to decide where to begin. If he started with the buildings on the outskirts, he could herd people toward the centre with little effort. The outlying buildings took light easily, whipping up the inferno of flame and smoke that created the terror he so wanted the people below him to feel. Lining up several buildings that lay along a rough curve, he swooped. His squeezed on his flame glands and let out a long tendril of flame that ignited each building and scorched the ground between.

He flew along an ever-decreasing perimeter, squirting jets of flame at anything made by man, taking satisfaction as fire rose. People ran out of the burning buildings, confused and terrified, just as Alpheratz desired. He considered killing them as he went, but he wanted them to have time to consider their fate, to know they were about to suffer and die. He wanted them to feel fear. Terror. Still, he held hope that when his vengeance was complete, he might find others like him somewhere in the world.

The people began to flee the conflagration, toward the centre of the settlement. He tightened his circle with each pass, herding them to their deaths. When only the cluster of buildings surrounding the central open space remained, he paused, allowing his flame glands a moment's rest. Spotting a sturdy-looking building, he glided down to perch on the apex of its roof. It flexed under his weight and a number of slates shattered, but it held him. The square below was filled with people, their eyes fixed on Alpheratz. He screeched, more for effect than out of true anger, and revelled in their terrified response. An arrow pinged off one of his scales, no more an irritation than the buzzing of a bee. Somewhere among the vermin beneath him, there was a brave one, not that it would matter.

He screeched again, accompanying it with flame. Cries of pain and prayers for aid filled the air, but it was all so much noise to Alpheratz. He breathed deep and emptied himself of fire until he could no longer see any people before him, only a raging inferno. The heat was so great that even his eyes stung. His task complete, he stretched his wings and gave them one great beat, letting the fire's heat lift him high over the village. He looked down, satisfied that once the flames had died, the destruction of the village would be complete. He turned toward his mountain, content that his work for the night was done.

He'd flapped his wings only twice more when he spotted another building in the distance, substantial enough to make it worthy of his time. More importantly, he spied two figures running toward it and altered course accordingly. He swooped low over them, letting them know that they had not escaped. Spinning about so he faced them, Alpheratz slammed onto the ground in front of the humans, who stopped, wide-eyed. They were a female and a male hatchling who barely reached her hip.

"Get behind me, Jacques," the female said.

The hatchling did as he was told, his fear-filled eyes wet with tears.

"Get away from us, you filthy bastard!" the female shouted, displaying the protective instinct with which most creatures treat their young.

Alpheratz ended their lives with a jet of flame so intense neither of them had time to scream, but felt no satisfaction. Indeed, he felt sick to the pit of his stomach. The image of the woman's defiant, terrified face burned in his mind. The love she showed, trying to protect her young even in the face of her own death, disturbed him. He thought of Nashira and his own hatchlings. Was this human female so different?

Hate fought with shame and regret with such fury that he thought his heart would come asunder. He launched himself into the air, desperate to be rid of the place, to take his mind elsewhere. The bigger building loomed in front of him and he hurled himself at it with every ounce of the raging turmoil inside him. He tore chunks of stone from the walls, burned it with flame, smashed his body against it, desiring to hurt himself as much as cause destruction. He sought oblivion in rage, but could not find it.

▲▲▲▲▲▲

Amaury stared out of the carriage window as it rattled along the cobbled streets toward the cathedral. He seemed to be spending a great deal of effort trying to distract himself from the dragon. It didn't work, however. To say he was worried was an understatement. He was a juggler who had thrown all his balls in the air, and he had no idea when they would come back down. The penalty for dropping one would be death.

Boudain the Tenth was too squeamish about breaking with a thousand years of law and tradition for Amaury to make him completely privy to his plans. The king couldn't understand that every omelette required eggs to be broken. He needed to be managed as carefully as the public.

Their relationship had been soured by Amaury leaking news of the dragon. There was no way to hide the Prince Bishop's involvement in that, and he would have to take his chastisement with good grace when it came. He would still have to watch out for the king's other advisors. They hungered for Amaury's power, and he would be damned before he let them have it.

He leaned back into his seat and drummed his fingers on the windowsill. When he was ready to announce the Order, he needed to be certain the king had no option but to agree with him. Covered in the glory of saving Mirabaya from a rampaging dragon, they would be seen as the sword and shield of the nation. As risky as it was, he knew his chosen course was the correct one. There would never be another opportunity so good.

The carriage came to a juddering halt outside the cathedral. Amaury didn't wait for an attendant to open the door. He was too eager to get to the archives and continue his studies. Every time he stepped into the vaulted, cavernous room beneath the cathedral, he learned something new. His mentor, the previous Prince Bishop, had been the first man in centuries to recognise the power that knowledge could give. Something of a zealot—not a trait Amaury would ever claim for himself—that knowledge had been anathema to him, despite the man's wish to assert the primacy of the church over the entire world.

For a time after his ascension, Amaury had not known what to do with the archive. Only after he had discovered Ysabeau's existence, and her talent, had he turned his mind to magic and how it could be used.

There had been a time when kings, princes, and dukes had heeded the words of the great prelates of the church. Now, in a time when Amaury's letters to even bishops in other countries went unanswered, the church's influence over the secular world was all but non-existent. He was less interested in the spiritual power of the church—far more so in the temporal.

Where once the church had been ruled by the Prince Bishop from Mirabay, in recent decades, the individual dioceses had grown increasingly independent. Each state sent its cardinal to Amaury's annual congress, but they no longer remained in Mirabaya year round, and their participation when present was lacklustre at best. Other than that, he rarely, if ever, heard from the other archbishops. Men of learning and influence amongst the people, they always had the ears of their rulers, and if Amaury could bring them back under his control, the power he could exercise would be enormous—far more than any local potentate could hope for. Mirabaya would be supreme, the physical support for the church as it spread its influence across the world, and the Order was key to that. Might was the only thing men with power understood, especially when it came to having to give up some of that power.

He swept through the cathedral's nave, giving only a curt nod to the eager deacon who had come out to greet him and paying little attention to the man's disappointment. He sped down the tight spiral staircase to the archive, focussed on his thoughts.

He was under no illusion that it had been anything but his political acumen that had won him the old king's ear, and it was the monarch's mental decline that had allowed him to build such an impressive power base so quickly. Amaury's predecessor, gods bless him, had been too much of a firebrand to gain much traction at court. He had been like the embarrassing uncle that families had to humour, but tried to distance themselves from.

Amaury thought of him more fondly than that. Had it not been for the previous Prince Bishop, Amaury had no idea where he would be now. Probably like so many other crippled swordsmen who had turned to the bottle or dream seed, who ultimately met their end on the Black Carpet, the illegal and often deadly underground duelling circuit. He didn't even have a country estate to retreat to—his father had taken it away from him when he lost in the Competition, favouring the younger brother over the severely wounded elder.

The church was universal, though, and the perfect vessel to exercise a type of power that did not end at national boundaries. Amaury did not see why he should pay court to a king, or seek to curry favour from a man entitled by birth, rather than by merit. It should be the other way around. Until Amaury gained a firm grip over the church and its bishops, that was not going to happen. So long as foreign bishops saw themselves as independent, their rulers were not going to pay attention to a Mirabayan priest, regardless of his title or the former authority of his office.

He had long wondered if there was a magical way to sway public opinion, and this was one of the things he kept an eye out for as he pored over the shelves in his private, forbidden library. It seemed like too much to hope for, considering how the College of Mages and all its people ended up.

He needed to focus on what he knew—manipulation of public opinion the old-fashioned way. Still, that was a task for the next day. That night was his, and his skin tingled in anticipation of what he might discover on the shelves.

Guillot had spent most of the previous evening doing the positions and had risen before dawn to pick up where he left off. By the time he joined the others for breakfast, he felt as though he was already halfway through his day. His shoulders complained of overuse. He had improved, but only marginally. Movements that had once come easily, had been fast and fluid, felt like they were lubricated with gravel.

Dal Sason looked up from where he was eating alone and gave Guillot a nod when he entered the room. Leverre and his people were sitting a noticeable distance away, talking quietly amongst themselves. They didn't react to Guillot's arrival. Guillot sat opposite dal Sason.

"How's the food?"

"Not bad," dal Sason said. "Sleep well?"

"Middling."

"I know what you're up to, by the way."

Guillot's gut twisted. "What do you mean?"

"You can fritter away as much coin as you like. It won't make the slightest difference to the Prince Bishop. It's said that he's richer than the king."

Guillot concealed a sigh of relief. "Perhaps, but I'd still prefer that I benefit from it, rather than him."

"Do you mind me asking: why all the ill feeling?"

"I do mind. It's none of your business."

Dal Sason blushed, but the innkeeper arrived in time to spare them an awkward moment. Gill ordered eggs, bacon, bread, and jam. It didn't even occur to him to ask for a glass of wine, which was something new.

"I expect we'll be arriving back in Villerauvais some time this evening?" dal Sason said.

"Something like that," Guillot said, regretting how sharp he had been. "Depends on whether our friends here have another day of hard riding in them."

Leverre overheard the remark. "We'll still be going long after you've dropped from the saddle," he said.

Guillot raised his glass of water. "I certainly hope so."

"As soon as you're done eating, we move," Leverre said.

Guillot turned back to dal Sason. "From the way he speaks, you'd almost think he was in charge."

Dal Sason chuckled. "You might think that, but actually, I am." Guillot frowned. As the alleged dragonslayer, he believed he was also leading the expedition. "I'm the only impartial party," dal Sason said. "Leverre wants to prove himself and his people. You want to . . . Well, I'm not sure what you want to do. All I'm interested in is seeing this threat to the kingdom extinguished."

"Impartial but for the substantial reward I'm sure the Prince Bishop is to recompense you with."

Dal Sason blushed but said nothing.

Guillot leaned back in his chair, not sure how to respond. It stung to be passed over. He had been the finest swordsman in the land, fought in several wars with distinction, and had been declared a hero three times over, but now, it all seemed to count for nothing. All that mattered was his membership in a social club for dissolute noblemen. What possible value could that have?

"Why do we have to go to Villerauvais, anyway?" Leverre said. "We have our plan."

"I need to get something," Guillot said. "We'll make Trelain not long after nightfall if we maintain our pace. A good night's sleep there, an early start, and we'll be in Villerauvais by noon. It won't delay us."

Leverre made to open his mouth, but Guillot fixed him with a stare that said the discussion was over.

Guillot had mixed feelings returning to Villerauvais. He was sober, in new clothes, and cleanly shaven. Quite possibly no one there would recognise him. He was afraid to learn if there had been many more attacks in his absence, and wondered how the people would greet his return. Might they have thought he had abandoned them?

When all this was over, if he still lived, he would change. He would invest time, money, and energy into the village and his demesne. At one time, he had harboured great plans for Villerauvais; when had they drifted into the ether? After the Darvarosian War? The Szavarian War? Or one of the others?

He should have left the city and taken Auroré back to Villerauvais after the wars, before he joined the Silver Circle. That was the moment everything started to slide downhill. Hindsight again. What a wonderful thing it was. It might be too late for his happiness, but that didn't mean it was too late for Villerauvais.

But it was.

Villerauvais was nothing more than an ash pit. Guillot stopped his horse and stared at it, unable to make sense of open space where buildings had stood since before he was born. The others stopped beside him.

"Is this it?" Leverre said.

"Gods, Guillot, I'm so sorry," dal Sason said.

"This was where your village was?" Leverre said.

Guillot nodded. "Yes." The word caught in his throat.

"Going to the city was the right choice, Guillot," dal Sason said. "There was nothing you could have done if you'd stayed here. If you'd been here, you'd be dead, and no help to anyone."

Guillot heard dal Sason's words from very far away. "I was no help to anyone as it was."

He urged his horse forward and scanned the remains, not sure what he was looking for. Little of anything remained beyond ash. When he got to the market square—the oldest part of the village, where stone had been used for construction, back when the Villerauvais seigneurs had been wealthier—there was a little more. Remnants of the buildings around the square stuck up like charred, skeletal ribs. The fire had been so hot that many of the stones had split into pieces.

"How long ago do you think this happened?" dal Sason said.

Leverre dismounted and waded into one of the ash piles, oblivious of the effect this had on his cream robes. He knelt and took up a handful.

"It's stone cold, but the ash looks fresh," Leverre said. "A day or two. Probably not long after you left."

"Any sign of survivors?" dal Sason said.

"What could have survived this?" Guillot said, his voice full of despair. "It was hot enough to break stone."

"The beast will most likely have moved on. What's the nearest settlement?"

"Montpareil," Guillot said, his voice hollow. "It's a little larger than Ville-rauvais."

"We should check there," Leverre said. "They might have suffered the same fate, but perhaps not. We might be able to stop it happening there." He studied Gill for a moment. "Maybe some survivors made it there."

"How?" Guillot said. "I've never seen destruction like it. Not even during the Szavarian War. How could anyone survive this?"

"We'll need to warn them if they're the next village in danger," dal Sason said.

Guillot turned his horse, looking for the manor house. He could see the house was gone. The dragon had burned it to the ground as well. Everything was gone. It felt as though the years he had spent there were nothing more than a drunken hallucination, the buildings, the people, all imagined. Yves, Jeanne, Philipe, Jacques. All the others. They had relied on him, looked to him for protection, and now they were ash. "I'll be ready to go in a few moments."

He rode to where his small townhouse had stood. Like all the other buildings, it was little more than a smudge on the ground. Dismounting, he walked through the burned debris, kicking at the ash with his foot until he struck something solid. He cleared away the ash, surprised to see the blue-grey sheen of Telastrian steel. The old sword trunk that he had kept by the door looked to be the only thing to have survived. The gold and silver decorations on its surface had melted away, but the Telastrian steel of the trunk itself looked sound.

He tried to open it, but it seemed welded shut. Likely some of the decorative metal had seeped into the joint and hardened. Guillot used his dagger to gouge at the seam, then pried open the trunk. Where the cloth lining had touched the sides of the trunk, it bore some minor scorch marks, but otherwise, the rare and prized metal had kept the contents safe. His ancient family sword and the Academy Sword of Honour were perfectly intact. He took them both out and clutched them to his chest, staring at the open space where there had been a wall bearing the painting of his wife.

The land beyond remained the same, but everything he knew was gone. The dragon had wiped from the landscape the efforts of generations of men and women. The swords were all that remained of the life he had lived there.

"How many of those do you have?" dal Sason said.

"Three," Guillot said. "You can have them if the dragon does for me." He returned to his horse and strapped them to its saddle. "I'm ready to go."

"Lead on," dal Sason said.

Guillot spurred his horse on, feeling Jeanne the Taverner's eyes burning into his back as he rode away.

CHAPTER
23

Montpareil was the perfect picture of a Mirabayan country village, bathed in moonlight, with the star-punctured sky and silhouetted mountains providing a breathtaking backdrop. The settlement was a cluster of buildings neatly tucked into the curve of a small river. A few of the buildings that surrounded the spire of the village's small church had the glow of light coming from their windows. Smoke drifted slowly skyward from the chimneys, and the water wheel on the mill turned lazily with a soothing *slosh* and *whoosh*.

Even in the dark, Guillot could see that the village was orderly and well maintained—the telltale signs of a diligent lord. It made him want to vomit. This was what Villerauvais should have been. This was what he should have made it.

"All looks well here," dal Sason said.

"It does," Leverre said. "They've been lucky so far."

Guillot felt a flash of anger. Why had the beast chosen his village? His home? What had anyone there done to deserve their fate? Montpareil was a bullying bastard. Why hadn't fate chosen to destroy his village? Guillot felt guilty, but couldn't dismiss the feeling of resentment.

"We should see if there's an inn or tavern that can put us up for the night," dal Sason said. "Might as well enjoy whatever comfort is available to us. We're not going dragon hunting at this hour."

"There's a proper inn here," Guillot said. "Montpareil is on the road, so people pass through. It might be a tight squeeze, but it'll take us all. Come on."

He led them into the town along the muddy lane that curved toward the cobbled, arcaded square that was the feature of all the towns in the region. Were it not for the good level of upkeep, he could be forgiven for mistaking it for Villerauvais. A faded sign swung from a metal bracket on the wall on one of the buildings, and Guillot pointed to it.

"That's the inn," Guillot said. "It's not Bauchard's, but the cook won't poison you, and the beds won't leave you with an itch. Probably."

Dal Sason nodded. "Leverre, have one of your people go in and fetch the stable boy."

Leverre didn't react for a moment, and Guillot wondered if dal Sason had over-stepped the mark. He found himself disappointed when Leverre nodded to Ginger—Brother Hallot—who obeyed the instruction without comment.

"You'll be taking a room to yourself again, Guillot?" dal Sason said.

"If Amaury is paying for it, I most certainly will. If they have one. Only after I've had a good dinner, though. I've got quite an appetite." He felt guilty thinking of his hunger. He felt guilty thinking of anything. His village and its inhabitants had been burned to death. They didn't get to be hungry anymore. Yet he still lived, and slaying their killer was his duty. One he feared he would almost certainly fail to execute. He had to try, though. Every moment the beast still lived insulted the memory of the people he had failed.

The stable boy arrived to take their horses with the sullen attitude of one who had believed his day's work to be over. Dismounted, Guillot and the others went into the inn. They were greeted by the smell of stale wine and smoke; the latter from a large, crackling fire that filled the room with welcome warmth.

"We need rooms," dal Sason said as he approached the innkeeper.

The innkeeper nodded. "How many?"

The banneret shrugged. "How many do you have free?"

"Four."

"We'll take the lot, then," dal Sason said.

Guillot chuckled. "It seems I'm a bad influence on you."

"I work for the king," dal Sason said. "The Prince Bishop's finances are of no concern to me. Right now, a hot meal and a good night's sleep are the only things that do. If we're well fed and rested, we'll be better able to do what we came out here to do."

"Are we too late for food?" Guillot said.

"Stove is still lit," the innkeeper said. "I can have something heated up for you."

"Excellent," dal Sason said. "We'll take it over by the fire."

"Won't be a moment, my Lord."

"Before you go," Guillot said.

"Be careful," dal Sason whispered. "Don't want to start a panic."

Gill nodded. "Has anyone come here from Villerauvais in the past couple of days?"

The innkeeper shrugged and shook his head. Gill's heart sank, but it had been a slim hope.

They walked over to a table by the fire and sat. Two of the Spurriers went to attend to the baggage, leaving only Short—Banneret Eston—and Sergeant Doyenne at the table. They both looked so young to Gill. Eston couldn't have been more than a year or two out of the Academy, while Doyenne didn't look much older.

"What brought you to the Order?" Guillot said to Doyenne, trying to take his mind off Villerauvais.

"Opportunity," she said. "They're few and far between for a woman. At least for those looking for a bit of adventure. The usual paths after university didn't take my fancy. This did."

Guillot nodded. "Sounds reasonable."

For a woman, education and the professions—medicine, bookkeeping, and the like—were the only paths to an independent life, and they weren't for everyone. He couldn't imagine a worse life than spending it doing something like lawyering, although on reflection, he supposed his past few years did come pretty close.

"Plus it means I get to wear a rapier like all the bannerets," Doyenne said.

"The Order can do that?" Guillot said, looking to Leverre. The law had always been that only bannerets could wear a rapier within city walls, but that didn't stop a variety of others from trying to get away with it.

"Many of us are bannerets," Leverre said. "The king gave us a dispensation for any who aren't."

"That was nice of him," Guillot said.

"It was necessary, if we're to fill the role he has in mind for us."

"What role is that, exactly?" Guillot said. "Does he find himself in need of replacing his old bunch of drunken lechers?"

Leverre's face reddened. "You were one of those drunken lechers, as I recall."

"I may have been a drunk, but I was never a lecher. And I resigned. Apparently the old king never got around to accepting it, though. Says a lot, really."

"Strange that you use the past tense when it comes to your drinking,"

Leverre said. "I heard you've spent the last half-decade at the bottom of a bottle."

"Makes for better company than fellas like you," Guillot said, his temper flaring.

"Gentlemen," dal Sason said. "It's neither the time, nor the place. We've got a job to do, and it's more likely to succeed if we get along. I'd ask you to apologise to one another, but I don't think that'll get us anywhere. Instead I'm going to ask you both to put it behind you and move on. Focus on what we've got ahead of us."

There was a strained silence. Guillot had always hated it when he couldn't defend his behaviour.

"I'm *telling* you to both move on," dal Sason said, with an edge to his voice that Guillot hadn't heard before.

"We don't have to like each other to work together," Guillot said. "I worked with the other Chevaliers for years, after all, without killing any of them. More's the pity."

Leverre snorted. "Do your job and we won't have any problems."

"Duelled a Competition winner, have you?" Guillot said. Even his anger couldn't stop him feeling ridiculous making the threat. He took a deep breath and tried to calm himself. "How in hells am I supposed to kill a dragon, anyway? Let it eat me and try to choke it on the way down?" Even as he spoke, he realised this was far from the worst of the ideas he'd had so far.

Eston let out a laugh that was cut short by a ferocious glare from the dark-eyed Sergeant Doyenne. Leverre maintained his humourless, impassive expression, a mix of boredom and constipation, while dal Sason shifted uncomfortably in his chair. Guillot could see that the same question had been occupying his mind.

"Have you . . . detected it yet?" Guillot said. "Are we even going in the right direction?"

"We are," Leverre said.

"You seem very certain," Guillot said. "You realise we're moving into mountainous terrain. The right way might not be the direct one."

"I realise that," Leverre said.

"So you know the area?" Guillot said, his suspicions rising. "If you're so sure we're on the right track."

Leverre shifted in his seat and looked at Doyenne. She gave an almost imperceptible shake of her head, but Guillot spotted it. "You know we're on the right track because you've been there before, haven't you?" Guillot said. "Have you tried to kill it already and failed?"

The expression on Leverre's face shifted slightly.

"No, that's not it, is it?" Guillot said.

"I really don't see this as being in any way constructive," dal Sason said.

"I think it's very constructive," Guillot said. "What were you doing up there?" he said to Leverre.

"We were on state business," Leverre said.

"You bastards let it out, didn't you?" Guillot said. The anger in his voice crackled like the log fire they sat beside. "You went poking your noses where they didn't belong, and you let it out." It took Guillot everything he had to restrain himself. If it came to blows, Leverre would likely kill him. "This is all your fault."

He turned his gaze to dal Sason. "I knew it was more than a coincidence when you turned up in the village at the same time all of this started happening. How long had you known about the dragon?"

"We took action as soon as we had an understanding of what was going on," dal Sason said. "It came as just as much of a shock to the king as it did for any of us." He paused for a moment. "My involvement only began when I was tasked with fetching you."

"I dare say the people of Villerauvais got quite a bit more of a shock than the king," Guillot said. Moments like these made having a sword strapped to his waist so much more dangerous.

"Yes, I . . . well, I've been meaning to say how sorry I am for your loss," dal Sason said. "We haven't had the time to consider what a traumatic blow that must be for you."

"You can shove your apology," Guillot said. "It doesn't repair the damage done. It certainly doesn't bring back the dead."

"Perhaps we should skip dinner and get some rest," dal Sason said. "It's been a long day. We can discuss how we're going to proceed with clear heads in the morning. Nothing has changed."

"To hells with that," Guillot said. "I want to know what happened, and now. How did all this start? I'm done with being kept in the dark."

Leverre cleared his throat and gave dal Sason a nod. "As you know, the Order is exploring ancient knowledge to help us progress more quickly. Our researchers uncovered information that indicated there were a number of locations that might contain objects or further information that would aid us.

It was on one of these exploratory missions that we first encountered the dragon."

"Encountered?" Guillot said.

"We roused it while exploring a large cavern in a mountain not far from here," Leverre said. "It killed all of my men, Banneret dal Villerauvais. It *ate* them. I can assure you I'm no stranger to loss caused by this beast. I want revenge on it just as much as you do."

Guillot sank back into his chair and thought for a moment, trying to push away his anger so he could think clearly. "What were you looking for?" Guillot said.

"That's not important," Leverre said. "It was simply something the Order's researchers thought might aid us."

Why would the Prince Bishop send men to a remote part of the country looking for an object if it was unimportant? Gill wondered. That could wait until another time, however.

"Fine," he said. "So you think this cave is where the beast lives?"

"I have no reason to think otherwise," Leverre said.

"Are you actually able to track it?" Guillot said.

"Possibly," Leverre said. "We haven't tried. We thought heading back to the cave would be the best way to start."

"Finally, we agree on something," Guillot said. "That covers the *where*, leaving us with the *how*. Anything on that subject that you've chosen not to share with me?" He glared at Leverre and dal Sason, but neither gave anything away.

"We're just as much in the dark on that as you are, Gill," dal Sason said. "That's why you were brought in. The king was hoping that there's still something about having been a Chevalier of the Silver Circle that will aid us. The initiation ceremony was said to have turned great swordsmen into great dragonslayers."

"When it was carried out by mages," Guillot said. "Not a bunch of drunken degenerates."

"There was still something of the mystical about it, though, was there not?" dal Sason said. "The Prince Bishop seems quite certain of that."

"He can be certain of whatever he likes," Guillot said. "It doesn't change anything. It was all a load of chanting, oath swearing, and drinking."

"Still, we'll take every little thing that we can," dal Sason said. "I don't understand the ins and outs of it, but there's the chance that some magic may still have been attached to the ceremony. If that doesn't make a difference, then we still have the greatest swordsman Mirabaya has ever produced in our arsenal. The rest of us aren't too bad either."

Guillot humphed. "You have to get close to use a sword. I can't see anyone getting close enough without getting eaten. There's a reason we use special long swords for boar hunting and spears to hunt belek."

"The simple fact of the matter is this, Gill," dal Sason said. "The king wanted to send a regiment to kill this beast. It took the Prince Bishop considerable effort to talk him around to sending a smaller group to investigate first. If we can kill it, wonderful. If not, we're to learn as much as we can and report back so that if and when the king does send a regiment, they are not lambs to the slaughter. Now that the people of Mirabay know about the beast, how do you think they would react to the news that it had destroyed a regiment of the king's finest soldiers?"

Dal Sason paused, but Guillot didn't need time to allow the idea to settle in, so he finished the point for him. "There would be panic, then riots," Guillot said. "The worst fear of every king. Aside from assassination, I suppose." It was the second time that evening he was forced to admit that dal Sason was correct. Whatever else about him, he had brains and knew how to use them.

"Right now, this dragon reaching Mirabay is the king's worst fear," dal Sason said. "Everyone wants to stop it, and stop it fast. Preferably before it kills anyone else."

The food arrived and conversation stopped as the innkeeper and the retasked stable boy set plates of steaming stew onto the table.

"Beef, slow cooked with wine, potatoes, and vegetables," the innkeeper said. "I hope you enjoy."

"I'm sure we will," dal Sason said.

"Have you heard any strange stories lately?" Guillot asked.

"What do you mean?" the innkeeper said.

"Anything unusual. Livestock being killed, buildings being burned. Anything like that."

"Now that you mention it," the innkeeper said, "Lord Montpareil rode out yesterday for Castle Brienne. The usual resupply wagons were overdue and he decided to find out what the problem was. The stores here were in danger of spoiling. We do most of our trade with the castle."

"When do you expect him back?" Guillot said.

The innkeeper shrugged. "Tomorrow? The day after. Soon I hope. The supplies won't last much longer, and we don't get paid if they're spoiled before they get to the castle."

"Thanks," Guillot said.

The innkeeper left them to their food, which they all attacked for several minutes before the conversation restarted.

"Where's Castle Brienne?" Leverre said.

Guillot shrugged. "It's one of the border pass forts. I'm not exactly sure where—I've never been."

"Do you think the dragon has attacked it?" dal Sason said.

"Your guess is as good as mine," Guillot said. "It's interesting that the innkeeper didn't say anything about the dragon, though. Or anything that might refer to it. Sounds like it hasn't made it this far yet, and neither has word of it."

"It means the beast's trail of destruction isn't as extensive as it might have been," Leverre said.

"There aren't many villages out here," Gill said. "News travels slowly. It could be days before anyone here knows what's happened at Villerauvais."

"Hopefully we'll be able to make sure it doesn't happen anywhere else. I'm going to turn in for the night," dal Sason said. "We should start early, I expect we've quite a bit of travelling to do to reach your mountain cave, Commander Leverre."

Guillot nodded, rose, and called for the innkeeper to lead them to their rooms. An early night would have been welcome, but he had a couple of hours of the positions to complete before he could put his head down.

CHAPTER
24

I have to admit," dal Drezony said, "that I'm very curious to see what you're capable of. I've never seen the Prince Bishop speak in quite so animated a way about any new recruit."

After a visit to the Order's quartermaster to get the uniforms she would need for her training and packing the garments away in her room, she went to the refectory for supper. As soon as Solène entered the long hall, lined from end to end by three rows of communal tables, dal Drezony had called her over. Solène had spent the better part of her adult life trying to be invisible, and being singled out as soon as she entered a room, with so many other people there, bothered her. The questioning made it even worse, but the smell of the food was enough to convince her it was worth staying.

She shrugged in response to dal Drezony. For her, being noticed had always meant trouble, but she realised that was something she was going to have to get over. *Forgettable* was the impression she had always sought to get across. Except for Trelain, where she had started to think she could make a life and a business. She could never forget where that had gotten her.

"After we eat, I thought you could give me a demonstration," dal Drezony said. "Give me an idea of where we'll be starting."

Solène shrugged again. "What do you want me to do?"

Dal Drezony laughed. "I don't know. What *can* you do? What did you do for the Prince Bishop?"

Pride would not allow Solène to repeat the same demonstration, but there were few things she could do intentionally. Looking along the table, she spotted an empty glass that no one was using. She focussed her thoughts, this time locking onto something different, something she had seen in the city, and had been wondering about ever since. She turned the glass upside down and stared at it. The air inside the bowl seemed to swirl and grow thicker, until it looked more like a liquid than a gas. Then it ignited into a light that bathed Solène and dal Drezony in a warm glow. Solène relaxed and smiled.

Dal Drezony watched in silence until the light faded, then disappeared. She had a pleased but bemused expression on her face.

"I saw the everlasting lamps when I got to the city," Solène said. "I've wanted to try making my own ever since."

"Magelamps," dal Drezony said. "They're called magelamps. And this was your first try at one?"

Solène nodded.

Dal Drezony let out a short laugh. "I wouldn't let the fading of the light bother you. No one here's been able to make them last very long either, and they've had a lot more practise. When did you stop concentrating on the light?"

"As soon as I made it," Solène said. "It's not much use if you have to concentrate on it the whole time, is it?"

Dal Drezony let out an incredulous bark of laughter. "No, I suppose it isn't. You've definitely not had any training? If you have, you can be honest. It won't get you in any trouble here."

Solène shook her head. "Where would I have gotten it?"

"Darvaros? Szavaria, perhaps? Although I've not heard of any of their mages who can do much more you just did. If they could, they'd have conquered us centuries ago. A good magelamp with a clean, bright light was once considered the pinnacle of the magical art. Every novice mage would have to make one to earn their title of magister. It's why we still have so many of them after all this time. Even in ideal conditions—perfect peace and quiet—I can't do much better than you just did. You know, the finest examples hint at the personality of their maker—the hue of the light, the way it swirls within the glass sphere." She chewed on a piece of bread as she stared at the upside-down glass. "To walk in here off the street and do that is beyond impressive. I can see why the Prince Bishop got so excited."

Solène felt the warmth of pride fill her, just as she had when people had returned to the bakery day after day saying her bread was the best they'd ever eaten. She didn't even notice that every eye in the refectory was on her. "I'd like to be able to make one that doesn't fade," she said.

"I expect you will achieve that, and sooner than any of us might have hoped. It's exciting to have you here. I think I'm going to learn as much from you as you do from us. We've studied so much of theory, but none of us have developed enough power to properly apply it. Exciting times lie ahead, Solène. For both of us. But enough about work—that will begin in the morning. I'll be calling on you after breakfast to get the day started, but for now I've kept you from your supper for too long!"

▲▲▲▲▲▲

Solène was a suspicious person. Having magical talent in a land where magic was illegal had made her so. It wasn't an enjoyable way to live, but her attitude had kept her alive. It made her question everything, and it was why she woke the next morning with a twist of nausea in her gut.

Everyone she had met the previous night had been welcoming and friendly, although she agreed with Seneschal dal Drezony that the bannerets were more self-assured than perhaps they should be. Nonetheless, they had given her the same welcome as everyone else, even if they did clearly think themselves the elite.

Food, comfort, friendliness—something inside her screamed that it was all too good to be true. She had spent too long trying to see the danger in everything to accept that she might have finally found her place in the world, and the fact that she had let her guard down the previous evening after so short a time there frightened her.

She had spoken to several novices who had been denounced for witchcraft, only to be secreted away to the Order for a new life. None had nearly the talent that she did, but their stories were much the same as her own. That didn't mean she was safe, though. No one gave so much without wanting something in return. That the Prince Bishop hoped to develop and capitalise on her ability was clear, but what that would mean in practise she did not know. The uncertainty made her feel sick.

With her stomach in knots, she had woken before dawn, but had skipped breakfast, choosing instead to sit on the edge of her bed, wondering what was to happen next. Would someone come for her? Should she be somewhere that she was unaware of? A knock on the door suggested the former. She opened it to Seneschal dal Drezony.

"Now for the bad news," the other woman said.

Solène's heart dropped.

"We have to go running with the bannerets," dal Drezony said. "Three mornings a week. No way out of it, sadly. Believe me, I hate running and I've tried everything I can think of."

Solène took a deep breath and relaxed. "You gave me a bit of a fright."

"Oh, be afraid. You haven't seen the pace we'll have to keep up with," dal Drezony said, smiling. "Uniform Number Four is the uniform for running. Get changed and meet me outside. Suffering shared is suffering halved. Or so I'm told."

Solène went to the trunk containing the uniforms the quartermaster had issued her. Each one came in its own linen bag with a large number on it. Dal Drezony's comment—"Number Four"—answered one of Solène's questions; it seemed the Order numbered its uniforms for different uses. She delved through the bags, realising she had two Number Twos, which she took to be the uniform for regular daily use, then found the one she was looking for.

Solène spilled the contents of Number Four onto her bed—light britches and vest, knee socks, and a light pair of white leather shoes. She changed, then met dal Drezony in the arcaded laneway. They walked in silence toward the front gate, where a large group of similarly attired people waited.

"It'll be nothing but pain at first," dal Drezony said, "but you'll get used to it quickly enough. I don't think I'd run more than a couple of steps in my life before I got here. Now it feels like I've run from one end of the kingdom to the other, but it's all part of the Prince Bishop's master plan—a strong, healthy body means a strong, healthy mind. I don't think he's wrong in that, but it's damned hard work."

Solène had run before, but not much, and only when trying to get away from something. It seemed they were the last two to arrive, as the group set off at a brisk pace as soon as they got there.

Dal Drezony stayed beside Solène as they ran—laps of the Priory around the inside of the walls—but thankfully didn't try to engage her in conversation. She began gasping for breath after only a short distance. It was both flattering and worrying that dal Drezony paid her such constant attention. Was she really that special? Would she really be able to do things no one else there could?

The burn in her legs and chest made it difficult to think, pushing her anxieties aside. Dal Drezony breathed hard but seemed comfortable with the pace. Several of the men, who had introduced themselves as bannerets the night before, were chatting and joking as they ran, as though it took no more effort than falling out of bed.

"How? Far?" Solène gasped, beginning to fear she would not be able to continue.

"There're still a few laps to go," dal Drezony said.

"I. Have. To. Walk," Solène said, reckoning death was more attractive than having to take one more stride.

"That's all right," dal Drezony said, slowing to a walk. "Don't want to kill you on your first day."

Solène stopped and doubled over, sucking in great breaths as the others continued on their way. "It gets easier?"

Dal Drezony laughed. "It does, I promise. Now, come on. If you stop for too long, it will be hard to start again. If we take the direct route back you'll have time to rest before lunch. You'll need to rest whenever you can, and keep the fuel coming in, or you won't have the energy to keep up with everything. The days are long here at the Priory, especially when you aren't used to them."

"Everything you do is dependent on the Fount," dal Drezony said.

Solène was walking with dal Drezony through one of the Priory's many courtyard gardens. She wore Uniform Number Two, as did most of the people around her: britches, boots, shirt, tunic, and robe. She had never worn britches before and they felt strange. Her legs were stiff and sore from the morning run, but walking seemed to help loosen them. It had taken her awhile to realise this was a lesson, not a casual stroll to ease aching legs.

"It's the energy of the world, and it can be found almost everywhere. In us, around us, wherever there is life. Certain things block it—thick stone, water. If you swim underwater, for instance, you won't be able to draw on the Fount. We don't know why that happens. Ordinarily, with a new novice, I'd have to spend quite some time teaching them to open their minds to the Fount. Happily, that isn't something I have to do with you—your connection to it already seems to be very strong."

"What does it look like?" she said.

"You mean you *haven't* seen it?" dal Drezony said.

Solène shrugged. She had no idea what the Fount was, nor had she ever felt it. She could simply do the things she could do.

"That comes as a surprise. Usually a novice needs to be able to see the Fount's manifestation before they can accept, and reach for it. Getting them to see it's the hard part."

"So what does it look like?"

Dal Drezony smiled. "A blue glow, covering everything. It's really quite beautiful. In order to draw on it, we must reach for it. To reach for it, we must see it. At least that's what we thought before you. I was right when I said we'd learn as much from you as you from us," dal Drezony said. "I can't shape magic unless I see the glow. Only when my mind is open to its existence, can I use it. It's too great a leap otherwise. For me, at least. And everyone else here. It requires quite a bit of concentration, so if you've got a better way, I want to learn."

Solène blushed. She didn't know why she could do the things she could do. "I don't know if I can teach you. I just want to do something, and it happens. Or it doesn't. It depends on what it is that I'm trying to do." After a moment's silence, she asked, "Is this how it will always be? Walks and conversations?"

"No, but for magic this is how we usually start. It helps the novice relax and slowly build up an understanding of, and familiarity with, the concepts they need to absorb. This in the afternoon, for now, and physical training—running, fencing, gymnastics—in the mornings.

"For you, this process will be faster, though. You already have a potent skill, so what we have to do is temper it. After that, your afternoons will be academic study, practise, and experimentation, and hopefully we will be able to develop your ability to its full potential. That's what we're all here to do, to keep pushing our boundaries and explore what is possible. If you hear any explosions over the course of the day, that's usually the reason. We've not had any serious accidents though, so don't worry."

CHAPTER
25

Solène was relieved that she didn't have to run the next morning, and felt settled enough to join her new comrades for breakfast. Her first fencing lesson was scheduled immediately afterward, and as instructed, she reported to the fencing salon, located in a long building lined with large bay windows too high from the ground for outsiders to see through. She had no idea what was about to happen, and felt uneasy as a result. Her light cream fencing clothes—Uniform Number Three—felt odd, tighter than any other clothing she'd ever worn, but the material had enough stretch to allow easy movement.

It felt peculiar at first. Without a robe, Solène felt oddly naked in her britches, but by the time she walked from the refectory to the training hall she had grown to like them. They certainly felt more practical than the long skirts she usually wore, and no one paid her the slightest attention, making it clear she did not stand out to anyone at the Priory.

The room that greeted her was impressive: an entire building dedicated to swordplay, with the beams and apex roof high above. The floor was of light-coloured wood, so well polished she could almost see her reflection in it. Several pairs of swordsmen and women fenced one another, clad in the same uniform Solène wore. They moved back and forth, their shoes thumping and squeaking on the floor as their blades clattered against one another. Fencing looked like it might be fun, and she felt her trepidation ease.

"Bastelle?"

It took Solène a moment to realise that the shout was directed at her. She looked over at a wiry man no taller than she was. His greying black hair was pulled back into a tight ponytail that gave him an intense look.

"Yes, I'm Solène from Bastelle. Brother Foulques?"

"*Banneret* Foulques," he said. "In my fencing salon, we use proper titles, so while you are within these walls, you call me Maestro. If you've got a title, tell me, and I'll use it. Otherwise, you're Novice Bastelle."

"You can call me Solène," she said.

"Did you run yesterday, Novice Bastelle?"

Solène nodded.

"What?"

"Yes I did, Maestro Foulques."

"Good. Now, the run. How're your legs?"

"Sore."

"Thought as much. It'll ease once you're warmed up." Selecting a sword from a rack on the wall, he walked over to her. "I presume you've never used one of these?"

Solène shook her head, then thought better of it. "No, Maestro."

"At least there won't be any bad habits to unlearn." He flipped the sword in his hand and presented it to her, handle first. "This is the lightest blade we have. It takes years of training to build the strength and stamina to use a heavier blade. We're not looking to make a banneret out of you, just to give you enough skill to use it if you really need to." He waved the handle at her, saying, "It's not going to bite. Not that end, anyway."

Hesitantly, Solène took the sword. The blade was long and slender, with a small, flat button at its tip. It looked flimsy, and she didn't like that he had chosen the lightest blade for her.

"We're not going to be having you running anyone through today," he said, noticing her staring at the blunt tip. "We start easy. Swordplay is all about movement. Footwork is of vital importance." Foulques turned and walked back to the sword rack, where he chose a more substantial blade for himself. "We're going to start with what we call 'the positions.' Just a few to start off with, focussing on your feet and posture. In time, you'll be doing them in your sleep. For now, we just want to get them into your head. And feet! Now, take your guard. Like this."

Solène watched as he adopted a balanced stance, with his knees flexed, and did her best to mimic him. She felt awkward as she tried to move her body into the Maestro's demonstrated position. No sooner had she managed the stance than he moved, taking three short steps forward, his feet ending up at the same angle as they had been at the beginning. No other part of him had moved and the tip of his sword had remained perfectly still. Solène's three steps forward were each different and she had to adjust her posture at the end, her sword waving about wildly all the time. She had barely finished moving when Foulques took three steps back, ending up where he had started, his movements looking like his body and legs were entirely separate.

She copied him again, giving up on trying to keep her sword still and eyes dead ahead, watching her feet and where they ended up compared to where she wanted them to be.

"Eyes up!" Foulques said. "Footwork is important, but you can't move your feet if you're dead. Always watch your opponent, or where he would be if you had one."

Solène started to nod—"Yes, Maestro."

"Ten times, back and forward," he said. "Slow. Precise. Train the movement into your body."

Solène started the set, feeling her already tired legs start to protest. Her arm and hand were also beginning to feel the strain of the unfamiliar position and weight. Now she was glad he had given her the light sword. She hadn't even swung the thing yet and already felt like it would pull her arm off. By the time she was halfway through the repetitions, beads of perspiration coated her forehead and her thighs burned. Swordplay, when she had seen it, looked fast and exciting, but this was tedious and slow and she couldn't help but feel disappointed. The moment she finished, she straightened up and lowered the sword; the release of tension in her shoulder was such a relief that she let out a sigh.

Foulques watched her with his arms akimbo. "Not too bad," he said. "You have natural athleticism, which gives you a head start, but you've let it lie fallow up until today, which means there is a lot of hard work to be done. Now, again!"

She had thought running would be the toughest part of life at the Priory, but it seemed she was wrong.

Solène sat in dal Drezony's office after lunch, waiting for the other woman to arrive to begin their lesson. It was a relief to think a gentle stroll through the Priory's gardens was the most taxing thing left between her, supper, and bed. Her legs ached with a dull burn that made it uncomfortable to sit still for too long, and she did her best not to think of tomorrow's morning run.

The office was a bright, airy room decorated in light and subtle shades. It very much spoke to dal Drezony's personality as Solène knew it. There was a perfect view of one of the peaceful courtyard gardens, with a stunning marble fountain at its centre. It was certainly the perfect place for quiet contemplation—something they seemed to do an awful lot of in the Order. So far, other than her encounter with Maestro Foulques, everything about the Order felt vague and directionless, as though people with talent were sent there in the hope that their magic would manifest and develop all by itself. She had to admit that it might not only be the Order causing her confusion. This was the first time in her adult life that she had not known what she was working toward; more than that, it was the first time her mind was not occupied with having to constantly look over her shoulder.

There were some papers on dal Drezony's desk, and Solène could not help but take a peek at the top sheet as she waited. The title caught her imagination instantly—"The Five Tests of Magical Competence." The page was upside down from her perspective, and she was just trying to decipher the first of the tests when dal Drezony entered the room.

"I'm sorry for keeping you waiting, but one of our talent scouts got picked up by the Intelligenciers late last night, and I had to get him released before they started interrogating him. Their methods can be severe, so I needed to get him out fast."

"I've seen them," Solène said. "And I've heard all about what they do."

"For people with our peculiar gifts, they're quite terrifying, but hopefully their days of witch hunting are limited. Once the Order is strong enough, the regulation and policing of magic use will fall to us and they will be able to focus on the spying, espionage, and assassination that they're more suited to. I'm assured that day is not far in coming. But back to more relevant things—how did you enjoy your session with Maestro Foulques?"

"It was . . . not like anything I've experienced before, but I enjoyed it. I can see why men are so drawn to it."

"Foulques can seem harsh, but I've grown very fond of him, and the skills he gives us may well save our lives one day. Our ability to draw on the Fount is not unlimited. The time might come when you have to rely on steel to save yourself."

Unable to either read the paper or contain her curiosity any longer, Solène pointed to the page on the table. "What are the Five Tests of Magical Competence?"

Dal Drezony frowned, then looked at her desk. "Ah, yes. I'm sorry, it hadn't occurred to me that you can read. It was something I thought we'd have to address."

Solène nodded. "I taught myself."

"Well, that puts us even farther ahead than I hoped. I worried that would be the thing that held you back the most. The Five Tests of Magical Competence—it's not the most inspiring title, but it's the best I could come up with, and it fits, so . . ." She shrugged. "It's something of a work in progress. Foulques has a pretty well-established set of criteria for judging ability with a sword, and academic tests are equally simple—either you know what you need to know, or you don't.

"Deciding when a novice has reached the ability level where we can let them out into the world and be confident that they aren't going to get themselves killed, or worse, cause a disaster that kills others, has proven to be more of a challenge. So we came up with five tests that would give us a good indication, and this is the current iteration." She spun the sheet around so Solène could get a better look.

The first test made her smile—to create a light that persisted after the caster had ceased to focus on it. She had done that on her first meeting with dal Drezony, and knew her next attempt would be even better.

The second was to lift a small object into the air and hold it steady for a certain amount of time. That sparked her imagination—she had never thought of trying something like that. Her use of magic had always been needs-based, and she had never needed to levitate something. Nonetheless, it didn't seem like such a difficult task, and she was confident she could do it.

The third task looked more challenging, and she could immediately see the relevance. It was to perform what it called "a push" while in a heavily distracting environment. The requirements seemed obvious enough, but she did wonder what a "heavily distracting environment" would involve.

"Heavily distracting?" Solène said.

"It's all well and good being able to shape magic in the serenity of the Priory, but you'll need to be able to do it, and control it, out in the real world too. Perhaps in a fight. We'll try to simulate that confusion in the test."

Solène nodded and looked at the next item on the list—the creation of a barrier that completely surrounds the caster and blocks both magical and physical attacks. The fifth and final test was called a "stilling." She looked at dal Drezony and raised an eyebrow.

"That's an interesting one," the woman said. "We discovered it in some old papers the Prince Bishop found, but we're not sure what it was used for. We can speculate, but the important thing for these purposes is that it's a complicated piece of magic that takes quite a bit of skill to shape. It slows the world around you, or at least the part of it you're focussing on. Time moves normally for the caster, and others if you're able to extend the effect to them, but that's very difficult. I sometimes wonder if I should try using it to help me get through all of this." She gestured to the pile of papers on the side of her desk.

Solène sat back in her chair and thought about it. Other than the first one, she hadn't attempted any of them. The challenge of trying to do them in a controlled way was an exciting prospect, and she wondered if she might be able to manage them all. She chewed her lip for a moment, then made her decision.

"When can I take the test?"

Dal Drezony laughed. "Well, I commend your eagerness, but as I explained, we have to be careful. Your talent is obvious, but there are huge dangers that you need to be aware of and trained to avoid. How far you've learned to use this talent is an entirely other matter, and it's my responsibility to help you develop it, and most importantly, learn how to control it. The greater the power, the greater the importance of control, and you are most certainly the most powerful mage I've encountered."

Solène blushed at the compliment, but wanted to take the tests even more. She had spent too long hiding from this. Now that she was free to explore it, patience was a very hard thing to come by.

"How can I show you that I have control?"

Dal Drezony laughed again. "Well, I suppose, by completing all the tests. Usually we know that a novice is going to be able to pass before allowing them to attempt them, but admittedly, these tests are new. There are a number of brothers and sisters here who I suspect might not be able to pass them even now. As I said, it's early days for us, and we're still trying to organise everything in the best way. For the first few years, there were no tests at all."

"I'd like to try," Solène said. "If I can't then I'm happy to spend as long as it takes to pass them, but I'd like to know where I stand now. How much work I need to do."

Dal Drezony chewed on her lip for a moment, her gaze drifting to her window, and the courtyard garden. After a moment, she nodded. "Very well. I'll make the arrangements and you can attempt them this afternoon. As you say, at the very least, we'll know what we have to work on. We'll meet again after supper at the crafting gallery. Will you be ready?"

Solène smiled, and nodded.

How did you even find your way out here the first time?" Guillot said. He stared up the narrow valley and shivered in the chill breeze. It had taken them the entire morning, since well before dawn, to get to the valley that led to the mountain Leverre said was home to the dragon.

"We have our methods," Leverre said.

"Remind me what you were looking for?" Guillot said.

Leverre glared at him. "I didn't tell you, and I'm not going to now for no other reason than it's a waste of our time."

"Whatever you say, Banneret-Commander Leverre."

Dal Sason cleared his throat. "I'd very much like to be there before nightfall. The uneven ground ahead will be treacherous in the dark."

It was barely noon, but with dal Sason, it was difficult to identify irony. Still, Guillot couldn't quite take the comment seriously. "I have to admit, the danger posed by the uneven ground does very little to bother me, all things considered," he said.

"Another thing we agree on," Leverre said. "We should camp soon. If we keep going, there won't be enough daylight left to fight the dragon when we reach its cave. I'd rather not face the thing in the dark."

"Indeed," Guillot said. "If we keep agreeing, we might end up friends."

Leverre gave him a thin-lipped smile, but said nothing.

"Let's find somewhere sheltered and out of sight to make camp," Guillot said. "If we're close to its home, we should stay hidden."

"There was a copse of trees not far from here, if I recall correctly," Leverre said. "It should give us enough cover."

"Lead on," dal Sason said.

Leverre took them into the valley along the track of a streambed. While the water was currently little more than a trickle, Guillot knew that during the spring thaw it would be a raging torrent capable of washing them back to where they had started. The ground grew rockier as they moved into the pass and the scree from the mountains rose on either side. He could feel his horse slipping on the rocks and had to admit that he was more concerned about a bad fall than he had led dal Sason to believe.

"That's the copse up ahead," Leverre said.

The trees were clustered in a hollow, safe from the howling winds that swept through the valley every winter, and far enough from the stream to avoid the torrents of meltwater every spring. They were the last trees in the valley, and there was something sad about their loneliness yet defiance in their continued existence in such a harsh and remote place. Guillot hoped their using it as a campsite wouldn't lead to the dragon burning it, and them, to ashes.

"It'll be a chilly night," Eston said when they gained the shelter of the trees.

"We won't freeze," Guillot said, "but if we light a fire, our flame-spurting friend might decide to come over and contribute. I'll take a night of discomfort over that, thanks."

"He's right," Leverre said. "While we're here, we have to be invisible."

They made their camp as comfortable as possible, piling pine needles up under their bedrolls and into mounds to give them shelter from the breeze. Guillot spotted Leverre standing at the edge of the copse, looking up at the mountainside. Making his way over, he followed Leverre's gaze up to a gaping maw in the mountain.

"It'll take time to get up there," Guillot said. "We'll be pretty exposed."

"Yes," Leverre said. "You'd be surprised how quick you can get back down when you've got a fire-breathing dragon chasing you, though."

Guillot let out a sober chuckle. "I'm sorry about your people. I've lost men in battle, and I know how hard it is."

Leverre nodded. "I'm sorry too. For your people. Your village. It was a horrible thing. Makes what we're doing here all the more important. No one intended any of this to happen. We had no way of knowing the creature was up there."

Guillot let out a grunt, not knowing what to say. Stopping the dragon was important, but he couldn't help feeling they were getting in way over their heads. If anyone was relying on him to have some miraculous superpower because he was a Chevalier of the Silver Circle, he feared they were going to be sorely disappointed. He had tried to recall the ceremony many times over the past few days, without much success.

"What's it like up there?" he asked.

"It's a huge cavern, pitch black. I think there's another chamber toward the back. The beast seemed to come out of there, but I didn't see myself. I was at the cavern mouth, overseeing the search."

"The dark will give us problems. We don't have many torches."

"We won't need them. I can fill the cavern with as much light as you want. Magic has its benefits."

"That brings me to my next question," Guillot said. "What can your people bring to the effort? Magically, I mean."

Leverre took a deep breath. "Magic is a new science. We can do a number of things that make life more convenient—move objects around, create light— but real power, like you hear of in stories about Imperial mages? We're a long way from being able to do anything close to that.

"That's what brought us up here. The Prince Bishop thought there might be something in this cave that could give us a boost. Instead, we lost several of our strongest and most promising mages, all dead before I knew what was happening. I'm not sure why it let me get away. It just sat down at the mouth of that cavern and watched me with its big, soulless eyes as I ran away. It was the most humiliating thing I've ever experienced."

Guillot felt awkward at Leverre's openness, though he supposed that if there was to be a rapprochement between them, now was the time.

"No one could expect you to have done differently," Guillot said. "I ran the first time I saw it too. It's a terrifying thing. Dragons have been the scary monster in children's stories for centuries. No one could expect to see one."

Leverre nodded. "No, I suppose not. To answer your question: we Spurriers can distract it, we can harry it, we will most likely be able to hurt it, but we don't possess the power to kill the beast."

"Thanks for being honest with me."

"To lie about that would simply get us both killed," Leverre said, then excused himself and returned to the campsite.

Guillot studied the black void in the mountainside, wondering if the beast was up there at that moment, resting in anticipation of destroying another village, or worse. He wondered if it suspected men were on their way to kill it, then wondered if it could even think. Did it know fear? At that moment, Guillot certainly did. The task ahead seemed as monumental as the mountain before him and no matter how hard he tried, he couldn't think of a way to complete it.

⋏⋏⋏⋏⋏⋏

Guillot felt like a condemned man when the light of day grew strong enough in their shady enclave to make it impossible to pretend to sleep any longer. He rolled out of his bed of blankets and pine needles and started preparing for the day. There was no chance of a campfire, and while he didn't like the idea of going up the mountain without a hot meal in his belly, he preferred it to the thought of being a hot meal in the dragon's belly.

Movement spread through the camp as the dragon hunters went about their morning routines in silence. Even dal Sason seemed to lack anything encouraging to say. He checked his gear, his face gone pale, as though realisation of what they intended to do had finally hit him.

Guillot drew his Sword of Honour and family sword from their sheaths and placed them on his blanket. The Sword of Honour, with a broader Telastrian blade, was something of a jack-of-all-trades. It would serve admirably on the battlefield or in most of the regular fighting a working banneret might set his hand to, but was too heavy to duel with, where speed meant the difference between life and death. Still, he wasn't sure it was the right weapon for this mission.

That left his family blade, Mourning. He had no idea of its age, only that it had been paired with a new, more fashionable hilt in his father's time, which in itself was not the first time it had been updated. The blade was broader at the base with a full-length fuller and lines that drew together at the tip in a smooth curve rather than the more angular design of the duelling blade. An ancestor, somewhere back in the almost forgotten mists of time, had been one of the founders of the Chevaliers of the Silver Circle, and Guillot had often wondered if the blade had been his. Might it already have tasted the blood of a dragon?

He picked it up and hefted it in his hand. He was much the same size as his father had been in his prime, and the handle couldn't have suited his hand much better if it had been made for him. The new hilt was tastefully done—it had been sent to Carlujko, the celebrated Ostian bladesmith, all the way on the other side of the Middle Sea, so the new Telastrian hilt would match the quality of the old, beautiful blade. While regular steel rusted over time, Telastrian steel aged like vintage wine, growing stronger and more beautiful. The swirling blue grain in the dark grey steel had developed a more vibrant hue with age, which made Guillot's other two newer swords pale by comparison.

Tightening his grip on the handle of the old sword, he chewed his lip. If Mourning hadn't already shed the blood of a dragon, then it was long beyond time. Perhaps the spirits of his ancestors would look down on him from the heavens favourably and aid him in his most dire moment. He laughed at how foolish this thought was, and how much more receptive he was to the teachings of the church and the benevolence of the gods now that he faced death.

"I'd love to know what can make you laugh on a morning like this," dal Sason said.

"Better to die laughing than screaming," Guillot said.

"That definitely isn't the cheery thought I was looking for," dal Sason said. "Are you near ready?"

"As ready as I'll ever be," Guillot said. "The others?"

"Likewise," Leverre said. "Although I'm beginning to wish we'd gone up the mountain in darkness. It might have been better to risk turning an ankle rather than be picked off one by one on that slope."

"Wouldn't make any difference," Guillot said as he started buckling on pieces of armour. "It was hunting around Villerauvais at night. I suspect it can see perfectly well in the dark."

"I wonder if it's too much to hope for that it doesn't see all that well in daylight," Sergeant Doyenne said.

"We can always hope," Guillot said. "If you wouldn't mind?" He raised his arms to expose the straps on his armour that were awkward to get to himself. Leverre stepped over and started tugging them tight.

"Hope for the best, prepare for the worst," Leverre said, giving the buckles one final pull. "Let's get to it. Nothing to be gained by putting it off any longer."

"Agreement again," Guillot said.

The group moved to the edge of the copse and surveyed the slope. Loose scree and boulders covered the steep mountainside. He couldn't see them all reaching the cavern in less than an hour, more likely two—a long time to be out in the open, on a surface impossible to move silently on.

"We should spread out," Guillot said.

"Sounds like a good idea," dal Sason said. "No point in making things any easier for it than we need to."

"Well, see you up there," Guillot said. "We can reconvene under the lip of the opening."

Everyone nodded in agreement and Guillot set off, leading the way. In addition to his old sword, he carried one of the modified belek spears. Intended to be used from the saddle, it was long and heavy and was awkward to haul up the mountainside. He felt it would be worth the effort, though. Every wrong choice, every concession to laziness, could be fatal.

Despite his best efforts, Guillot failed to keep his boot tops clear of the water when he crossed the stream, and they squelched as he walked. Dying with cold, wet feet didn't appeal at all. Added to his empty stomach, Gill expected he was about to have a particularly miserable experience.

His boots slipped on the loose stones as he started to tackle the slope and the cumbersome spear threw him off balance. It was too large to use as a walking stick, so he slung it over his shoulders and hung onto it with both hands in an effort to stay balanced. That worked, to a degree, but the scree shifted with each step, so he was breathing hard after only a few steps.

By the time he was halfway up, his thighs burned, and it felt as though the air wasn't thick enough to sustain him. He looked around and felt guilty disappointment to see the others making better progress than he, while looking as though they weren't finding the climb nearly so difficult. Before the day began, he had worried if he would be capable of fighting when he got to the top. Now he worried his heart might fail and he would drop dead before he even got close.

He wasn't going to be shown up by the others, however. At one time, other people had admired him, and he didn't intend to be considered an embarrassment now. He put his head down and drove with his legs, one step at a time, doing his best to ignore the distance he still had to cover.

CHAPTER
27

Solène arrived at the crafting gallery as the bell in the Priory's small campanile chimed the hour signalling the end of supper. She hadn't eaten—filled with nervous energy, she had no appetite. She hadn't been in the crafting gallery before, and found herself in a large, high-ceilinged room much like the fencing hall, but without the racks of training weapons.

She was surprised to see the Prince Bishop standing with dal Drezony and three magisters whom she had not yet met. Could his interest in her be that great? Other than those five, the hall was empty.

Dal Drezony walked over to welcome her. "Are you ready?"

Solène nodded, a flutter of nerves starting in her stomach.

"You are allowed to pass these tests one at a time, which means that anything you can do today will count and will be a remarkable achievement considering you've only just arrived."

Solène nodded again. "I'm ready," she said.

"Good." Dal Drezony turned back to the others. "We'll begin with the spell of perpetuating illumination."

It took Solène a moment to understand what dal Drezony meant, but once she did, she relaxed. She recalled dal Drezony saying the Fount looked like a blue glow, and as soon as the thought popped into her head, everything around her was bathed in blue, coruscating light—something she had never seen before. For an instant, she wondered why that had happened at just that moment, then pushed the thought from her mind and focussed on her task. She smiled with satisfaction as the Fount disappeared, leaving in its wake the golden light of the small, glowing orb—the one she had created without a container.

"What do I have to do next?" she said, turning to dal Drezony.

Dal Drezony smiled, her gaze locked on the light. Solène realised that the other woman had started to count the moment Solène had started to speak. After a moment, dal Drezony's smile grew wider.

"That will be sufficient," she said, then turned to the others. "I think we can consider that a pass?"

The three magisters nodded in agreement. Two men and a woman, they stood huddled together in their cream robes; their expressions inscrutable. Solène wondered if they were surprised, frightened, or indifferent, then realised she didn't care. She had seen and heard enough to know that the Prince Bishop's opinion was the only one that really mattered. Unfortunately, he was equally unreadable, staring at the magical light, which still showed no signs of diminishing. There was something discomfiting about the way he looked at it, but Solène couldn't put her finger on exactly what.

"We've left out some objects," dal Drezony said, gesturing. "For the levitation test, you must lift one—any one of your choosing—to a height no lower than your knee, and hold it there until I tell you to stop. You should try to keep it as motionless as you can."

Solène glanced at her light, which still shone brightly, boosting her confidence. Several dumbbells and weights of varying sizes had been laid out on the floor; she wondered if she should read anything into the selection. As soon as she focussed on her desire to lift, they all rose.

Surprised, she nearly gasped, trying to conceal her reaction from the watchers. The objects juddered in mid-air and she had to fight to regain her concentration. She brought the weights up until they were level with her eyes, then held them perfectly still. She had only intended to lift one, and the fact that they had all moved unnerved her.

While it was satisfying to have more power than she'd expected, the over-reach also indicated the lack of control dal Drezony had spoken of. At dal Drezony's nod, Solène lowered the weights to the floor. She felt a little light-headed and had to take a step to steady herself, but she didn't think anyone noticed.

"It was only necessary to lift one, but we appreciate the demonstration of what you can do," dal Drezony said. "Now, the third test. The push."

She drew Solène's attention to a large burlap sack filled with some sort of bulky material. "This approximates the weight of an average-sized man. You need to push it back a minimum of three paces."

Solène concentrated on the sack. She thought of Arnoul, of his hands reaching for her, and with a cry, she hurled her will against the sack, blasting it across the floor more than twice the required distance. When she had composed herself, she was relieved to see that she hadn't turned it into a pig.

"The barrier next," dal Drezony said.

The others remained conspicuously silent, closely watching every move Solène made. She did her best to ignore them, but it wasn't easy. This test gave her the most cause for concern. She had never attempted anything even close to creating any sort of "barrier" and had no idea where to start. She furrowed her brow. How did she do everything else? Desire seemed to be the key, and anything that made the desire stronger was a boon.

Closing her eyes, Solène imagined herself in the clearing on the road to Mirabay when they had encountered the highwaymen. One of them was pointing his small crossbow at her. She visualised his finger on the trigger, starting to press, the lever starting to move, the tense string waiting to fire the bolt. Even as she imagined the click of the trigger and the thrum of the bowstring, she allowed her instinct for survival to guide her mind. Her heart quickened.

"Impressive," dal Drezony said. "I've not seen one so strong as to be physically visible before."

Solène opened her eyes. A glowing blue hemisphere surrounded her.

"Your Grace, would you like to do the honours?" dal Drezony said.

The Prince Bishop smiled, and nodded.

"Maintain the shield now, Solène," dal Drezony said.

Panic flashed through her but Solène nodded. Would they actually do something like fire a quarrel at her? Would her shield stop it, or was it simply an illusion?

The Prince Bishop walked forward, drawing the dagger from his belt. Reversing the weapon, he tapped the pommel on the shield. There was a dull thud at the impact and the glowing blue energy indented at the point of contact, as though the dagger pressed against something soft. He pressed harder, but the shield didn't give. Solène's heart raced; she willed the shield to hold with all she was worth.

The Prince Bishop turned back to the others. "I can't get through," he said. "It's absolutely solid." He re-sheathed the dagger and returned to his earlier position. "Time for the final test," he said.

Relaxing, Solène released the shield. Her vision swam and it was all she could do to keep her balance. She forced a smile in dal Drezony's direction, though she couldn't really see the woman, just a blur. What was happening to her?

"The final test," dal Drezony said. "The stillness." She called out for an attendant, who came into the hall carrying a wooden cage. When he set it on the floor and opened it, a startled chicken ran out. Solène's vision had returned and she laughed when the animal dashed across as the floor. If she didn't manage to complete this test, someone would have quite a job chasing it down.

She thought about calming the chicken, with no effect. Changing her approach, she imagined it slowing down, as though it was wading through treacle. Gradually its movements became less frantic, until it moved as though it was getting sleepy and running out of energy. Solène realised everyone in the room was moving slowly. Dal Drezony was speaking, but her words were slurred and impossible to understand. Solène turned, intending to ask her to repeat herself, but the world grew dark and she fell to the floor.

Guillot was a sweaty mess by the time he reached the agreed-upon meeting spot near the entrance to the cavern. His undershirt was soaked through, his eyes stung, and his legs felt like jelly. The short time he had been wearing armour again had not been long enough to re-accustom him to it, nor was his fitness sufficient to carry the extra weight. He sat heavily on a large, flat rock near the others and prayed to any of the gods who would listen to help him recover quickly.

"You're looking a little worse for wear, Guillot," dal Sason said in a whisper. "Are you all right?"

Guillot cast him a sideways glance. Other than some extra colour to his cheeks, the banneret looked as though he had undertaken nothing more than a morning constitutional. The rest of them looked even fresher, and Guillot knew he couldn't put it down to age—Leverre was at least five or six years older than he. Forced to admit that he had been found wanting, he gave dal Sason a wry smile.

"I've not been as diligent with my training these past few years. Didn't expect to find myself on a dragon hunt. If I had, I'd have been sure to prepare."

"Brother Hallot will take care of that," Leverre said, his whisper sounding raspy. He nodded toward Guillot, looking at Hallot, and the red-haired Spurrier scrambled over the loose rocks to reach them.

"Try to relax," Hallot said. He closed his eyes and held his hands out, palms only a hair's breadth from Guillot's body, but not touching.

At first, Guillot felt nothing. Then—and it took a moment to be certain he was not imagining this—his heart slowed its pounding and his legs started to feel fresher. The stinging, gritty sensation around his eyes from a night of little sleep also disappeared. Soon he felt better than he could remember.

"Well, that's quite something," Guillot said, when Hallot opened his eyes and drew back his hands. "Does it work on hangovers too?"

Leverre let out a short laugh—the first time Guillot had heard him do so.

"It works on anything," Hallot said. "Comes in quite handy. Wish I'd been able to do it when I was at university, although you don't seem to be able to do it to yourself for whatever reason."

"Enough reminiscing," Leverre said, any vestige of good humour gone. "We need to get ready."

Leverre moved toward the cavern's entrance, stepping carefully in an effort to be as quiet as possible. When he drew close, he got down on his belly and crawled forward until he could peer inside. He lay still for a moment, and Guillot's heart quickened again as he wondered what the Spurrier might be seeing. As if in response, Leverre turned and silently mouthed the word "nothing." Guillot did not know whether to be elated or disappointed, but the former seemed to be claiming the victory.

"What do we do now?" dal Sason whispered.

Guillot shrugged. "Wait until it comes home?"

As he thought about it, lying in wait for the dragon somewhere was an attractive option. The element of surprise could tip the balance in their favour—if he discounted a great number of variables like potentially superior sight, smell, or hearing. The dragon might be able to hear the beating of his heart from miles away, for all he knew.

"We should go in and take a look," dal Sason said.

Guillot shrugged again. He had to admit dal Sason was probably right; it was foolish to come all that way and not at least have a snoop around. Standing, he gave Hallot a nod of approval when he realised how good his legs felt. Not only was the fatigue gone, they felt good and strong, much as they had when he had trained hard on a daily basis. Perhaps there was something to be said for magic after all. He didn't like the idea of men and women who could win battles with the power of their minds, or whatever they used, but healers who could do what Hallot had just done could change the world for the better. That much was undeniable.

Following Leverre's path, Guillot shuffled up beside the Brother-Commander at the edge of the entrance. Inside, he saw nothing but black, swirling darkness.

"You said something about a back chamber," Gill whispered. "Might it be resting in there?"

Leverre nodded. "That was where it was when we were last here. Might be this time, too. We'll need to be careful."

"What'll we do for light?" Guillot said. "Lighting the place up will wake it for sure if it is back there."

"Close your eyes," Leverre said. "This won't last long—things will take on a greenish tinge when it starts to fail, so come to me when that happens and I'll refresh it."

"Refresh what?"

"Close. Your. Eyes."

Guillot did, and felt Leverre touch a finger to his forehead.

"Open."

Guillot looked around the cavern in amazement. The interior of the cavern was covered in a coruscating blue glow. The walls themselves were the source of light, and although it was not bright, he could make out everything.

"You weren't lying when you said magic can make life easier, were you?" Guillot said.

Leverre raised his hands and shrugged, then resumed studying the cave. Guillot did likewise, quickly spotting a partially stripped set of ribs amid a pile of other bones that he could not specifically identify. They looked human, though, and Guillot suspected they were the remains of Leverre's previous command. He wondered how the man must feel to see them there, eaten and denied a proper funeral. If circumstances allowed, perhaps the dragon hunters would give the bodies a proper burial before returning home.

He continued to survey the cavern, but other than the bones, saw nothing of note, or, more importantly, nothing that indicated danger. He realised the others had gathered behind him, and technically, he was the dragonslayer, so . . .

"I'm going in for a closer look," he whispered.

Leverre nodded.

Guillot tested his grip on the spear, then hauled himself over the cavern's lip. He stood tall and took a deep breath before stepping forward into the beast's lair. Everything he did felt like one of the old Silver Circle stories, and he had to fight to silence the narrator in his head, who recounted every move he made, even when he scratched his arse. He couldn't quite see that making it into the tale of *their* adventure.

He continued into the cavern, doing his best to avoid the scattered bones while paying attention to everything around him. After a moment, he heard movement behind him, which was a relief—he didn't want to be stuck in the back of the cavern on his own when his magical night sight failed. He held the spear at guard and tracked his gaze with the tip, ready to strike at whatever came into view. However, there was nothing before him but rock.

He kept walking, his feet finally starting to remember their old precision of movement without conscious effort. When he was roughly in the centre of the cavern, he stopped and slowly turned around to look back at the others, who had ventured in behind him. Leverre gestured to the left and Guillot went that way. Although it was difficult to make out, the glow seemed to indicate a large passage into an antechamber. Entering the passage, he felt as if his stomach were being gnawed on by rats, so strong had his anxiety grown. He almost wished the beast would appear in front of him and get it over with. Despite Hallot's rejuvenative treatment, his heart was working far harder than it had been in a very long time, and the ever-building tension didn't help.

Rounding the corner, Gill was greeted with the antechamber. The empty antechamber. He let out a sigh of relief and took a quick look around, realising he had come to the back of the cavern—it went no farther. His gaze then returned to what he had been trying to ignore while seeing if there was any danger present. Shaped like an enormous bird's nest was a great pile of gold. Coins, goblets, plate—an example of almost anything that could be made from gold was present. He tried to pick up a coin, but it had been fused to the mass. There was more fortune there than any man could spend in ten lifetimes, but he would need a hammer and a chisel to get it out.

Satisfied that there was nothing else of note present—namely the dragon—Guillot headed back to the main chamber, walking more quickly and taking less care of his footing. He had gone only a few paces into the main chamber when he stubbed his toe on something hard and let out a swear. His heart jumped into his throat, and he scanned the room very carefully in case his exclamation had wakened a slumbering dragon that his initial inspection had missed. When he was satisfied there was no danger, he looked down at what he'd bumped into. The blue glow seemed different around it, not so intense, as though the object was sucking in the light around it.

He knelt, being careful of his spear, and prodded at the thing with a gloved hand. It seemed metallic and was partially buried. Curious, Guillot set down the spear and worked the object free. It was a small spherical pot with a flat bottom and an ornate rim that looked to be carved with symbols; he couldn't make them out in the odd blue light. It fit neatly into the palm of his hand.

To his mind, it was too small to be a drinking vessel—not for the quantities he usually drank, at least. Perhaps it had been used to store spices or something, and the lid had been lost. In the ethereal blue glow, the dull metal looked like pewter, or perhaps lead. In the old stories, dragons were said to have coveted precious metals like gold, silver, and platinum, and this was definitely not any of those.

When he held it closer, he realised there were swirling blue lines on its surface, just like the ones on his sword. He pulled the sword half out of its sheath and tapped the object against the hilt. It rang out like a soft, musical note—just like what happened any time two Telastrian blades were struck against one another—confirming his suspicion that the little bowl was indeed made of Telastrian steel. The blue lines on its surface seemed to be drawing in the glow of his night vision. The ethereal blue glow made the experience so surreal that he couldn't be sure he wasn't just imagining it. Nonetheless, it was a curious thing to see.

"What have you got there?" dal Sason said, approaching.

"I don't know. A small pot of some sort. Seems to be made of Telastrian steel. Worth an absolute fortune back in Mirabay, I reckon."

"Curious how it got here," dal Sason said.

"My thoughts exactly," Guillot said.

"Part of the dragon's haul of treasure?" dal Sason said.

Guillot laughed. "Oh, you haven't seen the half of it, but we've got a bigger fish to fry, so it'll have to wait. Leverre, can any of your people tell how long since the dragon was last here?"

"I don't know, but we can try." He and the other Spurriers conferred for a moment, then spread out around the cavern and began to do something that looked like they all badly needed to use the outhouse. Dal Sason gave Guillot an uncomfortable look. Guillot shrugged. After the way Hallot had freshened him up, he wasn't going to criticise magic any time soon.

Leverre opened his eyes and looked straight at Guillot. "It's been here recently," he said. He looked at the cup in Gill's hand. "What's that?"

"No idea," Gill said, dropping it into the purse on his belt. "Found it on the ground."

Leverre opened his mouth to say something, then abruptly turned his head to the cavern's entrance. "I think it's coming back!"

Guillot's heart started to race again. Part of his mind wanted to fall back on his substantial military training and experience, but the voice of doubt screamed that it was all irrelevant, that to use methods applied to other men would get them all burned to a crisp, eaten, then dropped from a great height to fertilise the valley below.

"Spread out," he said. "Try to take cover. If we can surprise it, all the better, but be prepared for the fact that it might already know we're here."

As he looked around for concealment, Gill realised the blue glow had faded and taken on a greenish tinge.

"Leverre," he said. "The glow is fading."

Leverre reached forward to touch Guillot's forehead just as the glaringly bright opening of the cavern was plunged into shade.

"Get down," Guillot shouted. He grabbed Leverre by the scruff of the neck even as the other man restored his night vision. They fell into the hollow of an outcrop of rock, Guillot letting out a groan as Leverre landed on top of him. The cavern exploded with light and heat as a jet of flame filled the air. Guillot could feel the touch of the super-heated air against his skin, but the outcrop they lay behind spared them from the worst of the blast. Someone had not been so lucky—Guillot could hear an agonised scream from somewhere. His heart sank as he wondered who it was. It sounded like a man's voice, but there was so much noise in the echoey cavern that he couldn't tell.

The flames continued for what seemed like an eternity. Gill squeezed his eyes shut as sizzling air rushed over him and wondered how long the beast could keep it up—surely it had to run out at some point?

"Are you all right?" Leverre shouted.

Even so close, it was a struggle to hear him. "Yes. You?"

"It's hot!"

"I'd noticed."

As suddenly as it had started, the fire stopped. The cavern fell completely silent; the blood thundering through Guillot's body was the only sound. He tried to breathe as quietly as he could, difficult though it was with Leverre's weight on top of him. Would the beast think they were all dead?

"What do we do now?" Leverre said.

Guillot opened his eyes. He could see smoke rising from Leverre's head where patches of hair had been singed. Patting his own head, Guillot was thankful to find he seemed to have been spared.

"I suppose we should try to kill it," he said. He looked at his belek spear, which had fallen nearby. The once-thick shaft had been charred to not much more than half its former size. "Do you reckon it has any fire left?"

Leverre looked at him, wide-eyed and silent. Guillot could hear the scratching of the dragon's feet as it came farther into the cavern. He shuffled out from under Leverre and rolled across the ground to grab the spear. With little alternative, he stood up and turned to face the dragon. Despite his best efforts, he could not stop himself from gasping at what he beheld.

The creature was huge, almost entirely filling the cavern mouth. It was covered in polished black scales, part serpent, part—he didn't how else to describe it. It stood on four limbs; two enormous wings were neatly folded on its back. Its tail was so long that the end still lay outside the cavern, and he could see several wicked-looking barbs on it. Poised on a long neck extending from muscular shoulders, its head resembled the shape of a dog's, with an elongated snout containing an array of razor-sharp teeth. A small horn rose at the tip of its nose between two large nostrils, and it had a pair of horns on the crown of its head that curved backwards into wicked points. Its eyes were huge amber orbs; Guillot saw they had black, slit pupils like a cat's, constantly changing size and shape as the beast regarded its surroundings.

Gill had to remind himself to breathe. He had grown up on stories of dragons, fearsome beasts that terrified children, but he had also known—as surely as he had known the sun would set each evening and rise the day following— that dragons were long dead. Until this moment, part of his mind still refused to believe what he had seen that night in Villerauvais, but now? Here it stood before him, and he was sober—he could not deny it. Despite his fear, he had to acknowledge what a magnificent creature it was. It seemed a shame to have to slay it, but everything about it was designed for the kill, from its fangs and horns to its talons and the barbs on its tail. It had killed so many people. People that had deserved better lives. He had failed them while they lived. If it took his death to make amends, so be it.

CHAPTER
29

Guillot surveyed the cavern to see if he could identify who had been caught in the flames. It was impossible to tell—he could make out some charred remains, and barely see the survivors taking cover behind rocks amidst all the smoke. He returned his attention to the dragon, who continued to ignore him. It was a curious thing to study the beast when it seemed to be unaware of his scrutiny. It sniffed at the air, causing the smoke to swirl against the backdrop of the cavern mouth. Guillot hefted the spear in his hand and swallowed hard.

"Hey!" he shouted.

The dragon's head snapped around to face him, pupils narrowing as it fixed its glowing amber eyes on him. It felt like the beast was staring into his soul. Guillot looked over the beast's body, wondering where to deliver his blow. The eyes were always a soft target, but unless the thrust was perfectly delivered and reached all the way to the brain, it would only enrage, not kill. A spear driven through the body was always a good bet. Living creatures had too many vital parts for such a strike not to hit anything important.

He targeted the dragon's chest and charged. He was wound tight with tension, and unleashing it was a great relief. Sparing a word of thanks for Hallot's healing magic, Guillot powered through each step. The dragon watched him approach, making no attempt to move. Was it confused? Or did it simply not care?

Guillot shouted in satisfaction as he felt the spear's tip strike home. The beast's scales were tough, like armour plate, and he felt the shaft flex as he tried to drive it through. With a great crack, the fire-damaged wood gave way and Guillot stumbled forward with nothing but a useless piece of lumber in his hand. With a tremendous blow, the air was knocked from his lungs and he was sent sailing through the air. He had enough time to decide that the dragon must have swiped at him with its paw, luckily without bringing its claws to bear, before he hit the ground with a clatter of metal plates.

Breathless from the impact, Guillot struggled to his hands and knees. The monster had turned to face him, and now bared its fangs, letting out a long, screeching hiss. Gasping, Gill finally managed to draw air into his lungs; he flung the remains of the spear shaft at the dragon. The cavern exploded into light and he felt hot air rush over him. With a burst of agility that would have done him credit on his finest day, Guillot flung himself to the side, his exposed skin stinging from the flame that passed through the space he had occupied a second before.

When the flame stopped, Gill checked himself over. He was grateful he hadn't been able to breathe during that last manoeuvre—the air sizzled with heat that would have seared his lungs had he drawn it in. His armour was blackened and blued from the heat, and would likely never be fit for public wear again, but he seemed to be physically intact. His night vision had failed during the fiery onslaught, so it was the war cry that alerted him to Leverre's attack. He heard the clatter of metal, and from the dragon's lack of reaction, assumed the strike had been ineffective. Its eyes glistened in the darkness, fixed on Guillot a moment longer before it turned away.

With the dragon's attention elsewhere, Guillot drew his sword and looked for a place to strike. He made for the dragon's flank and the join between body and wing. He heard a cry that could only have come from Leverre, then the voices of the others; an instant later they were all drowned out by the dragon's great, reverberating roar. The sound seemed to bounce off the cavern walls and assault Guillot's ears a dozen times.

Raising his sword with both hands, he made to stab the patch of softer-looking flesh where the dragon's wing connected to its body. The creature moved, putting his aim off, but the sword's tip bit into the dragon rather than glancing off its scales. He drove the blade in as deeply as he could, then pulled it out for a second strike. The dragon turned quickly, letting out another roar, and swiped at Guillot with its paw, but he managed to roll out of the way. As he did, he spotted Leverre lying on the cavern floor. The dragon turned away and lit the cavern with fire. Guillot couldn't hear any screams above the sound of the flames and the dragon's roaring. It disappeared into the smoke and darkness as he got to his feet. Guillot knew he had hurt it, but he didn't seem to have slowed it in the least. His body protested as he tried to stand straight, and his vision swam. He wished that he were anywhere else.

The cavern was becoming ever more choked with smoke and it was growing difficult to breathe. His throat burned and his eyes were streaming water. The smell of roasted meat was on the air, but Guillot did his best not to think about it. He tried to orient himself, but could not make sense of the hellish inferno before him. He had banged his head at some point and now struggled to think of what to do next.

He realised there was no way they could win in the cave. They had been fools to try to fight the beast in its lair. They had to get out or they would all die.

He went to Leverre, hacking on the thick smoke. Leverre was moving, but had been knocked senseless. Guillot sheathed his sword, grabbed the other man under the armpits, and dragged him toward the light of the cavern's mouth.

"Dal Sason!" he shouted. "We have to go." He wasn't sure if anyone heard him. The dragon continued to thrash about in the smoky darkness, occasionally issuing bursts of flame. When he reached the cavern mouth, Guillot laid Leverre on the ground and drew his sword, peering into the cave. He could just about make out the dragon, its lumbering shape causing great swirls in the smoke.

Every fibre of his being screamed at him not to plunge back in, but he knew how he would feel if he did not at least try to get the others out. He took a few deep breaths of sweet, fresh air, and then, covering his mouth with one hand, went back into the cavern.

After a few steps in near total darkness, he began to think this was an exercise in futility. Something struck him and he flinched, fearing it was a talon or that wickedly barbed tail. He felt no pain, so he patted himself down and was horrified to find his hand covered in sticky blood. For a moment he panicked, then, realising the object that had struck him was still at his feet, he knelt. It was Brother Quimper's head, and part of his torso.

Guillot fought down the urge to vomit. He had felt momentary flashes of panic on the battlefield, where his instincts demanded he turn and run. He had always overcome it, but never had he felt that compulsion so strongly as he did now. He couldn't see where the beast had gone, though the smoke was starting to clear.

He spotted movement not far away, and crept over, staying low and relying on the thicker smoke at the back of the cavern to shield him. He heard a groan and found dal Sason, lying on the ground not far from Banneret Eston.

Eston's skull was split in two, its contents spilling onto the rock below. It was a gruesome sight, but would have been a quick death. Dal Sason was still breathing and appeared to be free of any major injuries.

"Nicholas, can you hear me?" Guillot spoke quietly by the banneret's ear.

Dal Sason groaned, his breathing laboured. Guillot heard an angry rumble from the back of the cavern, followed by the sound of movement. He grabbed dal Sason and hauled him up onto his shoulders. He was convinced that Hallot was the source of that first agonised scream, and someone making such a sound does not survive it. He took a quick look around for Sergeant Doyenne, without success. There was something deeply unchivalrous about the idea of leaving without finding out her fate. He thought of calling out to her, but the risk of drawing the dragon's attention was too great.

At the cavern mouth, Guillot unceremoniously dumped dal Sason beside Leverre, who was starting to come to his senses. Dal Sason groaned again.

"Eston and Quimper are dead," Guillot told Leverre. "I think Hallot is too. I'm not sure about Doyenne."

Leverre nodded with an expression that said he knew Guillot was talking to him, but couldn't understand what he was saying.

Guillot cast a glance back into the smoke-filled cavern, hoping to see Doyenne stumble out of the gloom. He thought about asking Leverre for one of his magic touches of night sight, but knew at a look that the man was incapable at the moment. Guillot took a deep breath of fresh air, a panacea to his stinging throat, and sighed.

"I'll be back in a moment," he said.

▲▲▲▲▲▲

Guillot found Sergeant Doyenne at the back of the cavern. The setting sun had dropped to just the right height to fill the cavern with its failing light. It became clear that the notable absence of the dragon while Guillot was rescuing the others was down to Doyenne. The smoke had cleared, revealing the woman standing a few paces in front of the beast, which had, if Guillot were to attribute human expressions to it, a look of bewilderment on its face. Doyenne looked to be concentrating fiercely. Her feet were firmly planted on the cavern floor and she held one hand out in front of her, her index finger extended.

"Quickly," Guillot said, "we have to go."

Doyenne's eyes flicked to him for an instant before returning to the dragon. She seemed tired. Exhausted.

"You go," she said. "Get the others out if they still live."

"I'm not leaving you," Guillot said.

"I'm already dead. I'll hold it here as long as I can."

"What in hells do you mean?" Guillot said. "Come now, we can all get out."

"No, we can't," she said. "I've burned myself out and I'm not going to last much longer. Now go!"

There was such ferocity in her voice that Guillot didn't even consider disobeying. He ran back to the others. Leverre looked more alert and dal Sason showed improved signs of life.

"Where're the others?" Leverre said.

"Dead," Guillot said. "Doyenne is in there with the dragon. She wouldn't come out. Said she was already dead. Burned out. What in hells was she talking about?"

"I'll explain later," Leverre said, a grim look on his face. "We will be too if we don't get moving."

"Help me with dal Sason," Guillot said.

They each grabbed dal Sason under the arms, and with his feet dragging behind him, pulled him out of the cavern, and down the mountainside as quickly as they could.

Going downhill was easier than the reverse, but only marginally. With each step, the scree beneath their feet gave way and they slid several paces. That made for a fast descent, but Guillot expected a leg-breaking fall at any moment. He refused to look back for fear of what he might see; the sick feeling of wondering what had happened to that brave young woman kept him company the whole way.

Almost before he knew it, his feet were wet again, and they were pulling dal Sason across the river. Although he knew the sanctuary it offered was an illusion, there was something heartening about seeing the stand of trees where they had camped the previous night. The dragon could no doubt torch it, and them, with only a single breath, but Gill had convinced himself that once they reached it, they would be safe.

As soon as he reached the tree line, he collapsed to the ground, his face pressed into the dirt and the pine needles. Letting his mind focus on the prickly sensation, he tried to distance himself from the ordeal he had just been through.

"Are you all right?" Leverre asked.

"As all right as you can be after something like that," Guillot said. He allowed himself a moment longer to rest, then rolled over and sat up. He looked up at the cavern mouth from between the tree trunks. "Do you think it'll come after us?"

"It didn't the last time," Leverre said. "But who's to say. I saw you wound it. My sword just seemed to bounce off it."

"Lucky, I suppose," Guillot said. "Maybe it was the Telastrian steel?" He leaned over to check on dal Sason, who seemed to be breathing easier, but was still in bad shape. "Nicholas has seen better days."

"Nothing a session with a few of the Order's healers won't be able to fix," Leverre said. "I could do with one myself."

"You're not the only one," Guillot said, starting to notice all the bumps, bruises, and scrapes he had acquired now that the excitement was fading. "We should get away from here as quickly as we can."

"I'll send a pigeon from Trelain and get the Prince Bishop to dispatch help," Leverre said.

Guillot hauled himself to his feet. "Let's concentrate on getting ourselves to safety first."

CHAPTER
30

Solène felt groggy when she woke, as though her sleep had been interrupted in the midst of a particularly vivid dream. As she worked out what was reality, and what was imagined, she realised that dal Drezony was sitting at her bedside. She jumped in surprise.

"Oh, you're awake," dal Drezony said. "Such a relief. How do you feel?"

"Tired," Solène said. Her head was a muddle and her memory of the tests was fuzzy. "Did I pass the tests?"

Dal Drezony laughed. "Yes, with flying colours. The Prince Bishop was amazed by what you did. No one's managed to complete all the tests in one go before, and for that I have to apologise. The Prince Bishop wanted to see what you were capable of. I should have stepped in and stopped things, but I didn't, so I have to ask for your forgiveness."

Confused, Solène said, "You have it."

"I've so much to say to you right now, I really don't know where to start. The facts, I suppose."

Solène sat up on her elbows.

"You collapsed at the end of the test," dal Drezony said. "You were brought back to your rooms and have been watched constantly since."

"For how long?" Solène said.

"Since yesterday afternoon. All things considered, it could have been far worse. What happened to you is something we've come to call burnout. In the early days, it killed a couple of novices, so we've been careful about it ever since. We weren't sure if it would happen to you. I genuinely thought the tests lay well within your powers and was so eager to see what you're capable of. I didn't give it proper consideration. That was foolish and a mistake I won't be making again."

"I don't understand," Solène said. "What's 'burnout'?"

"We use the Fount to power our magic. As I told you before, it's anywhere that life is. It *is* life. It's within us, and is, as I and a number of others believe, what gives us our vital spark. However, when our internal reservoir of the Fount is drawn on too heavily, it affects us. A little will make you tired, a lot can cause you to lose consciousness, and even die.

"Part of what we train our novices to do is to draw on the Fount surrounding us, rather than the Fount within us. It's as though we use our own Fount as the spark to light the greater fire, but it at least means fatigue is the worst we have to worry about."

"So I drew on too much of my internal Fount?"

"Yes, I believe that to be the case."

"I had no idea that could happen," Solène said.

"You've probably never had to tax your magic so strenuously before, so it's never been an issue."

"I can remember being tired after using it a few times," Solène said, recalling how she had fallen asleep after her encounter with Arnoul.

"I should have brought it up earlier, but things have moved so quickly. I didn't think it would be important for some time yet." Dal Drezony drew a breath and smiled. "The Prince Bishop insists that you be initiated into the Order at once. On the one hand, he's right. There's no one else here even nearly as powerful as you. On the other, as long as you're untrained in managing your energy, you're as likely to kill yourself as achieve any of the feats he sees in your future."

Solène said nothing, still trying to understand.

"I'm not going to lie to you," dal Drezony said. "I argued against his decision as strenuously as I could, but at the end of the day, he is the Master of the Order, and his command has to be followed. I did convince him that you need more training, so you will attend on me daily to continue your education. Other than that, you will be given duties as an initiated Sister of the Order."

"What does that involve?" She was genuinely curious.

Dal Drezony smiled sadly. "Whatever the Prince Bishop says it does."

◢◢◢◣◣◣

Solène stood silently in the Priory's chapel. This was the not the first time she had felt life running faster than she could keep up with. Fleeing her village had terrified her—venturing out into the unknown, alone for the first time in her life. She wondered about her family often. They had been good, kind people who had loved her. They had reacted to her magic out of fear, and she found it difficult to blame them no matter how much it pained her.

A few weeks ago, she had been an apprentice baker who dreamed of opening her own bakery. Now she was dressed in magnificent cream robes with gold stitching, and the motif of the Order of the Golden Spur embroidered in heavy gold and silver wire on her chest. The Prince Bishop officiated the ceremony, and something about the way he looked at her made her uncomfortable. It was different than anything she had experienced before. Arnoul's glare had combined lust and hate; she had known what to expect from that, known she could deal with it.

That the Prince Bishop wanted something from her was obvious. He bore the expression of a hungry man staring at someone else's dinner—as if she had something he desperately wanted and he was trying to work out how to get it from her. As unnerving as that was, she wasn't so foolish as to not see the potential opportunity it brought. Considering her talent, she knew her life options were to live on the run and in fear, or remain at the Order. If she could work out what the Prince Bishop wanted, and how to give it to him at as little personal cost as possible, she could thrive there.

This was a dangerous option, however. If she could not deliver on whatever he expected from her, she was sure there would be consequences. The Order was not the simple, safe haven she had hoped it might be.

The Priory's chapel was the location for all of the Order's initiation ceremonies. Despite being headed by the Prince Bishop, dal Drezony had made it clear to Solène that the Order was not a religious organisation. Thus, Solène had not visited the chapel before. It was austere—cold stone, dark wood—a remnant of the Priory's earlier purpose. So rapidly did her mind race that she barely heard what the Prince Bishop said. Every so often he would pause for her response, which she gave with a nod of her head, as she had been instructed.

What if he wanted her to be a weapon? She'd had good reason to kill Arnoul for what he had tried to do to her, yet she had done something temporary to him that did little more than injure his dignity. She didn't think she had it in her to kill, and wouldn't be used as a weapon. What was her alternative, though? To run again?

"You are now an initiated Sister of the Order of the Golden Spur, and bear both the burdens and the benefits of that office," the Prince Bishop said, drawing her from her worries. "Go now, always mindful of your duties, and humble in the power you possess."

She nodded again, doing her best to avoid meeting his eyes, then walked from the chapel with dal Drezony at her side.

"How do you feel?" dal Drezony said when they reached daylight.

"No different than when I walked in," Solène said.

Dal Drezony laughed. "That sounds about right, but you're part of us now, and safe here. I can't tell you how much of a relief it was for me when I finally found my way here. My father used to not let me out of the house for fear I'd cast a spell on someone and end up on a pyre. Here, we can be who we are, explore it, and not fear what others may think. You don't have to worry about the Intelligenciers ever again. You're home."

Solène forced a smile. Until she knew what the Prince Bishop expected of her, she intended to reserve judgement.

Alpheratz lay in his cave, resting from the fight. He had expected his actions would eventually draw a response, so he was not entirely surprised by the encounter. Aside from the wound under his wing, it had been more of a learning experience than anything else. The humans who had woken him were taken unaware and were not powerful warriors. A group that had tracked him to his cave and attacked him should have been—but they were far weaker than he had expected. With the exception of the female at the end, who had strong magic and stronger courage, they were pathetic. The only wound he had taken was one of misfortune. Had the man who made the cut not had a Telastrian blade, Alpheratz knew he would have survived the encounter without even a scratch.

In one respect, it was disappointing. There had been glory in defeating the human warriors of old—"chevaliers" they had called themselves, although dragonkind had known them as "slayers." This battle had been little more than slaughter, and slaughter was something Alpheratz held a deep discomfort for. Each time he lay down to sleep, he saw the woman with the defiant eyes, and her offspring hiding behind her. Every time he thought of it, he felt shame. Shame that tore at the fibres of his heart. He thought of Nashira, and how she must have behaved when their hatchlings were attacked. The song of their souls had been the same—protect that which they loved. This wasn't the act of vermin.

What had he done? What was he doing? He was an enlightened dragon—a creature of magic and reason. This behaviour was beneath him. Beneath contempt. He banged his head against the cavern wall and let out an anguished cry. He had lost everything he knew, everything he loved, and his reaction had been to descend to unenlightened savagery. He cried out again. What was he supposed to do? How should he have reacted? Mankind had taken all from him. Where was the justice for that? The justice for Nashira and their hatchlings?

He knew the people who had wronged him were long dead. The people he had slain had never even seen a dragon before, let alone done one injury. There was no justice in killing them. Their spilled blood was his shame, his burden.

Mankind had grown weak. There was no glory in battle, nor honour in slaughter. He would do no more. The mountains stretched far to the west. He would depart the lands of men. He would find a new mountain and a new cave in a place no human could ever reach. Perhaps he might even find another of his kind, or perhaps some unhatched eggs that he could nurture to life. Hope was ever present in a world so huge.

Holding that thought in his mind, he found a peaceful sleep.

CHAPTER

31

A man wearing the Prince Bishop's livery waited outside her apartment when Solène returned after her evening meal. She had spent the day resting after the initiation, still feeling the effects of her overexertion during the tests.

"The Prince Bishop would like you to attend on him at the cathedral at seven bells. There is a carriage waiting at the gate to take you."

Dinner had started at six bells, which meant she was already either late, or very close to it. That wasn't the way she wanted to start things with him.

"Give me a moment to get my things," she said.

The messenger nodded and stepped back. Inside, clothes were spread everywhere—the past few days had been such a turmoil that she had not had time to keep anything organised. She looked about for her cloak—the new one she was entitled to wear as an initiate—and started digging through a mound of the novice robes that she had only needed for so brief a time. Finally she found what she was looking for and put it on as she headed out the door.

She rushed through the Priory's courtyards to the gate where the Prince Bishop's personal carriage awaited. She knew it was a continued sign of the importance he placed on her. She had never had to live up to expectations before, and was not finding her first taste of it at all palatable. Aside from it all, she felt awkward getting into such a plush conveyance.

The messenger sat up front with the driver, leaving her to the luxury of the interior in privacy. They jolted to a start and she could hear the driver shouting at the horses as the carriage accelerated down the road. Although it wasn't the most comfortable of rides, it was certainly exhilarating, as the carriage leaned over on its suspension springs rounding the corners.

The clatter of hooves and wheels on cobblestones signalled they were getting close—Solène had already learned that only the most central streets of the city were paved. Eventually, the carriage lurched to a stop with as much vigour as it had started. The messenger opened the door and held out a hand to help her down. It was treatment unlike any she had ever experienced. Only nobles and burgesses received such deference.

She followed the messenger into the cathedral's nave just as its great bell rang out seven times. It was a relief to have arrived on time, but the rushed journey left her feeling flustered, adding to her anxiety about the Prince Bishop.

He sat on a pew, making small talk with another churchman, who hung on the Prince Bishop's every word. When the Prince Bishop saw her, he actually looked relieved. He stood and walked toward her, stopping the other man mid-sentence.

"Your Grace," Solène said. "You wish to see me?"

"I do," he said. "I have something that I very much want to show you."

This innocuous statement was a relief, but Solène wondered what there might be in a cathedral that would be of interest to her. He led her to an alcove at the side of the nave, and then down a tight spiral staircase that must have brought them below the level of the river.

"The room I'm about to show you is a remnant of the building that was on this site before the cathedral was built," the Prince Bishop said. "It was used by the church in the days after the collapse of the Empire to collect and safeguard knowledge that my forebears knew would be lost in the turmoil that would follow. They were right. To the best of my knowledge, there is nowhere else in the world with so much material from old Imperial libraries."

Solène nodded, doing her best to seem interested while trying to work out where he was going with it.

"Much of the knowledge gathered here concerns the practise of magic," the Prince Bishop said. "Most of it, in fact."

They arrived at a large set of ancient double doors, which he unlocked and cast open. As soon as they had slammed to a halt, scores of magelamps illuminated down a long hallway lined with shelves. Solène's eyes widened. The vicar in Bastelle had a library in his church—it had consisted of one shelf. This place was enormous. To just count the tomes in this library would take weeks. Perhaps months. To read them? She wondered if a lifetime would be enough.

Books weren't the only things stored there. Many of the shelves she could see were more like honeycombs, with each little square niche containing what looked like a scroll.

"Impressive, isn't it," the Prince Bishop said. "I felt exactly the same way when I first saw it. I spend as much time as I can down here. So much forgotten knowledge. So much that the world actively shuns. If only they knew how much it could help them. Medicine, engineering, science—the knowledge here could take us into a new golden age. I hope that it will. This was where I came up with the idea for the Order."

"Why are you showing me this?" Solène said.

"Because I think you represent a great opportunity to usher in the new golden age in our lifetime. I have brought you here to learn. To acquire magical abilities that can make a real, positive difference in people's lives. To show them magic isn't all dark sorcery, that it can be an incredible force for good. I hope that one day soon, you'll be able to help your brothers and sisters advance more rapidly as well."

"I . . . I hope I do not disappoint," Solène said. What he spoke of appealed to her, but it was daunting. To be part of something so much bigger than herself, and to be expected to be such a huge influence on it, made her feel sick. "Where do I start?" Solène said.

The Prince Bishop laughed. "Wherever you want. I've set out some things that I've found particularly interesting, to start you off. Consider this library an adventure and follow wherever it leads you. The only rule is this: Before you try any magic, any at all, you must take it to Seneschal dal Drezony to discuss, and your first attempt at using it must be under her supervision. Do you understand?"

"Yes," Solène said.

"Good. My agreement with the seneschal stipulates that you spend mornings at the Priory—fencing, exercise, and lessons with her. The rest of the time, I expect you to spend here. There will be no other demands on you. You start tomorrow, but if you want to have a look around now, please do. There's something of a surprise awaiting you. I'll be disappointed if you can't overcome it, though." He smiled cryptically, but without malice. "My carriage will wait outside to take you back to the Priory whenever you're ready," he said as he turned to go.

Solène waited for the reverberating boom of the heavy doors closing behind him to subside before going over to look at the things he had left on a table. Her eyes widened when they fell on the text—it was unintelligible. It took her a moment to realise that it was written in old Imperial—essentially the language she spoke, but in a form over a thousand years old. That was the surprise, she assumed, and therefore her first test was to work out how to read it.

That could wait for the time being. She had never seen so many books in one place before. She hadn't even realised there *were* that many books. She spent her first hour wandering the shelves, occasionally taking down a volume for a closer look. They were all the same—every word in old Imperial. She would have to learn how to understand it, and quickly. She was too tired to start that evening, and daunted by the task that awaited her tomorrow.

▲▲▲▲▲▲

Amaury sat at his office desk and studied the note that had arrived by pigeon from Commander Leverre while he was showing Solène the archive. Sergeant Doyenne was a bad loss. He had sent her with Leverre so she could see the beast for herself, for before Solène, Doyenne was one of the Order's most powerful mages. She had, it seemed, demonstrated her strength and courage, but had lost her life.

As an intelligence-gathering exercise, it had been a success. They now knew more about their foe, primarily that it appeared to be vulnerable to Telastrian steel blades, and that it would not die easily. He would have to call in some diplomatic favours to get his hands on some Telastrian steel from the Ruripathians. Buying a blade was almost impossible—most bannerets who owned one would rather starve than sell it.

Losing Doyenne made him worried that killing the dragon might prove too great a challenge for the Order. He would have to direct Solène to seek information on dragons, and on offensive magic. He would also have to lean on dal Drezony to get Solène ready as quickly as possible. At his most optimistic, he reckoned they only had a matter of weeks before the dragon visited the first major settlement, and probably less. The time available to prepare her was best measured in hours rather than days.

His chief disappointment, one he had done his best to ignore until he had digested the rest of the information, was that Guillot still lived. Leverre stated that they needed the services of the best healer available. Perhaps Leverre was unable to do what the Prince Bishop required of him. Amaury made a note to send an assassin with the healer. It was a shame Ysabeau wasn't around to take care of Guillot. The certainty she brought to her assigned tasks would have been welcome at that moment. Hopefully the dragon had softened Gill up enough to make him an easy target.

All of this, however, was secondary to the line of text that had set his heart racing. They had found a small, cup-sized pot of Telastrian steel in the dragon's cave. Leverre had not been able to get a close look, but felt that it was almost certainly what they had been searching for. That seemed almost too much to hope for, but there were only two types of things made from Telastrian steel—sword blades, and objects that needed the metal's affinity to the Fount.

To Amaury, the Cup was the most important object in existence. It could change everything. He felt giddy at the possibility, and wondered if he should go to Trelain in person to take possession of the Cup. That might draw too much attention, however. He didn't want anyone else to know anything about the object.

With Solène in the Order, and the Cup soon to be his, it seemed as though everything was finally coming together. First, however, there was a dragon to deal with, and a stubborn drunk of a swordsman who would likely refuse to hand over the Cup. Leverre would have said in his message if he was unable to carry out his instructions, and even if he were, there was still dal Sason. He would tell the king Guillot was dead and that they had to move forward with the Order if they hoped to stop the dragon before it caused too much damage. This was risky; Amaury had no time to lose. Besides, it would soon be the truth, but with the added bonus that he would have the Cup and all that came with it.

CHAPTER

32

Leverre had sent a pigeon back to Mirabay from the gate house as soon as they reached Trelain. Loath as he was to have their failure reported, Gill was looking forward to meeting another of the Order's magical healers. He had fared better than the others, but every joint hurt and he was black and blue in more places than he could count. They had barely paused to take breath on the return journey—equally eager to make their report and get as far from the dragon as they could. The relentless pace had been hard on their already battered bodies—dal Sason had broken some ribs, Leverre complained of constant headaches, and Guillot felt like he'd been stampeded over. At times, the feather mattresses of the Black Drake inn were the only things that kept him going. Still, they were the lucky ones.

They had put dal Sason to bed and sent for a physician to ease his discomfort. Gill went down to the taproom to lose himself in the distractions to be found there, without much luck. The dragon was the only thing being talked about. News had arrived from Mirabay, making it official, and had been added to by the rumours seeping into the town from the countryside.

Travellers were talking about cutting short their stays, while the townsfolk were talking about leaving town until it was safe—and according to what he overheard, some already had. Others took the high ground of disbelief, thinking themselves too clever to be taken in by what had to be a joke. People were uncertain and confused. They knew they should be afraid, but couldn't quite believe the stories were true.

People whispered excitedly that the last of the Chevaliers of the Silver Circle had gone out to kill the beast. The Chevaliers' reputation was so famed that failure did not enter the people's minds. Unaware of the horrible deaths of Hallot, Quimper, Eston, and the ferociously heroic Sergeant Doyenne, the occupants of the taproom were eager to hear the story of the great slaying and to laud the only living dragonslayer. They hoped to see the great beast's head when it was brought back as a trophy.

Guillot wondered how they would react if they knew that the dragon was still very much alive and perhaps on its way to Trelain at that very moment. It didn't require a very active imagination to visualise the terror and panic, and all the things that went with them—rioting, looting, murder. Civic breakdown of the most severe kind. Once the dragon itself came into the mix, death and destruction on a mass scale could be added to the list.

He had failed again. Was it possible for a person to use up all their talent in their youth, leaving nothing for the remainder of their life? His mouth watered at the sight of an unfinished bottle of wine on the table next to him. He looked at his glass and jug of water and wanted to hurl them into the fire. Surely now, of all times, he could be forgiven a drink? What difference would it make anyway? It was unfair to have thought him capable of defeating a dragon. He was none of the things he had once been, just as the Chevaliers were none of the things they had once been by the time they went extinct.

He was reaching for the wine before he knew what he was doing. The bottle's mouth was against his lips an instant later, his nostrils filling with the bittersweet scent of ruby-red wine; the drips on the rim flooded his mouth with their rich flavour. He took a long gulp, draining what little remained in the bottle. A feeling of warmth wended its way down into his stomach, marking the wine's passage. An overwhelming sense of well-being followed. The tension in his shoulders and the tightness in his chest seemed to ease. Ever since they'd left the dragon's valley, he'd felt as though a cold hand had held his heart in a vice-like grip. Only now did that hand relax. His failure seemed to drift away from him, along with the pain of the destruction of Villerauvais, and the sorrow at Sergeant Doyenne's sacrifice.

He looked around for the barkeeper to order a bottle, but instead spotted the approaching Leverre, his face hollow, no doubt a result of the trauma of losing more people. Gill felt the blow himself, even though he had barely known them.

"I had begun to think the stories about you were untrue," Leverre said. "This is the first time I've seen you anywhere near a bottle."

Guillot blushed with shame. "It was here when I sat down," he said. "I was just going to call the barkeeper to take it away."

Leverre nodded in a way that said he didn't care if it was a lie or the truth.

"I'll be glad when the healers get here," he said, sitting down. "I can't seem to get rid of this headache. I've been chewing willow bark all evening, but it's not making the slightest difference."

"Bad blows to the head can be like that," Guillot said, growing angry with himself for having given in to the bottle. "I've had one or two that took days to ease off. You're lucky to have your healers."

"It's the way of the future. Once people get a taste for it, they'll never want to give it up."

"I've heard the same said of dream seed," Guillot said. *And wine*, he thought.

"Dream seed will make you feel good for a while, then kill you, but not before robbing you of everything that's worth having." Leverre lowered his voice. "Magic can bring an end to pain and suffering."

"It can also bring death, destruction, power-hungry despots."

"That was a thousand years ago and more," Leverre said, sitting back in his chair with a disgusted look on his face. "The Order has been specifically created to make sure that no one person can have too much power."

"I thought the Prince Bishop was the Order's master?"

"In name only. The real business is divided between the marshall, the seneschal, and the chancellor. We never agree on anything, so you won't have to worry about us trying to take over the world."

Guillot forced a laugh. "I have a great many things to worry about before I come to that one."

Leverre gave him a thin smile. "I'm sure you do."

Guillot took the small Telastrian steel cup from his purse and placed it on the table, spinning it between his fingers, trying to distract himself from having to talk to Leverre and to take his mind off the taste of wine. He still couldn't get his head around the reason why someone would use such an expensive metal to make a drinking cup.

"That's the thing you found in the cave, is it?" Leverre said. "What do you think it's for?"

Guillot suppressed a sigh, supposing he should have expected the inquiry. "No idea," he said. "I found it with the dragon's stash. It was the only thing that wasn't fused to the mass. Not sure why I took it. A souvenir, I suppose."

Leverre nodded, but didn't say anything. Guillot couldn't help but notice how he stared at it with far more curiosity than Guillot would have expected. It was Telastrian steel, so would bring a decent price should he choose to sell it, but beyond that it was unremarkable. He put it back in his purse and stood.

"I'm going out for a breath of air," he said. "I won't be long."

Guillot returned later that evening, having spent the time wandering the streets, watching the townsfolk react to the news of a dragon. For some it was business as usual—if they were concerned about being attacked, it didn't show. Others, mostly those with money, were reacting. When he passed by the houses of the wealthy, he saw carts and carriages being loaded. Likely those people had properties elsewhere, so their flight would be no great inconvenience. Guillot's failure would have little impact on them. As always, the most vulnerable would suffer most from his mistakes.

He went to dal Sason's room to see how he was doing, and found Leverre there as well. The local physician had paid one visit before disappearing from Trelain, so until the Prince Bishop sent help, dal Sason's care was left to Guillot and Leverre, who didn't seem to have a healing touch. The injured man had a little more colour in his cheeks, but in his usual pessimistic way, Guillot supposed that could be the first sign of fever.

"How are you feeling?" he said.

"Like I got run over by an ox cart," dal Sason said. "But I'll mend. What are we going to do now?"

Guillot shrugged and sat in one of the chairs by the bed. Dal Sason's chest was heavily strapped and his breathing sounded strained. Until a healer arrived, he would have to make do with the conventional treatment of bandages and a poultice the physician had given them. It smelled like horse piss.

"I'm going to Mirabaya to deliver my report in person." Leverre said. "I've never trusted pigeons. Too many things can go wrong. Hawks, cats . . ."

"What will you tell High Lord Prince Bishop Amaury?" Guillot said.

Leverre frowned. "That our attempt was unsuccessful, and we need to reconsider our approach."

"Long way to go to tell him we failed and got four people killed."

"We learned some things," Leverre said. "It wasn't a complete failure."

"It was an expensive way to learn that we didn't have a clue what we were doing," Guillot said, dropping his head into his hands and rubbing his temples. He thought of Sergeant Doyenne and the complete lack of fear in her voice, even though she knew she was about to die. He thought of all the people who had died at Villerauvais, and who knew how many others the dragon had already killed. How many more were to come? How many more had they failed?

Had he done something to anger the gods? Everyone knew they disliked hubris, and once upon a time his name had been big enough that perhaps they had noticed him, and were displeased with what they saw. He shook the thought from his head.

His father had always said that a man makes his own destiny, with a sword in his hand, and for everything positive Guillot had achieved in his life, that had been true. It was only when he'd started to take success for granted that things started to go wrong. He wondered when it had begun, when the polish on his career showed its first signs of tarnish. He'd always thought Auroré's death was the moment, but he knew in his heart that wasn't true.

No. It had been a cold, wet day on the other side of the Szavarian border months earlier, surrounded by dead men nearly as numerous as the blades of grass on the ground. He had come back to Mirabay bathed in as much glory as he had been in blood on the battlefield. Hero of Mirabaya, her most famous son, he was initiated into the Silver Circle, and took relief in the thought that he would never be sent to war again. Too much relief.

Since then, to be honest with himself, he had drifted. Into marriage, the Silver Circle, into all that came after. He had drifted into this mission, into the dragon's cave, and had even drifted to defeat. If he was to face the beast again, he had to take charge of himself. He had to be the man he once was, before life had dulled his edges. Could he find that man again? Did he still lurk within?

"When we try again," he said, "we can't go into it as if we're hunting a belek. We need to know more about it. To be better prepared."

"How do we go about doing that?" Leverre said.

"Like you said, we learned things. We have to sit and discuss exactly what we experienced. What worked. What didn't. We need to distill every little bit of information that we can, from start to finish. Every detail, no matter how trivial."

"You think it will make a difference?" Leverre said.

"It can't hurt," dal Sason said. "We can't go running to the Prince Bishop every time we run into an obstacle."

"Still," Leverre said. "I have to make sure he is updated on our situation."

"Run back to your master, then," Guillot said, his voice laden with frustration. He wondered if Amaury would delight in Gill's failure or if the danger was great enough to rob him of the pleasure.

Leverre's face darkened.

"Gentlemen, please," dal Sason said with a wheeze.

"I am part of a command structure, and I have orders to follow," Leverre said.

"If you need to return to the city," dal Sason said, "there's no point in wasting time. You should leave as soon as you feel ready."

"I'm ready now," Leverre said, rising to his feet.

Guillot might have found Leverre's thoughtless devotion to duty tedious—his willingness to set off on another journey after dark—but he had to acknowledge that there had been a time when he behaved the same way.

"I'll see to having your horse readied while you pack," he said, getting to his feet.

Leverre nodded in appreciation. "I'd like to take that odd little cup you found with me. Proof that we went into the cavern, if it's needed. There's also a slim chance we might be able to learn something from it."

"Like what?" Guillot said, surprised at Leverre's interest.

"I, well, that's what we'd be finding out. As you said, we can't leave anything out."

"It's a piece of Telastrian steel. It looks like a small cup, the type one might use with a flask. Other than the dragon being partial to a tipple, what do you think it's going to tell us that we don't already know?"

Leverre sighed. "I'm grasping at anything and everything. You should be too."

"All the same," Guillot said, his suspicions raised. "I think I'll hold on to it for the time being." Leverre had already admitted that the Spurriers had been looking for something magical when they first went to the cavern. Surely the little cup could not be it? It had been discarded on the cavern floor. Gill couldn't see anything interesting about it. Given that it had not earned a place on the gold pile, the dragon didn't seem to place any value on it either.

Leverre chewed his lip for a moment, then nodded. "If that's what you wish. I'll gather my things."

Guillot watched him walk away for a moment, wondering at his interest in an unremarkable object, before heading out to the stables to have Leverre's horse saddled.

CHAPTER

33

Solène returned to the archive as soon as she had finished her morning requirements at the Priory. She gathered a few volumes and folios at random, then sat and stared at them, willing them to make sense. Some passages were close enough to the modern script for her to eventually understand, but it was slow going, and there were large sections she couldn't make any sense of. At first, she thought this might be due to her lack of formal education, but it quickly became clear this was not the case—the old books were written in a different script to the one in modern usage.

After a while she went for a wander amongst the shelves, trying to clear her head, and hoping for inspiration. She had not gone far when she heard the doors boom open. Peeking out from behind a shelf, she saw the Prince Bishop walking toward her in his usual purposeful way, his pale blue-and-gold robes billowing out behind him.

"Solène," he said, his voice echoing down the cavernous groin-vault roof. "Come and join me, there's something we need to discuss."

She nodded, surprised to see him back so soon, and walked up the central aisle toward him. "Is there a problem?" she asked, concerned by the solemn expression on his face.

"Please, sit." He pulled out a chair for her. "I've some bad news," he said. "I understand you were very fond of Guillot dal Villerauvais. Sadly he, and some of your Brothers and Sisters, were killed in their effort to stop the dragon."

"I thought he was supposed to be some type of special dragonslayer?" she said. Few people had ever shown her kindness without expecting anything in return for it. She was deflated by the thought that he had been killed.

"He was," the Prince Bishop said. "At least we thought he was. The Chevaliers of the Silver Circle were renowned dragonslayers in their time, but it seems whatever skill or attributes they had were not passed down to the present day. We had no way of knowing. We all hoped he would be able to deliver the kingdom from this danger, and considering the beast was attacking his lands, Gill wanted to do something about it. We thought he was our best chance. Now the gauntlet has been passed to us."

"What do you mean?"

"Who else can stop a beast like this but the Order?" the Prince Bishop said.

"I thought you said several members of the Order were already killed trying to slay it?"

"They were, but they weren't you," the Prince Bishop said.

"You want *me* to slay a dragon?" Solène said, shocked at the idea.

"I feel that given a little more time, and the resources available in this library, you will be more than up to the task. Obviously you need to re-target your studies to locate material that will be of use."

"I don't know," Solène said. "This sounds too much for me." She started to feel light-headed. "A dragon? How am I supposed to survive that? I nearly killed myself completing the Order's tests."

"Calm down, Solène," the Prince Bishop said. "I've already lost more people than I care to. I'm not going to send you into anything that you won't be fully prepared for. It'll mean some hard work and late nights because we don't have much time, but when you go, you will be ready. You'll have the support of the entire Order. If the dragon gets to a large city like Mirabay, the death and destruction it could wreak is unthinkable. Everyone needs your help to stop this beast. One way or the other, we will be going out to face it, and I'd very much like to have you with us."

She studied his face. He seemed to be sincere, but she had encountered many men who had seemed sincere and had proven to be anything but. Still, if the Order must go out to face the dragon, what choice did she have? She was one of them, and if she expected the benefits, she should be prepared to share the burdens.

"I'll do what I can," she said. "I'll start to look for anything that might help."

"Thank you," the Prince Bishop said. "That's all I can ask."

She didn't have the heart to tell him that she hadn't worked out how to read anything in that huge library yet. Instead, she smiled and nodded.

◢◣◢◣◢◣◢◣

The Prince Bishop left in a hurry. In the time Solène had known him, it seemed he was always in a hurry. When he was gone, and she was once more in peace in the cavernous archive, she considered the alteration in her task. What the Prince Bishop proposed both thrilled and terrified her. She had never been a person of importance before, and now she had the most powerful man in the kingdom asking for her help. That she was expected to help slay a beast that had just killed the finest swordsman in the realm was less appealing.

She hadn't known Guillot well, but in their short acquaintance, he had done as much for her as any person she had ever encountered. More. He had walked into a furious mob and saved her from an unimaginably terrible death, and though life had made him bitter, he had never been anything but kind to her. There weren't enough men like him in the world, and now there was one less. She had long since stopped grieving for things that were lost to her, but she could not shake the sadness that gripped her when she thought of Gill reluctantly riding to do his duty, with each step of his horse carrying him toward his death.

No one else had done half so much for her. Dal Drezony and the Prince Bishop were doing their best to win her over, but only because she had something they wanted. From the start, Solène had realised that the Prince Bishop's benevolence to her would only last as long as he found her useful.

She took a deep breath and let it out with a sigh. No matter how honourable her intentions, they would not be enough to bring down a dragon. If she couldn't find an answer in that great, cavernous library of forbidden knowledge, she would almost certainly meet the same fate as Guillot.

One thing she had learned since being introduced to the archive was that there was no cataloguing system, nor any organisation. Everything seemed to have been randomly shelved. She didn't have the first idea of how to go about searching for information on dragons. She could search for years and not find anything. That left only the question of if and how magic might be of use. What kind of magic crafting would guide her to the information she needed? How could magic seek out something as abstract as written knowledge? Solène fought to gain control of her thoughts. Despite everything, she had always considered herself an ordinary person. How could an ordinary person achieve what others had failed to? Of course, she knew she wasn't ordinary, but she was only starting to accept she was capable of far more than she might think.

Taking a deep breath, Solène concentrated on dragons. Somewhere in the echoing cavern of a library, there was a thud. Wound tight, she jumped and almost let out a shriek of surprise. There was no one else down here and the door was at the opposite end of the room. She walked to the central aisle and peered down toward where the sound had come from. Magelamps mounted at the end of every shelf cast pools of warm light into the aisle, but between the shelves, darkness quickly reclaimed the territory. She collected the small hand lamp from the desk and advanced down the aisle as silently as she could.

As she walked, she considered the magical defensive options she had and took some comfort in having those thoughts primed as she advanced along the aisles. There was no other noise in the library now, other than that of her rapidly beating heart. Reaching the shelf where she thought the sound had come from, she quickly popped her head and the hand lamp around the corner.

A large book, bound in well-worn leather, lay on the floor. Letting out the breath she had been holding, Solène studied the vacant spot on the shelf above. The shelf was deep, so there was no reason for the volume to have fallen, unless whoever had put it there had done so carelessly. Considering every other book in that row was perfectly placed, that seemed unlikely.

She took another look up and down the main aisle to satisfy herself that there was no one sneaking up behind her, then walked to the book and knelt. She brushed some of the thick coating of dust from the cover, then opened it and read the title page. Her heart sank when she saw the text was in old Imperial. Nonetheless, she could make out one phrase in the title:

Seolfor Cercle.

Silver Circle. A chill ran over her skin. Had she somehow drawn it from the shelf? Used magic without realising it? If her control was so tenuous, what damage might she to do others, or herself, as she grew more powerful? So much potential, but so much danger.

She had other things to worry about first, though. She picked up the book and returned to her desk, wondering how she would go about deciphering it, and what it would tell her.

Solène stared at the book's cover page. She knew the Chevaliers had an ancient reputation as dragon fighters, so she could see the relevance. However, until she could understand the text, it didn't matter *how* relevant it was. If magic could find the book, perhaps it could help with this also? She started to read, reaching out to the Fount for aid. A few pages in and her hopes began to fade. It wasn't becoming any clearer.

She sat back in her chair and let out an exasperated breath. If the Prince Bishop had figured out how to read this, then surely she could.

Something dal Drezony had said popped into her mind—words focus thoughts, and sometimes speaking out loud could help shape magic. She leaned forward and began to read aloud in as stentorian a voice as she could muster. She chuckled at the way her voice boomed down the cavernous archive, but continued, enunciating each oddly sounding word with precision.

All the while, she tried to keep her mind open to the Fount, willing its energy to coat her words. Her skin began to tingle as she continued for several pages. She was so focussed on pronunciation and the Fount that it took some time before she realised the words were making sense. With a loud, maniacal laugh of victory, she returned to the beginning. The print on the page was no different to her eyes than a news sheet produced that morning. She could read the entire title now: *The Rule of the Order of the Silver Circle.*

The book started with an outline of the characteristics that should be expected of a Chevalier, and not a single one tallied with what she had heard of their modern counterparts. It moved from there to descriptions of their various uniforms, from attending at the Imperial court, the governor's court, all the way down to daily wear when likely to be seen in public.

After several pages her enthusiasm began to wane. She couldn't see how anything here was important—just rule after rule about how the Chevaliers were supposed to conduct themselves.

She drummed her fingers on the table and licked her lips. The air was dry, probably a good thing considering the presence of so many irreplaceable books. She made a mental note to bring a water skin with her in the future, then returned to the book. She flipped page after page, then stopped. Her eyes were locked on a chapter heading.

Initiation Rites for New Chevaliers.

She recalled the Prince Bishop mentioning that he thought the Chevaliers' dragon-slaying ability had something to do with their initiation rites. Solène started to read, carefully and slowly, and her eyes widened with fascination. The ceremony itself had religious undertones, the themes of which were familiar, as the same gods that were worshipped in Imperial times still prevailed. The involvement of the Imperial mages interested her the most, however.

Anyone with even the most cursory knowledge of history knew how bannerets came to be, as magically enhanced bodyguards for the Imperial mages. When the mages grew powerful and greedy, the bannerets rebelled. The ensuing war tore the Empire apart, but freed the people from the mages' tyranny. Magic was outlawed, while the bannerets took on legendary, heroic status. Although they were no longer magically enhanced, they remained an important part of society. Every parent of a son, to some degree, harboured the dream of seeing them go to an academy to earn their banner. It was the great leveller, something a man from the most humble of origins could earn if he worked hard enough and had the talent.

In theory, at least. Solène had come from a poor farming village and had never even seen a banneret until she went to Trelain. It was hard to imagine that any of them had come from backgrounds similar to hers.

Candidates for the Silver Circle, it seemed, were selected from experienced bannerets. Battle-hardened veterans who were considered among the best fighters alive. The text said the ceremony extolled virtues such as honour, mercy, and charity, but did not specify exactly what was said. Then the new initiate stepped forward to be anointed by an Imperial mage, a very high-ranked one it seemed, although Solène didn't recognise the title given. They placed a drop of water from a cup—a cup referred to with great reverence—on the initiate's tongue, and the initiate became a Chevalier of the Silver Circle, an already formidable warrior now somehow magically prepared to do battle with dragons and survive.

Her cynical eye was quick to separate ceremony from anything that might have a real effect, and the cup was what stood out. It was possible the Imperial mages had the power to materially improve the initiates—they had been capable of feats that gave Solène a headache just to think about. However, the one thing she had quickly come to understand was that Imperial mages viewed magic as a science. That had put them at odds with the lands the Empire had expanded into, where it was viewed as a mystical concept, the interaction of the gods with the physical world. Nothing about what they had done, or the methods the Order was trying to adopt from them, wasted time on ritual when it came to the actual use of magic. Everything was considered, measured, and recorded. The cup had to have some significance or power of its own.

Her first instinct was to seek out information on this cup, but she was exhausted from the effort of deciphering the text. Every morning at the Priory was an early one, and she needed to keep her mind rested and sharp if she didn't want to end up injuring herself. It would have to wait until tomorrow.

Guillot woke the morning after Leverre's departure and glanced out the window, wondering how long he had slept. It looked close to noon, but after the past couple of days, he reckoned he could be forgiven for sleeping late. Although his body still hurt in more places than he could count, he felt moderately refreshed.

He turned his mind to how he would spend the next few days until help arrived. Dal Sason wasn't going anywhere and Gill had no desire to sit at his bedside and make small talk when the man wasn't sleeping. He got up and dressed, then stopped in the doorway of his room. The sweet scent of wine and ale carried up on the warm air from the taproom. How long could he stay there without giving in to temptation? A few days. Possibly a week. Perhaps more? He had already cracked, albeit briefly, and today he felt a little more balanced than he had at that moment.

Dal Sason wasn't in any danger from his injuries. All he needed was rest until the Order's healers got there, and Gill couldn't do much to contribute to that. He drummed his fingers against his thigh for a moment, then headed for the stable yard. He needed something to keep him out of the taproom.

"Saddle my horse!"

After taking a few minutes to gather what he needed for the trip, Guillot was clattering out of the town gates on his horse, on his way back to Villerau-vais, or what was left of it. The village had been preying on his mind ever since they had discovered it burned to ashes. Part of him couldn't believe that was true, insisting that it was some horrible dream so vivid that it had remained with him when he woke. He needed to look through the remains—make sure that whatever he could find got a proper burial.

He had gone several miles before realising he hadn't told dal Sason he was leaving for a few days, and considered turning back. That would likely mean him remaining in Trelain overnight, and then who knew what would happen?

He had gone several more miles before he remembered the last time he had felt so strong a compulsion to return to Villerauvais, to return home. It was just after his judicial duel, when he had been handed his banner—the small, embroidered flag every banneret received on graduation and could fly as a mark of honour—in shreds, the greatest dishonour a swordsman could receive. Worse than everything else. Almost everything else. All he had worked for had been falling apart around him, like a great, beautiful house of cards collapsing in chaos, but he still had somewhere to run to. Now there was nothing. Nothing but a black smudge on the ground.

He wondered what the dragon was doing at that moment, how many villages it would destroy and how many people it would kill before they were ready to try to slay it once again. It occurred to him that he might cross its path on his trip back to Villerauvais, and the thought sent a shiver down his spine. Despite everything that had happened, despite the rut he had allowed himself to slide into, he wasn't ready to die. Killing the dragon was more important, however. If that meant dying, he had to make peace with that.

Gill arrived not long after nightfall. Were it not for the fact that he knew the area so well, he might have completely missed it—there were no features to tell a traveller by night that a village had once stood there. Whether it was the fear of ghosts, or respect for the dead, he stopped some distance from the ruins to make his camp for the night. Despite himself, he slept soundly. There was, it seemed, something to be said for complete exhaustion.

▲▲▲▲▲

When Gill crawled out from his blankets the next morning and surveyed the place that had once been his home, he was dismayed. It was hard to believe that only days before, people had made their homes there. He circled the village, staying well clear of what would have been the town's boundary. How long would it be, he wondered, before grass and weeds reclaimed the ground? The task of digging through the ash to find bones would take days, or even weeks. He was no priest, so any words he said before putting them in the ground would have been hollow. It occurred to him that a far better tribute was to complete the task he had set himself. Kill the beast. Avenge his people.

He urged his horse in the direction of the manor house and spurred it to a slow trot. He could tell even from a distance that it had suffered the same fate as the town, but there were items in the house that were important to his family—jewellery, heirlooms, and such—and curiosity dictated that he at least check to see if any had survived.

With so many memories of the place—a building that had stood for centuries before he was born and which, he had thought, would stand for centuries to come—it was discomfiting to not see it there. It had been a stone structure, so he'd expected more of it to remain standing. With all the timber support—once concealed under carpets and behind plastered walls—burned away, it seemed to have simply fallen apart, the great chunks of cut limestone lying haphazardly around what had been gardens when his mother lived.

He tried to picture where everything had been, the study, the lounge, the kitchen—that was easy, as its great stone fireplace stood a lonely vigil in the centre of the ruin. The rest had nothing to mark its presence but Guillot's memory. He stepped over fallen stones into what had been the hall, his boots crunching on the cinders beneath his feet. He felt the numb anguish that often preceded tears, but none came. He had not lived in the house since he was a child, nor had he even visited it with any regularity, but he could not have predicted the effect its destruction had on him. So long as it had remained, there had been hope that one day he would come out of the shadows and properly take on the mantle of Seigneur of Villerauvais. Now that would never happen.

What could he do? Make another futile attempt against the dragon to prove he wasn't a coward? Would a heroic death redeem his destroyed reputation? Gill wandered through the remains, kicking at the ash and bits of debris, occasionally seeing something vaguely recognisable and trying to remember the last time he'd seen it intact. He had not gone far before he found himself staring down a flight of stone steps leading into darkness below.

At first Guillot thought he had reached the kitchen, beneath which there was a small wine cellar and ice store, but a quick glance at the lonely fireplace told him he was about where his father's study had been. He frowned and stared down the dark stairway, rummaging through the clutter of his memory for any old cellar he might have forgotten about. He had spent a lot of time in his father's study as a boy, playing with tin soldiers on the rug while his father worked at his desk. He couldn't remember any door other than the one that led in and out of the room, nor could he remember any flight of stairs leading to a second cellar. If he'd known it was there, he would have explored it—he had been a very curious child.

He went down several steps, his right hand instinctively resting on the handle of his sword, then stopped, realising that whatever was down there would be hidden by the darkness. He skipped back up the steps, thinking that having Leverre around would have been useful at that moment. A few minutes of kicking around in the ash turned up some fragments of wood. A few moments hunched over the pile with his tinder box got a fire going, and soon enough his makeshift torch was bright enough to be of use.

Shielding the flame with his hand, Guillot descended the stairs. His first obstacle was a heavy oak door reinforced with riveted iron bands. It was badly scorched, but had otherwise survived the dragon's wrath intact. What had not survived the passage of time was a handle of any sort. Where Guillot would have expected to find one, there was only a small, round hole in the wood. It invited him to stick a finger through, and considering that he was in the perceived safety of what was once his family home, he was tempted to do exactly that. The voice of caution screamed in his ear, however; as a boy, he had heard too many tales of children putting their hands where they didn't belong, and being trapped by evil spirits, sorcerers, monsters, or whatever the story's villain happened to be.

He took his dagger from its sheath and carefully probed the hole. Quite why anyone would want to booby-trap a cellar door was the question, and after several moments, he was confident nothing waited on the other side to take off his finger. He knelt by the hole and peered in, trying to cast as much of the torch's light in as he could. He could see the void in the centre of the door where the old locking mechanism had been sandwiched, but it too was gone, with what looked like a wedge of wood in its place. He poked at it with his dagger for a moment, but it was hammered in tight, and time had sealed it to the surrounding wood.

He stood, and with impulsive abandon, put his boot to the door. The dry oak gave with a loud crack and the door creaked open. He took a deep breath and waved his torch into the open doorway.

CHAPTER 35

Solène regretted not having sought more mentions of the cup before she left the archive the previous evening—she had tossed and turned all night thinking about it, and had barely a thought for anything else all morning, much to Maestro Foulques's displeasure. Even dal Drezony had grown impatient with her, and sent her off for an early lunch when it was obvious her mind was irretrievably elsewhere.

She reached for the Fount as soon as she got to the archive, and in actively looking for it, realised how weak it was down there. Remembering dal Drezony explaining that underground, surrounded by rock, the Fount would be dulled, she felt a sense of satisfaction that she could now sense this for herself. Weak though it might be, there was plenty of magical energy available for what Solène wanted to do. She focussed on her desire for information on an old, magical cup, imagining it contained in a folio of papers, then in a scroll, and finally in a book. Though she held each thought for several moments, there was no result.

Adding thoughts of the Chevaliers to the mix, she tried again. The clump of leather-bound paper hitting the floor brought a smile to Solène's face as she walked toward the sound. What awaited her looked like a ledger. A neat, clerical hand had inscribed a list of names—none of which she recognised—with dates beside them. These too looked unfamiliar, leading her to assume that this was how they had recorded dates during Imperial times. She flipped several pages and discovered that she held bound correspondence; the ledger at the beginning was a record of sender, recipient, and the date of sending. She noticed two vacant spots on the shelf. One from this book; the other, she assumed, something the Prince Bishop had taken to study.

Back at her desk, she dived straight in. The letters discussed the possession of an ancient artefact that had been in the safekeeping of the Imperial

College of Mages since the first days of the Empire. The writers were considering moving it to Mirabensis—Mirabaya as it had been known back then. It took a moment for the pieces to come together in her mind—if it had been used to initiate the Chevaliers, it must have ended up in Mirabaya. She decided to follow the thread carefully, to learn all she could.

There was a subtext to the letters, which in the earlier part of the tome at least seemed to be between only two correspondents, one at the Imperial capital, Vellin-Ilora, and the other, quite possibly in the chamber where she now sat. It felt voyeuristic to think she might be on the very spot where some of the letters were written, to be peering into someone's private thoughts and concerns, albeit from one and a half millennia away.

The Mirabayan writer appealed to his superior in Vellin-Ilora for assistance in a crisis, the specifics of which were not detailed. Solène presumed this was because the circumstances were well known to both of them, though each mention irritated her as they offered only hints. According to this man, the situation was so dire, it called for the use of the *Amatus Cup*. Solène was familiar with the name *Amatus*. He was the first mage, the man who began the science of magic.

The correspondent in Vellin-Ilora was reluctant to resort to the Cup. It seemed even at that point, there was some doubt as to whether it actually did anything, or if it were simply an object that had assumed importance from its association with a hero of the past. Either way, they did not want it leaving Vellin-Ilora unless absolutely necessary.

Solène let out a sigh of satisfaction as she turned a page and finally saw mention of the cause of the great crisis. At that moment she felt a great affinity with the man who might have written the letter not far from where she now sat, for their problem was the same. Dragons.

The letters continued, with the Mirabayan correspondent pointing out that he was sending copies to the emperor himself. He said the Cup was never used, and was no longer needed by the College of Mages. He went on to detail how it could benefit the men being sent to deal with the crisis, how it could be used to grant them the additional abilities they needed.

So that was it—the answer she was looking for. The Cup could give a man or woman additional powers and skills. If they were going to all those lengths to find a weapon to defeat the dragons, it meant the weapons they already had weren't up to the job. They had to create a new type of banneret because neither the old ones, nor the most powerful mages, were able to defeat the beasts.

That presented a problem, though. How was she supposed to defeat a dragon if the powerful mages of old couldn't manage it?

She skipped through the remaining letters, pausing only to read one signed by the emperor. It stated that the Cup would be transported to Mirabensis for use by a new organisation of bannerets dedicated to the fight against dragons and under the full supervision of the College of Mages—the Chevaliers of the Silver Circle. That explained the presence of mages at the initiation ceremony. It also confirmed the Cup was sent to Mirabay.

The correspondence ended with a letter outlining the delivery process—shipment from Vellin-Ilora to the Port of Mirabensis, then transport up the River Vosges to Mirabay. When Solène closed the book, some questions had been answered, but an equal number of new ones had arisen. If the Cup had reached Mirabay, where was it now? If they found it, how would they use it?

Finding the Cup, if it still existed, seemed to be the next course for her research, if she hoped to bring the Prince Bishop information he could use. Once they had the Cup, then they could worry about figuring out what to do with it.

Perhaps records of the Silver Circle would provide the answers she needed. She stood and reached for the Fount, focussing her thoughts on the Silver Circle, the Amatus Cup, on books, documents, and scrolls, and on various things such records might be called. She waited for the familiar sound of a falling book, but there was nothing. She tried again, and noticed the book on the Chevaliers' rule twitch on the desk, but nothing else. One final try, more forceful than any of the others, left her feeling dizzy. She sat, wondering what to do next.

CHAPTER
36

The light from Guillot's flickering torch was an eerie companion as it jumped around the walls of the cellar, in one moment casting things in a warm orange light and in the next, abandoning them to darkness. He wished he had a magelamp; there had been several in the manor house, but it was unlikely any had survived the fire. With the meagre light he had, it was difficult to tell the size of the space, but it was large, with walls of finely cut stone and a groin-vault ceiling. Care and considerable expense had gone into the construction, making the fact that it had been sealed up all the more intriguing.

He had the fleeting worry that it was to keep something from getting out, but he doubted his family would have continued to live there if something dangerous lay beneath their feet. Even if that had been the case, it would be long dead.

A face appeared out of the darkness and a shriek of fright left Gill's mouth before he could stop it. The initial flash of panic subsided as he realised what he was looking at, but it took several more moments for his heart to slow. It was, of course, a statue. Composure reclaimed, he stepped closer for a better look. The work was outstanding, and the life-size statue was an equal to any of the monuments he had seen in Mirabay. The features were so lifelike it was as though a living man had been turned into marble. The figure was of a man of a similar age to Guillot—certainly no older than forty. His tight, neat beard was definitely not of the current fashion, and his hair was styled in thick curls.

The stone face's expression was serene—almost angelic—but as Guillot took in the rest of the statue, he realised this was a monument to a man of war. He wore armour of an unusual style, and a broad-bladed sword with a single cross-guard was strapped to his waist. A museum in Mirabay contained old Imperial-era statues, and this reminded Gill of them. Why would anyone want to shut up such a work in the darkness of a cellar? Indeed, what was a statue like that doing in a place like Villerauvais at all? Guillot's eyes widened when he spotted something that the inconsistent and flickering light of his torch had not revealed until now—a circle of silver metal on the armour's marble breastplate.

Waving the torch, Guillot gasped to see another statue standing beyond the first, and another beyond that. Despite the frustrating lack of light, he worked his way along the line of statues, which were arrayed with their backs to the left wall of the room, filling the spaces between the ornate pillars that supported the roof. He counted six before stopping. He had not reached the end of the room, which he still could not even see in the torchlight. Turning, he plunged into the darkness, heading for the wall on the other side, counting paces as he went. At twelve, he found himself staring into the face of another statue—which was flanked by still more. How many were there?

His torch flickered and the flame dwindled. It had eaten away at the wood and he knew soon it would die altogether. He didn't want to be stuck down there when it did, so after a final look at the statue before him, he made his way back to the entrance.

Guillot's eyes protested at the daylight when he emerged from the cellar and he shielded them with one hand. In the other, the torch sputtered out in a tendril of black smoke from a meagre glowing ember at its tip. His mind raced, his imagination particularly grabbed by the silver circle on the statue's breastplate. He had always known a distant ancestor of his was a founding member of the Silver Circle, but the cellar seemed to indicate far more than that. Why would an individual Chevalier keep statues of his comrades in a crypt below his manor house? If there had even been a manor house there when the crypt was built. The masonry below looked old, very old, and far more substantial than the house had been. The older parts of the house had gone back at least a dozen generations. Why would something this large have been built so far from the capital?

He sat on the top step, staring down into the darkness. He went through the possibilities, from as mundane as discovering more about his family heritage, to discovering a great dragon-slaying sword of wonder. He knew the latter was too much to hope for, but the discovery excited him in a way he had not felt in a very long time, and he was glad of the distraction from dwelling on his rash failure and the loss of so many lives.

First, he needed a better light source. He could return to Trelain to fetch a proper lantern, but that would take up too much time. There was no chance of finding anything of use in the village, so he would have to make do with whatever he could find. He could ride to a nearby stand of trees to cut some wood, but it would be green, and the smoke it gave off would fill the cellar until it became a homemade version of the dragon's cave. He realised he hadn't checked the kitchen cellar. Something might have survived down there.

Nursing the remaining smouldering fragments from his first torch, he hurried to the stairwell by the lonely fireplace. The stairway's construction was startlingly similar to that of the secret cellar. He had been down into it countless times, but had never considered it might be much older than the rest of the house. His hope that there would be something useful stemmed from the fact that it was deep below ground—which kept the wine at optimum temperature and slowed the melting of the ice in the cold-room annex. When he was a child, each winter men brought great blocks of ice down from the mountains, packed in insulating straw, and lowered them into the cellar through a hatch somewhere on the grounds, probably long overgrown now.

He had gone only a few steps before the glow of the ember at the end of his stick was the only light he had. However, he knew his way around, so it was enough to let him find what he was looking for. He laughed in satisfaction when he found the brandy rack. There were a couple of bottles remaining, and they were intact, protected from the heat of the fire by the depth at which they were stored. He pulled a large section of planking from an empty rack, tucked a brandy bottle under his arm, and reached daylight just as the glowing ember started to burn his hand.

He dropped the ember, set down his bottle, and made for his horse. Taking a blanket from his saddlebag, he cut two large sections from it. He broke the plank into two thick, baton-length pieces, and wrapped a piece of cloth around one end of each one. Finally, he uncorked the brandy bottle. The smell hit him almost instantly and he hesitated for a moment, but his curiosity at what lay below overwhelmed his fading need for alcohol. He liberally doused the cloth in the brandy until the label on the bottle caught his eye and he grimaced when he saw the date.

At over two hundred years old, the bottle would have been worth at least a hundred crowns in Mirabay, and it seemed like a shameful waste to set it afire. However, needs must, and he was glad that he had not known of the bottle's existence when Jeanne had cut off his access to wine.

Returning to the remnant of his first torch, Guillot touched one of the new torches to its fading glow. With some gentle blowing, the flame took hold, coating the soaked cloth in a refined blue flame. That done, he returned to the secret cellar—the alcohol-powered flame cast far more light into the darkness than his previous torch, but made for an eerier experience. The first few statues on either side of the chamber were visible, continuing their timeless vigil. Newly revealed were the frescoes painted on the walls behind them.

Although Guillot knew he could never be accused of being an art aficionado, he liked to think he had a discerning eye, and to him, the quality of the painting was exceptional—easily on par with the statuary—and would do credit to a great museum or even the king's palace. They depicted great battles between man and dragon, and Guillot noted that some of the Chevaliers depicted in the scenes bore a strong resemblance to the statues before them. What tragedy had led to them being hidden here for who knew how long? He advanced down the cellar—might it more appropriately be called a hall?— eager to see what lay at the far end. Armed with a spare torch and the bottle of fuel, which he was trying not to think of as drinkable alcohol, he had no fear of being caught down there in the absolute darkness.

He walked past rank after rank of noble-looking statues, his predecessors in the Silver Circle. He wondered what they would think of what the Silver Circle had become—or if, stories to the contrary, perhaps that was what it had been like all along. The silver ring pressed into the breastplate of each statue's armour was new to Guillot. Neither he nor any of the Chevaliers he had known had one on their ceremonial or service armour, not that the latter saw a great deal of wear, and wondered when they stopped using it.

Guillot reckoned he was well beyond the boundaries of the old house when the end of the space appeared out of the gloom. When he approached the feature at the end of the hall—two more statues flanking what looked like an altar of some kind—his jaw dropped.

One of the statues held out an open hand, palm up; its other hand held a stick, or straw. A small object resting on the open palm caught Gill's attention. Despite it being carved from marble, he knew it. Small, nearly spherical, with an inscribed rim. He scrabbled in his purse and coaxed out the odd little cup he'd found in the dragon's cave. There could be no mistaking it, they were one and the same.

Reaching up, Guillot placed the cup next to its stone doppelgänger. Of course, there might have been many such cups. Perhaps it was the preferred style at one time? Why anyone would make a cup from Telastrian steel was a mystery to him, but a mystery that might be starting to reveal itself.

What significance did this scene—the two statues, and the altar—have to the old Chevaliers? What role did the cup play? How had it ended up in the dragon's cavern? He shook his head and rubbed his brow. As fascinating as it was, it raised more questions but answered none. It also occurred to Guillot that Leverre had been very interested in taking possession of the cup. At the time Guillot had found it irritating and curious, but not enough to become overly suspicious. Now, though, it made him wonder. Did Leverre know more about it than he had let on? Once again he felt as though there was far more going on than he was aware of. It wasn't a feeling he liked, and if past experience was anything to go by, it usually ended badly for him. It was what he hated about Mirabay, why he had left, and why it took a dragon attack to get him to go back.

He doubted there would be any way to determine the meaning of what he was looking at or to learn anything about the silly-looking little cup. So much had been forgotten. If the Chevaliers had stayed true to themselves, it was unlikely Guillot would be the only one left, and the dragon would likely be dead.

He circled the room, studying the frescoes. Perhaps if they were contemporary to the actions depicted, they would give him a hint as to how the old Chevaliers achieved their supposedly great feats. He was quickly disappointed; they were far more style than substance. Men didn't defeat something so terrifying as a dragon while looking as though they were hoping to make a dinner engagement that evening.

He looked around the hidden cellar and swore. How did all the pieces fit together? He spent hours studying the paintings and statues, then camped out by the house, prepared to continue his exploration the next morning.

CHAPTER
37

Solène woke to the discomfort of her face pressed against a hard surface. She sat up abruptly, disoriented, and took a moment to work out where she was. The archive. She wondered how long she had been asleep, but since she was underground, there was no way to tell what time it was. Day or night, she was famished, so she headed for the exit.

As she walked, the concerns she had fallen asleep with returned. The Silver Circle were empowered by drinking from an ancient cup, the location of which was unknown; mages did not seem to have been able to kill dragons by themselves. How little to show for a day's work! Having discovered how to read the documents and to locate what she was looking for quickly were significant achievements, but she could only find something as long as she knew *what* she was looking for.

She walked up the spiral steps to the cathedral, legs stiff and protesting from the hours spent at the desk. Light came in through the stained-glass windows, so she must have slept through the night. She hoped her absence at the Priory that morning wouldn't get her into trouble. She had planned to call at a café near the cathedral for something to eat before returning to the archive, but now wondered if she should go back to the Priory first.

Her attention was caught by the sharp footfalls of a grey-haired man who had just entered the cathedral, the door shutting behind him with a reverberating boom. His cloak billowed, revealing the Prince Bishop's livery.

"Sister dal Bastelle," he called.

It took Solène's sleep-deprived mind a moment to realise he was referring to her. "Yes?"

"Good. I called at the Priory first, but they told me you weren't there. The Prince Bishop wishes for you to attend on him at the palace to update him on your progress."

It seemed the Prince Bishop wasn't the most patient of men, and it worried her how little she had to give him. The man stood looking at her hopefully.

"Now?" she said.

"That would be perfect. I have a carriage waiting."

"I was hoping to get something to eat."

"I'm sure the palace kitchens will be able to provide you with far better fare than anything you can find on the Isle."

Clearly, he wasn't going to accept any delay and he was right that the food in the palace was going to be better than any of the cafés, plus, she wouldn't have to pay for it. She nodded and followed him out of the cathedral.

The carriage waiting outside wasn't the Prince Bishop's personal vehicle, but Solène knew it wasn't a good idea to get too used to such treatment—it had simply been the honey to catch the fly. She was, at least, allowed the privacy of the cabin, as the messenger sat outside with the driver. The seats weren't cushioned, and there was no gilding in sight, but it still beat having to walk through dirty streets to the palace. She watched the city speed by, but without the interest she'd once had. She was quickly coming to realise that everything in Mirabay had a price higher than it first seemed.

The carriage came to a halt outside the palace gate, and Solène didn't wait for anyone to open the door for her. Pushing it open, she hopped down and paced toward the palace doors. She had no idea what she would say to the Prince Bishop. How would he take the news that their only source of salvation was a cup that had been lost for a millennium and was unlikely to ever be found again? Unless there were a magical way to find it, which she had not yet figured out.

She breezed past the guards at the door with only the briefest interaction, so caught up in her thoughts that she walked straight into a man she recognised—Commander Leverre.

"Commander Leverre, isn't it?" Solène said. "You were with Gill, weren't you? I didn't realise you were already back in the city." She could see his confusion. "I'm sorry. We haven't met. I am—was—a friend of Gill's. My name is Solène. Initiate Solène."

"Well met, Initiate," he said, only now taking in her uniform. "I'm just returned." His eyes were red and he looked like he hadn't slept in several days.

"I was very upset to hear about Guillot. I hope you weren't too badly injured in the fight."

Leverre frowned. "He came out of it better than the rest of us. I have a constant headache, and there are the brothers and sisters we lost in the fight to remember, but I thank you for your concern."

Solène's mind spun and she opened her mouth to speak, then thought better of it and smiled. Leverre gave her a curt nod.

"If you'll excuse me," he said. "I'm keen for a hot meal and a warm bed."

She watched him until he disappeared into the sunlight beyond the great double doors. She chewed on her lip. Had the Prince Bishop been mistaken about who had died? It didn't seem like the type of mistake a man as fastidious as he would make. On instinct, she knew she had been lied to.

Why would the Prince Bishop lie to her about Guillot? She considered asking him about it, but it occurred to her that there might be more to be gained by playing along for the time being. She knew the Prince Bishop had an agenda, but she didn't know its goal, or where she would fit in when that point was reached.

The walk from the palace doors to the Prince Bishop's offices seemed far shorter than it had the last time—too short, in fact. She found herself outside the door to the antechamber—used as an office by the Prince Bishop's secretary—before she had a clear idea of the strategy she wanted to adopt. There were too many people passing by—from servants to courtiers—for her to loiter for long. She knocked, and was commanded to enter.

The Prince Bishop's personal secretary whisked Solène straight through to his master's office, where the Prince Bishop stood staring out the window. He remained in his silent vigil, not acknowledging her arrival until the secretary had left and closed the door behind him.

"Have you discovered anything of use?" he asked, without turning.

Solène shifted the weight between her feet. "I have, but I fear it might not be enough."

"I still want to hear it."

Solène took a deep breath and made her decision. The less he thought she knew, the better. "I've found some records documenting the early days of the Silver Circle. They make mention of a cup used to anoint the new Chevaliers under the supervision of the College of Mages. It supposedly ended up in Mirabaya. Perhaps if we could find it and learn how to use it . . ."

She paused to gauge his reaction, but his gaze remained fixed on whatever he was looking at below—perhaps one of the palace gardens. The silence grew until Solène wondered if she should say something else, for no reason other than to fill the space.

"I had heard of special initiation rites," the Prince Bishop said at last. "I had hoped that something of them might have carried over to the present day—my reason for sending Guillot on the mission in the first place. Now I see the modern rite omitted the key component."

Seeing her chance, Solène threw caution to the wind. "I was wondering. Guillot showed me a great deal of kindness, and, well, I know he doesn't have anyone to mourn or remember him, so I thought perhaps I could repay his kindness in that way. Do you know . . . how it happened? I mean, was it quick? Did he suffer?"

The Prince Bishop turned to face her with an abruptness that startled her. "I believe it was instantaneous and bravely met," he said. "Dwelling on such things never does anyone any good." He walked to his chair, sat down, and steepled his fingers.

She studied him closely. Now that he had confirmed the lie, Solène knew there was more to him involving Guillot in his plans than she had thought. What would he do if he were caught not only in the initial lie, but in compounding it? Surely Leverre had given the Prince Bishop a complete report on what had happened? Why, then, did the Prince Bishop continue to perpetuate a lie when a simple claim of incomplete information would have swept the matter to one side? Unless he intended that the lie never be found out.

She felt the blood drain from her face as what that meant dawned on her.

"Solène? Are you all right?"

She forced a smile. "Yes, thank you. I've not had much sleep the last couple of days."

The Prince Bishop nodded. "It certainly looks that way. Go back to the Priory and get some rest. You can continue your investigations tomorrow. A hot meal and an early night will put you to rights."

She smiled again and nodded. "I expect so." Gazing around the room, she saw a pile of books in the corner. They looked old, like those she had spent the last few days surrounded by. She decided to ask a risky question. "Have you heard any mention of this cup before? It was referred to as the Amatus Cup. Any hints of how to track it down would be a big help."

The Prince Bishop frowned for a moment as though in deep concentration. "No, I'm afraid not. If I come across anything, I'll be sure to let you know."

Suspicious, Solène reached for the Fount and focussed her thoughts on the Cup and the Silver Circle. She let out a surprised cough when she saw the books twitch.

The Prince Bishop gave her an inquiring look.

"I'm sorry, my Lord," she said. "I'm fit to drop. If I might be excused?"

"Of course," he said.

With a false smile, she left the room as calmly as possible. She took a deep breath when the door closed behind her, but was startled when she realised the Prince Bishop's secretary was staring at her. She gave him a curt nod, then left, walking quickly.

Questions, questions, questions, she thought as she headed for her waiting carriage. *Why are there always so many questions and so few answers?* That the Prince Bishop was keeping something from her came as no great surprise. She gave her driver a wave, told him to take her to the Priory, and hopped into the carriage. It struck her as odd how quickly she was becoming accustomed to such things. As he pulled away one thought plagued her. If Guillot wasn't already dead, then he soon would be. But why, and could she stop it from happening?

Leverre was the only man who could shed light on it all. She was certain she would find him back at the Priory. Once she knew where Guillot was, she could somehow get a warning to him that the Prince Bishop did not intend to let him live. Was she being paranoid? She chewed her lip. Part of her said it had to be a mistake, but her gut told her there was something wrong. She hoped Leverre had some answers. She tapped her foot against the side of the carriage and willed it to go faster.

⁂

As soon as Solène arrived at the Priory, she asked for directions to Commander Leverre's quarters. Even though it was the height of the day, and the Priory was as buzzing with activity as it got, there was still a serenity about the place that was completely absent in the city. It had been her home for only a handful of days, yet she had already developed an affection for it. In the pit of her stomach, however, she could not help but feel her time there was already nearing its end.

Officer accommodation was not far removed from that provided for sisters, brothers, corporals, or sergeants, although their barrack houses were in a quieter part of the Priory's grounds. More than enough time had passed since she'd encountered him at the palace for him to have eaten and gone to bed, and he hadn't struck her as the type of man who would take kindly to having his sleep interrupted. There was no time to delay, however, so she marched up to his door and pounded on it.

After a moment she heard noise from inside, then the door creaked open.

"What is it?" Leverre said, looking ruffled.

"I'm sorry to disturb you, Commander, but I wanted to ask you a few things."

For a moment she thought he was going to turn her away, but then he nodded, although he did not move to let her in.

"You're certain Guillot wasn't hurt? It's just that, well, I don't have very many people I can call a friend, and I'm worried about him."

Leverre nodded. "He had barely a scratch on him when I left them in Trelain."

"Where is he, exactly?"

He frowned, and she worried that she'd overstepped the mark.

"The Black Drake. It's a classy spot, so I doubt he'll get himself into any trouble there unless he goes looking for it."

"And the beast?"

"Guillot got one good cut at it, but that's about it. I expect the injury won't bother it for too long."

Solène grimaced. It wasn't much for the cost of four lives. "I'm sorry about your people."

"Our people, Sister."

Solène smiled. "Of course. But I didn't know them."

"The Order and its members are intended for dangerous work. When we join, we accept the fact that one day our duties may cost us our lives. For them, that day came. For the rest of us, it's waiting out there."

"Still, it can never be easy."

"It isn't."

Silence fell—Solène felt awkward but Leverre seemed comfortable. Feeling she had exhausted him as an avenue for information, she turned, preparing to leave.

"You really do care for him, don't you," Leverre said before she could take a step.

"He saved my life when I was nothing but a stranger in a bad situation," she said. "So yes, I do."

"He saved mine, too," Leverre said. His face was knotted as though he was struggling with a difficult thought. "Men are on their way to Trelain to kill him," he blurted out.

"What?" Solène said, allowing her surprise to conceal the fact that he had confirmed her worst suspicion.

"It's complicated, but the Prince Bishop wants Guillot's failure to be complete, so he can bring the Order out into the open as the country's saviour."

"And for complete failure he needs Gill dead?"

Leverre nodded slowly, his face twisting into an uncomfortable grimace.

"Why are you telling me?"

"Because it's the right thing to do. I was supposed to make sure he didn't come back from the cave alive. But that *wasn't* the right thing to do, so I didn't do it. What are you going to do now that you know?"

"I'm going to warn him," Solène said, incredulous at the idea that there was anything else *to* do. His eyes narrowed. "I wouldn't recommend trying to stop me."

Leverre's face split into a weary smile, the first time she had seen him look anything other than sullen. "I've no intention of trying to stop you. I wouldn't have told you if I was going to. It'll mean going against the Prince Bishop. That mightn't go so well for you."

The reality of her intended action had not escaped her, but she had chosen not to think about that. "I know," she said, at last allowing the fact that she could not return to the Priory, or the safety of the Order, to sink in. She would have to go back to her old life, constantly looking over her shoulder—now with one of the most powerful men in the country as her enemy.

"If we're to beat the men the Prince Bishop has sent to Trelain, we'll need to get moving."

"What do you mean *we*?" Solène said.

"Like I said, he saved my life too. I owe him more than sending a slip of a girl to give him a warning."

She glowered at him, but he didn't seem to notice.

"Get some travelling rations together for both of us, and anything else that you need," he said. "Keep it to a minimum, though. We'll need to move fast. Meet me at the stables in fifteen minutes."

CHAPTER
38

Gill returned to the underground chamber as soon as he woke the next day. He discovered another door at the back of what he was coming to think of as a nave, tucked behind the statues depicting the ceremony. He tried to ignore the judgemental stares of the marble Chevaliers as he investigated the new doors. All the while, he was plagued by the question of what a replica of the little cup he had found in a dragon's cave was doing in a chapel under his family home.

Though it was dry and cool down there—its suitability for storing wine was not lost on him—the newly discovered wooden door had grown far more brittle than the one he had forced open to get into the chapel. At a firm push, it splintered from its hinges, clattering to the ground with an echoing din and such a cloud of dust that Guillot coughed and spluttered before retreating into the larger room until it subsided.

At first he thought the new space was empty, but after the air cleared a little more, he could make out plaques lining the wall. That they were funerary was immediately obvious to him—he had seen their like many times before, including in the family mausoleum that now lay in a pile of rubble somewhere above his head. He held his torch up to the nearest plaque, engraved with finely chiselled lettering in a language he could not read. The letter forms were similar to those he knew, but distorted. The spellings were strange, with letters clustered together in unusual ways. He tried sounding out the words but they refused to make sense.

The next plaque was the same, as was the third. He was about to curse when he spotted something he recognised on the fourth plaque—a name he knew. *Valdamar.* It sent a chill down his spine. The lettering was odd, but when he looked past that, the word was there, as clear as day, dancing in the flickering red light of his torch.

There wasn't a boy or girl in Mirabaya who didn't know that name. *Valdamar—Blade of the Morning Mist*. One of the most famous of the dragon-slaying Chevaliers, Guillot could remember his father telling him at least a dozen stories about Valdamar. One for each of the dragons he was reputed to have slain. He was said to have come from a rural province, one known for being misty and mysterious, but more importantly, one known for being plagued by dragons. It occurred to Guillot that Villerauvais was almost perpetually shrouded in mist in spring and autumn. He had never considered a connection before, but now? What was someone like Valdamar doing buried here? While there was a family legend about descent from one of the founders of the Silver Circle, Valdamar had lived later, during the fall of the Empire and the early days of the kingdom. He was one of the last great Imperial Knights. After his generation, the Silver Circle became what Guillot knew it as.

Gill reflected that his own life was a microcosm of the Silver Circle's history. In disgrace, with his purpose gone, he had filled his time emptying bottles. How had those giants of men, who had lived their lives doing deeds that would be talked of for more than a thousand years, settled into ordinary lives when those days were gone? How do you accept that the great purpose of your life was past?

He had been given a second chance, a reprieve the Silver Circle never got. Stopping this dragon was *his* great life's purpose, but it had come to him when he was least ready for it. He looked at Valdamar's tomb marker and smiled forlornly. If it had come at any other time, would it have been a true test?

He walked through the rest of the crypt, but he only recognised Valdamar's name. One hero among many, the only one to be remembered. There was tragedy in that. Considering that Valdamar's tomb had not been given precedence over any of the others, it was difficult to believe they had not done anything to distinguish themselves. Perhaps the years and retellings had handed their tales to another hero.

The back wall was carved with text from ceiling to floor. The inscription was flanked on either side by representations of the two figures he had seen near the altar in the previous room—the supplicant knight, and the majestic, robed figure holding a cup in one hand and a small stick in the other. It was clearly an anointing ceremony of some sort. Guillot himself had been through one when he joined the Chevaliers, although the cup he had been handed had been far larger and never seemed to empty.

He cast his eyes over the carved words but could not understand them.

Occasionally a word might seem familiar, but not enough to make sense of it. Whatever was written there would have to remain a mystery, at least for the time being. If he survived all that was to come, perhaps he would be able to find someone at the university in Mirabay who could read such things.

With one final look around—his gaze lingering on Valdamar's tomb—Guillot knew it was time to get back to Trelain. It seemed there was nothing more for him to discover here, although the secret chambers left him with many questions.

Trelain had a bleak atmosphere when Guillot returned, worse even than when he had departed. He suspected that word had leaked of the injured man recuperating in the Black Drake, and that he was the survivor of an ill-fated dragon-slaying attempt. Guillot could smell fear on the air. The streets were emptier, and much of the activity was of people preparing for the worst—shutting up properties, hurrying about as though every moment in the open put them in further danger. People had been unsure before. Now they were afraid.

There were still plenty of villages between the dragon and Trelain—as far as he knew—and it could happily feed and destroy its way through the countryside for weeks before reaching the city. That wouldn't matter, though. Soon the panic would start and everyone who could go, would.

He didn't expect the Order's healers to arrive until that evening at the earliest—more likely at some point the next day. While he still felt better than he had before, thanks to Brother Hallot, the battering he had taken in the dragon's cave had taken a toll. Another round of healing might bring him back to his best, which was an appealing thought. It gave him hope that he could prevail, although, despite the gravity of the situation, he couldn't help but feel it would be cheating. It was odd how daft notions of honour and fidelity stuck in your head, even after a lifetime of seeing their gaping flaws in the cold light of reality.

He wondered what Valdamar would have made of such thoughts. The perfect hero, the man to model oneself on. True, brave, and just. Guillot wondered if he had ever kicked a man in the balls during a fight, or slid a dagger into an enemy's back on the battlefield. He shook his head. There was no shame in looking for an edge when the stakes were mortal. The old Chevaliers were rumoured to have been given magical gifts by the Imperial sorcerers. If

Amaury's warrior mages could do the same for him, he would welcome it with open arms.

The stable boy appeared as if by magic as soon as Guillot entered the stable yard at the Black Drake. He slid down from the horse and tossed the lad a penny before heading inside. A hot meal, a bath if one could be rustled up, then sleep. To his surprise, dal Sason was sitting by the fire.

"Feeling better then?" Guillot said, trying to muster as much cheer in his voice as he could.

Dal Sason turned to look at him, a grimace of pain twisting his face.

"Not feeling better then," Guillot commented.

"I've broken ribs. What do you think?"

Guillot shrugged and sat. "What's good to eat tonight?"

"Where in hells have you been?"

"I went for a ride."

"You've been gone for two days."

"It was a long ride," Guillot said.

"I thought you'd run off. Thought your nerve had gone."

"Thanks for the vote of confidence."

Dal Sason fell silent for a moment. "Sorry. That was unfair."

"Understandable enough. It seems like half the town's getting ready to leave."

"Word must have gotten out that we didn't kill it."

Guillot nodded. "Surprised the panic hasn't spread faster."

"As soon as word of its next attack gets here, things will get ugly fast. It's up to us to try to stop that."

"I know," Guillot said. "Do you really think we're up to it?"

"We have to try," dal Sason said.

Guillot laughed. They'd done that once already, and it hadn't gone so well. "Is it worth it?"

"Worth what?" dal Sason said.

"Whatever the Prince Bishop is paying you. Is it enough?"

Dal Sason gave a sad smile. "In our line of work, is it ever enough?"

CHAPTER
39

Solène rocked gently from side to side as the horse trotted along the road toward Trelain. She had done the vast majority of her wandering on foot, with only the occasional ride in a cart or wagon. She didn't think she would ever feel entirely comfortable on horseback, perched just high enough for the drop to look daunting.

She didn't know how to feel about returning to Trelain. On the one hand, the growing sense of misgiving that had been twisting in her stomach for the past few days was gone. She had realised there was a problem, and now she was doing something about it. However, the last time she was in Trelain, the townsfolk had wanted to burn her at the stake. She was torn between the desire to spur the horse to a gallop to get to Guillot all the sooner, and turning around and fleeing from trouble. People tended to have short memories, but she knew she risked her life by returning to the city.

Leverre was not proving the most talkative of travelling companions—although after all he had been through, and after having ridden through the night, he must have been utterly exhausted—so Solène was left to stew in her own thoughts. She tried to use the time to connect all the pieces of information she'd gathered, with little success.

"How did he save your life?"

The voice came as such a surprise that Solène jumped in her saddle.

"Pardon?"

"Guillot. What did he do that saved your life?"

Solène felt anxious when she thought about it. That day was the closest she had come to death. "The townsfolk discovered I could do magic," Solène said. Leverre grunted an acknowledgement. "They were going to burn me." Admitting it out loud doused her in emotion, and she could feel a lump form in her throat. She had never spoken about it before, never acknowledged to herself how close she had come to a terrifying and agonising death. She had tried to take it in her stride, filing it away in her mind with all the other daily hardships of life when you have no one, have nothing. She'd be damned if she shed a tear in front of Leverre, however. He was both her superior officer—if that mattered anymore—and one of the surliest people she had ever met. She refused to show weakness to him.

"I saw a witch burned when I was a child," Leverre said. "I'll never forget it. I've been to war twice. I've seen horrible things; friends cut to pieces, a field littered with so many dead it made a butcher's house smell like a rose garden, but watching that woman die was the worst thing I've ever seen. I hoped the Order would change all of that, but I'm not so sure anymore." He sighed. "I could already do things, you see. Small things—nothing like what I'm told you're able to do. After the burning, I hid that part of myself, pushed it so far down it was all but gone when the Prince Bishop finally found me.

"I always wondered why he sponsored me for the Academy. My father was a blacksmith. Not too many blacksmith's sons go to the Academy. I worked hard, almost forgot about the *touch*, as I used to call it. After the Academy, it was the army. Then, one day, the Prince Bishop called on me, told me he always knew that there was more to me than meets the eye, and brought me into the Order. There were no more than twenty or thirty in it then, a mix of scholars from the university, like Seneschal dal Drezony, soldiers like me, and one or two other talented strays he'd found along the way. Like you, I suppose. No offence."

Solène laughed. "None taken. *Stray* describes me pretty well, I think. What did he do for you? Guillot, I mean, when he saved you?"

Leverre took a deep breath and let it out slowly. "In truth, I'm not really sure. I took a bad knock on the head. That monster really rang my bell!" He chuckled. "When sense started to come back, Gill was hauling me into the daylight. Hallot, Quimper, and Eston were dead. Doyenne and dal Sason were still fighting, but she didn't make it out. Dal Sason wouldn't have either, if it wasn't for Gill."

"He's an interesting man," Solène said. "I'd like to get to know him better." Leverre looked over at her and raised an eyebrow. "I mean, it sounds like he has quite a history."

Leverre let out a laugh that sounded like a sick dog barking. "He certainly has that. He was once considered the best swordsman in the world. In fact, he was—he won the Competition. If that wasn't enough, he was the great hero on the third day at Heilsbrun in the Ventish Wars. Led a charge that took a bridge that thousands had died fighting over the previous two days. We might well still be there fighting for it if he hadn't. Stories of the things men do in battle are usually talked up afterward, but that one wasn't. I was there. Seeing him go across that bridge, knowing he was a Mirabayan, well, it was really something. Filled you with whatever it takes to convince a man to charge at a pike wall. Charge we did, and run they did. It really was something."

He had a gentle smile on his face, but he wiped it off as soon as he saw her looking at him.

"He came back from the Ventish Wars a hero. He was a legend by the time he came back from the Szavarian War. I didn't see action in that one. Then the king had him inducted into the Silver Circle and appointed him royal champion. He married the most beautiful woman in the kingdom, protected the king—what more could a man of arms ask for?" He chuckled. "It was all downhill for him after that, though. He's lost his wife, his child, his banner. For a man like him, that's everything. It makes me sick to see what he became, but you can't blame him for it, I suppose. There's something ironic in the kingdom having broken its greatest swordsman before it needed him the most, don't you think?"

This time, Solène raised an eyebrow. "I'm not sure if it would have made any difference."

"What do you mean?"

"I was doing some research for the Prince Bishop. The old Chevaliers, the dragonslayers, they were magically enhanced. Even then a lot of them were killed, taking on dragons."

"Killing a dragon is never going to be an easy thing, no matter what advantages you have."

"What about Gill and the Prince Bishop? What is it between them?"

Leverre shrugged. "I don't know, aside from the fact that they were friends once. The Prince Bishop is a banneret. Was a swordsman in his youth. Then he got hurt and life took him in a different direction. Not sure when they fell out, but there's certainly no love lost between them."

Solène chewed her lip for a moment. "Do you know anything about a cup?"

"A cup?"

"An ancient one. One that might have some magical significance. I've seen it called the Amatus Cup, and I think there's a chance it might still be in Mirabaya somewhere." She watched him as she spoke, and could tell from his quickly hidden reaction that he knew what she was talking about.

"I don't . . ." He took a deep breath and let it out with a sigh. "It's what we were looking for the first time we went up to the dragon's cave. When we woke it up."

Solène's jaw dropped. She felt her heart race with excitement. Did he have some of the answers she was looking for? "Why were you looking for it?"

"The Prince Bishop wanted it," Leverre said, with the fervour of a man seeking to unload a great burden. "He said it was vital to the Order's success. So much of what we're doing comes from the ancient Imperial documents that he's dug up that this mission didn't seem all that unusual. It made sense that there might be something old and hidden out there which would come in useful."

"What does it do?"

Leverre chuckled. "I didn't need to know that to find it, so he didn't tell me."

"And how were you going to find it? What led you to the cave?" Questions were coming to her faster than her mouth could get them out.

He looked over at her. "You're all questions. What is it to you?"

"The Prince Bishop wanted me to find information that would help us kill the dragon. I think the Cup might be what we're looking for."

Leverre laughed. "Our days of working for the Prince Bishop are well and truly over. Take my word for it. He's not a man who forgives. Or forgets. Once we've warned Gill, we'll both need to disappear."

"The beast still needs to be killed," she said. "Not for him, but for all the people who'll be slaughtered if someone doesn't. It might as well be us. We might be able to help Gill do it. The Cup might be of use in that. Is there any chance that we can find it?"

Leverre looked away from her and out to the horizon. "The Prince Bishop told me that it would create an incredibly dense concentration of the Fount, that someone with my familiarity with the Fount would be able to sense it against the background noise of all that energy, whereas a novice wouldn't. He was right. I could feel it the moment I walked into the dragon's cave. It was like a tight knot of threads in a sheet of perfectly woven silk."

"Do you think it's still up there?"

Leverre laughed. "No. Gill has it. He picked it up when we were in the cave."

"Guillot *has* it?" Solène said.

He looked at her, a curious expression on his face. "Yes, he does. I'm certain. I saw him with it. I could feel that same knot of energy coming from it when he showed it to me."

Solène slumped in her saddle, vacillating between intense feelings of relief and disbelief. If they already had the Cup, perhaps the solution to their problem was close at hand—assuming they could figure out how to use it.

There might be an answer in the archive—or in the books in the Prince Bishop's office. She would have to turn back now if she wanted to look, leaving Guillot to his fate. There was a chance he would be able to defend himself, but even the greatest swordsman in the world, at his peak, was as vulnerable to an unexpected knife in the back as anyone else.

She shook her head to dismiss the thought. Guillot was the only man alive who knew what was said at the Silver Circle's initiation. She needed to know everything he could remember about it. It was a slim hope, but the only one she had. Casting magic on a person was very different from casting it on an object. Even if it was well intended, the things that could go wrong were legion.

CHAPTER
40

Late the next afternoon, when they were not far from Trelain, Solène spotted a group of riders on the road ahead, going in the same direction as them. Everyone else they had passed had been going the other way—fleeing the dragon. This group was different, and it looked as though they were wearing matching cream travelling cloaks, just like the ones she and Leverre wore. She looked at him, slumped in his saddle, drifting in and out of sleep. He had spent several hard days on the road with almost no rest, and it amazed her that he had held up as well as he had.

"Leverre."

He grunted.

"Up ahead."

He snapped upright, his eyes wide. "That's them."

"I know. That's why I woke you."

He squinted. "Five. No, six. More than I was expecting."

"Gill was the best swordsman in the world. The Prince Bishop isn't likely to take any chances."

Leverre grunted again. "If they're actually Order people, I'd say Dreue and Gamet are with them. They're the most suited for this type of work. Vicious bastards, both of them. They'd both be rotting in a dungeon somewhere if the Prince Bishop hadn't found a use for them."

"That sounds encouraging," Solène said sarcastically. "What do we do now?"

"There's two options as I see it. The first is, we ride up to them and pretend the Prince Bishop sent us to fetch them back to Mirabay. We'll have to go back with them, though, so Gill won't get a warning. It buys time though, and maybe we could get word to him by pigeon or private messenger."

"You think that'll work?"

"Probably not. Gamet's sharp as a tack and suspicious as a cuckold. He'll expect sealed, written orders. I would too."

"What's the second option?"

"We make sure they don't reach Trelain."

"You mean *kill* them?"

"Did you think we were coming here to convince them of the error of their ways? This was always going to come down to violence, either here and now, or later, in Trelain."

Solène nodded. Another reality she had put off considering. Now she lived in a world where men were willing to kill one another to get what they wanted. It struck her as odd how life at the top of the ladder so closely resembled life at the bottom.

"Could we not drop out of sight and follow them? Wait until we reach Gill, to boost our numbers?"

Leverre shook his head. "If we've seen them, they've seen us. They'll have seen our robes too. In hindsight, we should have worn something different, but it's too late to do anything about that now. They'll think it odd if brothers and sisters of the Order don't ride up to meet them. You can see that they've already slowed. They're expecting us to join them."

"Let's do that, then. Join them, and ride with them to Trelain."

"Gamet's the Order's chancellor. We're equal in rank, so I have no authority over him. He'll expect to see our orders. If we don't have any, he'll want to know why."

"So we make something up."

"He's not the type to fall for something like that. Gamet's a vicious thug, but he knows what the Order's done for him, and what it can do for him, so he follows the rules like he wrote them himself."

She stared at the group long enough to confirm that the distance between them was closing.

"What do I need to do?" she said.

"You haven't had enough training with a sword to be any use in that regard," Leverre said. "But if what I hear about you is true, that would be putting you to waste."

Solène's stomach twisted with nerves. She'd used magic to defend herself before, but this felt different. Now she would be the attacker, using it as a weapon, not a shield.

"I'm not sure I can," she said.

"You passed your tests, didn't you?"

She nodded.

"Then you can. Instinct will guide you to what you need in a situation like this."

She nodded again, gaze locked on the riders ahead of them.

"We'll ride up to them all friendly," Leverre said. "We need to get close, and I'd rather do that without crossbow bolts flying through the air. I don't think any of them are strong enough to do serious damage with magic, but in the heat of the moment, you never know, so keep your wits about you and be prepared to hit anyone who looks like they might be trying to rustle something up."

Solène's hands felt cold, and she realised they were shaking.

"Are you all right?" Leverre said.

She nodded, but the action didn't come as easily as she would have liked.

"You can do this," he said. "We can do this. If we want to stop them from killing Gill, it's what needs to be done." He paused for a moment. "Are you ready?"

"I am," she said, with far more resolve in her voice than she'd thought she could muster.

"Good. We ride up nice and relaxed. On my signal, let fly with everything you have."

"Everything I have," Solène repeated.

"Let's go."

"Wait, what's your signal?"

Leverre was already riding ahead. "I haven't decided yet, but you'll know it when you see it!"

She urged her horse on and caught up with him, trying to appear nonchalant to the group ahead. Her skin crawled as she imagined their eyes on her, and she tried to think about anything other than what she had to do. She feared that if she thought about it too much, when it came time, she would freeze.

As they got closer, Leverre held up a hand. At first she felt a flash of panic that it was his signal and it was time to act, but she realised it was merely a salutation.

"Brother-Chancellor Gamet! Is that you?" Leverre shouted.

The Spurriers had stopped and turned to welcome people they thought were their brother and sister in arms. Something about their ruse felt underhanded to Solène, but when stakes were as high as they were, she supposed nothing was out of the question.

"Leverre! What are you doing out here?" one of them shouted.

As they neared, Solène began to make out faces. There was a woman about her own age, whom Solène had seen eating in the refectory. At the time, she had thought she looked friendly. Realising the woman was looking at her, she swallowed hard and broke eye contact. They would never be friends now. If everything went well, Solène would never even know her name.

Another was a young man she had seen training in the fencing hall. He was quick and had looked impressive, and she had hoped to one day match him in skill. He was dangerous. Somewhere in her, she decided he would be the first to go. That she had just chosen someone to kill made her want to vomit. The grim knowledge that either everyone in front of her would be dead in the next few minutes, or she would, was of little consolation.

She tried to return her attention to Leverre, who was chatting with Gamet as though they were old friends. She supposed that in a way, they were. Despite her effort, all she could think about was the tempest of emotion twisting inside her. She wondered if this was how everyone felt before going into battle. If so, how could anyone choose to make a career of it? How could anyone, after even a single taste, want anything to do with it ever again?

When the fight at last started, it happened so fast she nearly missed it, despite having been waiting for it. Leverre drew his sword and cut Gamet down in one flashing sweep that sprayed blood across Solène's face and her pristine cream clothes. In a panic, she searched the group for the man she decided would be first. He was already moving, reacting far faster than Solène. With a roar born from the desire to survive that frightened even her, she drew on the Fount, careful to avoid tapping her own reservoir, and directed it all at him.

Where there had been a young man dressed head to toe in the Order's cream cloth, there was now nothing but an empty saddle. She squinted, wondering what had happened. What she had done?

She realised the saddle and the horse's back were drenched in a thick layer of sticky blood and viscera, and it was all she could do not to be sick.

One of the others stared, mouth agape, at where their comrade had just been. To her surprise, they were dressed in red now—it took her a moment to work out why. Then she pushed the thought from her head as quickly as it had entered.

A flashing sword cut through the air, so close to her face that she could feel the breeze of its passage. Some deep-rooted instinct for survival had caused her to flinch, but her attacker closed the distance and she knew she would not be able to dodge a second time. Without thinking, she extended her hand and roared again, a hoarse, bestial sound that was alien to her. Her attacker momentarily became a smudge of cream and red in the air, then he too was gone, coating everything around him in a misting of blood.

She felt a violent tug on her, but there was no one touching her. It felt as though something had grabbed her soul and was trying to pull it from her body. Looking around frantically, she saw the woman, hand outstretched, her face a picture of concentration. Solène felt the tug again, then more distress than she had ever known. She lashed out again, not in hate or rage, but in anguish. It was a terrible thing she was doing, but she felt compelled to continue. She fed the pain of her soul into her focus and in an instant the young woman was nothing more than a red stain.

Feeling cold and dizzy, Solène realised she hadn't been able to separate herself from the Fount during the third attack. Though she was reeling, only she and Leverre remained in the saddle. Three bodies lay in the road; there was nothing left of the others but blood. There was a look of grim satisfaction on his face but she felt awful.

How could there not have been a better way? How could she have been capable of what she did? Had it always lurked within her, waiting for a chance to come out? What if she couldn't stop it the next time she felt danger? She had not chosen to turn Arnoul into a pig, she had done it instinctively. Might this be what she did the next time she acted on instinct? She retched, bringing up nothing but bitter bile. She looked up, shamed by both what she had done, and for being sick. Leverre nodded to her with a thin smile.

"Well done."

She burst into tears.

"It's always like this the first time," Leverre said. "Just let it out. You'll feel better after."

She did her best to smile and hold it in despite his advice. She had never been one to show weakness to others, but the confused rage of emotion inside of her threatened to overcome her well-trained resolve. Her body shuddered with every contained sob. Cold spread through her body and every limb felt heavy.

"We should get moving," he said. "There's nothing to be gained by staying here any longer. It'd be just my luck for the king's Highway Rangers to show up now."

She wanted to ask what to do about the bodies, but it was all she could do to nod and follow him. The air stank of the metallic tang of blood, and she had to admit she would be glad to be as far from the place as possible.

They reached a small river crossed by a bridge that was barely large enough to warrant the name. It was not far from where they had fought, but Solène could go no farther without some rest. She knew if she hadn't managed to separate herself from the Fount that one time, she wouldn't even have made it this far.

"I have to stop," she said.

"We can rest a short while," Leverre said. "We should clean up too. We can't go into Trelain looking as we do."

She looked down at her robes, now a dark rusty red for the most part, crusted with the dried blood of those she killed. Wearing them made her skin crawl and she suddenly couldn't wait to be rid of them. Sliding off her horse, Solène went to the water's edge and started scrubbing the blood from her still-shaking hands. She thought she might fall into the water from sheer exhaustion, and wondered what Leverre would say if she asked to rest for a while. Her head swam with fatigue now that the excitement of the fight had faded. She knew the magic she had used had taken a heavy toll on her. It was only right that it did. *Killing should never come easily,* she thought. Looking for him, she saw that Leverre had yet to dismount.

"What's wrong?" she said.

"Nothing." He swung his leg over the horse's back and grimaced in pain. He let out a loud groan as he lowered himself to the ground. His hand went to his side as he walked to the water.

"Were you wounded?"

"A cut, nothing more," he said. "I've had far wor—" He tumbled to the shingle riverbank with a rattle of loose stones.

Solène rushed to his side and used a wet corner of her robe to wipe the dried blood from his face. His skin was pale—almost deathly so. "Felix," she said, sprinkling a handful of water on his cheek.

His eyelids flickered, then lifted slowly.

"Thank the gods," she said. "Let me take a look at your cut."

She took the dagger from his belt to cut his bloody tunic, exposing that part of his belly. She saw a dark, narrow slit, a handspan long, oozing dark blood at a prodigious rate.

"Did this just start now?" she said. "When you got down from the horse?"

He shook his head grimly.

"I haven't taken any healing instruction. What do I do?"

He spluttered out a laugh. "Neither have I. The Prince Bishop didn't recruit me for my bedside manner."

"I have to stop this bleeding. I have to fix this or you're going to die."

"I think it was too late for that the minute the blade came out. There's only so much magic can do."

"I can do more magic than most," she said.

"Try, then," he said. "After that fight we just had, I'd be surprised if you could set light to dry grass."

She had no idea where to start. She was so tired she could barely hold a thought. How could she hope to shape the Fount? Crafting magic on someone needed so much focus, plus an absolute certainty of what you wanted to achieve. It was why healing was the most specialised school of magic at the Priory. It was easy to cast a forceful blow, or, as she had just discovered, do far more than that when the intent was destruction. Healing was all finesse, and Solène had no idea how to wield her talent as anything other than a club.

"You must know something. Tell me. Anything."

He murmured something, but she couldn't quite make it out.

"What?"

"A letter," he said, the words coming between laboured breaths. "I left a letter at the Priory saying I had to stop them from killing Gill. Said it was a matter of personal honour, that he'd saved my life. You don't need to take any blame for it."

Tears streamed down her face. She pressed her fingers down on either side of the wound and reached out for the Fount. It seemed distant, and the farther she stretched, the more it receded, always staying in view, but just beyond her grasp. Trying made her dizziness worse. She squeezed her eyes tight, concentrating for all she was worth. She went through all the exercises dal Drezony had taught her, but none had any effect. She looked within, to her own reservoir. It was depleted—dangerously so—but she had to try.

Drawing on it, Solène focussed her thoughts again, willing Leverre's body to heal itself. He groaned in pain and she flinched. Was she making it worse?

Panic welled up in her gut. She closed her eyes and concentrated with every fibre of her being as she tried again. She could feel Leverre's body tense, then relax. When she opened her eyes, Leverre's eyes were empty, staring up at a sky they could not see, just like those of the men and women they had left to the crows on the road.

She rolled onto her back and let her mind drift. She hadn't saved him. She might have made his last moments worse. She tried to cry, but had no more tears, no more strength. She struggled to breathe, as though her lungs were too exhausted to continue working. When her eyelids slid shut, she didn't have the strength to open them again.

CHAPTER 41

Solène woke with a start. Confused, she had to fight through the muddle of her mind to recall where she was. The river. The bridge. Leverre's body, next to her. She took some small comfort in the knowledge that the threat to Guillot had been stopped. The sun was dipping below the horizon, and she still felt exhausted, so she concluded she had not slept for long. The horses were eating grass close by, so she hauled herself up and into the saddle.

She cast a glance back at Leverre's body, knowing she didn't have the strength to bury him and still reach Trelain. She could send someone for him when she got there. She clung to the saddle with all her strength, and urged the horse on.

⁂

Guillot sat by the fire in the Black Drake, alone with his thoughts. He had not shared more than a few words with dal Sason since getting back from Ville-rauvais. The wait for Leverre to return was becoming unbearable. Guillot had even begun to consider loading himself up on brandy and riding back to the dragon's cave for another try.

He supposed he was being a little unfair on dal Sason for keeping to his room. He had broken a few ribs himself, years before, and remembered only too well how painful it was. Even taking a breath was something you came to dread. The sooner the Order's healers arrived, the better it would be. Too much time spent thinking about what he had still to do wasn't good for his sanity or his courage. A fast horse could get him to Humberland in no more than a week, and the dragon could be someone else's problem.

Thinking further, he supposed the entire western seaboard could fall within the dragon's range—fleeing would only delay the inevitable. The best option was to ride for the coast and take a ship for anywhere in the east. There were legends of dragons in the northern mountains on the far side of the Middle Sea, though. He hadn't heard the same said for the south, so that might work. He couldn't abide Ostians, so it would have to be farther south. Auracia might work, but the independent city-states spent most of their time fighting one another, and when not doing that, teaming up to find someone else to fight. The chances of getting drawn into their squabbles were too great, so he crossed Auracia off his mental list.

That left Shandahar, famed for its seraglios . . . although someone had told him they frowned on alcohol, so that meant Shandahar was out also. The Spice Isles had pirates, but also a tasty sugar spirit called rhon, and clement weather for most of the year. He could learn to sail a brig, and make his life trading and adventuring between the isles. Still, pirates, and as romantic as it sounded, it was a dangerous part of the world. He crossed the Spice Isles off the list. Humberland in the north saw rain for two-thirds of the year, so he didn't consider it for more than a moment. That left the far east, countries forgotten since the days of the Empire. He wouldn't be able to speak the language, and was too old to learn new things, so that was off the list too.

That left Jahar or Darvaros. Jahar was filled with hot jungles, and Darvaros, arid plains. Neither particularly took his fancy. No, he was destined to be in Mirabaya, and if he wished to enjoy a long and content life here, he would have to deal with the dragon. He had just turned his mind back to that problem when the door opened, sending a blast of cool, fresh air through the taproom.

"Guillot?"

He turned, startled by the use of his name. Solène walked toward him, looking exhausted and wearing cream clothes liberally splattered with blood.

"Solène? What are you doing here? Are you all right? Did the Prince Bishop send you? Where's Leverre?"

"Hold on," she said. "Let me sit and catch my breath. I've been riding hard all day."

She slumped into the chair opposite him and he thought she was about to pass out. He waved to the barkeep, who brought over a carafe of water and a couple of glasses. Guillot filled one and pushed it over to Solène. She drained it, then nodded to the empty glass. He refilled it, wishing he could find that level of satisfaction in the tasteless liquid.

"Leverre was with me, but he's dead," she said between gulps. "The Prince

Bishop sent men to kill you. We chased them down and stopped them, but they killed Leverre."

Guillot arched an eyebrow and leaned back in his chair. "I know Amaury doesn't like me—rest assured I've little love for him myself—but try to have me killed?"

She nodded. "It's a long story. Complicated, too, but the gist of it is he was going to have you killed, blame it on the dragon, then use your failure to give the people a reason to welcome the Order and its mages with open arms."

"All right, I can sort of see how that makes sense," Guillot said, still trying to digest the news. "You stopped the assassins though?"

"We did," she said, and let out a series of great, wracking sobs. "I killed three people. I used magic to do it."

Guillot leaned forward and placed a hand on her shoulder. "If they were on their way to murder me, it was the right thing to do. We live in a world where sometimes people need killing. It's never easy, and it never feels good— at least, it shouldn't—but sometimes it needs to be done."

"I know," she said. "I . . . I just had no idea how it would happen. The way I did it, I mean. It was horrible. So horrible. You can't imagine."

He gave her a wry smile, thinking back to a day many years before, and a bridge filled with men. He didn't have to imagine—he simply remembered.

She did her best to stifle her tears.

"The horror of it will fade with time," Guillot said. "I promise you that."

"I don't care," she said. "I never want to have to do anything like that again. I'll never use magic to kill again. Never."

"There are things worth killing for. You saved my life by doing what you did, and I'm grateful to you. If you're lucky, perhaps you'll never have to kill again, but now you know what it's like, and that you can if you have to. Never say never."

She shrugged. "Where's Nicholas?"

"He's up in his room, licking his wounds," Guillot said. "He got knocked about pretty badly by the dragon."

"Leverre said he broke some ribs?"

"Three at least, I'd say," Guillot said. "Is there anything you can do for him? Have they taught you how to heal? His condition has worsened and I'm start-ing to worry about him."

She shook her head. "People are complicated things. It's easy to make a mess of it if you don't know what you're doing. I might be able to ease his pain a little, but I need some rest first. An hour should do."

Gill nodded. "Might be best if you don't mention what's happened, or that the Prince Bishop wants me dead."

"I'm in complete agreement with you on that," she said.

Guillot nodded. "I'll get a room readied for you."

Solène willed away the gentle knocking on her door, but as awareness returned, she remembered what needed to be done. It was dark outside, so he hadn't let her sleep through until morning. She got up, put on her robe, which the inn's staff had cleaned, and answered the door. Gill stood there, a sheepish look on his face.

"I gave you as long as I dared," he said. "Dal Sason's looking worse and having trouble breathing." He led Solène into dal Sason's room.

"I've brought you a visitor," he said, flopping down onto a wicker-backed chair.

"Solène? What are you doing here?" he said, gasping the words out between laboured breaths.

"I'm here to help," she said, casting Guillot a guilty look.

"You'd best take a look at my ribs then," dal Sason said. "They hurt something awful."

Moving to beside the bed, she pulled back his bandage. The right side of his chest was a variety of colours from black to yellow, and she could clearly see the location of each of the breaks. She had only seen a wound turn bad once—when a miller's apprentice in Bastelle got a hand caught in the mill's gear wheel—but the boy's flesh looked exactly like dal Sason's. The mill had taken his hand, then the rot had taken his arm to the shoulder. The visiting physician had cut it off, saying it was the only way to save the lad. It hadn't worked.

There was no cutting off a chunk of dal Sason's chest, however. She felt a chill run across her skin as it occurred to her that in saving Guillot, in killing the assassins and their party, she might have condemned dal Sason to death. One of them had to have been a healer, who would have been able to fix him with only a treatment or two. No regular physician would be able to do a thing for him if he had the rot. There were no more healers coming, and unless she did something, he was a dead man.

"How are you feeling?" she said, as she glanced at Guillot. She could see that he recognised the serious expression on her face.

"Rotten," dal Sason said. "Worse today, if anything. The pain is unbelievable at times. It eased off for a while, but it's so hot and tight down my right side now, that I can barely move. Or breathe."

"I'm going to fetch some cold water. Ice, if they have any. Cooling it down will help, then I'll see what I can do. Gill, will you give me a hand?"

He nodded, his own expression grave. As soon as they got outside, with the door closed behind them, she stopped.

"I'm no healer," she said, "but even I can see the wounds inside him have turned bad. Without help, it's going to get worse. Probably kill him. Who knows how much other damage was done to his insides."

"What do we do, then?" Guillot said. "Shall I ask around for another physician?"

"I don't think that will help. He's already seen one, hasn't he?" Guillot nodded. "And yet he's worse now."

"I see what you mean," Guillot said. "Are you willing to help him?"

"I could end up doing more harm than good," she said. Her stomach twisted with fear as she remembered the pain Leverre had felt during his final moments. "I understand the principle of what I'm supposed to do, but that's as far as it goes."

"Well, if he's going to die without help, it might be that anything you do that speeds him to that end would be a mercy. But there's a chance you'll be able to help him. Perhaps even save him. I'm willing to take it."

"Do you think he would be?" she said, torn between the desire to help and the fear of making it worse.

"We can ask, but it might make him suspicious. Why would the Prince Bishop send an untested healer?"

Solène thought for a moment. If she could kill, surely she could heal? Leverre had been willing to let her try, though sadly, that hadn't gone well. Still, dal Sason's injuries weren't as severe, and hopefully would require less powerful intervention. She could start off by trying to cleanse him of the infection, and all being well, go from there. She couldn't do much harm if she adopted that approach, and though harsh, there was sense in what Gill said.

"I'll try," she said. "I need to rest more first, though. And eat a good meal.

The journey took a lot out of me. Without more rest I can't guarantee I won't make him worse. A few more hours aren't likely to significantly change his situation."

"Agreed," Gill said. "Eat, then rest. We can start in the morning. I'll fetch ice and water to help with the fever and take care of him until then."

She nodded, and could already feel her mouth start to water at the thought of a good dinner.

Solène awoke late the next morning. The combination of an overly large meal, followed by a full night's sleep in a warm bed, had left her feeling almost normal. At moments, she could almost forget the events of the past few days, and her role in them.

Gill was asleep on the wooden chair when she went into dal Sason's room, snoring gently and completely oblivious to her arrival. She thought about waking him, but there was nothing he could do to help. Magical healing didn't require any other intervention. If done right, it was soothing, pain free, and completely restorative. If done wrong?

She walked quietly to dal Sason's bedside and sat. He was asleep, but there was nothing peaceful about it. He twitched and moaned, and she could see from his colour and sweat-matted hair that fever had set in. She took a deep breath and held her hand out, above his chest. She closed her eyes and reached for the Fount. It was waiting for her, easily within reach now. It always seemed to be so much stronger in towns and cities. She noticed a clump of energy in Gill's purse—just like Leverre had described. That must be the Cup. They would need to talk about that later—

She shuddered, realising that her mind had wandered, and returned her focus to what needed to be done. Distraction was disastrous in magic, all the more so when healing—she could end up hastening the infection's spread, or worse. She knew she was still a long way from having the mental discipline she needed, but she was ready to try. She focussed on a desire to heal. She thought of a fever fading, of dal Sason's skin cooling. She thought of rotting flesh returning to a healthy state.

Releasing her hold on the Fount, Solène opened her eyes, fearful of what she might see. Dal Sason's face was not nearly as flushed as it had been when she had first sat down beside him. His expression was of a man more at ease. She closed her eyes again and repeated the process, extending her thoughts to bones knitting and becoming strong, of normal, healthy blood flow restored to damaged tissues. Her mind flashed back to the moment she had turned a woman from person to a spray of blood and bits of flesh. Dal Sason let out a pained groan and Solène jumped in fright, her heart racing, remembering the moment before Leverre had died.

She took a deep breath to steady herself and looked dal Sason over, but it appeared that whatever had caused his distress had been momentary. She let out a sigh of relief and sat, cursing herself for allowing horrific memories to intrude on her thoughts. This was why healing was considered such an expert magical art. The slightest distraction, the slightest drop in focus, and the patient could suffer immeasurably. The precision needed to target specific internal injuries required an encyclopaedic knowledge of anatomy as well as incredible skill. It was why she was only willing to risk treatment in the most general way.

Calmer, she steadied her thoughts, pushing anything that was not in the here and now far to the back of her mind. She felt the Fount start to flow into her as she willed her magic to grow stronger. She furrowed her brow and squeezed her eyes shut, holding on to that single thought. The danger was that desiring to maintain only one, pure thought often led to thinking about the act of thinking, which in itself was a distraction. She gave it one last effort, then stopped. She wished healing could be as simple as killing. If it were, surely the world would be a much better place.

She opened her eyes to take in her work. Dal Sason's colour was back to normal and he slept peacefully, with an expression of great comfort on his face.

"I didn't want to disturb you," Guillot said.

She jumped in fright but managed not to shriek. "You startled me," she said. "I thought you were asleep."

"I was, until near the end. You looked so focussed on the task I didn't want to cause you to make a mistake." He chuckled. "I was almost afraid to breathe. He looks well, though. Better than he has since before the cave. To my eye it seems as though it worked."

"I think it has," Solène said. "I hope. His body's been through a lot of trauma though, so he'll still need rest. I daren't do any more for fear of undoing what I've managed. I'm too new to all this to chance my luck."

"A sound view," Guillot said. "Why don't we leave him to it and get some breakfast. I'm starving, and I dare say you are too."

▲▲▲▲▲▲

They ate in silence until Guillot felt the rumble in his belly start to give way to a feeling of contentment. The food in the Black Drake was good, and he realised he was tending to overeat. A few more days at the Black Drake, and he would need to let his belt out a notch or two.

"I was hoping that there might be more help coming from the city to deal with the dragon," he said, finally breaking the silence. "I assume that won't be coming now?"

She shook her head. "No."

"I'll have to make do then."

"You're going to go after it again?" she said.

"What choice do I have? I'm sure Nicholas will help when he's better. We know what to expect now. It might go better for us this time."

"The Cup," she said. "With everything that's happened, I'd almost forgotten. Leverre said you found a cup in the dragon's cave."

"Yyyeeessss . . ." Guillot said. First Leverre's interest in it, now hers. His suspicion was reaching its boiling point.

"Do you still have it?"

"I do," Guillot said reluctantly. Having found the statues in the chambers beneath his ruined manor, he was doubly suspicious of the Order's interest in the cup. "Why are you all so interested in a little Telastrian steel pot?"

"It's much more than that," she said. "At least I think it is. If it's what I've read about."

He studied her for a moment, then decided he could trust her as much as anyone. She had killed people on his behalf, after all. He took the cup out of his purse and set it on the table, next to the salt and pepper shakers, where it looked much like a sugar bowl.

A look of intense concentration spread across Solène's face before she let out a gasp. "That's it," she said. "Just as Leverre described—like a knot of threads in a sheet of silk."

"I would very much like to know why Leverre was so interested in it, and why you know about it at all," Guillot said.

"It's a very ancient artefact. The histories say it's what gave mankind true magical power. It's called the Amatus Cup, after—"

"Yes, I know who Amatus was. You're saying this was his?"

"No. The histories say he was the one to discover it, that it's how he got his power and ushered in the golden age of magic."

"And it got to a dragon's cave how, exactly?"

"Your guess is as good as mine. What I do know is that it was used in the Silver Circle's initiation ritual. I found a book of letters between an Imperial official and the Imperial court, requesting that it be made available to help them fight dragons. In the ritual, a mage placed a drop of water on the tongue of the initiate, did something to focus the Fount in a particular way, and created a magically enhanced, dragon-slaying Chevalier of the Silver Circle."

"I know," Guillot said.

Solène frowned. "How?"

"Well, I suspected as much." He described the rooms he had found under his old manor house, the paintings, the statues, watching closely to see what she made of it all. He watched her chew her lip, then realised he had left something out entirely. "There was old writing. I expect I'll need to find a schol—"

"I can read it," she said. "From what you've said, that might be where the ceremony happened. The inscription might tell me how the ceremony was conducted—what was said. That's the key. The drop from the Cup will give you power, but I don't know what kind. It could be anything. Improved speed, strength, intelligence, the ability to pat your head and rub your tummy at the same time.

"In the ritual, the mages channelled it toward something specific, and that's the key. They knew what was needed to fight a dragon—they'd been trying and failing for some time. There's no reason why I can't shape the power in the same way."

"For me?"

"Of course you," she said. "Who else? I can't cast it on myself. At least, I don't think I can, and I barely know one end of a sword from the other."

"Maybe it was magic that did it, not a sword."

"Surely then it would have been *Magisters of the Silver Circle*, not *Chevaliers*?"

"Good point."

"We need to go there. I need to see the inscriptions."

"Should we wait for dal Sason?" Guillot said, hoping she would say no.

"I suppose we should."

He groaned inwardly. "When he's awake then."

CHAPTER
43

Nicholas lay in bed, thinking. He had overheard some of what Solène and Guillot had whispered to one another while they thought him asleep. In reality, he had gone from a tormented half sleep of feverish nightmares to feeling perfectly well in the blink of an eye. He had too much experience of how the world worked to reveal to anyone that he was healthy again, until he was ready.

Leverre had returned to the city and was now dead. Neither he nor the dragon had killed Guillot, which meant the task fell to him. It was disappointing that Leverre hadn't managed it; Nicholas had hoped that he wouldn't be called on to do it, for the simple reason that he liked Gill. Assassination wasn't a good way for a man like Guillot to go, but Nicholas knew that his job might not always tally with what he found tasteful. Still, there were many things in life he found distasteful that he could do nothing about, and if he didn't look out for himself, no one else would. He had said he would do it, had taken the money, and desperately wanted what that money would bring—the return of his family's estates and status. That meant he would do it.

Moral quandaries dealt with, he returned to trying to make sense of what was going on and how best to proceed with his task. Nicholas had expected two things to happen after they returned to Trelain. First, Leverre would kill Guillot, leaving the way open for the Prince Bishop to announce the Order as the saviours of Mirabaya. Then he had expected a combat-strength detachment of Spurriers to arrive, to heal him so he could lead them to the dragon. They would kill it and fulfill the Prince Bishop's promise to the people.

Clearly something had gone wrong, and he didn't know what.

He chewed the matter over for a moment, and came to the conclusion that the dearth of information didn't matter. He had his orders, and in the absence of instructions to the contrary, the correct course was to follow them. He stretched his arm, shoulder, and neck, and smiled broadly when he completed the movement entirely free of pain. The girl had worked wonders, though the amount of power she appeared to wield was a concern. He had no desire to die in the execution of his duty, and he knew she would side with Gill in the event of a fight.

He would have to wait until they were apart, and if necessary, kill them both. He knew the Prince Bishop wouldn't be happy with the loss of his protégé, but Nicholas felt confident that her presence in Trelain wasn't on the Prince Bishop's orders. If she was as strong as she seemed to be, she posed too big a threat to be allowed to live if there was even a hint of uncertainty as to her loyalty. Both Solène and Gill had to die.

He swung his feet out of bed and sat up, rotating his shoulder as he did. It was amazing how quickly one became accustomed to debilitating pain. With each revolution he expected the agonising grind of broken bone to spear through him. That it did not was an enjoyable novelty. He dressed quickly and strapped on his sword belt.

Nicholas didn't think of himself as an assassin, though that was the role he found himself playing most often. There was a way of doing things in polite society, and if someone needed a nobleman or banneret killed, it was frowned upon to do it with a dagger in a dark alley. Nicholas had found his niche quickly after leaving the Academy: "Duellist for hire" was the way he preferred to think of himself. If his clients wanted only to draw blood, he would draw blood. If they wanted to maim, he would maim. If they wanted to kill, he would oblige. The Prince Bishop's patronage would change his life, and he couldn't afford to fail.

Killing Guillot would be a different matter, however. Given Gill's reputation, Nicholas considered using a dagger and striking when it was least expected. However, while cleaner living over the past couple of weeks had cleaned the rust off Gill's edges, Nicholas was confident that he was still a long way from the man he had once been. A somewhat recovered has-been alcoholic should not give him too much trouble. Unfortunately, Guillot wasn't alone.

He smiled as he adjusted his tunic and pulled on his cloak. What was the witchcraft accuser's name again? Nicholas struggled to remember details about the man who had accused Solène of witchcraft. That encounter seemed like it had taken place long ago—the details were fuzzy in his memory. He slipped out of the Black Drake unseen, revelling in the pleasure of being out of doors and pain free. Perhaps revisiting the scene would jog his memory. Concealed under the hood of his cloak, Nicholas made the short walk from the inn to the small town square where the mob had tried to burn Solène.

It was a very different place now, virtually empty rather than filled with a bloodthirsty crowd. Remembering where he had been on his previous visit, albeit on horseback, he moved to that spot. He visualised Gill riding forward, his horse brazenly shoving people out of the way. He recalled the imperious, utterly confident way Guillot had commanded someone to tell him what was going on and the unquestioning obedience of the townspeople in response.

Unfocussing his eyes, Nicholas receded into his mind, placing himself back at that moment: the crowd, the noise, the atmosphere of anger and bloodlust. Guillot's forceful questioning. The man who had denounced Solène.

Arnoul. Arnoul, Master of the Tanners' Guild. Nicholas smiled to himself and grabbed a passer-by.

"The Tanners' Guild house. Where is it?"

"Jerome's Square, my Lord," the man said, looking uneasy at Nicholas's unexpected attack. He pointed in the direction. "Can't miss it."

Nicholas let the man go and set off without even considering an apology. The sooner he was done with this, the sooner he could return to Mirabay to reap his reward. Once he'd reclaimed his ancestral home and lands, there would be no more fighting other men's duels. And no more dragon-slaying. No amount of gold or promotion could tempt him to repeat that folly.

Jerome's Square was not far and the Tanners' house was well marked and easily found. Entering, Nicholas found a clerk working at a desk. "The Master of the Guild," Nicholas said. "I wish to speak with him."

"He's very busy," the clerk said. "Leave a calling card and we'll arrange an appointment."

"I'll see him now," Nicholas said, his temper flaring, "or I'll drag you out into the street and beat your impertinent teeth from your face." He pushed back his cloak to free the hilt of his sword.

The clerk looked up, his eyes widening when he realised that he wasn't dealing with a commoner. "Apologies, my Lord. I'll see if he's available."

"Do that," Nicholas said, taking a seat on a bench by the door.

Arnoul wasn't long in coming. Nicholas recognised him from the day on the square, although he looked less rattled than he had on that day. The piggy eyes were the same.

Nicholas stood.

"My Lord," Arnoul said. "If you'd like to come this way, I'll do my best to see to whatever you need."

"I haven't the time," Nicholas said. "I've come to deliver a message. A few weeks ago, you accused a young woman of witchcraft." Arnoul's face reddened. "She's back in town. Staying at the Black Drake. She hasn't been punished and likely won't be unless someone does something about it. I don't know how much longer she'll be there, so I suggest you move quickly." Arnoul's eyes narrowed and he licked his lips before speaking.

"I thank you, my Lord. If you'll give me leave, I'll attend to it at once."

"By all means," Nicholas said. "I don't want to see justice go unserved."

Nicholas walked out of the Tanners' house and headed for the Black Drake. He still hadn't decided on how he wanted to deal with Gill. If Gill was with Solène when Arnoul and his lackeys turned up, he would fight to protect her, and with her magic added to the mix, it could get messy. Very messy.

Ideally the two would be apart when it happened, then Nicholas could draw Guillot into a duel. He hoped Arnoul's anger at what Solène had done to him was still smouldering hot enough to inspire him to immediate action, but Nicholas supposed waiting a day or so wouldn't make a great deal of difference. The dragon might torch a few more villages, but that wasn't really his concern. So long as it was stopped before it got to Mirabay, or to his own village and demesne at Sason, he didn't give a damn. Even wiping Trelain off the map wouldn't be the worst thing to happen. It was a dirty hole of a town with nothing to commend it, as far as he was aware.

Nearing the Black Drake, he loitered in a small alleyway opposite, curious to see if something would grow from the seeds he had sown. The easiest way to kill someone was if a good distraction kept the target from thinking of their own situation. That principle held true just as much in duels as it did in an outright assassination. If some blood spilled unnecessarily along the way, he wasn't going to lose any sleep over it.

He didn't have to wait long before he saw a crowd of men coming down the street. They were nine strong, and several held weapons of some sort—a club, a smith's hammer, a short sword. He felt a momentary pang of sympathy for the staff at the Black Drake, who were accustomed to a certain standard of client. None of the men marching on it at that moment came even close to fitting the bill. It wasn't going to be a pretty scene, nor a pleasant experience for anyone standing in the mob's way.

Nicholas stole across the street to the stable yard, then into the Black Drake and up the back stairs to Gill's room; there he collected Gill's sword, which hung in its scabbard from a bedpost. Then he took up a position where he could overlook the taproom. He could see Gill and Solène sitting at a table, likely waiting for him to wake so they could get on with whatever they planned to do next.

The inn's front door slammed open and the mob barged in, Arnoul at their head, brandishing a walking stick with a large, polished head that suggested it was designed for more than just walking.

"There she is," he roared, pointing to a visibly surprised Solène. "Take her."

The behaviour of bullies never ceased to amuse Nicholas. The chief bully, the one with the greatest desire for the end result, always kept the greatest distance, always had others carry out their aims. In certain ways Arnoul was similar to the Prince Bishop, Nicholas reflected. Both were men of influence within their spheres, and both had something to offer the men doing their bidding. It was a sad reflection on the world, he thought, that no matter how high you rose, base instinct and behaviour would always out. Still, when you understood the way of the world, you could thrive in it, and Nicholas had always prided himself on clearly seeing how things worked.

Guillot had jumped to his feet, his hand instinctively going for his sword, which was not there. It wasn't the done thing to wear a sword in the taproom of a respectable establishment. There were plenty of inns where to go without one was an act of idiocy, but the Black Drake was not one of them. Gill stared down the men Arnoul had commanded to seize Solène, and something of a standoff developed as they tried to work out how much of a danger he represented. Nicholas allowed the standoff to continue a moment longer before making his way down to the taproom.

"Gentlemen, please," he said, trying to ignore the rising tension he felt. Although Guillot was toothless, Nicholas had no real idea what Solène was capable of. "Master Arnoul, you may take the witch. However, her companion is to be left to me."

CHAPTER
44

"What in hells are you playing at, dal Sason?" Guillot said. The absence of a sword at his side felt like a stinging wound. The best weapon he had to hand was the chair he had just been sitting on. And Solène. After the trauma of killing for the first time, another confrontation was the last thing she needed, though her spirits had lifted considerably when she successfully used her magical gifts to heal dal Sason. Guillot worried that having to kill again so soon might break her.

"It's a long, complicated story that I really couldn't be bothered to go into," dal Sason said. "Suffice to say, she's going to be taken away, then you and I are going to have a chat."

"Now might be a good time to conjure something up," Guillot said.

Solène looked terrified, then her expression hardened, giving him hope that she would magic the whole situation away. His heart sank when she shook her head. "I won't," she said. "I can't."

"You can't let them take you," Guillot said. "You know what happened the last time."

She gave him a sad smile. "I do, but I don't care. It's better than the alternative. I won't kill again. Not ever."

"Well, now that we've got that out of the way," dal Sason said. "Master Arnoul?" He nodded at Solène.

Arnoul barked another order, and his men, emboldened, grabbed her and started to haul her to the door. Guillot took a step forward, taking a firm grip on the chair. Solène shook her head again, but dal Sason's blade at his throat stopped Gill from lifting it and charging. Laughing harshly, the men manhandled Solène out of the taproom, leaving Guillot and dal Sason alone—anyone not involved had long since fled.

"What now?" Guillot said.

"Let's go out into the stable yard."

With a sword point at his throat, Guillot couldn't argue. He had been around long enough to know that opportunity presented itself at the most unexpected moments. He nodded gently, careful not to cut himself on dal Sason's blade.

Outside, he was greeted by cool air and the harsh tang of horse dung. A few paces from the inn's door, he turned to face dal Sason, looking around him for anything he might be able to use as a weapon. There was only a half-full pail of water. Or perhaps night soil.

"So, we're here," Guillot said.

"Didn't want anyone else to see this," dal Sason said. "When the announcement is made, you'll have died a hero's death at the dragon's claws."

"The Academy must really be dropping its standards if it's producing graduates willing to kill in cold blood," Guillot said, hoping to bait him.

"Oh, come on," dal Sason said. "That's the most facile thing I've ever heard. The Academy's been producing cold-blooded killers for centuries. Honour is only for rich boys who never have to get their hands dirty."

"Sason a bit of a shit-hole then?" Guillot said.

Dal Sason merely smiled. "Far from it," he said. "Sadly, my father managed to gamble most of it away. Honour is simply a dish that I cannot afford."

"So being the Prince Bishop's little errand boy means you'll get it all back?"

"Something like that," dal Sason said, throwing Guillot his sword.

Guillot caught it, more surprised than ever. "I'm not sure I follow what's going on here."

Dal Sason smiled. "I've always wanted to fight a Competition winner. I'll be even happier to kill one."

"Find Briché, then. I hear he's let himself slide even worse than I have. So fat that you could thrust backwards and still hit him."

Dal Sason burst into an attack, in no way distracted by Guillot's effort at humour. Gill danced back across the cobbles of the stable yard, parrying dal Sason's expert attacks, all the while hoping there wasn't a steaming pile of horse manure stacked up behind him. There were far better ways to go than bleeding out on a heap of horse shit.

Dal Sason overreached and Guillot pounced on the opportunity, countering and firing in thrusts as quickly as he could, driving dal Sason back toward the inn.

"So you haven't drunk it all away, then," dal Sason said.

"Sorry to disappoint you," Guillot said, thrusting as fast as he could. It was he who was disappointed, however, when he saw how easily dal Sason parried it.

He backed away to slow things down. Already his chest heaved and his arm burned. It was difficult to accept that he was long past the best he would ever be. More difficult still to accept that he might die because of it. Dal Sason was younger, in better practise, and hadn't spent the last few years looking into a bottle. Gill sucked in great breaths, but knew it would take more than a few gasps of air to get him through the next few moments.

Dal Sason advanced, attempting to close the distance, but Guillot didn't give him the satisfaction of controlling the fight and backed off, staying out of range.

"Don't tell me you're afraid to die," dal Sason said nastily. "From the state I found you in, I'm surprised you don't welcome it. Looked as though you were waiting for it to come and the sooner the better."

Guillot wiped the sweat from his brow and kept backtracking, knowing there wasn't much farther to go before he'd run into the wall of the stable. He had seen swordsmen behave like dal Sason—he'd even done it himself. When you are so confident of victory, when you are so certain that you have the measure of your opponent, like a cat, you start to toy with them, to revel in your mastery of a life-or-death situation. You know you have faced another in a mortal dance, and triumphed.

Dal Sason attacked again, lunging in a smooth, powerful movement. Solène had done too good a job healing him. Why hadn't she left even a little crack in one of his ribs? Guillot parried and spun to the side, hoping to get around dal Sason so he would be able to retreat toward the other side of the courtyard. He needed time to think—something in precious short supply during a duel.

He saw the way the fight was going as well as dal Sason. It was only a matter of time before he missed a parry and was skewered. He wasn't so prideful as to believe he could push for victory solely by gritting down and relying on his speed and skill. Both had long since departed him. He was still good, he would allow himself that much, but dal Sason was better.

Dal Sason came at him again. He parried and tried to riposte, but the parry had left him so off balance that he stumbled and missed his target by so much that dal Sason didn't even bother to try to defend himself.

"How sad," dal Sason said. "I'm only sorry I didn't get to see you in your prime so I'd have something to compare to this sorry exhibition."

"I thought you did see me?" Guillot said.

Dal Sason smiled and shrugged. "I've never been a particularly good liar. I always forget what I've told people."

"Occupational hazard," Guillot said, edging back toward the tavern, wondering if he could run faster than dal Sason. Probably not, and even if he could, he would allow himself to sink only so far. Better to die on the sword, even considered a drunken disgrace, than to live as a coward. He wasn't willing to simply roll over for the assassin, though. The smug grin on dal Sason's face, his absolute certainty of victory, was galling.

Dal Sason attacked again, but Guillot could tell there was no intent behind it. It was more a demonstration attack, showing perfect form, without commitment to the kill. It was an insult, and Guillot could tell by the look on the other man's face that dal Sason planned to toy with him until he was too tired to even lift his sword, then make the killing cut at his leisure. And that was Guillot's answer.

He waited for the next attack and made a haphazard effort to parry. It wasn't the parry of a completely exhausted man, but indicated that he was nearly there. He followed it with a slow, wobbly lunge. Dal Sason simply stepped aside and laughed. He didn't even bother coming in with a riposte, though Guillot had left himself dangerously open. That had been a gamble, but dal Sason's inaction proved his suspicion correct. He retreated again, breathing heavily—that much, at least, wasn't an act. He stood with his sword en garde, but the point wavering around as though he were halfway through his third bottle of wine.

Dal Sason thrust twice, probing attacks that Guillot limply parried, making sure to bring his sword slowly back to guard. The moment was near. Dal Sason's eyes narrowed, and he exploded into a series of powerful attacks, cutting at Guillot rather than thrusting. Gill shied back from the first, parried the second, then riposted with everything he had left. His sword was buried up to the hilt in dal Sason's chest before the younger man realised what had happened.

"Not so slow after all," Guillot said. He pulled his sword out with a twist to make certain dal Sason wouldn't come at him again. Dal Sason dropped to his knees, sword falling from his limp fingers. Blood bubbled from the corners of his mouth and he fell to the muddy cobbles.

"I was beginning to think you were all right," Guillot said. "Seems my judgement is as bad as it ever was."

He stood over dal Sason until the life left the banneret's eyes. As his excitement faded, Guillot felt light-headed. He realised he had pushed his body far beyond what it was able for. He balanced on his sword, sweat dribbling from the end of his nose. His heart started to slow, then jumped back to full speed as he recalled Solène. He had to free her from Arnoul's mob. After the fight he had just been in he didn't fancy his chances, but he had to at least try.

He had no idea where they would take her—they would need several hours to build a pyre big enough to kill someone, so they would need to put her somewhere for safekeeping.

An uncertain face stared at him from the street entrance to the stable yard.

"I was about to help you," Solène said, "but you didn't need it." She walked into the courtyard and stood looking down at dal Sason's body. "It would have saved us both a lot of bother if I'd let him die of his injuries, wouldn't it?"

"I know I'm a cynical git," Guillot said, "but I meant it when I said that the world is a better place without some people in it." He looked at her sharply. "How did you get free?"

She shrugged. "Just because I won't use magic to kill doesn't mean I won't use it to protect myself."

He raised an eyebrow.

"We should ready the horses and leave. I want to see the secret room you told me about. Also, it won't be long before nine sheep become nine very angry men again. I'd like to be far away from here before that happens."

Guillot laughed and called for the stable boy.

PART THREE

Seeing sheep ambling about on Trelain's main street was not terribly un-usual—it happened every market day—but for Guillot, knowing that only minutes earlier they had been an angry mob made it a very bizarre experience. Solène didn't cast the animals so much as a glance as they rode out of the town, but Guillot's eyes were glued to them, wondering what it would look like when they turned back into people. He wondered at the confusion it would cause, and how people would react. On consideration, he was glad they wouldn't be around to find out for themselves.

That Amaury thought himself so powerful that he could dispose of people at his convenience was enraging. That he had sent someone to kill Gill was even more so. Amaury had always been an arrogant little shit, but Guillot had to admit that he had been too, in his younger days, which was probably why he and the Prince Bishop had been friends once upon a time.

His first taste of battle had begun to knock that arrogance out of him. His second had finished the job. Gone were the legion of adoring fans lining the arena at the Competition. Gone was the glamour, the excitement, the cere-mony. It was all blood, guts, mud, and watching people you knew and con-sidered friends getting chopped to bits and dying in agony, far from home and the people they loved. All a big attitude did on the battlefield was get you killed. It had nearly done for him, but he prided himself in having been self-aware enough to learn his lesson quickly. He might have been better with a sword than the men around him, but he didn't have eyes in the back of his head, and when he needed them, his comrades were there.

Amaury never learned that lesson. The injury he sustained in the Compe-tition's quarterfinal—from a blow Guillot had delivered—had ended his days with a sword in hand. It struck Gill that his former friend had probably re-sented him since their days at the Academy, where he had been the big fish until Guillot came along. Since then, despite his best efforts, Amaury had always been second-best.

With the power he had now, and the resentment he seemed to harbour, Guillot was surprised that Amaury hadn't sent a hired sword to pay a call on him before, one night when he was lost in the bottom of a bottle. Perhaps out of sight was out of mind, and it wasn't as if Amaury hadn't been occupying himself in other ways, climbing the slippery slope of power.

If Guillot survived what he had to do next, he would pay a visit to the Prince Bishop. Despite the other man's old injury, Guillot would call him out.

"I'm not going to turn you into a sheep, you know," Solène said, after a long silence.

Guillot smiled. "Sorry, lost in my thoughts is all. Do you really think my death would have been enough to make the people accept the presence of mages?"

Solène shrugged. "The Prince Bishop's been pushing the story of the last Chevalier of the Silver Circle riding off to slay the dragon and save the nation pretty hard. People are convinced that you'll do it. If you do, you'll be very, very famous."

"No pressure, then," Guillot said. "Still, he might get his wish."

"We'll find what we need in this secret room," Solène said. "If we don't, perhaps there'll be enough that I can cobble something together that will give you what you need."

"That's not the most confidence-inspiring thing you've ever said."

"Many things can be done to a soldier to make them better. Meddling with a body is tricky, and I've not done anything like that before—no one alive has. Instructions would be better than experimenting."

"I'm in complete agreement with that," Guillot said.

"Still, it went well with dal Sason. That's something, although it is easier to fix what was broken than change things to work differently."

"You're really not filling me with any enthusiasm for this idea. I think I'd rather take my chances with the dragon. It didn't get me the last time . . ."

She chewed on her lip and stared into the distance. "You're right. It's risky to try without instructions. It could take years of trial and error to get the ritual right, and even longer to determine and formulate the enhancements most suited to dragon fighting. Best to just face it with your armour and sword. Like you said, that kept you alive the last time."

He thought about the plates bundled up on the saddle behind him. The heat of the dragon's flame had made the metal brittle. It was little better than the ceremonial suits made of paste they used to wear in his Silver Circle days. "When you put it like that," Guillot said.

⏣

They crested the rise leading to the piles of rubble that had once been the old manor house of Villerauvais. Guillot realised that this was a sight he would never grow used to. He wondered if he should rebuild, but what was the point? Villerauvais was gone. Without the village, there was no seigneur, and no need for a manor house. Assuming he survived the ordeals he had before him. If the dragon wasn't enough, he now felt compelled to deal with the Prince Bishop, and that wasn't the act of a man looking forward to a long life.

"What did it look like before?" Solène said.

"It was taller." He realised he was being churlish, but the feeling of failure at seeing every part of his heritage wiped out was profound. "It was never much of a place compared to some. Villerauvais wasn't a rich province, but the house was probably grander than the place deserved. It was larger once, but parts were knocked down over the years as they fell out of use and into disrepair."

"How old was it?"

"The remains you see? I don't really know. My family first came out here during the Empire."

"One of them helped found the Silver Circle?"

"Supposedly, although after what I found under the ruin, I'm more inclined to believe it. I think Valdamar is buried down there. At least, there's a tomb with his name on it."

They let their horses graze on the lawn by the remains of the house, and Guillot escorted Solène down the steps to the hidden chambers.

"This is it," he said, gesturing to the broken door at the bottom of the stairwell. "I bought a lantern in Trelain. Let me fetch it."

Solène raised an eyebrow.

Guillot smiled sheepishly. "Oh, of course. Well, let's go in then."

They walked into the inky pool of darkness. Solène muttered something under her breath and an orb of cool white light appeared above them, growing in strength until the muttering stopped. Light fell on the first part of the chamber, illuminating the first few statues.

"Do different spells have different words you have to learn?" Guillot said.

"No. They don't need words at all, really. Magic is shaped with thoughts.

Sometimes words give form to thoughts. When you're good enough, and can control your mind precisely, you don't need them. Sometimes I find speaking them aloud helps me focus on what I want to achieve."

He nodded slowly. "Well, this is it. The altar is at the far end, the tombs in the chamber beyond."

She cast another orb of light, then another, until the whole chamber was as bright as if the roof had been lifted off, letting in the sun.

"These are magnificent," she said, walking forward to take a closer look at the statues.

"I presume they were all Chevaliers," he said. "The paintings are even more impressive."

"They are," Solène said, moving closer to one. "There's a lot of magic here. It's why everything's in such good condition. This looks as if it was painted yesterday."

"I hadn't thought of that," Guillot said. "I didn't have nearly so much light the last time I was here."

"If the paintings were protected against the elements, maybe everything here was." She advanced down the chamber until she reached the altar, and the two statues depicting the ritual with the Cup.

"I've seen this before," she said. "In the *Rule of the Chevaliers of the Silver Circle*, the only text about them that I was able to find. It had a drawing of a ceremony where a magister placed a drop from the cup on the initiate's tongue."

"What would happen if you drank a whole cupful?"

She shrugged. "I'm not sure if the quantity you drink matters, only the intended result. Maybe it does, though. Who knows? Best stick to what they did."

"Would there be any harm in trying?"

"I might end up turning you into a puddle of gore with only a drop, and you want to try drinking the whole thing?" she said.

"I take your point. The engraving is in the next chamber."

They went through, and Solène created another orb of light. It made the room seem far smaller than it had when Guillot had nothing but a flickering torch to light his way.

"That's Valdamar's tomb?" she said, nodding toward it.

"It belongs to someone with that name, anyway."

"My father used to tell me stories about him," Solène said.

"Mine too," Guillot said.

"Do you think one of those statues outside is of him?"

"I reckon so."

She reached out and placed her hand against the memorial plaque, as though touching it would somehow give her greater connection to a man long dead.

"The engraving is on that wall there," Guillot said.

As Solène glanced over and furrowed her brow, another sphere of light appeared, making each carving clear and precise.

"This is how they used to write Imperial," she said. "Back in the days of the Empire."

"When did you learn how to read it?"

"A few days ago." She shrugged. "Magic has its uses."

"Is it what we're looking for?"

She remained silent for a moment, her eyes tracking along the lines of writing. Then she smiled. "It is."

Guillot felt a wave of relief. Not only would he not have to run the gauntlet of magical experimentation, he would not be marching to almost certain death the next time he went dragon hunting.

"What does it do?" he said.

She chewed her lip for a moment. "I . . . I'm not really sure. I thought it would make you faster, stronger, more resilient, but I can't see how any of what's written here would do any of that."

He shrugged. "I suppose there's only one way to find out."

"You're willing to take the chance?"

"Whatever it was doesn't seem to have killed any of them," he said, nodding toward Valdamar's tomb. "At least, not right away."

"You have the Cup?"

"Of course," he said. "Does it matter what we fill it with?" Now seemed as good as any a time to allow himself a sip of something potent.

"The engraving says *the purest water*. Know of any pure water around here?"

Setting his disappointment aside, he nodded. "There's a stream not far from here. It comes down from the mountains uninterrupted. It's as fresh a water source as you're likely to find."

"I want to look around a little more first. See if there's anything else here that might be of use."

In the improved light she had created, she surveyed the tombs one by one, and then, satisfied she had not missed anything, they returned to the main chamber.

"It's like a hall of heroes," she said. The rows of statues, with the magnificent paintings behind them, now illuminated to their full glory, made for an impressive sight. "They went to a lot of trouble to create the magic that keeps this place in good condition. For a spell to last so long, the power they had must have been immeasurable. Look!" She pointed to the feet of the statues. There were small nameplates engraved into the bases. "Andalon," she said. "Ixten," she added, pointing to another. "Valdamar. It's amazing to think they were all here."

"Even more amazing to think I spent my childhood living above it all and never knew."

She walked up to the painting behind Valdamar's statue and studied it so closely her nose almost pressed against it. "There's something odd here," she said. She closed her eyes, frowning in concentration.

The room filled with the sound of grinding stone, and the painting slid back from the wall, opening a passageway into a chamber behind.

Guillot shook his head, amazed. "What did you do?"

"There's a lot of magic down here. I influenced it. Shall we take a look?"

He walked forward eagerly, then stopped, one foot in mid-air. "What if there's a trap?"

"A trap?"

"Well, if they're trying to protect something down here, maybe they took precautions to make sure the wrong people didn't find it?" Guillot said.

"That strikes me as paranoid."

"I'd rather be paranoid than in the bottom of a pit of spikes."

Solène sighed and closed her eyes for a moment. "I can't feel anything unusual in there—no hidden empty spaces or concentrations of magic."

"You can do that?"

Solène nodded. "The Fount lines objects. If there's an open space, I can feel the way the Fount's shape changes. That's how I knew there was something behind the painting."

"Still," Guillot said, "let's be careful. There might not be a trap, but that doesn't mean it's safe. This space is old, and the house above it has been destroyed. The structure might not be as stable as it seems."

She nodded and Guillot advanced into the passage revealed behind the painting. It was dark at first, but then one of Solène's light spheres appeared overhead and his jaw dropped.

Before him stood a wooden mannequin wearing the most magnificent suit of armour he had ever seen. He walked up to it, careful to watch where he placed his feet. The idea of a trap still hadn't left his mind, although he was now equally worried about the roof falling down on him. Surrounding the armour were other things a warrior might use on a daily basis—a saddle, a chest, and a wooden stand that looked as though it was intended to hold a sword, but which was empty.

"What's in there?" Solène called.

"Come and see. It's safe. I think."

He heard her come in behind him as he took a closer look at the armour. It was made from Telastrian steel, something he had never seen before. He had never known it to be used for anything other than blades—until he had found the Cup. He couldn't even begin to imagine the value of an entire suit of armour made from the precious metal. What was more, the workmanship was magnificent. It wasn't of a fashionable style, but if it fit him, it would likely serve him far better than the scorched suit packed in his saddlebags.

As if the natural beauty of the metal was not enough, the armour was finely engraved and inlaid with a brighter metal that Guillot took to be silver. It seemed that whatever magic had kept the place secure for so long had stopped the metal from tarnishing.

"There's another chamber behind the next statue," she said. "And the one after. I think it's safe to assume there's one behind each of them. What do you think they were for?"

"This looks like Valdamar's private chamber, where he kept his war gear when he wasn't using it," Guillot said. "I suppose they each had their own room. I'd still like to know why it's here at all, under my family home."

"What's in the chest?" Solène said.

Guillot lifted the lid with his foot, expecting a crossbow bolt to whizz out of a hole in the wall. The chest creaked open, but there was no bolt.

"Papers," he said, with disappointment. "In perfect condition, though. Like everything else here."

Solène walked to the chest and picked over them. "This is a diary," she said. "Valdamar's personal diary."

"I'm sure there are minstrels who would pay a king's ransom to get their hands on that! The forgotten stories would keep them in pride of place at any court in the country for the rest of their days."

"A king's ransom isn't what I'm interested in right now," Solène said. "If you've anything you want to do, this might take me a little while." She sat cross-legged next to the chest and took out a sheaf of papers.

"No," he said, sitting beside her. "You can give me the highlights as you go."

CHAPTER
46

Guillot left her and wandered around the chamber as Solène read in silence. Either Valdamar hadn't been particularly fastidious in recounting his great deeds, or there wasn't much worth repeating in his papers. His equipment was interesting, however. There was a clutch of finely made spears with heads of Telastrian steel, barbed in a style he hadn't seen before. He felt a pang of disappointment as he stared at the vacant space on the sword stand. He would have loved to get his hands on Valdamar's sword. Solène cleared her throat to get his attention, then spoke.

"There's only a little bit about the ritual, as best I can see, but I know why all of this is here."

"Really?"

"There was a castle here once. This was the Chevaliers' hall, where they were initiated, where they kept their equipment and prepared for battle. The initiation rite wasn't an initiation rite at all. Well, it was, but its effect was short-lived, and the ceremony had to be repeated each time they went out to face a dragon. The mages must really have been worried about the Chevaliers growing too powerful."

"That doesn't explain why it was *here*."

"It was their headquarters—or was intended to be. These pages talk about its construction as a base close to where they were operating. It makes sense, if this is where they were operating all the time."

"I suppose so," Guillot said.

"They were transporting the Cup out here to allow that. I'm not sure why the mages let them bring it out here, but they did in the end. Much of the Silver Circle's treasure was in the same convoy. It was attacked by two dragons. Valdamar says the gold in the strongboxes attracted them, but the Amatus Cup was taken along with it." She shuffled through the papers.

"The Silver Circle seems to have gone into decline straight after. This place never became the headquarters they'd intended it to be. They weren't able to properly initiate any new recruits and the existing Chevaliers had to make do with the residual effects of their . . . treatments. They tried to get the Cup back, but never found it.

"Valdamar lists off the names—*the names*—of the dragons they managed to kill along the way, but always with far greater casualties than when they had the Cup. The castle was destroyed in the mage wars and the remaining Chevaliers turned their attention to helping establish the new kingdom of Mirabaya. That's the end of it. They must have put protections on this hall to keep it safe, probably intending to resume the search for the Cup once the wars ended and the country was stable again.

"It doesn't look like they ever came back, though. Not while they lived, anyway."

"I suppose the Silver Circle had its place at court," Guillot said, "and there weren't many dragons left—if any. The new Chevaliers probably didn't have much interest in living the life of danger that the old ones did, nor spending all their time out here in the middle of nowhere. My generation of Chevaliers certainly didn't, duelling field notwithstanding."

"I'm going to go through the other chambers to see if there's anything else useful," Solène said, "but I think I have everything that I need to carry out the ceremony. The words will focus my thoughts on shaping the magic in the desired way, and then we'll be as ready as we'll ever be."

"*I'll* be as ready as I'll ever be," Guillot said. "Whatever protection it provides won't extend to you. There's never any mention of mages helping to fight dragons, and there must be a reason for that. There's no need for you to put yourself in danger as well. If it does everything it's supposed to do, I'm sure that I'll be fine."

Solène's face darkened. "We can discuss it on the road," she said. "There's still a lot of work to do here."

▲▲▲▲▲

Guillot could only resist the temptation to try Valdamar's armour on for so long. With Solène working her way through the side chambers, he was largely left to his own devices. He spent some time ogling the perfectly preserved weaponry and armour, some of which were impressive indeed, Ixten's in particular. He was reputed to have been a giant of a man, and judging by his armour, it seemed as though the stories had done little to exaggerate his size. He must have stood at least a full head taller than Guillot.

Although all the other suits were equals to Valdamar's in quality, only his looked even close to Gill's size. He stole back to the first secret chamber they had opened, and started putting it on. Dressing oneself in armour was never an easy task—a fact that had kept squires in work for centuries. By the time Guillot had the breastplate on, he wondered exactly how many squires Valdamar might actually have had.

He worked through the pieces in the well-practised routine he had always followed. He managed most of it himself, but there were a couple of buckles he couldn't get tight enough. He called out to Solène, who appeared a moment later.

"If you wouldn't mind?" he said.

He felt the buckles pull tight.

"It suits you," Solène said.

Guillot turned around, blushing. "I, well, I was curious to see if it would fit."

"It looks almost perfect. If it's better than what you have, I see no reason not to use it," she said.

"I think it's better than anything anyone has." He moved his arms and twisted to test the fit, surprised that there were no pinches or impediments. It was light too, far lighter than regular steel.

"Well, then, I doubt Valdamar would mind. I suspect you're already using his sword."

He cast a glance at the empty sword holder beside the mannequin. "What do you mean?"

"Come and see."

She led him back to the painting at the chamber's entrance and pointed at the sword in Valdamar's hand.

Guillot leaned close and squinted to make out the detail. The hilt was completely different—in Imperial times they had favoured a plain cross-guard, rather than the elaborate swept hilts and ringed guards currently used. The painting clearly showed the blade was Telastrian steel, but as Guillot studied it, he saw the hint of a familiar etching along the fuller.

"Gods alive," he said. He drew his old family blade from its sheath and looked at it. As a child, he had often wondered what the barely legible etching on the blade said, but he'd long since concluded it was the maker's mark. "Can you read what it says?"

"Of course," she said. He handed it to her, and she studied it. "Blade of the Morning Mist. First Among Twenty."

"Blade of the Morning Mist," Guillot said, his skin tingling. *Morning*, not *Mourning*, as he had always thought it to be called. Valdamar was called the *Blade of the Morning Mist* in the stories, but the tales must have altered with time. In the magical light Solène had cast, Guillot could see how the sword had earned its name. The blue and grey of the Telastrian steel swirled down the length of the blade like the mist that rolled across the pastures on a spring morning.

"The swords in the other rooms are numbered too," Solène said. "There are twenty of them in all."

"Valdamar's was the first."

"Yours was the first," she said.

"I knew it was old," Guillot said. "I never thought it might be that old, though. Nor that it might have been Valdamar's. It's humbling."

"This is no time to be humble," Solène said. "Is there anything else here you think might be useful?"

He nodded to the clutch of spears. "The heads on those spears are Telastrian. I'll take them too."

Solène said, "I've learned all I'm going to here. It's time for the ritual."

Guillot nodded.

"You still want to go through with it?"

"Is there any alternative?" Solène shrugged. "You're confident that you can do it?"

She nodded.

"Well, let's head to the river and get our pure water."

It hadn't occurred to Guillot to take the armour off before they left the remains of the old Silver Circle castle. It felt more comfortable than the armour he'd worn when facing the dragon and he felt more secure wearing a suit that had been made specifically for a veteran dragonslayer. Nonetheless, he couldn't help but feel a little pompous wearing Valdamar's armour, and sheepish at having been using his sword without realising.

The stream was only a short ride from the remains of the manor. Guillot had spent nearly every summer's day there fishing when he was a boy, but now realised he hadn't been there since before he left Villerauvais for the Academy. He remembered running to the river after each morning's lessons, usually swishing a stick through the air, imagining himself chasing dragons that were terrified by his ferocity. Now he was sitting in Valdamar's armour, wearing his sword, and readying himself to do battle with a beast he never thought he would lay eyes on. How could the world change so quickly?

Solène dismounted and crouched at the riverbank. She scooped up a handful of water, sniffed it, then drank.

"This will do," she said.

Guillot nodded and dismounted easily. A well-made suit of armour was not nearly so cumbersome as people thought, with the plates fitting the body's shape and the weight evenly distributed so that when fit and trained, you could wear it for several hours before starting to feel the burden. Valdamar's armour was on an entirely different level, however. It felt no different from a light suit of summer linen, yet he knew the Telastrian steel would perform better than anything made by the best smiths in Mirabay. He felt like a fraud wearing it—like a boy putting on his father's shoes and pretending to be a man.

He took the Cup from his purse and handed it to her. How odd to think such a small object could grant such power. She dipped it into the stream, filling it with water, then pulled a reed from the riverbank.

"Are you ready?"

"As ready as I'll ever be," Guillot said.

He stood straight and tried to relax, but his shoulders and chest were tight with tension. She stepped closer, then dipped the tip of the reed into the water. Guillot closed his eyes, opened his mouth, and extended his tongue, as he had when his nanny had administered medicine when he was a child. He did his best not to shudder when he felt the cool droplet hit his tongue. He could hear Solène whispering, but couldn't make out her words. His heart raced as he waited to feel the magic take effect.

As the rhythmic cadence of Solène's words continued, Gill wondered if every tick, itch, and sensation he felt had something to do with magic. Eventually she fell silent. He waited a moment longer, then opened one eye. She watched him expectantly.

"Is that it?" he said.

"I've finished," she said. "How do you feel?"

"No different. Did it work?"

She shrugged. "I'm sure I did everything right, but I don't know how to tell."

"Is the Cup broken?"

She laughed. "It doesn't work like that. It takes a lot of effort to destroy something magical. How else do you think all of the magelamps in the city have lasted so long?"

A shiver of concern ran across his skin. What if it hadn't worked? One way or the other, this would be the last time he would face the dragon. One of them would be dead at the end of the encounter. After sitting around waiting for death for so long, it seemed inconvenient that he would realise his great desire for life so strongly when faced with the task he had.

"Is there any way we can test it?" he said. "Before I go into the cave?"

"You know as much as I do about all of this. I don't even understand what the words were channelling. I could feel the magic shape, but I don't know what it will do."

He took a deep breath and let it out slowly. "I don't feel any different."

"There's no reason you would," Solène said, "until the magic starts to affect you, which might only happen when it has to."

"Like when the dragon's trying to bite my head off?"

She nodded. "Not an ideal time to be testing it, but that's the way magic works. We use it and shape it, but we never fully control it. Or understand it."

"Well, I suppose we should go and find out," Guillot said.

CHAPTER
47

Alpheratz had waited until he felt the wound beneath his wing was healed enough for prolonged flight before setting off. He was well fed and could go weeks before needing to eat again. Pausing at the mouth of his cave, he looked out across the landscape. He had hatched in the cave, and this view was the first thing he had seen every day of his life. It saddened him to think that the world had moved on, that his place was no longer here, but he had to accept it. Change was the great tragedy of a creature that enjoyed a lifespan measured in millennia.

He spread his wings and grimaced at the tight, painful sensation in his side. It would take some time to loosen the muscle. He stepped into the void and let himself fall until the pressure of the air was enough to carry his weight. He didn't allow himself a backward glance—there was too much pain and regret, not only at what had happened, but at what he had become.

When he took a deep breath of the crisp mountain air, his eyes widened. He smelled something familiar, something that jogged a memory deep in the recesses of his mind. Something he had not smelled since waking. He inhaled deeply again, allowing the scent to fill his nostrils. It was the tang of magic, but a particular flavour of magic. It was a slayer.

His heart raced. Here was a person worthy of his vengeance. Slayers were the root of all the evil that had been brought down on dragonkind. This was a person he could kill, a person whose death would balance the scales of justice.

He glided around in a wide arc, conserving every ounce of energy for the fight to come. Narrowing his eyes, Alpheratz looked down the valley. A long way off, he spotted two riders approaching.

Riding back into the valley to the dragon's cave was an odd feeling, like repeating an act of stupidity even though you've long since realised what a bad idea it was the first time. The fact that he had undergone an ancient magical ritual that might or might not have worked did little to quell the butterflies in Guillot's stomach, but the sense of foreboding and unfinished business that had lingered with him for days finally felt as though it was being addressed. It was a small mercy, but one he happily clung to.

"What do you think it does?" Guillot said, asking again in the hope an answer would distract him from his anxiety, or at least give him a shred of hope to cling to.

Solène shrugged.

"Best guess?"

She looked at him seriously. "Something that helps you kill a dragon."

Guillot burst into laughter. It took him a moment to get it under control, his nerves feeding the chuckles. He spotted the stand of trees where they had camped and retreated to, and his laughter came to an abrupt halt. He looked up the mountain to the dark void on its side.

"That's it," he said, nodding to it with his head.

"It's amazing to think a dragon lives there. I'm still not sure I believe it."

"It's certainly something that needs to be seen to be believed," Guillot said, "although I think I could have happily gone to my grave never having had the pleasure."

"It's quite a climb to get up there," Solène said. "Should we rest first?"

Guillot shook his head. "I want to get to it. Brother Hallot gave me a touch of something—energy, or stamina, I think—the last time. If you can repeat that, it will get me up there ready to go."

"Should be simple enough," Solène said. "Do you have everything else you need?"

He took one of the Telastrian spears from its fastening on his saddle and checked the edge on its head. It was perfect, as Telastrian steel edges always were, and he hoped it would be of more use than the spear he had hauled up the mountainside the last time. "I think so. Come with me as far as the mouth of the cave so you can get rid of the fatigue after the climb."

"I can do more than that," she said.

"I'm sure you can, but who's the anointed dragonslayer? Enough people have died up there already. If everything works as it's supposed to, I won't need your help. If I do, well, then you'll have another opportunity to earn the drag-

onslayer title for yourself. I want you to head straight back down to the valley's entrance. If I don't join you by nightfall, I won't be coming. Get straight
back to Mirabay and make sure that bastard Amaury sends an army to deal
with it once and for all."

She nodded. Just then a strange sensation passed over him, as though
something was trying to pull his insides out of his body. He wavered in the
saddle, and Solène gave him a curious look.

"Are you all right?"

"I think so," he said, recovering his balance. "Felt a bit odd for a moment.
Like something was pulling on my insides. It's passed now."

"You're sure?"

He looked about, still puzzled by the sensation. The direction of the pull
had felt very specific, but when he looked that way, he saw nothing. "I am."
He was considering the sensation, when the day darkened. He looked up again
to see what was blocking the sun—a silhouette that would turn the bowels of
the bravest of men to water.

"Damn the gods to the three hells," Guillot said.

"What'll we do?" Solène said.

"Forget about the plan, for a start," Guillot said, looking up to the beast
that hovered above them, still but for the lazy beat of its great wings.

"How will we get at it up there?" she said.

"I don't think that'll be a problem," Guillot said. "Do your best to keep
moving and stay out of its range. Ideally by riding for Mirabay as fast as
you can."

"I'm not leaving you," she said, as she tried to keep her horse calm.

Guillot could feel his horse grow skittish beneath him. His own resolve
wasn't too far behind. He drew his sword, for no reason other than to do something familiar and comforting. He felt his heart leap into his throat when the
dragon drew in its wings and dropped like a stone from the heavens.

Guillot felt fear tingle across his skin like a colony of dancing ants. He remained locked in place, trying to decide which god to pray to, before remembering that he didn't believe in any of them. They certainly hadn't ever helped
him before. Out of the corner of his eye, he could see that Solène was frozen
as well. He slapped the rump of her horse with the flat of his blade.

"Ride!" he shouted, before kicking his own mount with his heels.

He craned his neck to see where the dragon was while he tried to work out
where to go. Plenty of valley remained, but he needed to come up with some

kind of plan, and fast. The horse thundered along the turf with little urging—she wanted to be away from the dragon just as much as Guillot did. He wondered if she would be cooperative when the time came to turn to face it.

Another backward glance confirmed the dragon was coming after him, wings outstretched, gliding silently along like a great, dark shadow of death. He knew the flame would be next. The hairs on the back of his neck shrivelled in anticipation. Unwilling to run his horse to exhaustion, he brought her to a halt and turned. His sword felt like a reed in the wind when he stared at the beast gliding toward him.

It was huge; he could not hope to stand against it. He almost wished he were back in the cave, where its size had seemed less imposing. It was all teeth, claws, and wickedly sharp horns, things concealed by the gloom and smoke in the cave. Then, had he seen all that was now before him with such clarity, he would likely have lost his nerve and fled. Now he felt resigned to what needed to be done and what his fate would likely be.

Guillot spurred the horse into a gallop, overcoming its resistance to charging toward the dragon's fangs and glowing eyes. He expected a burst of flame to end him at any moment. He re-sheathed his sword, feeling naive for having drawn it in panic, then took hold of the spear with his right hand and brought it to bear. It had been a long time since he had thrown a spear, but with a target as large as the dragon, he could hardly miss.

Still, unsure of the power of his arm, he waited until the dragon was so close he could smell its breath, a mix of rotting meat and naphtha. Gill stood up in his stirrups and with a great roar, hurled the spear with every ounce of strength he had. The spear flew true, but disappeared into a jet of flame.

Reacting as quickly as he could, Guillot urged his horse to the right, but she was not fast enough. The horse screamed as the fire burned her. She had galloped a number of paces before Gill could look back and assess her injury. Her rump was scorched, yet he had felt nothing—no heat, no pain. Had the superb Telastrian armour protected him? Had he turned out of the way in time? Or was this the boon the Silver Circle had enjoyed—a resistance to flame?

He wheeled the horse around and saw the dragon turning in a long, lazy arc through the sky, its black scales shimmering in the sunlight like fine mail armour. He spotted Solène some distance away, watching everything as it unfolded. Frustrated that she had not taken his advice to head down the valley, he waved at her and pointed, but she ignored him. He had no time to argue with her; he returned his attention to the dragon, which was completing its turn back toward him.

His horse whickered but held steady beneath him. They had both survived the dragon's first pass and been emboldened by the experience. He reached for another spear even as he tried to see if the first one had struck true. He wasn't sure what else to do. The initiation hadn't implanted dragon-killing instructions in his mind.

He urged his horse on again until she was heading toward the dragon at full gallop. The pounding of his heart syncopated with the thundering of her hooves and he felt the excitement of battle flush through his veins. To think that he was doing as Valdamar had once done, charging a dragon, spear in hand—to be doing something no man alive ever had, was a thrill like none other. A vestige of his former self wondered if stories would be written about this fight, if he would someday be as legendary as Valdamar, Andalon, and the others.

The dragon let out a shrieking roar that stabbed into Guillot's ears. He raised his spear once more, smiling at the sight of the previous one sticking out of the beast's side. More confident now, he waited, spear poised to strike. Perhaps this would be the one to bring it to the ground.

Still he waited, until the dragon was so close that it filled the sky. He drew back his arm, preparing to release his spear, then felt a thud on his armour. Something yanked up on his body and his feet came free of the stirrups. He looked down and saw his rapidly shrinking horse come to a confused halt. Panic threatened to overwhelm his already racing heart as the beast's wings beat down, sending them ever higher. He tried to twist around in its grip, but was held firm in the creature's razor-like talons. Were it not for Valdamar's armour, he thought, he would have been pierced through. As it was, the claws barely made a dent.

Realising that he still held his spear, he stabbed at the dragon's flank, but the strike had no power. The weapon glanced off the glittering black scales and was wrenched from his grip. He watched it tumble back to the ground, which was dropping away rapidly, and was terror-struck, knowing what lay in store for him if the dragon let go. It occurred to him that was exactly what it intended.

He grabbed a smooth, curving talon just as the dragon released its grip. Despite his best effort, Gill could feel his leather-gauntleted hand slide toward its tip. He gripped with every bit of strength and dangled from the talon. The beast craned its head down to look at him, and its lips twisted. It shook its foot, and Guillot's hold slipped right to the talon's end. The dragon lifted its foot again for what would undoubtedly be a final shake, bringing Gill close to the spear he had stuck into the dragon. He hurled himself at it desperately. His right hand fell short, but with a desperate twist, he caught the end of the shaft with his left.

The dragon roared in frustration. Guillot cast his atheism to one side and prayed to every god and ancestor he could remember that the spear would hold fast. He got both hands on to it and pulled himself up as the dragon started to buck and twist through the air. With each movement, Guillot expected the spear to pull free, but its Telastrian barbs held firm. He knew he could only hold on for so long, but he could think of no way to encourage the beast to land. Not alive, at least.

He twisted his left arm around the spear, then drew his legs and feet up to do the same. Releasing the shaft with his right hand, Guillot drew his sword.

Even with the benefit of daylight, it was difficult to spot a weak point in the dragon's scales. He had been lucky with the spear, but didn't dare trying to stab into the same spot for fear of cutting the spearhead loose.

The dragon thrashed and bucked in an effort to throw Guillot free. It scrabbled with its feet, trying to catch him with its talons, but Guillot had managed to find himself a spot the dragon couldn't reach. As he swung back and forward, clinging to the spear shaft for dear life, Gill looked desperately for an inviting target. He wondered where the beast's heart might be and if his sword was long enough to reach it. However, a destroyed heart might kill the beast instantly, dropping them both out of the sky, and Guillot still clung to the hope that he might survive the battle.

The lungs would be better. Making it hard for the beast to breathe might force it to the ground. He hoped. This left him with the same problem as the heart—where were they, and would he be able to reach them? He watched the dragon's huge chest expand and contract with each breath, and knew that was where to strike. As the dragon's chest filled with air, Gill struck at the exposed join between two scales, pushing the blade in up to its hilt.

The dragon screeched and bucked with such violence that Guillot lost his grip on the sword. He clamped both arms and legs around the spear shaft, hoping to avoid a plunging death to the valley below. The dragon's breathing became raspy and wet, giving Guillot hope that his sword—now firmly out of reach—had struck home. The beast ceased its contortions, stretched out its wings, and its thrashing climb became a smooth, gliding descent.

Wind whistled past Guillot's ears, and he wished that he had a free hand to shelter his eyes. All he could do was turn his head away and hope the wind's growing force didn't pull him from the spear. Blood splattered into his face from the wound on the dragon's chest. Its salty, bitter tang gave Guillot hope. If he could make the monster bleed, he could kill it. He would have to get his sword back, however. Assuming he survived the landing.

The ground approached at an alarming rate, and Guillot began to worry that he had overdone his thrust into the dragon's chest. Perhaps he had struck its heart as well. Their speed continued to grow until Guillot was moving far faster than he ever had, faster than he thought possible. If they hit the ground at that rate, there wouldn't even be enough of him left to scrape up. At least it would be quick. He gasped as the ground filled his view, and turned his head, bracing for the impact. At the last moment, the dragon angled its wings and slowed, touching down as lightly as a feather.

It took Gill a moment to realise they had landed. Panting, he had to pull his hands from the spear shaft. He had been holding on so tightly that his fingers had locked in place. He backed away from the dragon while it groped at the sword with one of its talons. Never one to let an opportunity pass, Guillot looked for anything he could use as a weapon. Other than a few fist-sized rocks, there was nothing but the dagger on his belt. He drew it, feeling ridiculous—he might as well spit at the beast. The dragon finally caught the sword's hilt with one of its claws and pulled the blade free, then looked at Guillot and hissed in defiance, as if saying that he might have hurt it, but not enough. It paced forward, slowly and carefully, like a cat stalking a mouse. There was nowhere to run, nowhere to hide, and with only a dagger, no way to fight. He gritted his teeth and met the dragon's murderous gaze.

"Gill!"

He looked around. Solène sat atop her horse, holding his last spear. She threw it to him and he grabbed for it like a starving man reaching for a morsel of food, now delighted that she had ignored his entreaty to flee. He turned to face the dragon, feeling that the spear in his hands put him back in the fight. He was immediately greeted with an inferno that carried in it every bit of the dragon's rage.

Guillot stood, engulfed by flame, expecting death to take him, but it did not come. The visor of his helmet was up, and he could feel the fury of the heat on his face, but took no harm from it. The super-heated air felt as though it had weight, like coursing water flowing over him. He forced himself forward, against its flow, until the flame stopped.

The dragon's expressive face showed concern, coupled with amazement that Gill was still alive. The blast of flame had clearly taken a toll on the beast. Guillot wondered if it was starting to question the outcome of the fight.

He launched himself forward, leading with his spear. The dragon swatted at him, but Guillot changed his line of attack and passed beneath the dragon's talons. It leaped back with surprising agility and Guillot ran harmlessly past. His path took him near the wound he'd made with his sword. Blood gushed from it with the beast's every movement. Pivoting, Gill tried to drive the spear into the same spot, but the dragon twisted out of the way.

Guillot paused for a moment to catch his breath. Sweat stung his eyes, and his chest heaved. He charged at the dragon again. It looked as though it was going to fire flame at him, but Guillot no longer feared he would burn.

The dragon lunged forward and snapped its great jaws at him, forcing him to roll to the side. He clambered to his feet in time enough to get out of the way of its tail, which ripped through the air with all the sizzle of a drover's whip.

Guillot charged at the monster again, gasping for breath. Even at his fittest, a fight like this would have pushed him hard. The tip of his spear struck one of the armour-like scales and skittered to one side. He stumbled, his weight too far forward, and fell flat on his face. He rolled onto his back in time to see the dragon's talons coming for him. Another roll got him almost clear—the edge of one talon screeched along his armour and into the join between plates. It cut into his flesh, sending a jolt of pain through him. Guillot wrenched himself away and struggled to his feet.

The dragon's tail slammed into his back with a deafening bang, sending

Guillot flying. He hit the ground with a crunch, his eyes and mouth filling with grit. He scrambled up, spitting and blinking to try to clear the dirt so he could see and breathe. By the time he could, the dragon was close again. Exhausted, he struggled to bring the spear to bear once more. His armour, which had felt so light, now weighed on him as though it was crudely cut lead. Blood streamed from his wound and he was starting to feel dizzy.

One last charge, he thought, *and let the gods decide how the dice will fall.* No one could expect more of him than that. He levelled the spear and ran, shouting with all he had. The dragon reared back on its hind legs, then pounced. The spearhead hit its scales but did not penetrate. The impact knocked Gill to the ground again and he was too weary to get up. Rolling over, he looked up at the hulking great beast above him.

Blood flowed more strongly from the sword wound, coursing in pulses with each beat of the dragon's heart. Guillot wished that he had the strength to strike at it again, but his arm was numb and he couldn't even feel the spear that was still in his grasp. He was spent.

The dragon shifted to one side, then collapsed, shaking the ground on impact. Guillot remained where he was, taking comfort in the simple act of breathing and not having to fight for his life. The sun shone on his face, its gentle warmth a welcome change from the furnace-like heat of the dragon's breath.

Another shadow fell over him.

"It's dead," Solène said.

"Did you kill it?" Guillot said, confused.

"You did. A clean strike to its heart. It just took it awhile to realise that it was dead."

Guillot groaned. "I was aiming for its lungs."

Solène laughed. She knelt beside him and placed a hand on his chest. A wave of relief spread through his body. Tired, stinging muscles were refreshed. Aches and strains faded. His wound felt less severe, though it was still bleeding. He propped himself up on one elbow and looked at the dragon, motionless on the ground. For a moment Guillot was struck by the tragedy that something so unique and so magnificent had to be killed. He didn't feel a rush of victory or achievement, just shame. That didn't detract from the fact that it had needed to be done. Nonetheless, he couldn't muster any pride in the act.

He wondered how Valdamar had felt after slaying his first dragon.

When he got to his feet, Solène handed him his sword, hilt first. "I picked this up," she said.

He thanked her and took it. He pulled a handful of grass from the ground and did his best to clean the blade before sheathing it. The feeling of the grass in his hands made him realise that he had worn through the palms of his leather gauntlets, probably while gripping the spear shaft to keep from falling to his death.

"What do we do now?" Solène said.

He shrugged. "We take proof of what we've done back to Trelain. After that? Whatever we want."

She raised an eyebrow.

"The Prince Bishop won't be able to touch us. We're the heroes who slew the dragon that terrified the whole country. When we ride into Trelain with the dragon's head, everyone will know it's dead and that we're the ones that killed it."

"That's it then?"

Guillot smiled. "Oh no," he said. "That's definitely not it. I said he couldn't touch us. I didn't say we couldn't touch him."

CHAPTER
49

The cave had not felt movement nor heard sound in centuries. Since its last inhabitant had left, never to return, it had been a place of stillness and silence. It was not empty, however. A cluster of three eggs sat, huddled together, on a pile of gold coins melted into a solid mass. Now one of the eggs twitched, knocking against its neighbour, which also twitched. In moments, all the eggs were moving, their nascent inhabitants stirring for the first time.

Both the sound and movement were meagre, but grew steadily, ending a state of stasis that had existed for a millennium. The first egg split with a crack that echoed through the cave and a baby dragon pushed its snout through the gap, taking its first breath of air.